— THE BOOK OF —

MARY

THE UNTOLD STORY OF MARY, MOTHER OF JESUS

A NOVEL BY
ALAN GOLD

First published in 2020 by Golden Wren Publishing Ltd. Sydney, Australia.

© Alan Gold, 2020

The moral rights of the author have been asserted.

Title: The book of Mary
Author: Alan Gold

Paperback ISBN: 978-0-6487102-5-7
EBook ISBN: 978-0-6487102-4-0

Subject: Historical religious fiction
Visit our website – www.goldenwrenpublishing.com

All enquiries should be made to the publisher at:
rebecca@goldenwrenpublishing.com

This is a work of fiction. It does not present itself to readers as a work of theology, philosophy or belief. It is a story. All of the names, characters, places, events, locales, and incidents are based on works of Jewish and Christian writers. The details of the Essene community are based loosely on the writings of the Jewish, and later Roman, historian, Josephus, as well as later writers concerning the community at Qumran. All else is a product of the author's imagination.

www.goldenwrenpublishing.com

A BRIEF EXPLANATION OF NAMES AND DATES

Throughout this novel, the terms 'BC' (Before Christ) and 'AD' (Anno Domini...the Year of Our Lord) are not used.

Instead, dates in Israel are referred to by their more standard academic definition as 'BCE' – Before the Common Era – and 'CE' – Common Era.

Dates in Rome are given as the year in which a particular Emperor first ascended the throne.

Certain names have been used to accord to how characters would have been called in their day.

Jesus would have been known as Jeshua; Mary would have been known as Miriam.

CONTENTS

Sephoris, north of Galilee 5 BCE – The final year of the reign of Herod the Great

The appearance of just one would have meant nothing to her; she could have ignored it and viewed it as a random and unknowable act of Almighty Yahweh in the sky. Two still could have been a coincidence, and although she began to feel a growing concern, like when storm clouds gather over the Great Sea, there was no real reason for her to say a blessing or to feel genuine alarm. But three was a different matter. The sudden and unexpected appearance of three mighty vultures circling in a column in the sky, presage a catastrophe.

Three was the number the old women talked about under their breath, whispering its significance as they gathered in the town square to dye cloth or to fill the communal cooking pot for the people to take food when the Sabbath arrived. When she approached them to try to hear what they were saying, they fell into silence, and told her that this was no place for a child, and to go back to her father's house. But hiding behind a wall, she sometimes heard snippets of their talk. Three, they said, had magic attached to it and could mean good, or evil. There were the three sons of Noah, then there was Abraham, Isaac and Jacob, the three founders of the faith of the Jews, and didn't the seer Balaam beat his donkey three times. And although the old women didn't mention him, Miriam herself remembered the prophet Jonah inside the large fish for three days and three nights?

So it must be a sign from Almighty God in Heaven, Yahweh, that when three vultures gathered in the same sky, it presaged a catastrophe. It could mean loss of a creature of the Divine, either animal or human; it could mean sickness or injury or even death.

Yes, the girl realized. Three was a terrible sign. But when she looked up in the sky again, she was suddenly horrified. Now there were four and when four and more appeared together in the same sky, wheeling around in a gigantic column which stretched up to the heavens – and then she counted at least seven others circling in a distant field – the idea of chance evaporated, and certainty took over; the certainty of sudden illness or death, the certainty of someone in her town mourning irreplaceable loss and heartache.

Miriam stared at the huge, ugly birds, one above the other, gliding in perfect intersecting circles in the sky, and she knew that one of her town's animals – or maybe, may God prevent her thinking bad thoughts, it could be a resident of the town – was injured or had died and at this very moment, Yahweh was gathering the soul into His bosom.

But then her distress at the sight of the birds of prey left her, and the courage for which she was renowned throughout the village made her consider doing something which her father would say was foolhardy and hazardous, but which her heart told her she had to do. Staring at them, Miriam thought to herself that if the vultures were still circling and hadn't landed in order to use their viciously sharp beaks and claws to tear the flesh from some hapless sheep or maybe a little child in distress, God's creature might still be alive and she could dash across the fields to rescue it. Then she would carry it home, and one of the shepherds or even the town's wise men might tend to its ailments and make it better.

Miriam was resting with Elizabeth and two others. They had met in Nathan's field overlooking the town after working since dawn that morning in preparing the house and the food for the Sabbath, and as was the custom, before it fell dark, the girls gathered in one field, the boys gathered in another and they spoke about whatever took their fancy.

The girls were supposed to talk about the meaning of God's Sabbath, but talk inevitably turned towards boys. And when the sky darkened and before the stars began to shine, before the ram's horn was blown by the Priest to signify the start of the Sabbath, they would rise, kiss, bid each other a peaceful and happy Sabbath, and enter their households for their fathers' blessing.

But today was different. To the sudden consternation of her friends, Miriam stood suddenly from the blanket where she and three other girls had been sitting cross-legged playing bones and stones and talking to wait for the sound of the Sabbath, and dashed down the hill towards the river. She heard her friends call after her in surprise, but she knew that if she told them what she was going to do, they'd try to stop her, for their parents would never allow them to interfere with these awful and dangerous scavenger birds. And if she was beyond the confines of the town when the Sabbath had been declared, the consequences could be horrible.

Within moments, Miriam was leaping over tussocks of grass and avoiding rocks as she neared the bridge which spanned the tributary of the great Jordan river further to the East. Crossing it, she said a swift blessing at seeing flowing water for the first time that day, and she heard her heavy footfall echoing on the planks of wood from which the bridge was made. She raced up the eastern bank, her heart now pounding with the effort and the sudden sense of fear and consternation. Her parents had forbidden her ever to go near to where vultures which were feeding on carrion, for fear they would turn and attack her, and these birds were fully half her size.

But as she ran up the river bank and approached the field over which she'd seen the birds circling, her mind centered on the reality that they still hadn't landed, which meant that she wasn't contravening her parent's instructions, or taking undue risks.

It was the field of Simeon, he who tendered to the crops, and it was still full of the stalks and remnants of the wheat which he'd planted the previous season and whose ears were now filling the town granary. Now he was letting Gad's flock of sheep agist in return for a daily part measure of sheep's milk.

Miriam slowed down as she entered Simeon's field, both from exhaustion and a growing sense of caution. She looked around, trying to see a fallen or stricken animal. What she feared more than anything was the prospect of discovering a friend from her town who had fallen from illness and injury and was dying. More than anything, she hated death. Her father Joachim told her that death was nothing more than a continuation of life with the Eternal One, Blessed be He; but Miriam was more like her mother Hannah, who felt such a weight of sadness when she did her duty and sat with a dead person on the night before the funeral.

And then Miriam heard it bleating. The frantic cry of lamb, just a few weeks old. She walked on and saw it struggling. It had separated from its mother, and somehow had fallen into a deep hollow where once a huge tree had grown. Nearby, its mother was frantically talking to it, telling it to climb out, but one look told Miriam that the little animal was too exhausted to continue trying. It was lying down now, accepting its fate, waiting for Yahweh to take its soul and to end its suffering.

In anger at the cruelty of the vultures, Miriam picked up a stick she found in the field, and flung it into the sky to scare off the birds, but they were much too high, and the stick fell harmlessly back towards the tributary deep in the valley.

Cautiously, Miriam walked over to the hollow where the lamb had become trapped. She jumped down, calling out calming words, and then began to sing the little animal a song she'd learned earlier that week from the older women in the town. It was about love and babies and it had made them laugh when they'd taught it to her. Miriam thought that the lamb might find it funny.

She slid both hands beneath its small warm body, feeling its heart pounding in a crazed drum beat, and she easily lifted it up into her arms. It didn't even try to struggle or object. Maybe it knew it had to accept whatever happened to it, or maybe it realized that Miriam was there to help it, and it surrendered into her arms. Whispering into its ear, Miriam climbed out of the hollow, and carried it over to where its mother was standing.

At first, the ewe raced toward her, trying to butt Miriam away, pushing her back towards the hollow, not understanding what she was doing, but when Miriam put the lamb down close to her teat, the mother simply stood there, and allowed the little thing to suckle on her. Miriam stood and watched mother and baby for some minutes, and then looked up into the sky. Four of the seven vultures had already flown away. Soon the others would leave, realizing that their feast had been taken from them. She shook her head in wonder. According to the Rabbi in her town, everything alive was Yahweh's creature and had a soul which was joined to that of the Eternal One, Blessed be He. So if the vultures were God's creatures and had souls, why did Miriam find them so repellent? Why was she so horrified by spiders and snakes when they were God's creatures? Didn't the Prophets in the days of the Old Temple preach of the Oneness of all things? Yet looking at the vultures disappearing into the distance to find some other dead body on which to feast, she shuddered, and wondered just what Yahweh was thinking when he created them.

Smiling, Miriam said a blessing over the mother and baby sheep. Then she ran back towards Sephoris, conscious that the sun was already low in the sky and getting perilously close to the tops of the hills of the Western edge of the valley in which her town was situated. Soon it would be below the level of the hills as it continued its journey towards the great sea. Then three stars would appear in the sky and the day of the Sabbath would be declared by the Priest blowing on the ram's horn. If she was outside of her town when she heard the blowing of the Shofar, she would be in terrible trouble with her parents for breaching the rules of the Sabbath. And she knew that it wasn't just God who would be angry with her for denying the laws of His Sabbath, but if she was caught by a Roman patrol she would be in dire trouble. It was said that girls who were captured by the Romans were raped by every single one of the 80 men in the Century, and then they were shipped off to Rome to be auctioned as slaves.

With a terrible fear in her heart, suddenly realizing how reckless she'd been, Miriam ran like the desert wind back towards her town. Yes, her parents were strict in their observance of the Lord's will, but somehow the Lord's will didn't extend to the Roman soldiers who were worse than the vultures. The danger of her being out at night would terrify her parents, and even if she told them that she'd just performed a mitzvah by saving the life of a lamb, it wouldn't mollify them. They'd still punish her.

As she ran at reckless speed towards her town, even though it had been enlarged with the new Roman garrison and the amphitheaters and the baths, she thought how life had changed in the past few years. Sephoris these days was more a city than a town, and cruel men with iron weapons and metal heels wandered its streets as though it was their own.

She looked into the distance and saw a Century of the invaders marching in double file. It frightened her because she realized that at any moment, the curfew would be declared, and the gates shut. Then, regardless of the Priests and Rabbis sounding the shofar, she wouldn't be able to enter her own village, and her life would be in mortal peril; and even if she did manage to get to the gate before it closed, she'd still be in danger of becoming the plaything of the Romans. Her heart pounded as she ran down the hillside and hastened towards the gate.

+

Joachim of Sephoris held the goblet of wine high above his head, and remained silent as his lips parted in silent prayer. Miriam tried to read what his face was saying, but his lips were obscured by the shadow which the prayer shawl cast over his mouth. So, she strained in the silence to try to hear his whisper to the Almighty One, Blessed be He.

"Hear me Yahweh, God of Abraham, Isaac and Jacob. I, your faithful servant Joachim son of Alchanan beseech you; bless this, my family, and keep them safe from harm and disease; make Miriam and Rachel and Esther, fruit of my seed, bear male fruit in their time; bless my dear Hannah and keep her safe when she is not in my sight; and bless this town of Sephoris and keep its men true and faithful to the ancient ways, Your holy ways. Bless our crops and our animals, and make the Roman soldiers, whose iron feet trample Your sacred soil, leave Judaea and Samaria never to return to this land of milk and honey which you gave to Israel, Your people."

She had always had excellent hearing, but didn't dare tell her father that she had been able to overhear the private prayer he had said to the Almighty One.

Before Joachim put down the goblet and lowered the prayer shawl from his head to his shoulders, he whispered another prayer. *"And please, Yahweh, make my Miriam more responsible and stop her taking the risks she's taking."*

Miriam flushed in embarrassment, praying that none of the others heard what her father had just said. She buried her face in her hands as though she was praying. Then she heard him walk around the table and lay his hand on the heads of his three daughters each in turn according to their age. For each one, he said a different blessing. Miriam, being the oldest and so the first, closed her eyes and bowed her head deeper as she felt her father's warm hand, fingers outstretched, on the top of her head.

"Lord God," he said, his voice sonorous and melodic, "make Your light shine onto this child Miriam, now become a woman. Make her life sweet and peaceful and free from pain..." She thought he'd finished her blessing, and opened her eyes, but closed them immediately when he said, "...and make her coming betrothal to Malachai son of Belazel rich and bountiful and free of debt and enable her to produce many of the sons which you have seen fit, in your infinite wisdom, to deny to me."

"Joachim!" hissed his wife Hannah. "Don't dare criticize Yahweh."

"Is this the same Yahweh who allows Romans to enter our town? Whose iron feet tread on our sacred ground and build obscene buildings where Alexander Jannaeus the Hashmonean planted the first trees and created this town which is our home?" he demanded.

In growing fury, Hannah looked at him and said, "The Alexander Jannaeus who worshipped the Greek invaders of our lands, and killed hundreds of Jews just for fun? Joachim, don't make a mockery of the Sabbath. Just bless the girls and let us get on with our meal!"

Joachim apologized to God and his wife. Then he removed his hand and kissed Miriam on the forehead before he moved around to Rachel who was the next eldest. But Miriam didn't hear the way in which he blessed her, because the thought of her coming betrothal to Malachai and her best friend, his sister Elizabeth, made her feel warm and comforted. She liked Malachai very much, and thought he'd make a suitable husband. But most of all, she loved Elizabeth, with whom she had grown since childhood. Elizabeth was fond of Zachary, and for a month now the two girls had been planning a double wedding. But Zachary wasn't as keen on Elizabeth and in her heart, Miriam knew that he had his eye on her; but she would never do anything to hurt Elizabeth so when Zachary smiled at her, Miriam never gave him a moment's hope that she was anything but his friend, and in love with Malachai. On the blanket, before she had run like a whirlwind to rescue the lamb, Elizabeth had been telling Miriam how she'd love to have a son with Zachary, and she'd call him Jonathan and she would ensure that he grew in the ways of God.

When Joachim returned to his place, he held up his wine goblet again, said a blessing over the wine, "Blessed are you, Oh Lord, our God, Master and King and Ruler of the Earth and the Moon and the Sun and the Stars, who have brought forth grape in its season and have given us the bounty of this sacred wine."

He drank a deep draft, and gave the goblet to Hannah, who sipped it, and passed it to Miriam, who passed it to her younger sister. When all had drunk the Sabbath wine, Joachim tore apart the steaming loaf which Hannah had purchased from the town baker just before the stars shone to herald the arrival of the Sabbath.

"Lord God Yahweh, blessed are You, King of the Heavens, who has enabled me to break this bread and to feed my family."

He tore off a chunk each for his wife and his daughters, and then Esther as the youngest daughter rose and brought the lentil stew to the table. As next youngest, Rachel gave her father a spoonful of the stew, then her mother and then her older sister Miriam. When they were all served, Joachim stood again, and spread his arms outstretched across the table.

"Yahweh, for these, Your bounties and blessings, we give You praise and thank You for Your kindness."

Everybody said 'Amen' and then began to eat. Joachim looked at his family, and asked softly, "Does anybody have anything to tell me?"

The two sisters looked at each other. Miriam continued to look down at her plate. When the silence became oppressive, Joachim said, "I was outside at our well, washing my face and hands in preparation for the Sabbath, when I thought I saw a young woman at the top of the opposite valley, running as though chased by a demon. Perhaps I was wrong."

Miriam looked at her father and mother and told them what she'd done. She admitted that she had been reckless, but that she wanted to save the lamb from the vultures.

Joachim nodded gravely, but said, "And what if it hadn't been a lamb, Miriam? What if a patrol of Roman soldiers had killed a rebel or a Rabbi? They might still have been in the area where you performed your *mitzvah*, and your running into them could have..." His words trailed off as they all thought of the hideous reality of Miriam being captured by the invaders.

She slept well that night. When she awoke, Miriam and her sisters kissed their father farewell as he left the house in the early morning of the Sabbath day and walked down the hill to the Synagogue building. He took a path which skirted around the new Roman baths and amphitheaters that had been built in the center of the town, looking at them in disgust. The Rabbis had reached an accommodation with the Romans, so that from the arrival of Sabbath on the evening of the sixth day of the week, and throughout the seventh day of rest and prayer until the evening of the seventh day, the Romans merely carried out their patrols and didn't bother the residents of Sephoris. But despite the relative quiet in the town, Joachim was still angry from the time when he left his home until the moment that he arrived in the Synagogue and immersed himself in the ancient laws of Moses.

Miriam watched him as he, and all the other men of the town entered the stone building. Then she went inside, and sat down to play with a new set of knucklebones which she had been given by the parents of her friend Elizabeth, and saw with joy how clear and easy to read were the letters on all of the facets the dice. She gathered her sisters, and they began to throw the dice in the air, trying to make words as they came to rest on the blanket. It was the only day of the week where she was not allowed to do any work, and the enforced day of rest revived her mind and her spirits.

After only a short while, Miriam became bored with dice, so she left her younger sisters to play and went for a walk around the town, carefully avoiding anywhere that the Roman soldiers might be congregating. She dropped in on her dearest friend Elizabeth to spend some time and to tell her of her rescue of the lamb the previous day.

The two of them walked within the boundaries of the town, as Yahweh demanded, but it still enabled them to saunter up the hill to where Malachai lived, in the hope that he might already have returned from praying in the Synagogue. But the house was quiet, and Miriam and Elizabeth didn't want to disturb the peace of the family's Sabbath.

When they returned to the lower section of the town, it was already approaching the middle of the day when the men would leave the

Synagogue after the morning prayers, and would begin to wend their ways to their homes for the midday meal. Miriam kissed Elizabeth and walked quickly back to her house.

Even from the pathway, Miriam could smell the delicious aroma of a lamb stew. Most of the women of the town took food from the communal pot as Moses' law prevented them from lighting a fire, but her mother prepared the food the day before, and tendered the fire under the family cauldron during the night, so she remained faithful to the law.

And Miriam was eager to eat the midday meal, because once a week, when the family ate the delicious cubes of meat nestled seductively in the thick dark aromatic juices, she would daydream. She would ponder what it must be like to be King Herod and live in a glorious palace in Jerusalem or by the shores of the Dead Sea, and to have servants and slaves do all his bidding; to have meat every day and fruit brought to him on huge golden platters, and to eat freely of the milk of a cow which a slave had churned into cream or butter. How wonderful life would be if she had all that given to her.

But then she forced herself to stop thinking such thoughts, because Moses the Lawgiver who had brought the Torah from Sinai had told the Israelites that it was one of the sins against Yahweh to covet that which your neighbor had, even if your neighbor, like Herod, was descended from the Edomites, dwellers who lived in the wasteland beyond Jerusalem and Jericho and were never at peace, but spent their lives wandering into and out of the awful Negev Desert.

So she said a blessing over the water and washed her hands and face before entering the house, and felt the heat from the recently stirred embers which her mother had assiduously kept alive all night.

She helped her mother and sisters put out the bowls and spoons and break the bread into segments, which she distributed to each member of the family. And they waited until their father returned from the Synagogue.

When they were eating their meal, Miriam suddenly lost her appetite. She looked in horror as her father repeated what he'd already said twice. She glanced in trepidation at her mother hoping that she would argue, and then back to her father, but the full import of his pronouncement had already made itself understood to her, and she was reeling at the way in which her life had suddenly plunged into the darkness of a nightmare.

"I'm assured by the Rabbi of his town that Yosef is a good man. A righteous man. Yosef has wealth and a secure business as a carpenter. He and his family originally came from Bethlehem where he was born, but moved to Nazareth because the town's old carpenter had died, and it would improve their circumstances. Since then, he has prospered, and is a man of stature. His wife Melcha died during the month of Tammuz, ninety days ago. They had been married for twenty six years, and with her, Yahweh had blessed the couple with six children, two girls and four boys. But now that she is dead, the Priests of Nazareth have told him that as one of the generations of King David, it's incumbent upon him to take himself another wife and to continue the line. They've looked favorably on you, Miriam. He is of the line of David. There could be no greater honor for our family."

"But I'm already betrothed. To Malachai. I don't want another husband," she said, her voice beginning to break as tears welled up in her eyes.

"Miriam, you aren't betrothed until your union is blessed by the Priests and until a dowry is negotiated. And as the eldest daughter of this house, you will do as you are commanded, both by the Priests and by your father," said her mother. Miriam looked in shock at her mother Hannah and could see the pain in her eyes. But she knew her mother had to show a unified front with her husband, and so wasn't surprised. "And Nazareth is only a day's journey from here, so we'll see you several times during the year. Yosef will treat you well, and he won't expect much of you, for he has a servant who will do things for you in his house, which is more than your father has been able to provide," said Hannah.

Her throat was dry and the taste of the lamb stew had become bitter in her mouth. She'd hoped and expected her mother to support her in denying the injunction of the Priests, but she was siding with her father. He'd told her the news when he'd returned from the synagogue. It had been discussed between the priests, who had informed her father of their decision, and he had agreed.

"But I don't want to leave Sephoris. I don't want to leave my friends," Miriam said.

"Sephoris is becoming more of a Roman town than a place where Jews used to live in peace to worship Yahweh," said Joachim. Your mother and I cannot move from here, but I hope that my daughters will find new lives away from where these barbarians have decided to station themselves."

It didn't mollify her grief. "But I want to marry Malachai and have children here; his children." Miriam felt her eyes beginning to fill with tears. "I don't know this Yosef. And he's old. I don't want to be married to an old man."

"He's not old. He's only six years older than your father," Hannah told her.

Rachel began to whimper. "I don't want Miriam to leave," she said between sobs. "I want her to stay here."

Now Esther, the youngest of the daughters, began to cry, and in fury Joachim slammed down his fist on the table, and shouted, "How dare you disturb the Lord's Sabbath with your whimpering. Enough of this talk. We will sit in silence and finish our meal. Then I will return to the Synagogue and continue my prayers, after which I will continue my discussions with the Priest and the Rabbi who have traveled here all the way from Nazareth to honor our house and betroth Miriam to Yosef. By the end of today, I will have determined what dowry must be paid to Yosef, and then the arrangement will be concluded. And that is the end of it!"

Silenced, the mother and her three daughters sat rigidly as Joachim continued to eat his lamb stew. Secretively and cautiously, Hannah pressed her finger to her lips to forbid Miriam from saying anything which might further enrage Joachim's mood. The girl knew when to remain silent, but underneath her breath, speaking to the ears of Yahweh, she said, *"I will not marry this man. I just won't!"*

+

They lay together in the open field, their work done, their tasks completed. They had lain together once before, when Miriam had allowed him to touch and kiss her breasts, but when she could feel both Malachai and herself become unnaturally excited and her face had flushed crimson, she forced his hand away, sitting up suddenly, feeling faint and giddy. Since then, and it was only four months earlier, Miriam had been very cautious about how she had greeted and spent time with Malachai.

But circumstances had changed, and within the week, she was to leave Sephoris and marry a man she'd neither met, nor in whom she had the remotest interest. A man forty years older than her! A man with six children, all but two of whom were older than Miriam. How would she cope? How would she exert motherly control over the children and gain their respect as their new mother? How could she leave Malachai, the young man she had decided to marry and who, she believed, was approved by her father?

They lay in silence, looking up at the vast cloudless sky whose canopy was the entire valley, from eastern to western hilltop. They had been silent since Miriam had led Malachai gently into the field in order to explain to him how their lives would now change so dramatically as a result of her father's decision. At first he had said nothing, but looked at her in shock and disbelief. Then, he'd become angry and demanded that she do everything in her power to reverse her father's decision, that she refuse his will, that he and she would stand together before Joachim and tell him that no such marriage would be taking place, because Miriam and Malachai were already betrothed in mind and spirit, if not in law.

And then his eyes had brightened with a sudden and brilliant epiphany. He'd stood and paced the field, and told her that they would marry...that day...immediately. That as a result of their wedding, there could be no prospect of her marrying this Yosef the carpenter of Nazareth.

But she had tempered his excitement with the reality that without her father's blessing and a suitable dowry to Malachai's parents, no Priest or Rabbi would marry them. So Malachai suggested that they ask the Roman authorities to marry them, but Miriam absolutely rejected this, saying that she would never stray from her worship of Yahweh; and the Jewish court, the Sanhedrin, would never accept the legality of that marriage. So finally, he accepted his fate and with resignation, lay down beside her.

The clouds which came in from the south slowly rose up and ambled across the sky, and Miriam felt increasingly drowsy. She was very weary late in the afternoon of the first day of the week. She'd hardly slept that Sabbath eve, and when she woke up on the first morning of the week, all her housework and her work in the fields had been as though she had lead weights tied to her limbs.

Laying with Malachai in the fields, she closed her eyes in the late afternoon warmth and began to drift. In her dreams, she felt Malachai kissing her, felt his arms caressing her body, and she liked it. She knew she was smiling, although she was asleep. And in her dreams, she felt him touching other parts of her body, parts which she'd forbidden him to touch in earlier times. But now that she was to be married to another, she didn't want to stop him and although she thought she was asleep, she was enjoying what he was doing. She felt him rub himself along her leg, back and forth, back and forth as though his legs were caressing hers, and then he kissed her and cried out her name and the sound of his voice made her suddenly awake and look at him. His hair was ruffled, his face was red and sweating, but his eyes showed both love and fear.

She drew him to her and kissed him, and pushed his body off of hers. As sleep left her, reality began to press upon her mind. The dreaming state in which she'd felt so warm and comforted was now gone, and again she looked up and saw the blue sky, the white scudding clouds and the outline of the distant hills. But she was concerned that Malachai's face was frowning in anxiety and Miriam wondered what could be wrong.

"What is it? What's the matter?" she asked him gently, yawning and stretching. But all he said to her was "I'm sorry. I'm so sorry." Failing to understand, Miriam sat up and realized that her clothes were awry. She began to straighten them, when the gentle late afternoon breeze wafted across the exposed skin of the upper part of her leg close to her womanliness, and she felt it was wet. Hastily, she pulled her garment across her naked skin, worried that perhaps she had begun her monthly blood flow, and he would see it. But when she looked, she realized that it was wet from Malachai's seed, which he'd spilled at the top of her leg. She reeled back, and Malachai moved away, trying to hide his shame and embarrassment.

She could barely say the words, but she knew she had to. "Am I still intact?" she whispered.

Malachai nodded, but couldn't look at her. "Yes, you came into this field like a virgin. And a virgin you remain. I swear."

Miriam stood, and shook her head in horror when she realized that he had used her body for his pleasure without her permission. Shocked and disgusted, she looked at him, but he had hidden his face in his hands in the shame which was suffusing his mind.

"How could you? Malachai, how could you do this to me?" she demanded.

But he heard nothing, his hands blocking out all sensation. And in tears Miriam began to run back to the town, but with the wind in her ears, she barely heard Malachai's plaintive shout, "I didn't put it in, Miriam. I swear before Yahweh I didn't put it in..."

+

As she walked towards the Synagogue where she would meet her future husband for the very first time, she wondered why she was so afraid? Miriam always did Yahweh's will, as she was doing now. She always put her faith and trust in Yahweh, as she was now. So why was she so frightened? It didn't make sense.

The Synagogue was tiny; far smaller than the magnificent Synagogue in Sephoris. And the town of Nazareth was tiny as well, with hardly any streets running this way and that, and an insignificant central square with no seats or benches or even a reservoir to quench the thirst of people or animals in the hot sun.

But at least the presence of Roman rule was not apparent; indeed, although Nazareth was close to The Way of the Sea, the ancient route for travelers and merchants which ran between Damascus and Egypt, it was apparently of such little significance to anyone other than Nazarenes that the Romans had ignored it altogether and had concentrated their influence in the area on Sephoris.

But it was a pleasant enough little village, and although it was high in the hills, and the air smelled cleaner than the air in her town, and even though she could look back and see mountains in the far distance, Miriam still felt a sense of disappointing as she walked into the village. Where were the young people? Where were the shops and craftsmen's workbenches? Where were the lovely buildings? She'd never been this far from Sephoris in all her life, and if this was what the rest of the world had to offer, she'd much prefer to stay in her home.

They entered the Synagogue, and her father put his hand up to touch the lintel and the tiny jar which held the lamb's blood and the segment from the scroll which told of the Exodus from Egypt. Then he kissed the hand which had been so blessed by the touch. Miriam followed her father's actions and kissed her hand, saying a quick blessing before she walked through the curtain in front of the door of the Synagogue.

They entered, and Miriam tried to peer through the dark. And then she saw him. It must be him, for he stood in the center of the Synagogue, and was surrounded by well-wishers. He was looking at her in expectation and excitement.

There was a kindness in his face, a gentleness which appealed to her. Even though he was grey-haired there was still a sense of youthfulness and what most pleased her was that his eyes were full of wisdom and beauty. More than anything about a man, she loved kindly eyes. Her father Joachim, for all his strictness with his daughters, had kindly eyes.

Yet her heart was still pounding in anxiety, which surely meant that her unwillingness to marry this man was manifesting. So why, if she was a good daughter of Yahweh, was she so worried? Surely, as her father had been telling her all along the journey, Yahweh's will would prevail, and she would find happiness in a union which had been blessed by the Priests and Rabbis of both Sephoris and of Nazareth. For Yosef was of the line of King David, and the honor to Miriam's family was immense.

And now they met, face to face. Her voice quivering, she walked with her father from the outer row of stone benches towards the center where the Holy scrolls were placed, and she said to him, "I, Miriam of Sephoris, daughter of Joachim, son of Alchanan, daughter of Hannah of the generations of the tribe of Judah, greet as my husband Yosef son of Jacob, son of Eliahu of the generations of King David. I swear by Yahweh that I will respect you and defend you against your enemies and that I will diligently perform the duties which is your right to expect of a Jewish wife."

"And I, Yosef, son of Jacob and of the generations of David, greet you Miriam of Sephoris as my wife. I swear by Yahweh that I will honor you as your husband and will protect you and make the goodness and kindness of the world shine upon you."

The Nazarene Rabbi, listening carefully to the respect in which Miriam had greeted her future husband, was satisfied that this was a suitable wife for a man of Yosef's stature, the carpenter of the town and a man who owned property and fields in the vicinity. A man in whose body ran the seed of the greatest of all the Jewish Kings, David of blessed memory.

"The dowry having been agreed, I, Abraham ben Simeon, Rabbi of the School of Hillel and teacher and leader of the people of Nazareth, do hereby give my consent for the wedding contract to be drawn up between these two people and for the nuptials to be consecrated within the month of Shevat in the Synagogue of Sephoris. I have chosen this month for the wedding, because according to Rabbi Hillel under whom I have studied, and who is one of the greatest sages our nation has ever produced, the month of Shevat is the time of the new year for trees, and this augurs well for a wedding between this older man and this younger woman. For he is as sturdy and mighty as a cedar, and she is as young as a sapling and together they will make many children grow and prosper until all Israel is a strong forest and able to deny the progress of our enemies. So, my children, with this permission, I pray to Yahweh that you two will live in peace and harmony for years without end."

The many people from Nazareth who were gathered in the Synagogue to greet the girl and her father, crowded round and congratulated Miriam and Joachim, assuring them that they would make the long journey down into the valley to Sephoris and would celebrate with the conjoined families.

As the men took Joachim and Yosef aside to talk with them, the women crowded around Miriam and bombarded her with questions about her interests and her family connections, she saw four women and two men sitting in a back bench. They were apart from the others, as though they were observers gazing at a spectacle. But when she looked closely at them, she saw that the four women were looking at her in more than mere curiosity; one was frowning, one was scowling, one was shaking her head in wonder and one appeared to be sneering. One of the two men merely stared between his legs at the floor. Only the youngest of the six, a boy of not more than fourteen years, was smiling directly at her. She knew that these were her new family. And her heart sank in distress.

She was determined that she would be a good and encouraging wife to Yosef; that she would put all thoughts about Malachai and even her friendships in Sephoris out of her mind so that she could become a proper faithful Jewish wife, even of a man she would never previously have considered marrying, a man she would obey, but never love.

+

On the night of their marriage, when eventually they were alone together and he had tried and failed to enter her body, she had reassured him that it was exhaustion and the excitement of the wedding that had caused his failure. It was a freezing cold night and so she also said that the weather wasn't conducive to a man's vigor.

But when those excuses and reasons could no longer be used in the following week, and the week after that when the weather brightened, and despite his strenuous efforts night after night, she had shouldered the blame for his incapability, and told him that it was because of her unattractiveness that he'd found it so impossible to fulfil his husbandly obligation to enter her body. He'd denied this, telling her that he found her very pleasing and desirable. So Miriam told him it must be a feeling of guilt that he had married so soon after the death of his wife Melcha, and Yosef accepted this reasoning, and slept soundly. And this was to Miriam's relief, for even though she'd been married for over a month, she found the prospect of making love to Yosef something which she did not relish.

But now a worry began to grow in Miriam's mind. For some time, she had felt odd tickles and twinges in her stomach and back and couldn't understand the reason. Then, for several mornings in the past week, she'd had to rise quickly from their bed and run outside of the house to vomit into the bed of flowers.

While she was waiting in the line of women for the village baker to put out the newly baked bread, she mentioned her problem in passing one day to an elderly matron, a friend of Yosef's, who understood the mysteries of the body and used herbs and medicines to cure illnesses; but instead of re-assuring her, she'd said with a grin that Miriam was probably with child, and that Yosef was to be congratulated. She cackled that many in the village had taken wagers that he was no longer capable, and those who had bet against him would be angry with her because now they would lose their money.

In a state of confusion and concern, Miriam returned to her home with the bread. Yosef immediately knew from the worry in her face that there was a problem. Gently, he asked her what was troubling her, and without even considering the consequences, she told him what the old medicine woman had said.

At first, he laughed and told her that she must have misunderstood. But when she repeated the symptoms she'd explained to the old woman, Yosef became increasingly concerned. He asked further questions, and with each answer, he reacted more and more in shock and amazement. The amiability disappeared, and now he was the angry father, the older husband who suddenly realized that he'd been made to look like a complete fool.

As the understanding of his situation became increasingly clear, there followed a terrible row about how she'd been given to him as a virgin, yet she was nothing of the sort. He even called her a harlot and a wanton woman, which made Miriam furious and storm out of the house into their garden. He ordered her to return to the house, but she refused, and sat on the edge of the escarpment, looking out to the distant Mediterranean Sea. Eventually, after more than two hours of silent hostility, Yosef was forced to come out of the house and speak with his wife.

"You are a girl who I took into my house on the advice of my Priests, and I was told..."

"Now listen to me, Yosef," Miriam said sternly. He hadn't seen a face as determined or furious as hers in many years, not since his wife had refused to move from Nazareth to Jerusalem when he wanted to re-orientate his life. "I came to you as a virgin. I am still a virgin. No man has been inside me. Yes, I've had a close and dear friend, a boy of Sephoris, and we were very..." She sought for the right word so as not to exacerbate her husband's anger any further, "...passionate. But he respected me and he didn't make love to me. I am as whole and pure as I was when I was born. I swear to Yahweh that I have no idea how this has happened. But..."

And she dissolved into tears of fear and confusion. Yosef was suddenly upset. He had heard that sometimes healthy young girls did indeed become pregnant without the boy being responsible; and if this had happened, then surely it was a sign from Yahweh. But how could he be sure?

She started to recover, but continued to protest that she was a virgin when she married, and that she still was, despite being wed for many weeks. The innocence of her face, and the hurt in her eyes calmed Yosef down, and although still angry at her deception, he realized that he was trapped by his circumstance.

The coldness between them continued for the morning, and when, at lunch, Yosef walked out of the front rooms to go to the back part of their house facing the roadway where his carpentry was done, Miriam sat for long moments in silence, wondering what had happened to her. Her mind immediately thought of Malachai and how he'd spilled his seed, like Onan of the Bible. But he'd spilled his seed so close to where her legs parted, to where her womanness began. She knew he hadn't penetrated her, because there had been no bleeding. So what in the name of God Almighty in Heaven could have happened to make her be with child? How could she become pregnant when no man had known her?

In her tears, she didn't hear Yosef return and stand in the doorway.

"Miriam," he said, his voice as gentle as the way in which he was looking at her. She looked up and saw him silhouetted in the outside light. "Miriam, listen to me. You swear that you have not been with another man. I want to believe you, and I think in your heart you believe it, and so I will believe it too. Maybe in one of my fumbling attempts to be a husband to you, I have spilled some of my seed, and it has gone within you. But whatever is the truth, be assured that this will be known only to the two of us. I will support you in all things, and I will call this infant mine, whether it is of my seed or not. Because for you to be...to have been with...for it to be known...I'll be the laughing stock of Nazareth, and..."

"It is of your seed, Yosef," she said quickly. "No matter what you might think of me, no man has known me before our marriage. Of this, I swear by Yahweh and the future wellbeing of my child. My body has never been entered, by you or by any other man. I was and still am a virgin."

"Virgins don't become pregnant," he said softly.

"I know. But let any of the old women of the village, any doctor or priest examine me, and they will tell you that my covering hasn't broken and I am still intact. I have never bled from breaking my covering, only from my monthly woman's flow. I swear it to you."

"Then how...?" "I don't know, unless as you said, it was you... somehow..." "Yes, yes, I understand. But listen to me carefully, Miriam, because my reputation is in jeopardy. I am a man of a good name and I won't have my name bandied around by gossips and old wives that Yosef of Nazareth isn't capable..."

She interrupted him, "And I am also of a good name, Yosef, and nobody will say that I have acted against the will of Yahweh or my parents or my husband. I too must be protected from your accusations. Is that understood?"

He nodded. "Nobody in Nazareth or in Sephoris must know or even suspect that this child is born of any other father than me. And I will never make any accusations against you. But it is my reputation as your husband that must be protected. You as my wife are a reflection upon my good name. Is that clearly understand?" he said, his voice rising in demand.

"It's not!" she said, her voice rising in anger. "I am your wife, but my good name is just as important to me."

"I understand that. But assure me that you will tell nobody that you are still intact." She nodded and agreed. "Good," he responded.

"When you are more certain that a baby is within you, we will tell my children. You will send word to your father and mother. If the child is a boy, he will be called Jeshua which means Yahweh is Our Salvation. If it is a girl, she will be called Avigail, which means My Father is Joy. Then nobody will question my child's parentage."

He smiled at her. She fought against the uprise in anger she suddenly felt towards her husband but understood the concessions he had made to her. Another husband would have been sent her back to her parents in humiliation. There might even been calls from the priests for her stoning as an adulteress. At least she didn't have to suffer that. She smiled back and nodded again. She prayed that the feelings in her stomach and her sickness in the morning was only an ailment, and that she wasn't pregnant. But then, why had her bleeding not started as they normally did in the beginning of the month?

CHAPTER TWO

The Court of Caesar Augustus, Rome 23rd year of the reign

"I won't have it, I tell you," he shouted, tossing the vellum scroll across the marble floor, where it skidded at the foot of a surprised matron of the Roman court who wondered whether or not she should bend down and retrieve it. Her husband sneaked a look at her, and she knew to stand still until the Emperor's fury abated.

When he saw where the book had landed, and fearing that the matron might pick it up and contaminate her mind with its filth and obscenity, the Princeps of the Roman Empire, Caesar Augustus, snapped his finger and ordered a servant to go across the room and retrieve the manuscript.

"But Caesar, it isn't a book of..."

"Don't tell me what this book is, or isn't. I've read bits of it, and I won't have it! I won't. It's filth. Disgusting. I won't have some poet corrupting the morals of young Roman men and women. Listen carefully to me...before I came to power, Rome was a city full of orgies and licentiousness and married men and women sleeping with other people's wives and that sort of disgraceful behavior. It's taken me twenty years to bring a sense of decency and order into the city, and I won't have this...this...poet defiling the minds of young boys and girls with his disgraceful rubbish. All this talk about seduction and deflowering virgins. I won't have it. I'm warning you, and you can warn him. Tell him to write like Virgil or Horace or like your niece Sulpicia or tell him to get out of the city and write his poems for the wild men of Africa or the savages of Germania.

"Why can't he write like the great men of Rome, like Virgil or Horace? They were mischievous and funny and loved to poke fun at me and the citizens, but they weren't dirty and sordid. All of Rome laughed at their wickedness. They were terrible to the farmers and the soldiers, but their minds were Roman minds, not like this fellow, this...what's his name?"

"Ovid, great Caesar. His name is Ovid," said his Greek slave and counsellor. Though Augustus was furious, involuntarily he found himself smiling when he remembered his delight at the satires of Virgin and Horace, two of the great poets of the Empire, greatly missed in Rome since their deaths.

"Look, Marcus Valerius Messalla, this Ovid is a clever fellow and he can certainly write well. No denying that! But I won't have him writing this filth in Rome. Tell him that if he continues, I'll banish him to the furthest reaches of the Empire. I'll send him to northern Gaul or to Syria or the Armenian Sea. Go back, Marcus Valerius, and tell him that I'm very displeased, and that I'll be true to my word."

Forgetting his need for caution, Marcus Valerius shouted out "Oh! For the sake of the Gods who watch over us, Caesar, how can you even contemplate exiling this man? He's Rome's greatest poet?" Marcus Valerius surprised those listening, but the frustration in his voice was evident. "It's obvious that you haven't properly read or understood any of Ovid's poetry, but you've just made up your mind that he's writing filth, and he's offended your sense of propriety. Read his works, and you'll see what I mean."

Stunned by Marcus Valerius' imprudent language, Augustus looked around the room to see how others had reacted. He was known as a Princeps who welcomed disputation and argument in his court and often held public shouting matches with his advisors, reckoning that a heated discussion was the best way to arrive at the most sensible answer to a problem. But rarely did Augustus allow debate or argument over issues of the city's morals, and he thought he'd made it quite clear to Marcus Valerius that Ovid's love poetry offended him, and that meant that it offended all of Rome.

Changing his voice, his tone becoming serious. "Marcus Valerius Messalla, I have patronized the arts, especially poetry, since I first came to power. I've built the greatest buildings in the history of the Republic and the Empire. I have paid a fortune out of my own pocket to poets and artists and sculptors in order to glorify Rome and all of its distant possessions. But I will not have some provincial from Sulmo bringing disgrace to my court, my city, my country or my Empire. Now listen to me, and listen very carefully, Marcus Valerius Messalla. I know that you, yourself, are patron to many artists and poets. I commend you for that. But the poet has to write respectable material. Satire certainly, because we should laugh at ourselves and not take the things we do too seriously...love poetry for sure, because poets can make love with words which will last much longer than the feeling of a kiss...beautiful descriptions will be welcome, because those not fortunate enough to be able to see Rome can read of her beauty and magnificence through the words of writers and poets...and poets can especially glorifying our great victories in battles against the barbarian, so that the feeling of the battle will last beyond the bodies left rotting on the battle field. But that is as far as I will allow it to go. Nobody in Rome can expect to write filth and foul and outrageous obscenities talking of seducing girls, without risking my very great wrath."

Marcus Valerius Messalla looked up and was about to continue his argument, when he saw the look on Augustus' face, and thought better of saying anything further. He felt his wife beside him stiffening, warning him to remain silent at all costs.

"The Poet Publius Ovidius Naso will desist from any more of this filth, or I will order his exile. That is my ruling. Is that understood?"

Marcus Valerius nodded, bowed, and the husband and wife, patrons and providers to the theatre and the arts of Rome, beat a hasty retreat from the Audience Chamber. Caesar Augustus breathed a huge sigh of relief. He hated these interchanges about morals. Rome was still such a hotbed of prostitution, with painted women flooding in from all throughout the Empire in order to earn good money servicing not only Roman citizens, but also the thousands of traders and artisans and travelers who had made the city so overcrowded with denizens of an altogether unsuitable sort. These whores, some of whom came from the distant provinces, were ruining families by seducing husbands away from their duties to their family. And Caesar would put a stop to it.

Now that Marcus Valerius Messalla had scurried off, no doubt to tell Ovid the good news that he'd been saved from exile provided he did what he was told, Caesar Augustus had more important things to deal with. One thing was the status of his wife's son, Tiberius. She was pressing him to force Tiberius to return from Rhodes and to join the Imperial family. Since he'd divorced his wife, he'd been a difficult man to deal with; churlish, arrogant, ungrateful and temperamental. But worst of all was his surliness, as though his mouth was always full of sour milk.

In many ways, though, Livia was right, because Tiberius was a brilliant general and had many outstanding successes in the field; he was loved by his army, and his decision to go into self-imposed exile had been very upsetting. Livia had forced Tiberius to divorce the women whom he loved so dearly, his wife Vipsania, and to marry instead Julia, the widow of his close friend, Agrippa. Even though Julia was Augustus' daughter through his first wife, Scribonia, Augustus knew that the marriage would be a disaster and loveless; yet for reasons which still defied him, he had agreed to Livia's demands, and caused great unhappiness for several people.

Livia wanted Augustus to adopt Tiberias not just as his step-son, which he already was, but as his blood son, thereby guaranteeing him the succession to the Imperial Purple; and he probably would accede to his wife's wishes one day. But he would make her wait and suffer the discomfort which were her reward for her many intrigues.

But the succession and Tiberias' status was only one thing on his agenda for today; the other was taxes, and making sure that the Empire, even in its most distant reaches, paid its fair share in his administration of its affairs. Keeping an army in Germania, and in Gaul, and in Syria and in Armenia was hideously expensive, and the local inhabitants simply had to pay their fair share for the protection he afforded them.

The last census he'd organized, sixteen years after Julius' assassination when Augustus was already all-powerful, had raised a fortune for the Empire; and now, twenty or more years later, it was time for another. Not only did a census enable him to know how many people lived in his Empire, but it also told him the extent of the money which would flood into the Roman treasury in the forthcoming three or four years; that would enable him to determine how large his army should be, which wars he could afford to fight, and which public buildings he had the money to construct.

His advisor waiting patiently in the anteroom of the Audience Hall, Publicus Quirinius Secundus, had all the facts and figures

Augustus would need. But the big question was the cost of organizing the census. Would he raise more from his attempt to tax the people, than he would spend in the effort?

Since coming to power, Augustus had completely revolutionized the administration of the Empire, and had appointed good, honest, and decent men to provincial governorships, and beneath them procurators and prefects to administer the different regions of the governor's domain. In the past the Empire's administration had been conducted exclusively from Rome; and that had led to massive loss of revenue, corruption, nepotism and gross inefficiency.

In order to ensure that his world-wide empire ran smoothly, Caesar Augustus had appointed brilliant administrators to advise him, and through him, the Senate, on the best way of making the Empire flourish. They had suggested moving the administration from the center, and giving major responsibilities to skilled bureaucrats in six regions; these bureaucrats...sometimes members of the Roman aristocracy, sometimes brilliant and successful military generals, and sometimes ordinary men who had worked their way into a position of great significance because of their skill at organization, were appointed to large regions which they were appointed to run on behalf of Caesar and the Senate; however, Augustus never appointed a man because he'd bought the office or because he was known to a close friend of the Emperor. What Augustus wanted in the regions was to have trusted men who would do the right thing for Rome.

And now that he had his Empire running smoothly, he had to know how many people were in it, so that he could pay for his grand design. From previous correspondence, he knew that Publicus Quirinius had a big problem with the enormity of the task of organizing the census. He'd said that a census should be undertaken in North Africa, Egypt, Gaul, those parts of Germania under Roman control, and the East as far as Syria. But in his letter, he had begged Caesar not to try to undertake the census in Syria or beyond, especially the lands to the South of Syria, for those lands contained the province of Judea, and there would be terrible trouble for King Herod if such a census and additional taxation was imposed on the barbaric and undisciplined people of that formidable desert land.

But Augustus had made up his mind, and he would tell Publicus Quirinius so. He fortified himself for the next interview with a goblet of wine, and nodded to his servant to admit Publicus. As the little bald sycophant walked forward, he bowed constantly towards the throne; more than anything, Augustus hated sycophants, time-servers, nepotists those who had attained high position without brains or work. He sighed and prepared himself for a long and detailed – and terribly boring – debate about facts and figures and costs. 'Oh dear,' he thought, 'Why did administrators have to make administration so boring?'

CHAPTER THREE

Nazareth, Judea 4 BCE

Three of her step-children greeted the news of Miriam's pregnancy in shocked silence. Two in profound disdain. Only James, younger than Miriam by a year, greeted her news with undisguised joy as they carried the bucket of water from the well. He dropped the bucket, splashing cold water over her feet, hugged and kissed her and wished her the blessings of Yahweh, and told her that her news would bring blessings to his house and respect for his father.

Out of reverence for their father, they had all kissed Miriam and brought her gifts of eggs and honey in a basket made from hyssop and myrtle, but she could tell from their reaction to her that it was a gift not of friendship, but of duty. Only James seemed genuinely and openly delighted and took her hand and told her that he'd make the best step-brother a boy had ever had, and that he'd protect the child with his life and ensure that he or she never wanted for anything. Miriam hugged him, and whispered thanks and a blessing into his ear.

The sickness ended in the third month of her pregnancy, now quite apparent to her and her husband by the small bulge in her belly. He no longer looked at her in anger or disappointment, but as a loving husband looks at his ailing wife. He'd even begun to believe that the child might very well be his, and that his juices might have somehow flowed into her without either of them realizing it; for aside from the question over the parentage of her baby, Miriam was in every other respect the model wife...reverential, obedient, charming, and a fitting companion for a man of importance who was the carpenter to the village.

Visiting her a week after she'd entrusted James with the mission of walking down to Sephoris to tell her parents Hannah and Joachim the news, they had returned to Nazareth with the boy, and told her and Yosef how delighted they were that their daughter had fulfilled her marital expectations so quickly and promised Miriam a truly excellent gift when the baby was born. Yosef beamed and accepted their congratulations; but knowing him as well as she did, Miriam knew that there was not complete joy in her husband's heart. For the arrival of her parents had again opened up doubts about who and what Miriam might have been in Sephoris before they were betrothed.

Later, on their first night in Nazareth, Yosef and Miriam and her parents sat down to eat a meal in celebration of their arrival, and of the news of Miriam's pregnancy. She made a stew of barley and oats, in which cow's meat had been braised. Despite the cold, and in order to make room for the new arrivals, Yosef's children agreed to be seated at the table outside of the house and eat their meal. When they had eaten and drunk wine and blessed the union and the coming baby, Joachim said, "It's not good for you that your baby will be born in the month of Tishri."

Miriam looked at him in surprise. "Why not?" she asked.

"Because of the Census. Yosef was born in Bethlehem, and you and he will have to return there. The Romans say that the officers of the Census will arrive here in the month of Nissan, and so by the time they've taken the census in Jerusalem and then begin to move north to other towns, they'll probably arrive in Bethlehem by Tishri. That's just when you'll be having the baby. The days will be pleasantly warm, but the nights can be very cold. And I don't like the idea of your traveling when you're so heavily pregnant."

"What census?" asked Yosef.

Joachim realized that Nazareth was off the beaten track, and that news wouldn't reach the village as quickly as it reached Sephoris. News of the census was all over Jerusalem and Sephoris and the other major cities; the Roman soldiers were angry that they'd have a huge additional workload and would have to travel into the wild and remote areas and would have to face the Zealots and the Sicarii and the other Jews resisting their rule in parts of the land where the rebels had the advantage. Many Roman soldiers would die, just because the Emperor Augustus wanted to know how many subjects he commanded. Everybody thought it was madness to try to take a census in such a wild and remote province of the Roman Empire as Judea, but despite the advice he'd been given, Caesar Augustus was insistent that all of his subjects must be known to him if they were to feel a part of the grandeur of Rome; only then, he had reasoned, would the true benefits of Roman citizenship be understood by all of the world.

Apologizing for making the assumption that the people of Nazareth would have known of such an event, he explained, "This is a propitious year for the Romans. The city was founded 750 years ago, and this is the 60th year of the life of Augustus. So excited are the Roman Senate because of the peace which Augustus had brought to the empire that, according to the Centurion in Sephoris, the Senate is going to crown Caesar *Pater Patriae*, the Father of the Nation. In honor of this event, the Caesar in Rome has decreed that he will register all inhabitants of the world by recording their names. The Romans soldiers to whom we speak say it's only to find out how many people are in the Empire, and where they live; but I think it's just for him to be able to raise taxes so that nobody will be able to avoid paying them."

Yosef shook his head in amazement. "But there's already been a census. Twenty years ago. I remember it clearly, because I had an urgent job to be done on renewing the frame of a house which had been burnt down. The people were desperate, and yet I was forced to leave my home and spend days just to travel back to Bethlehem to be counted. Surely you're wrong, Joachim? Why would Augustus Caesar conduct another census so soon?"

Joachim shook his head. "I'm only telling you what the Romans have told us in Sephoris. Privately, they've told us that the first census of Augustus was so successful in raising money from the empire, that he has instructed it be done once in every generation."

"But why does this involve Miriam? She was born in Sephoris. That's where she must return."

Joachim shook his head. "No, a wife will travel with her husband to the place of his birth. That's the Roman law. What will you do if Miriam is due to give birth when you're traveling? How will you manage? Such a journey could endanger the life of the child," said Joachim.

"Yahweh will provide. And anyway, Bethlehem is only nine days journey, and we'll rest every night on the way so that we don't tire Miriam out."

But Hannah looked concerned. "Surely if you make a plea to the Roman authorities, they'll understand that a woman who will be as pregnant as Miriam can't undertake such a long journey."

Yosef reached over the table and held Hannah's hand. "Dear friend," he said, "the Roman authorities make no exception for age or pregnancy or weariness. They aren't the friends of the Jews. They hate us with all their hearts and wish to see us suffer. They despise us because we won't worship their gods. They're worse than the Greeks who defiled our Temples a hundred years ago. The name of Hyrcanus will be cursed forever for inviting them into our country for his own aggrandizement."

"What!" shouted Joachim, "It was the Roman General Pompey who invaded God's sacred land, may Yahweh cause his evil soul to be tormented for ever and ever."

"Nonsense, Joachim," said Yosef, "Aristobulus was our rightful king and would have defended us, but his brother Hyrcanus coveted the throne, and used General Pompey and his army to depose him. Now we have the Romans with their feet on our necks and not a moment of freedom in our lives and because of them the Sadducees are in charge of the Temple. Despite what the Greeks did to us by defiling our Temple with statues of their gods, I'd rather have the Greeks than the Romans. At least the Greeks were intelligent and could be reasoned with; but the Romans are cruel and evil and know only war and fighting. Had Aristobulus not lost the throne, then Judah and Israel would have..."

Joachim rose from his seat in order to rebut what Yosef was saying, but Hannah said, "Please, both of you. No arguments about the Romans or the Greeks or the Egyptians or the Midianites or anything to do with politics on this joyous night. You can argue about Rome and Egypt and all the world tomorrow and the day after and the day after that for all I care, but we're here to celebrate the happy news of our daughter's great fortune, and we shouldn't sully this feast with talk of ancient times and who did what to whom."

"Ancient? It was only sixty years ago. And if it hadn't been for Hyrcanus and Pompey, and then Augustus Caesar..." Joachim began, but Hannah gave him that special look reserved for her private censure, and he stopped talking.

But despite Hannah's entreaties, a mood of despair descended on the table. It was so easy in Nazareth, so far from the events of the world, to forget about the Roman occupation of their lands. Cruelty was rampant in the towns and the countryside, and there were stories even reaching the heights of Nazareth of old women who were trampled to death because they couldn't get out of the way of a column of Roman soldiers in time; or other stories of youths who were simply playing in their streets and they were abducted by Roman slave traders under the watchful eye of some Centurion who was obviously being bribed to ignore what was happening. Valuable farmland and their crops on the outskirts of Jewish cities were being destroyed to make way for Roman encampments and dwelling houses. Roman soldiers would steal from a street trader, and if the hapless man complained, he'd be beaten severely, sometimes to death. At regular intervals, farms were invaded by Roman soldiers under the orders of the Centurions and they stole the provisions of the family, so starvation would have been inevitable during the harsh winter months had not other families shared their meagre stores.

And now, Miriam realized, she would have to risk not just her own life but the life of her newborn baby by traveling to Bethlehem, the other end of the country, just because her husband Yosef had been born there. Could her life become any worse, she wondered?

She had never before traveled so far to the south of her country. Nor had she ever realized how the Romans and the *publicani* were ruining the lives of ordinary Israelites. There weren't any gates or bridges between Sephoris and Nazareth, and so there was no opportunity for a publican to set up a toll and impose a tax on the movement of people or goods or produce. But the moment she and Yosef stepped out onto the Highway of the Kings which led to Jerusalem, they came across rapacious publican after grasping publican who demanded a shekel here and a silver coin there because he'd been given control of that part of the road.

Usually Miriam argued with the publicans and told them that all they had on them was a few bekahs, but half a shekel wasn't of interest to the *publicani*, who occasionally would get their ruffians and bodyguards to search Yosef's belongings. Had Miriam not been secreting their money in a purse close to her large stomach, daring the guards to strip and search a pregnant woman, they would have lost all their money before they were even a quarter of the way to Jerusalem.

At the beginning of their journey, Yosef explained to her that these local *publicanis* were former slaves, or low-born Romans, or even Romanized Israelites who had purchased a particular section of road, or a border crossing, from more important *publicani*, who themselves purchased an entire area of land from Knights in Rome who themselves purchased the country from the Emperor. As long as the Emperor Augustus received his yearly tribute from a country and from people he despised, he didn't much care how the underlings in this distant part of his domain exploited their people.

And the effect was that the citizens were being crushed by the military might of Rome's soldiers and the financial larceny of the publicans and other tax collectors. Nothing, and nobody, could move in Israel or Judah without incurring heavy taxes. While she was living in her home in Sephoris, she hadn't realized the burdens under which the Jews lived. But now, traveling towards Jerusalem, it all became horribly clear to her. The further she traveled into Israel, the further she was from the safety and security of her home, the more she began to distrust, then despise the Romans and their acolytes. She had no idea of the damage which they were doing to her nation. But something inside her, some inner voice, told her that once she was no longer pregnant, once she was free again, she had to do something about it.

Yet despite the burdens of being stopped many times a day to pay taxes, Miriam was still filled with excitement at the prospect of seeing David's city. She would be in Bethlehem for the counting of the census, but Jerusalem was so close. Ever since she had been a little girl, and her father Joachim had spoken to her about Jerusalem and the Temple of Solomon and the High Priest and whispering the sacred and unknowable proper name of Yahweh, she had always wanted to be a part of it, to see it with her eyes, and not in her imagination.

She wanted to see the Urim and the Thummim, the twelve sacred stones within the High Priest's breastplate through which Yahweh made his will known to the Jewish people. She wanted to revel in the sacred rituals and hear the unknowable words of mystery which would reveal the truth about God and Heaven and all the other things which occupied her mind while she was falling asleep. She wanted to be near to the men who were near to Yahweh.

Her father disdained this new Temple because it had been built by Herod, but what did Miriam care if Solomon's Temple had been knocked down by the Babylonians and rebuilt by that evil old Idumaean, King Herod? Even her father, skeptical as he was, admitted the new one was just as grand and magnificent, burning white in the sun of the high mountains of Jerusalem.

She was so inexperienced in the ways of the world. She relished those times when traders came to Sephoris and sometimes would be invited into the house by Joachim for a meal; then she would bombard them with questions about what different cities were like, what sorts of people lived there, what they did, and what they thought. Sometimes, when she was really lucky, her father would invite in some merchants or traders from a caravan which was en route from Tyre or Siddon to Alexandria in Egypt. Then she would spend the entire night asking about the Egyptians and their rituals, or about the Phoenicians and the type of gods they worshipped. And no matter how much they explained it to her, Miriam couldn't understand how intelligent men and women could worship suns and moons and wind and rain and thunder when the creation of the One and Only True God, Yahweh was all around for everybody to see.

Sometimes, her mind spun for days afterwards about the things they described, and Miriam determined that one day, she would join a caravan and travel beyond Sephoris, and she would leave Judea and Israel and travel the world.

But the furthest she had traveled until now was to Nazareth to marry her husband; and with her marriage, it seemed as though any thoughts she might have had of traveling were now impossible to realize. And now that the Romans were everywhere in the Galilee, Yosef wouldn't allow her to stray far from her house, and he could never leave Nazareth because he was so busy as a carpenter. Which made this journey particularly special, because even though she was heavily pregnant, and a married woman, the thought of going to

Bethlehem, so close to Jerusalem, excited her, despite the danger of the Romans.

But her real dream, her goal, was to go to Jerusalem and stand on the Temple Mount in order to see if Yahweh was present. Maybe, without anybody seeing her, she could creep into the Holy of Holies, the *Kadosh ha Kadeshim* and, although she knew that it was empty and devoid of the lost Tablets which Moses had brought down from Sinai, to see if Yahweh was present. Of course, that was an impossible dream for her to realize because anybody except for the High Priest of the Cohanim who was caught in there would suffer death by stoning, so it would remain her dream.

She was beside herself with excitement at the prospect of seeing the newly expanded Temple, the *Beit ha Mikdash*, which had been renovated by King Herod on the site of the old Temple which, in its turn, had been built on the ruins of Solomon's Temple when the Jews had returned from exile in Babylon. The Temple which Herod had renovated had been a rude and rough one, unfit for the worship of a god like Yahweh, and Herod had determined that to earn the love of his new people, he would raise taxes to extend the Temple and make it grander than the Temple which the great King Solomon had built.

And it wasn't only the building which Miriam wanted to see, but also the priests in their magnificent robes and jewels, and to watch them sacrifice animals in the name of the Lord; to smell the smoke of incense and inhale the roasting flesh of animals offered up to propitiate God; oh, just to see the Priests and their servants, the Levites, in their fine crowns and their robes.

But it wasn't to be. Despite her wail of disappointment, Yosef had decreed otherwise, and in her condition, with a baby kicking inside her and feeling exhausted all the while, with her arms and ankles swelling up, she was in no state to argue with her husband. So she wasn't allowed to visit Jerusalem. Instead, Yosef had ordered that because of the anger and rebellion against the Roman rule in the city, it would be safer if they slept for the night in the Kedron valley outside the walls, and then skirted David's city to the south and onto the road to Bethlehem, just two days journey from Jerusalem.

Fortunately, Yosef had allowed her to travel on a donkey from Nazareth, which had made her journey much easier, though the undulations of the donkey's back as it traversed the ruts in the path made her feel as though she was in a boat on the Sea of Galilee, and its occasional stumble when its hooves landed on a rock and pitched her off the beast's back were making her feel constantly ill-at-ease, concerned about the effect this journey could be having upon the baby within her belly.

It was already evening on the sixth day of their journey from Nazareth, and Yosef was talking about pitching his camp for the night, when they rounded a bend in the road and he stopped walking. Instinctively, the donkey, led by a rope, also stopped. Miriam, whose eyes were transfixed by the sheer cliffs close by the road which plunged deep into ravines on the eastern side of the mountain range which they were traversing, looked at her husband to see why he wasn't walking any longer. And then, ahead of them on a nearby hill, as though some divine hand had draped a series of gigantic white candles onto the mountain top, stood Jerusalem, David's city, *Ir Shalom*, the City of Peace, the City of Inheritance. And as the evening sun sank beyond the hills towards the Great Sea in the Middle of the Earth, it looked as though the divine candles on the tops of the mountain were alive with flames burning in their towers.

Yosef turned and smiled at Miriam. "Jerusalem!" he said softly. "The Temple of Herod in that huge building on the outer edge of the city, near to the north wall. But I don't remember it this way. The last time I was here, twenty years ago, the city hadn't spread this far to the north..." He pointed to the walls, "...and these walls. I remember one wall, but not this second huge wall around the city. And those...," he said, pointing to two huge round towers which seemed to stretch upwards to try to touch the sky, "...those must be the Antonia fortress and the Citadel that I've heard so much about. People are already calling it the Tower of David in sorrow for the great king's disappointment, because Yahweh forbad David from building his Temple here because he had killed so many in war. It was left to his son King Solomon to begin building a Temple which would be a proper house for the Tablets which Moses the Lawgiver brought down from the Mountain of Sinai..."

Miriam was irritated whenever Yosef explained matters of the Torah with which she was equally as familiar as was he. But she allowed her irritation to pass because she was transfixed by her first look at Jerusalem. It was huge, magnificent, wondrous. Herod had built a palace in Sephoris, which she thought was the most wonderful building she'd ever seen; but compared to Jerusalem, it was nothing more than a shed where the cattle were kept in the winter.

She realized that she was staring at Jerusalem open-mouthed in awe at both its size and its beauty. "It's the most wonderful city in the world," she told her husband. "I know you said that we can't enter it, but I have to see it. I must," she demanded.

He nodded. He also wanted to enter the city and see what changes King Herod had made since the last time he'd been here all those years ago. "When we return from Bethlehem and the census, it's possible that there will be fewer Romans in Jerusalem. They'll probably be in other cities conducting the will of the Emperor. Maybe it'll be safer on our return journey to enter the city and spend a day looking around."

It was a major concession, and Miriam was overwhelmed by excitement; but she knew enough to remain silent, and not to press her luck further by asking additional favors of her husband. Yosef tugged on the rope, and the donkey jerked forward. "They say that there's a hippodrome for horse races, and a huge marketplace where all the produce from every city in the world can be purchased; and they say that there's a magnificent theatre where actors perform plays. Not Jewish plays, of course, but Roman and Greek plays. King Herod entertains the Governors and the Procurators and important visitors, and they say that there are a thousand slaves who serve at his banquets."

Miriam shook her head in disbelief. She kicked the donkey forward, impelling it towards Bethlehem; for the sooner they arrived and registered and had her baby, the sooner they could return here to visit Jerusalem. And if Yosef thought that they were only going to spend one day there, he was very much mistaken. She had never seen Jerusalem before, and the likelihood is that she would never see it again. Her dreams of traveling to other parts of the Roman world disappeared when she married and became a wife to Yosef. That, she accepted. So if this was the only benefit she would ever receive in her entire life by marrying a Nazarene who was born in Bethlehem, then she intended to make the most of her opportunity.

They walked on and descended into the Kedron Valley to the east of Jerusalem. At the foot of the mountain on which the city was built, with the vast walls soaring above them towards heaven itself, they set up their modest encampment within sight of the Tomb of the Prophet Zachariah.

As Yosef unburdened the donkey and began setting out the straw mats and blankets on which they would sleep, Miriam began gathering wood from the valley floor to start the fire. She would knead flour and water quickly and make some bread which, when baked in their small, portable oven, she would spread liberally with butter and honey. Then she would boil some eggs which Yosef had found in a wild hen's nest during the morning. That, with some herbs she'd found on the side of a hill, plus some root vegetables she'd picked up along the way and some wine she'd brought from home should make a wonderful meal.

Miriam busied herself with gathering kindling and then larger twigs. Because of the census, there had been so many travelers through the valley recently that wood wasn't as easy to find as it was in the hills around Nazareth; but she found sufficient, and within moments, the fire was warming both her and the oven in which she would cook the bread. From the food sacks, she took out two scoops of millet flour and one of wheat flour, and poured oil onto them, mixing them around until it was a paste. Then she added milk and some water until it was of the right consistency. Miriam then kneaded the dough through her hands and fingers until it was of sufficient thickness and strength to be placed onto the warm floor of the oven. The mixture immediately began to sizzle and spit and bubble, and the delicious aromas of fresh bread rose up into the evening sky. Yosef turned at the smell and smiled at her. His stomach groaned at the smell of food, and he walked over to Miriam, and said a blessing over the food which they would soon consume.

As a treat for having reached the landmark of Jerusalem, Yosef opened one of the saddlebags, and took out some dried fish which he had brought with him from Nazareth in order to give Miriam sufficient healthy food for her baby, now almost full-grown within her belly and ready to be born; he cut two generous slices, removed some bones, and gave them to her.

They sat and ate the bread and fish, the eggs mixed with the herbs and the softened roots and drank the wine in silence, glad not to be moving, happy to be within sight of the walls of Jerusalem.

When their meal was finished, and they had said their thanksgiving prayers, Miriam asked Yosef if, just this once, he would wash the plates and utensils, as she particularly wanted to visit the Tomb of Zachariah. He encouraged to her to walk across to the Tomb but cautioned her about strangers and robbers who might be in the Valley waiting to take advantage of travelers.

But she wasn't concerned. From the dozens of fires which were blazing or being started, Miriam realized that there were hundreds of travelers on the road for the Census who had made camp for the night in the Valley, and she knew that were she to be assaulted, she would just need to scream, and many men would come running to her aid.

The Tomb was a funny, square mausoleum, with some columns and a roof like a tiny Greek Temple. Yet it was the burial place of one of the greatest men in the history of all of Israel. Zachariah's prophesies in the time of the Persians had always struck a chord deep within her. It was Zachariah, and his friend Haggai who demanded that Solomon's Temple be rebuilt. Zachariah said that until this was done, the coming Age of Yahweh would never happen, and the Jewish people would always wander in eternal darkness. On many nights, when she was alone in her room, Miriam would read parts of the scroll of Zachariah in which he told of his visions of the end of the world and of the four horsemen who would foreshadow the arrival of the Messiah, of Yahweh's return to sit in His kingdom of Jerusalem, and of the proper re-building of Solomon's Temple.

He had written words which showed her that what had been constructed by Herod was done, not for Yahweh, but in order to impress the Romans. Though magnificent, Herod's was not a proper Temple built by the Jews, for the Jews! Zachariah had written that when a true temple was built, and the last block was put into place,

Yahweh would descend from the Heavens with Moses and Aaron to sit in His House, and then and only then would all the world recognize Yahweh as Israel's True God.

She fell to her knees before the Tomb and prayed a long and silent prayer for Zacharia to protect her and her baby child, and to help the people of Israel rid their land of the Romans once and for all time.

+

She awoke not with the cold, but through a vibration in the floor of the valley. A rumbling. Like an earthquake she'd once experience, many years earlier, which had shaken houses and caused pots to fall from shelves. But this was a deeper rumbling; it seemed to come in waves and grew stronger and more persistent the more she wakened into consciousness.

Miriam sat bolt upright in the early morning light, and in the northern end of the valley, she saw clouds of dust. Yosef was already sitting up, still huddled in his blanket, looking north to try to understand what was the disturbance to God's quiet on such a beautiful morning.

And then they saw them! A *centuria* of about eighty or ninety Roman soldiers led by ten horsemen. At the head of the column was a Centurion riding in a chariot, weaving in and out of the huddled Jewish travelers who were still asleep on the floor of the valley, the horsemen riding behind him and finally the leather-clad soldiers running in menacing uniform lines.

"Quickly, Miriam," said Yosef. "We must get out of their way and hide among the trees."

But she didn't move.

"Miriam," said Yosef as he gathered the blankets and started to pack the mule. "Get up quickly."

But still she sat there, looking in increasing anger at the armed force which was coming quickly towards her. Jewish travelers in the path of the Romans were scampering out of their way, but Miriam refused to move. Her prayers to Zachariah the previous night, and her dreams when he'd visited her in her sleep, made her feel angry at the invasion of her resting place.

"Miriam!" shouted Yosef as he led the donkey up a short path away from the valley floor. "Come here now!"

She stood, but didn't move. Instead, she felt herself impelled to action, to refuse the arbitrary commands of the Romans; to demand her rights as an Israelite woman who was given the privilege of living in this land by Yahweh Himself. Who did these Romans think that they were, riding on Yahweh's land, telling the Chosen People to move out of their way!

Miriam positioned herself in the path of the Roman *centuria*, directly in front of the charioteer and the following horsemen as they rode towards her.

Assuming that his wife was following him, Yosef found a safe place behind some bushes, and tethered the donkey. Then he turned, and Yosef realized in horror that Miriam, still down on the floor of the valley, had not followed him, but instead had stationed herself right in the place to which the Army was riding at a manic pace.

He screamed her name in growing panic, but Miriam didn't even turn to acknowledge him. Instead, she stared directly at the Charioteer who was riding towards her in a fury of dust and antagonism. Surprised that a Jewish woman hadn't scampered out of his way, the Roman soldier reined his chariot to a halt and skidded on the dust and detritus in front of her, his horses rearing up and neighing in anger. He could easily have ridden over or around her, but he recognized resistance when he saw it, and he knew how to deal with it.

"In the name of the Senate and the People of Rome, I command you to move aside for Caesar's army," he shouted at Miriam.

Suddenly terrified and realizing the stupidity of what she had done, Miriam's immediate instinct was to run towards Yosef. But at the very moment when her legs seemed like water, a vision of the Prophet Zachariah came suddenly into her mind, and she gained courage. And her courage increased when she saw the look of arrogance in the Roman's eye.

"Can't the Roman army go around a lone woman who is heavy with a child?" she asked.

And then the soldier noticed that she was, indeed, so pregnant that she would soon give birth. "Woman," he said, "I don't wish you harm. Not in your condition. Move aside and let me and my men pass."

From a distance, she heard Yosef's plaintive cry of her name, but she ignored him. She saw other Jews in the bushes staring at her.

"This is my land, Roman. My feet have more right to be here than your iron wheels. My ancestors lived here a thousand years before Rome was even a dream. If you want to travel in my land, you will have to go around me."

By now, the Roman *centuria* had caught up with their commander and the horsemen who followed him. Grateful of the rest, they stood panting behind him, leaning on their spears, catching their breath. All he had to do was to strike her dead with his sword and continue. But there was something about this woman which made him stop in wonder. Her eyes were suffused with a light which he hadn't seen before. Other Jews cowered when he looked at them; but this woman stared directly at him, almost daring him to raise his strong arm against her feebleness.

"You know I could arrest you and imprison you in the Jerusalem fortress for rebellion against the Roman Army," he told her. But his voice carried no conviction.

Miriam smiled and nodded at him. "And no doubt Caesar Augustus would reward you handsomely for your bravery against an unarmed Israelite woman who is nine months pregnant."

He burst out laughing. He turned to his men, and shouted, "Here stands the first truly brave Jewish woman I've ever met. On this first and last occasion, in deference to a pregnant woman and the life she bears inside of her, Rome will give way to Israel."

His men laughed, and the Roman soldier looked at Miriam, saying, "May your God continue to protect you." He whipped his horse around her. Miriam stood there as the chariot trundled past her, followed by the cavalry and then the *centuria* who ran to follow.

She was still standing, stock still, when the Romans were already in the distance and Yosef returned to stand before her.

He was going to admonish her severely, but he looked into her eyes and there was a spirit there which he'd never seen before. Her eyes were more alive and animated than he'd ever seen them.

"Miriam?"

"Yosef, last night, the Prophet Zachariah came to me. In a dream. He told me that I will give birth to a great man who will save the Jews from Rome. Who will rebuild the Temple of Solomon as God meant it to be. Who will cleanse this land of ungodly ways. Yosef, the Prophet told me that I must stand against the Romans, and begin the work which my son will complete. And I did it. You saw me. I was terrified, but I remembered the words of the Prophet and I knew that I wouldn't be hurt."

Yosef felt his heart pounding. He heard other Jews moving towards him; to congratulate him and Miriam on their bravery. But he couldn't find any words to say, other than "Yahweh is great. Praise be to Yahweh."

CHAPTER FOUR

Beit Lehem, A town a day's walk south of Jerusalem

Never in her young life did she think that she would experience such a depth of pain. Never did she believe that her body could be so far beyond her control, contorted in waves of agony which she thought would tear her apart and leave her and her baby dead. Indeed, at moments when her contractions were at their worst, death was what she wished for. Her mother had told her of the pain of bearing a child, a result of the guilt of Mother Eve in her disobeying of Yahweh and seduction of Father Adam to commit the sin of knowledge, but nobody had ever said that it would be as overwhelmingly horrible as this! Was Eve *really* that evil to deserve such punishment from Yahweh? She herself had been seduced by a serpent and in her confusion had told Adam of wonders of the fruit of the Tree of Knowledge...but Miriam's thoughts about the first scroll of the Books of Moses suddenly collapsed into a miasma of pain and she screamed as the knives and hot staves again assaulted her back and belly and thighs.

As one wave of contractions subsided and before another began, she clasped Yosef's hands and begged him to bring her the help of a midwife or even the wife of the man in whose house they had been taken in as guests. He'd never witnessed the births of his other children; he'd never been a traveler before or been on the road when his late wife was pregnant. So his horror at Miriam's birth pains impelled him into action, but when he stood to run out of the room to fetch some help, the next contraction began, and she pulled him back to grip his hand in an effort to share the pain she was feeling with him. The touch of his hand soothed her but didn't make the pain disappear.

Avishag, the wife of Benjamin, son of Menasseh of Beit Lechem, walked hurriedly from her house to the shed where Jewish custom decreed that she and her husband had to accommodate visitors and travelers and guests who were on the road. She was frankly fed up with accommodating unwanted and unexpected guests. If it wasn't the Festival of Booths, it was the Celebration of the Passover and the

Flight from Egypt, or some other reason the Ancients had decreed that a Jewish house must offer hospitality to travelers.

And now she was forced to obey the Law and give over her house to strangers because of this ridiculous Roman census. Not the most generous of women, Avishag had become increasingly annoyed at the numbers of travelers who had flooded into Beit Lechem because of the census, and who her husband Benjamin insisted must be given hospitality. She knew Jewish customs and traditions as well as he, and so she made the outer buildings as comfortable as possible; but by the time the tenth man and woman had come and gone, her patience was nearly at an end; until the arrival of the poor girl from Nazareth who was ghostly white and in imminent danger of giving birth on her doorstep.

Seeing her and her much older husband standing there looking exhausted and on the point of collapsing, Avishag had pushed Benjamin out of the way, and immediately helped the girl to the outhouse, laid her down on a blanket, ordered her husband to soothe her brow and cool her body with water, and set to in the kitchen by boiling water and preparing cloth for the baby. As Miriam's screams increased in pitch and intensity, Avishag knew that birth was only hours away.

Leaving her house and walking down the path to the outhouse where food was stored for the winter months, Avishag carried a bowl of hot water which the poor young woman would need to wash away the blood and afterbirth when the baby was born. Her husband Benjamin was fussing and fretting in the doorway, looking in at the scene in concern. She nudged him to one side, entered the dimly-lit barn, and barked an order to Yosef to move aside.

"How bad are the pains?" she asked Miriam. It was an unnecessary question, because from the look on the poor child's face, they were at their very peak, racking her entire body with their misery. Avishag remembered with a shudder her own pains when her first child was born. All she had wanted was the Angel of Death to descend, end the curse of Eve, and give her relief from the misery.

The older woman told Yosef to go outside, and when the two women were alone, Avishag gently lifted Miriam's clothes, and saw that the baby's head was already visible. God only knew how she'd managed to walk to the doorstep when she was already in labor.

Because the girl's mother wasn't here thanks to the damnable census, Avishag knew that she'd have to act in her place. Miriam's elderly husband was useless, as were all men, and so Avishag sat her up, and forced her onto her knees still breathing deeply to expel the air as though she was blowing dust away from the table. And so they continued, with increasing pain and agony, until suddenly there was enough of the baby visible outside of Miriam for Avishag to gently twist the baby's head, cautiously pull the infant from the young woman's body, and ease out the afterbirth. Miriam, utterly spent and near to losing consciousness, fell back onto the mat, and began to cry in relief that the pain had suddenly disappeared.

Avishag tied the cord, ensured that the little boy had all his limbs and fingers, wiped his eyes and nose with warm water, and wrapped him tightly in a swaddling cloth, and handed him to Miriam. The infant, a perfect little boy, lay inert and lifeless until Avishag pinched him hard on his ankle. Then he winced, the full gusto of life entered his body, and he emitted a scream easily as loud as his mother's had been, which he continued almost without taking a breath. Miriam looked up, and despite her exhaustion, she smiled broadly when she saw her baby.

For the first time since she'd met the young woman late on the previous night, Miriam's eyes didn't wear a mask of pain; instead, she smiled at Avishag and her dry lips mouthed the words 'thank you.' But it was when Miriam first saw her baby, and when the normally stern and uncompromising Avishag witnessed the depth of love the young woman felt, that the dam of tears was breached, and Miriam sobbed and hugged the infant she called Jeshua and cried and laughed and kissed him and thanked Avishag again, all at the same moment. The two women hugged in their shared instant of giving life, and kissed each other.

"You have a son," Avishag said to Yosef when she felt his presence behind her. "A fine young man with strong lungs. He is complete with all God's parts...arms and legs and all else which will enable him to grow into a man. A treasure for all Israel. May Yahweh bless him and his family, and make His Holy countenance shine forth and help the little lad to prosper and grow and be a strength for our nation. May the Holy One, Blessed be He, make him like Moses and Aaron and grant him a strong right hand and an arm outstretched to protect widows and orphans, the poor and the homeless, especially in these dark and evil times."

Yosef and Benjamin, standing over the bed and looking down at the mother and child, said together "Amen."

"So," said Benjamin after Yosef and Miriam had had enough time looking at, and fondling their child, "let's pour some cups of wine and say a proper blessing to Yahweh for this miracle. Yosef, follow me and we'll see how many cups we can empty together. You, my friend, have had a hard time with all your worry about Miriam's safety; you need to drown your troubles with some festivities. And with all these travelers and strangers on the roads, and with the Romans breathing down our necks, it'll be good to get drunk and forget our predicament."

As the men left the outhouse, leaving Miriam and Jeshua alone, all Avishag could do was to grin and shrug. They were getting drunk because of all Yosef's hard work. She couldn't help but smile. It was the way of the world.

+

The screams which erupted from the bed chamber didn't even cause a ripple of concern on any of the faces of the courtiers, priests, Roman officials, Jewish noblemen or visitors from other realms. In the cool atmosphere of the marble palace, the noises of pain wafted away with the gentle late summer breezes. Even when they grew louder and louder as the agony gripped the King's body in yet another spasm, or Herod suffered yet another excruciating paroxysm or seizure of his muscles or bowels or belly and he roared like a wounded mountain lion, nobody paid his screams the slightest bit of attention.

They had heard the screeching before. Many times before. The screams never ceased. Even since Yahweh had afflicted King Herod with a multiplicity of diseases and ailments, he had been in constant pain. Doctor after doctor had tried to cure him and their failure had been greeted by their summary executions. Some were roasted slowly to death over an open fire, affording the watching Herod some amusement if not relief; some were thrown from the high walls of the Palace; some were pegged to stakes in the desert to be desiccated by the sun and then eaten to death by mountain lions or stung by scorpions. But because of Herod's treatment of his doctors, there were now almost none left in the land, for so many wise men and doctors, especially those who lived in Jerusalem and nearby towns, had all fled to Egypt in fear of being visited by Herod's Captain, and ordered to attend upon his master.

So Herod, who would probably not see the beginning his seventieth year on earth, lay in baths of cold asses milk or tubs of warm oil in a futile attempt to cure the breakdown of his kidneys, his skin, his liver, and his private parts. As though the pain in the rest of his body wasn't sufficient punishment from Yahweh, the visible disintegration of his manhood was a sign that God hated him and that he hated God. His penis and scrotum, those parts of his body which had served him well throughout all his long life, were now weak and risible remnants of his Kingship, visibly festering and rotting before his very eyes and stinking to such an extent that only those who were ordered to, could bear to be close to him.

Many words were forbidden in Herod's presence, and his courtiers, and even some of the lesser Romans who were attached to his court, had learned from hard experience, not to use them. There was never to be any sentence in which the word 'death' occurred; or 'illness'; or 'pain'. Or any word which might be used to intimate to Herod that others beyond the confines of his Palace knew of his suffering. For he believed with fervent passion that if word got out to the Israelites that Herod was in pain from his illnesses and on his deathbed, his ten wives and fifteen children, all of whom would claim the Kingdom, would hover like vultures regardless of which one he nominated. And doubtless many...perhaps all...who learned of his weakened condition would draw close and happily stick a knife into his ribs.

As the pains subsided, his mind cleared, and King Herod was carried from the bath of oil to his bedchamber. He lay there, swathed in towels, and was able to think clearly once again. How had it all come to this? When he'd been a young man, he'd been a soldier and a horseman and a lover; he'd ridden camels across the desert for an entire day without feeling even a twinge of pain in his body; he'd been the first into a battle and would take his sword against twenty men before breaking into a sweat; he would stand before his people and would command their attention just by the magnificence of his voice or his demeanor; and when he looked at a young woman, within moments his manhood would stand to attention with the rigidity of an eager young Palace guard and he'd have her bedded by evening and their love making would last all through the night. How many of the women he'd had during the night and early parts of the morning, had been unable to rise or walk away from his bedchamber, whereas he was enthused with vigor and would spring into action and command the day.

Yet here he now lay, an old man in a diseased and rotting body. Herod, sad, pain-racked, depleted and contaminated, who for some reason they still called 'Great.' A shadow of the man he once was, swaddled in wet oily towels as though he were an infant. He knew he was despised, feared. In his younger day, he had relished the fear he put into people. Yet now, all he wanted was to be loved by his chosen people. All he wished for was that the people of Israel and for the god he had chosen as his own, Yahweh, would love him. His every waking moment, since imploring the Caesar in Rome to make him King of the Jews, had been devoted to glorifying Israel and making his realm into the most celebrated in the entire Roman empire.

But no matter what he'd done, no matter who he had had to kill to get his way and protect the longevity of his rule, he could never get the Israelites to love him. Hadn't he given these ungrateful Jews a new Temple, new towns, enlarged the borders by capturing neighboring nations, built entire new harbors for their ships, new roads and new marketplaces? Had he not invited the Romans in as protectors from the Parthians when they set up Antigonas as the King of the Jews? Had he not managed to escape and beg the Romans to nominate him as ruler of the Jews and had they not done his bidding? Who else could bend the great Roman Empire to do his bidding? Nobody! Only Herod.

Yet despite the glory he'd brought to the realm, the Jews never accepted him, just because he was born an Idumænean from the desert kingdom of the Edoms; just because his people were nomads and wanderers and desert traders, shepherds and animal herders, these arrogant city-dwelling Jews looked down upon them and treated them with contempt.

He'd even divorced his wife Doris to marry Mariamne, granddaughter of the Jews' beloved King John Hyrcanus. She was his perfect wife, for she was born a Hasmonean princess and even to this day, despite his many other wives, he still loved her dearly and passionately. Because of her entreaties, he'd made many treacherous Hasmoneans into his courtiers and given them great wealth in his court even though many had tried to stab him in the back. But it was all to no avail, for the more he did for his people, the more they despised him.

The question of succession had plagued him for years. He recalled the nights he'd spent walking the walls and battlements of his Palace, thinking who should be King when Yahweh called him into the sky. Antipater, his son by Doris? Aristobulus or Alexander, his sons by Mariamne? Well, it was too late for them. He'd had them strangled! Both of them! His own sons! It had been painful, but they'd deserved it. They'd called him a shameless old man who died his hair and they'd intrigued with the captains of the army to overthrow him; so they had to die, sons or not! How long ago had he given orders for them to be strangled? Three years? And since then, his body was increasingly racked by aches and pains, and his manhood, his very manhood which had satisfied all the needs of each and every one of his ten wives and countless servants, was turning black and festering in front of his very eyes.

As the pains began to grow again, a servant gave him a potion of tamarix, garlic and pomegranate which he drank down in one draft. He was exhausted from yet another day of fighting the pains; when would Yahweh make the medicines work and give him respite from his daily misery? The potions, drafts and medicines he was given didn't seem to relieve the symptoms at all.

During the day, he'd conducted just one meeting, and yet he could barely concentrate on what was happening around him. The audience had been with a provincial governor, who had come to pay him tribute, but even that had exhausted him. The gift the man had brought was a spice box made of Mother of Pearl. The nacre was covered in finely wrought gold filigree with lapis lazuli and diamonds in the lid. In itself, it was exquisite, but when Herod opened it, he found two vials containing the priceless imperial purple. Even he, used to receiving wonderful tributes, was amazed. These vials contained liquid taken from the rare murex shell found only in Phoenicia and allowed to be used only by the Caesars in Rome as dyes for their robes. The box and its contents were worth a fortune, so in return, he'd granted the governor taxation rights on imports at a small port in the province of Joppa where few boats landed, so it wasn't a major concession in return for what must have cost the governor a year's worth of income. The governor had stolen the wealth of his people in taxes to pay for Herod's gift, and now Herod was rewarding him in his pocket by giving him a concession over the port. It was a good deal. Only the people would suffer.

When he was younger, he would have been excited at the beautiful gift, and would have used it as a weapon of seduction in his conquest of the wife or daughter of an important man; but now, even when he first held the gift, he immediately lost interest in it as the pains spread from his back, through his belly to his arms and legs. What had his life come to?

He could feel himself slipping into unconsciousness again. Waves of nausea swept over him as the room began to spin. Voices were all around him, yet he knew he was alone except for a servant whose tongue had been cut out so he could repeat nothing of what he overheard.

Today, the voices were so clear. *"Jews hate you,"* they said. *"Israel wants to see you dead."* It was youngsters who were saying these things. *"No spawn of Herod will inherit your kingdom when you die. Instead a child will be born who will steal your wealth, and you will be forgotten."*

Who was saying these things? Sounded like young voices. Like the voices of children. Well, for saying such things, they would die. All of them!

"Kill all of the children of Israel," he screamed to his captains, to his soldiers, to his courtiers. His voice hoarse from the potion and the pain, he yelled for all to hear, "Kill them all. Especially the newborn children. Every child in the land is to die for daring to say such things." Not a soul responded, so he screamed again, "Nobody will take my kingdom from me. Let them all die. Kill all of Israel's children! I command it."

Those who were in parts of the Palace close to his bedchamber heard him shouting and listened to what he was saying. The looked at each other frowning, and repeated, *"Kill the children of Israel?"*

They laughed. He was old and sick and demented. He gave such orders all the while. In earlier days people had obeyed for fear of losing their own lives unless his orders were to be followed to the letter. But these days, his orders were treated with contempt and never inscribed into law. What could the old bastard do about their disobedience? He couldn't even walk. So he ranted and raved, and was ignored. Everybody was waiting for his death, so why obey a man when he had the strength of a pigeon, and he was just a pathetic, sick old carcass to whom nobody gave any serious consideration any longer.

"Kill all of the children of Israel," one of the courtiers repeated, his voice taking on a mocking semblance of Herod's croak. He looked at the captain of his army. The soldier smiled and shook his head. "Mad!" said the soldier, and laughed. "Mad as a Prophet. He'll soon be gone. Then we can all rest in peace."

"Aye," said the courtier, "but who comes after?"

+

Miriam looked in horror at Neriah, Avishag's sister, and asked her to repeat the information.

"King Herod has issued an instruction to have all the children of Israel born in the past year put to death," Neriah said. "I didn't believe it myself at first, but my husband, who is a cook in the Palace, heard it from one of Herod's trusted sycophants. People laughed and didn't appear to take it seriously, but there are so many people around Herod these days who want his blessing to succeed him when he dies, that you never know what will happen. Antipater, Herod's son by Doris is exiled in Rome, but there are rumors which say that now Herod is dying, Antipater is returning. He'll do anything for his father's favor, and if he arrives and hears that his father's orders haven't been carried out, he could do it himself.

"I tell you, Miriam, you must leave this accursed land. Yahweh has deserted us and left His people to the hands of the Romans and the Idumaeneans, and we are lost. We, the people whom He brought out of Egypt and to whom He gave the land of Israel as an inheritance! Now we are abandoned. Go to another land, Miriam, to save your child. Go far from this country to a land where the people live in freedom. Return when Yahweh returns to His land."

"All the children?" she asked, still too stunned to fully comprehend the news which Avishag's sister had brought. "But how could he kill all the children? Why would he kill all the children?"

"They say he has had a vision. In his mortification, he hears voices. And the voices were of the young and the poor, and they told him that he would be soon die, and that he would be replaced as King, not by one of his brood, but by a poor and simple child. An Israelite child."

"He would kill all of our children?" she repeated, this time more to herself than the horrified listeners in the room, trying to comprehend the enormity of what Neriah has been saying. "He would murder..."

Neriah nodded. "He's done it before and he'll do it again before he dies and his body is eaten by worms. He kills without a moment's thought. He once heard that students of a particular Rabbi were making fun of him, and he had a huge fire built in the center of their town, and all of them were thrown alive into the flames. I could tell you more, but with a baby just a week old, you're not in any condition to hear such things. But I came tonight to warn you and Yosef to leave Israel, to go to Esbus or Peraea or Ituraea or even Phoenicia. Maybe as far as Egypt. But you must leave and make your lives outside of Israel in order to protect the life of your baby."

Neriah bent down and kissed Jeshua, who was sleeping soundly in his mother's arms. She said a blessing over him, and then turned and walked towards the door of the house. "May Yahweh bless the inhabitants of this home and make it safe from those of our rulers by whose grace we should be protected. May Yahweh bring a swift and merciful end to our suffering."

They all said their 'Amens', and when Yosef and Miriam were alone with Benjamin and Avishag, they talked about what should be done.

"My husband and I are not in Herod's eyes," said Avishag. "Our children are grown and live in their own homes and their children, thank God, are too old to be in danger from Herod; so there is less reason for us to flee than there is for you and your baby. Whether you should go depends on whether what Neriah said is true. I know she told the truth for she is my sister, but she may be repeating gossip which is false. Still, even if it was the ravings of a madman, these are murderous times, and if you ask my opinion, you should err on the side of caution."

Yosef nodded in agreement. "I will send word to my family and yours, Miriam. I will explain that we will not return to Nazareth until Herod is dead. I will tell our family and friends that we have traveled to Egypt and out of his reach."

"Egypt?" she asked, stunned by Yosef deciding on a country which was so far away.

He nodded. "The Prophet Hosea said, *'When Israel was a child, I loved him, and out of Egypt I called my son.'* To me, this is a sign that Yahweh has left Israel and is now in Egypt and is calling to our son Jeshua and to us as his parents to join him in the land from which our forefathers were exiled."

Horrified at the prospect of more travel, and of not returning to her home in Galilee, Miriam said archly, "But husband, surely the prophet meant that God, in Israel, was calling to us to leave Egypt. Surely this is why our father Moses brought us out of the Land of our bondage."

Yosef smiled, and shook his head gently, "No my love. Moses our Father brought us out of Egypt, but Israel has been stolen from us by Herod and the Romans. I believe that Hosea the Prophet foretold that our child Jeshua will be loved by Yahweh in Egypt and is calling for him to come. We shall go there, Miriam, where it is safe from Herod and his breed. When Herod dies...when Yahweh returns to Israel...and when peace settles on this land, then we will return."

Miriam was stunned by her sudden reversal of fortunes. It was not a woman's place to argue further with her husband, but she couldn't allow Yosef to take her so far away from her home just because of the ravings of a lunatic king. Yes, Herod was a violent and dangerous man who had killed many Israelites, including his own sons and some of his wives. He was a monster who had married ten women and had spawned numerous children, but any father who could put to death his own sons Aristobulus and Alexander, would easily put to death all the first-born children of Israel just as Moses had done in Egypt when the Pharaoh had refused God's orders to let his people Israel go free.

And it was then that Miriam stopped breathing and listening to her husband's words, for she suddenly realized that this could be a test from Yahweh Himself. Could her own son, her newborn babe, her darling Jeshua, have been sent by God to become a second Moses? Could her son save the Children of Israel from the monstrosities of the Romans and of the family of King Herod? Was this why he was born to her even though she hadn't known a man's body? Her body tingled with the sudden realization that the Holy *Ruach*, the spirit of God, might be in the room with her. Could Yahweh Himself be looking down upon such a humble and ordinary woman laying in an outhouse, and directly guiding her thoughts and her actions? Could Jeshua be a holy child, and not just an ordinary child? Could he be another Moses, another Isaiah, another Elijah? Her throat dried at the thought of what could be, and she was overwhelmed by fear and incomprehension. She was just an ordinary Jewish girl. Why would Yahweh have chosen her? Yet the mothers of Isaiah and Elijah, Moses and Joshua had been ordinary Jewish women.

She knew to remain silent and not make these thoughts known, or Yosef would say that she was suffering a fit of the mind and would lock her in her room until sanity had been restored. So she looked at her husband and smiled and nodded.

Yet there was something which almost forced her to share her thoughts with Yosef, but to do so would make him think that childbirth had driven her mad. She wanted to argue with him about going to Egypt, but caution stilled her tongue. For in her heart, she accepted that he was right, and now even Yahweh Himself was telling her to go. Yosef's interpretation was based on his understanding of Herod and the realities of what Israel had become, for why would God, the father and protector of Israel, allow a monster like Herod to rule over His people were He still in residence. No, she realized, God the Father must have left the land of Israel and was in Egypt. And perhaps her son's birth was a sign from Yahweh Himself.

The prophets had foretold it. Hadn't the Prophet Micah said *"But you, Beth Lechem Ephratah, though you be little among the thousands of Judah, yet out of you shall he come forth unto me that is to be ruler in Israel; whose goings forth have been from of old, from everlasting."*

And hadn't the great Prophet Isaiah himself written, *"For unto us a child is born, unto us a son is given: and the government shall be upon his shoulder: and his name shall be called Wonderful, Counsellor, The mighty God, The everlasting Father, The Prince of Peace."*

And didn't Isaiah himself predict that there would come forth a rod out of the stem of Jesse, and a Branch shall grow out of his roots, and wasn't Yosef himself from the stem of Jesse, father of King David? And finally, and most important, hadn't Isaiah said, *"Therefore the Lord himself shall give you a sign; Behold, a pure young woman shall conceive, and bear a son, and shall call His name Immanuel."*

Could the prophet have meant a virgin, instead of a young woman? And could he have called her offspring Immanuel because it meant *'God is with us'*. Perhaps instead she should have called her son Immanuel and not Jeshua. Yet Jeshua meant 'savior' so...so...her mind couldn't even begin to encompass the possibilities.

She lay back still exhausted. For a young woman who, until the previous year, had never traveled further than the fields around Sephoris, she was not only seeing Jerusalem and Beit Lechem and other parts of Israel for the first time; but now she was going to see Egypt, the land of the Pharaohs and the Pyramids and the Sphinxes. As the wives of the ancient Israelites had left their home during a time of famine to travel to Egypt, so she too would leave her home with her newborn babe and travel to Egypt in the hope of finding a good and kindly ruler who would protect them from the madness which had overtaken her nation.

Her mind was ablaze with the prospects, of fear and uncertainty, and yet with a certain excitement that, unlike her friends in Sephoris, she would see the entire world before she returned.

And then her baby Jeshua stirred and he began to mewl, his mouth seeking her breast. She looked down at him, stroked his chubby cheek, and fed the infant. Yosef smiled as he saw the love and devotion in Miriam's eyes as she looked at the baby. But as Miriam took Jeshua to her breast and stroked his delicate head, she was thinking very different thoughts than those of her husband. She was beginning to see the child not as her baby, but as an infant who belonged to all Israel.

CHAPTER FIVE

Elephantine Island, Egypt the year 4 BCE

Like Moses in the bulrushes of ancient Egypt, in the time before the Exodus from the cruel Pharaoh Ramses whom their Prophets said was the enslaver of the Israelite tribes, Miriam had placed her infant son in a cradle of reeds, a basket which now floated beside her in the water. The tiny crib was tethered to a jetty where boats which the Egyptians called *feluccas* plied back and forth from the western bank of the Nile to the Island of Elephantine, carrying the Island's supplies. Miriam was happy to place little Jeshua in the cradle so that the gentle waves which lapped the Island's edge lulled him to sleep. The site she chose, at the footings of an ancient bridge, long ago destroyed by a torrential flood and which had once connected the Island to the mainland, was too shallow for large river fish, and she felt a degree of safety for her child.

At first, Yosef had been very worried about keeping little Jeshua in a crib in the water. He warned her of the Nile crocodiles which infested this part of the river, hideous creatures which swam lazily and meandered too and fro with only their eyes and snouts visible as they watched everything from the middle of the river. No part of the mighty Nile River was too shallow for them, for unlike the fishes of the deep, these crocodiles swam at the surface of the water, but could breathe air when they waded onto the shore. They were a terrifying menace, and every year, all people who lived close to the shores of the river would suddenly hear a heart-rending scream, and know that an invisible crocodile had suddenly rushed out of the water and dragged some terrified man or woman or child, or some animal come to drink at the water's edge, and was now rolling its body around the creature to drown it.

Crocodiles sometimes appeared just to be drifting with the current as though they were asleep, and that was when they were at their most threatening. In the first days of their arrival at Elephantine, Yosef and Mirim had been warned by other members of the Jewish community to be constantly wary of unseen dangers which lay beneath the surface of the water, because crocodiles would suddenly burst out of the water and run up the bank to fix their massive jaws on the leg of an unwary child or an animal which was kneeling down to drink, drag him down into the river and dance with him until he drowned in agony and exhaustion.

But that wasn't Yosef's only concern; he was also scared of the river horses, which the Romans called *hippopotami*, huge animals which also swam in this part of the river; these were truly monstrous beasts from the deepest regions of Gehenna, with massive faces and legs and bodies which looked as though they were covered with the same armor as the Roman soldiers wore when they walked through a town. It was said that their breath was the foulest in all creation, and one breath, could turn a man into stone.

Once, when Yosef and his family had first arrived in Egypt, they had witnessed a fight between a river horse and a crocodile. It had been utterly terrifying, and the middle of the normally placid water looked as though it was boiling. Within minutes, there was a huge red stain from the beast's blood, and as though from nowhere, other crocodiles appeared from the margins of the water and swam to participate in the unexpected feast. And then large snakes also swam out from their holes in the river's banks. It was a hideous scene, too painful for them to watch. Yet the Egyptians looked on and cheered with every struggle of the two beasts. As she walked away, Miriam commented to Yosef, "At least we in Israel only have one crocodile, and he will soon die in his palace."

The thought of the fight between the river horse and the crocodile had made Miriam very cautious, and from that moment onwards, she had watched the water like an eagle, alert to any movement, any disturbance in the surface or the current which would indicate a beast swimming towards her. The slightest concern and she would pull on the tether, grasp Jeshua, and run into the center of the Island to the safety of the Temple of the Word of Yahweh. It was located at a place which the local Jews called Yeb.

+

Living in the land of Israel, a land in which rain only fell occasionally, and where the rivers were little more than streams, Miriam had never seen a river as vast as the Nile, which ran through the heart of Egypt and which flooded every year, inundating the land with life-giving nutriments and blessing its people and its crops for the growing season. On its banks, as far as the eye could see to the horizon, were fields of wheat and barley, watered by clever channels which the ancients had dug from the river's edge into the furthest ranges where the crops were grown. Because the river lay lower than the land, bullocks were used to turn vast wooden wheels whose little buckets pulled the water from the Nile and deposited it into the channels, where it ran to give life to the crops. Never had she seen anything as brilliant as the work of these Egyptians. This system of irrigation was especially important when the sun was at its fiercest and the river level dropped in the summer. Miriam was constantly amazed by such ingenuity, such originality.

Miriam often came here to the gentle banks of the Nile. She had been told that during the spring and summer months, when the river rose dramatically and flooded its banks, its water tasted sweet and pure, and ran swiftly northwards to the distant sea. Nobody knew where the sudden vast volumes of additional water came from. Some said that it was the winter gods, crying for the loss of their domain; others said that it was the melting snow from the distant and unscalable mountains. But as the weather warmed, the slow flowing and mildly behaved river rose and rose until the water spilled over its banks into the adjoining countryside and drenched everything in its path as far as the eye could see. And then, once the ground was wet and like a bog, the water slowly receded and as if by a miracle of Yahweh the crops started to grow, wheat and corn, fruits and olives, and there was enough to feed everybody and much of Rome and its people as well.

Egypt was an amazing country, filled with extraordinary people. Even from the time when she crossed its border, she knew that she was entering an exotic and fabulous land, the sort of place which is the source of travelers' stories. And as she rode her donkey and carried baby Jeshua, with Yosef walking the long distance into the heart of the new land, they were amazed by the different kinds of people whom they passed. Some looked just like Israelites and yet they spoke a language much of which Miriam couldn't understand except for certain words and phrases; when she asked, she was told that the language was Greek; others told her that they were speaking Koine; others still that they met were Roman and spoke Latin, which she was just beginning to understand. The travelers whom she understood the best were those who spoke Koine, similar to the language of the Greeks who had conquered Israel a few hundred years earlier, but with many Hebrew words added. And of course, most spoke Egyptian, which Miriam found very difficult to comprehend.

Having been here for three months, however, she was now beginning to understand some of the more common words, and only the other day, she had been able to ask a woman if she could purchase some river fish in order to make an evening meal for herself and her family.

She and Yosef had made Elephantine their home. Somehow, they felt safer on an Island in the middle of the Nile, thinking it would be harder for Herod's henchmen to find them than if they were living in one of the large Egyptian cities which they were told were full of spies and where whispers at night could mean imprisonment and death in the morning. While it was not a proper home to them like Sephoris or Nazareth, the large Jewish population of Elephantine was friendly, and welcomed them with open arms, especially eager to hear news of Israel and the evil of Herod. And Yosef's trade as a carpenter was especially welcome.

The Island of Elephantine housed an ancient community of Jews who claimed to have been there for five centuries, ever since the Babylonians under their king Nebuchadnezzar of cursed name had swept over the Land of Israel and caused such horrors. The Jews who fled into Egypt had built a large Temple, similar to the Temple in Jerusalem. When Miriam and Yosef left Israel hurriedly to escape the madman, they had traveled on back roads through Gaza and the Sinai Wilderness into the delta of the Nile and then to Elephantine. Not knowing where they were going, except south and west towards the setting sun, they had been following the advice of travelers they'd met along the way who told them of this distant but important community of their co-religionists; never, though, did they believe that the community would be as large and as flourishing. And to their amazement, the community seemed to live side by side, and very happily, with the priests who worshipped the cult shrine of the ram-headed Egyptian deity Khnum. Although domestic gods and false idols were still worshipped in private in the homes of many Jews in Israel, despite what Elijah had done to Jezebel when she'd tried to introduce her pagan Phoenician gods, the Pharisee rabbis and Sadducee Priests of Israel took a very dim view of such idolatry. The Rabbis were always shouting and screaming about transgressions when they found an example of a Jew who had turned his eyes from the Lord God.

The Jews of Elephantine had taken Yosef and his family into their homes and given them food and shelter. In return, Yosef had worked as a carpenter, and restored much of the wooden bench-work and the stand for the scrolls of the Torah to the delight of the Rabbis of Elephantine and their congregants. The Pharisee Rabbis of this community were unlike those in Israel; they were not at odds with the Priests of the Temple and seemed to share much of the responsibility for the religion.

Miriam and Yosef had been given a small house in which to live, more of a shelter. It was in the orchard of a rich merchant who made his living by purchasing gold from the distant mines of Nubia and using it to barter for the excess wheat which the farmers grew in years of plenty. This he stored in huge grain sheds and storage houses and paid his men to guard it day and night against both rats and people. When the winter came, he released the stocks of grain to the Royal Household and to the Pharaoh's bakers and made a lot of money. He also traded in the red stone which was quarried from nearby, and which was used for the tall columns which the Greeks called *obeliskos*.

He was a kind man who took pity on them when he heard that they had escaped from the insanity of Herod and gave them the shelter in a large and comfortable shed in his orchard. In return, Miriam helped out in the kitchen of the master's house, cleaned the merchant's rooms along with other servants, and attended on his wife when she went to the markets on the western shore at Syene.

At first, Miriam had been unwilling to travel to Syene. Though she'd never been to Egypt before, she knew of Syene from the Scrolls of the Prophet Ezekiel, who had written, *'The land of Egypt will become a desolation and waste. Then they will know that I am the Lord. Because you said, "the Nile is mine, and I have made it. Therefore, behold, I am against you and against your rivers, and I will make the land of Egypt an utter waste and desolation, from Migdol to Syene and even to the border of Ethiopia.'*

But the mistress of the house had assured that Syene was a gentle and peaceful town and the markets there were rich with excellent produce. So she went. All of this was so new to her. Miriam had never worked at cleaning a house for another person and found the experience interesting and rewarding. In her father's home in Sephoris, and in her own home in Nazareth, she had done her own cleaning, washing and preparation of meals; but when she had to attend to these duties for another person, she gave more thought as to what she was doing.

She particularly enjoyed cooking for the merchant and his family, because she was able to experiment with different foods, not only from Egypt, but also with meats or vegetables which Yosef didn't allow her to serve because of his dislike of the taste. Egypt was a land of great richness and interest. She hadn't before eaten many of the fruits and foods which were plentiful in this country. She particularly enjoyed the bread made from barley, but she found the millet bread to be too harsh for her tastes. For Yosef, she made stews from lentils, beans and peas in which she put the meat of lamb when it was available. And as a special treat, when he had been working hard, she would give him a plate of orange and pomegranate and the fruit of the date and dûm palm.

One of the meals she particularly enjoyed creating, once she'd been shown how to make it, was an Alexandrian Loaf. Named after some ancient conqueror of Egypt called Alexander, who people said came from Greece or Macedon or somewhere, he had created his meal in the city which he founded on the shore of the Great Sea. He'd even name a city after himself and built some palace where scrolls and books were kept.

The first time she ate it, she was allowed to watch how Judit the cook made it for the household. She then made it the following day for Yosef, who said that he liked it very much, and congratulated her on her new skills. When Judit made it, she simply took an already baked loaf, and removed almost all of the bread inside. Then she sprinkled it with a mixture of the juice of a lemon mixed in water. In a stone mortar, Judit ground pepper from India, garlic, mint, honey, oil and more water. She then stuffed the hollowed-out loaf with the cooked liver of chickens, recently cooked strips of the meat of cows, seeds, cumin, slices of onion, and other vegetables. She poured the ground spices into the hollow to fill in the spaces, returned the end of the loaf, and bound it together with cord. Then she placed it in an oven to heat it up and served it with more vegetables. It had become the wealthy family's favorite food, and having served it to Yosef, she knew it would soon become his. How she was going to keep putting in the pepper from India, the most expensive spice she'd ever heard of, Miriam had no idea. The first time she'd eaten it, she'd coughed, and her eyes had run with tears; but then it's hot but subtle taste began to warm and excite her mouth and the food tasted more alive than she'd ever known. Soon, she was asking Judit's permission to take small amounts home so that she could spice her husband's food with it. Yosef's reaction had been different to hers. He had tasted the vitalized food, smiled, and eaten with a new gusto. But Miriam knew she mustn't abuse Judit's good nature, as the pepper spice was fiercely expensive, and the absence of anything more than a pinch could be noticed by the wife.

The longer Miriam and Yosef stayed in Egypt, the more they became accustomed to the way of life there. Although the Romans were present in the large towns, they were somehow friendlier and less domineering than they were in Israel. Egypt supplied much of Rome with its wheat, and so the trading nations and their people were generally able to tolerate each other. And on the Island of Elephantine, because it was so far south of the main cities of Egypt, the Roman presence was less noticeable.

She and Yosef had even talked about whether they should make their life in Egypt. It was an interesting idea, because Yosef could earn a very good living as a carpenter, and Jeshua would grow up in a rich and prosperous community. But they put the idea out of their minds, for Miriam missed her family, and Yosef knew that, as she became increasingly familiar with Egypt and its newness faded into routine, Miriam would shortly become homesick for Sephoris and Nazareth, and would want to return to show her family their little baby. And in the forefront of their minds was the fact that the Lord Yahweh had given Israel to the Hebrew people, and that it was their duty to live in the land and make it prosper. But silently, and only ever to herself, Miriam kept thinking about the meaning of Jeshua's birth, musing over the thoughts which had flooded her mind while she was still recovering in the outdoor barn in Beth Lechem. Could Yahweh have given Jeshua to her, and to the Jewish people, to lead them out of their misery, out of Roman occupation, and into a better world?

These were some of the problems which she was musing upon when she was tending to Jeshua sleeping in his cradle on a hilltop overlooking the River Nile. A recent sighting of a huge crocodile in the weed and rushes across the bank had frightened her, and until it disappeared upstream, or was caught and killed by fishermen, she determined not to go too close to the river. The dangers, for the unwary, were extraordinary.

As she lay on the mat, her eyes closed against the sun, she noticed a sudden darkness, as if a shadow had passed across the face of the orb. Shielding her eyes, she looked up, and was shocked to see a man standing above her. She immediately sat up, and looked towards the crib, where Jeshua was sleeping soundly.

"I'm sorry I frightened you, Lady," said the man. "I was crossing the field to return to my Temple, when I noticed you. There are vultures in the sky, and I was concerned that you were hurt."

She sat up and saw clearly now that he was a man in his old age, and didn't pose a threat to her or her baby.

"How old is your baby?" he asked.

Now that she was no longer lying prostrate, she felt more confident. He was thin and wiry, and she knew with certainty that one puff of wind from the Nile would blow him over. She invited him to sit, and poured him a cup of wine, which he accepted gratefully on such a hot day.

"My baby is not yet a year old, yet he walks and is beginning to say little things, not just sounds, but he also likes to sleep," she said. "His name is Jeshua."

"A Hebrew child," said the old man. "Then not one created by my God, Khnum."

"I'm sorry, Sir, but I haven't heard of your god. There are so many gods in this country, that it's difficult for me..."

The old man smiled. "There's no reason why you, being a Hebrew, should have heard of the God Khnum. He is the god of the Nile, and every year, when the Nile floods, my god Khnum brings silt and clay in the water, which he lays down on the land. It brings food to the soil, but it also brings the next generation of children. The clay which Khnum brings from the heavens in the floodwaters, he uses at his potter's wheel to make into the tiny beings which he then places into the wombs of young women who become mothers. That's why we priests of Khnum call our god the Divine Potter. My name in our language means *'He who smiles on the God Khnum.'*"

Miriam smiled. Even after living here for nearly a year, she still found Egyptian names impossible to pronounce.

"In my Hebrew faith, my child was implanted in my womb by our God, Yahweh. My child's name is Jeshua, which in my language means *God saves his people*. My name is Miriam, which in my language means a rebellious person, which I'm not. But I was named by my parents after the sister of our father Moses. Our legends tell us that Miriam watched over her infant brother when his mother Yocheved placed him in a cradle in the waters of the Nile after the Pharaoh Ramses decreed that all Hebrew boys must die."

The old Egyptian nodded, and said, "And in Egyptian, the name means *'beloved of the gods.'*

And then the old man seemed to become pensive and looked up into the cloudless blue sky. He seemed to recall something from his distant past. "The Pharaoh Ramses. He lived more than a thousand years ago. He was a great Pharaoh. But this man Moses. I recall now. He was a prince in the palace of Thutmose the Second, before the great schism."

"I don't know, Sir," Miriam told him. "But you must know of the great schism, the one caused by you Jews." She shook her head. The old man breathed deeply. "It is said that you people, you Hebrews, nearly caused the downfall of Egypt. You people do not believe in the many gods in which we Egyptians believe. Nor as do the Greeks and the Romans. You believe in one god."

Miriam nodded. "Yes, our God is Yahweh, the one true God."

"A hundred years after the Pharaoh Thutmose was forced by this man Moses to allow the Hebrew people to return to their land of Israel, one of our Pharaohs, whose name is cursed through the centuries, rid us of all the gods, and of all the priests, who he arrested and imprisoned. This Pharaoh, whose cursed name is Akhenaten, which means Successful Man for the Sun God Aten, only allowed one god to be worshipped. He said that the vision came to him and followed the exile of you Hebrews taking with you your one god.

"Many priests and their families were enslaved and murdered by this evil madman Pharaoh, who even moved the capital of Egypt from Thebes to a new city which he built, now in ruins, called Amarna. And fortunately, after his death, his son, Tutankhamun, rid himself of his father's heresy and brought back all the gods, especially the great god, Amun," said the old man.

Shocked, Miriam was concerned, "But are you blaming us for this misfortune? Are you saying it was the Hebrews?"

The old man smiled, and finished his wine. "No. I blame the Pharaoh's wife Nefertiti, who some say was the mother of the Pharaoh Tutankhamun, though many say it was Kiya, one of the accursed Akhenaten's other wives. It is impossible to tell, because Akhenaten's hieroglyphs have been chiseled out of the stele. But it was Akhenaten's favorite wife Nefertiti who our priests and sages believe whispered into the ear of the king to follow the Hebrews and worship their god, the disc of the Sun."

Confused, Miriam said, "But our God Yahweh isn't the sun. It was he who created the sun; and the stars; and the heavens and the earth. Our books, taken from the mountain we call Sinai in the desert, tell us clearly that our God is invisible and that he is everywhere. And nowhere."

Now it was the old priest's turn to be confused. "But if he is invisible, how do you know what he looks like? How can you worship him? He may be in front of you or behind...or nowhere. I don't understand."

"It's hard to explain. I've seen the idols you worship for your gods. The god with the head of a crocodile, with the body of a raven, or as a lion or a cat. But we have no such God, because our Yahweh ordered us not to worship idols or statues. We can only worship our god in our minds."

The priest nodded, trying to understand, but failing to see how one could worship nothing. He stood, bowed to Miriam, and said, "Go in peace to your husband and family, Miriam, who is called in my tongue the beloved of god. And may your invisible god protect you and your son, whose name in your language is 'God saves his people.'"

The decision to return to Israel was made for them one morning, when Miriam was about to take Jeshua to the water for his joyous time in the crib, something which the young baby loved. Miriam particularly loved the look of peace and happiness on his face as he lay on his back, and experienced the gentle lulling waves rock the crib from side to side.

As she carried babe and basket and walked the hundred paces out of the orchard to the water's edge, she was distracted by a gathering of men and women on the steps of the Temple. Always conscious of problems which resulted in the gathering of crowds and the Roman's hatred of unofficial and threatening multitudes, she cautiously remained in the orchard and watched what was happening. Suddenly, she saw Yosef emerge from the Temple and burst through the crowd. He ran towards their home. Completely out of character, he was shouting at the top of his voice, "Miriam. Miriam."

Terrified that a catastrophe was about to befall her, she ran carrying the baby in his crib to the perimeter of their orchard home.

"Wonderful news. Herod is dead. Miriam, Herod is dead. A messenger from Israel. From Jerusalem. The evil one is dead. Now we can return to Israel."

Her heart missed a beat. It wasn't a catastrophe. It wasn't bad news. She could go home. She said to her sleeping child, "Jeshua, we're going home. We're going to Israel, where you will grow and become as good a man as your father."

CHAPTER SIX

Nazareth, the land of Israel, the year 9 CE

The feeling had been growing within her the past three or four years. It began with a sense that he was quicker, more alert than the other children. Brighter, somehow! Oh, she knew that all mothers said this, but whereas other children in the village took time to comprehend or reason, Jeshua seemed to have an instinctive understanding and appreciation before she or Yosef needed to explain something.

It was only small things, of course; when she was finishing washing their clothes at the stream, she would turn and suddenly find that Jeshua had brought two baskets to put them in, rather then the one she had thought was necessary; and he was right. Or there were times when she'd think about talking to him concerning some topic or other, and without her saying a word, he'd suddenly address not just the issue, but gave the answer. It was as though he was inside her mind, and knew what she was thinking.

When she saw the way he watched her so intently, she knew that her son was different from other children. And as Jeshua grew into an active and intelligent boy, soon to be the newest of the young men of the village, the difference between him and the other children of Nazareth became increasingly stark; and there were many things which differentiated Jeshua from the other children and identify him as odd and beyond the normal.

Different in his interests, his seriousness, his desire to know everything; different in the way he sought out Yosef to watch him craft wood or make furniture in preference to going out into the fields and playing with the other young girls and boys of town. Different, even, in the way he would touch the now-mature wood before Yosef sculpted it into furniture, his hands following the patterns of the grain, his eyes delighting in the knots and whorls and the way the bark had darkened and stiffened with age and desiccation. Sometimes, Yosef had told her, he'd even caught Jeshua silently praying to Yahweh and thanking Him for giving up His living tree to become furniture and of use to someone in the village.

Yosef even remarked on it one morning to Miriam. He told her of the other day when the two of them had been in a field, and they'd seen a tall and ancient oak tree. Amazed by its tall stature and the beauty of its branches, Jeshua had been transfixed.

"This oak," the boy had said to his father, "is a symbol of the similarity and the difference between us."

Not understanding, Yosef asked what the boy meant. "We both look at the same tree, father. I see our heritage, and the fact that Yahweh loves His people so much, that he has planted this tree to give us shade and for us to appreciate the beauty of His kingdom. You look at the same tree and you see a table and chairs, a bed and the wood which supports the roof and the walls of a house. And since you've been teaching me the trade of the carpenter, I now see both God's, and your world through my own eyes."

Since that moment, Yosef had told Miriam, he now no longer thought of wood as dead. Instead, his young son had opened his eyes to the continuity of the Lord's realm; now he saw through his son's eyes that what once lived and grew under Yahwehs sky, would continue to live even in death and had a different purpose. It was an amazing insight into the work that he'd been doing all his life.

And even more astounding was when Jeshua picked up a large piece of wood which Yosef was going to fashion into an order from a villager, and simply by looking at it for a moment or two, Jeshua would suggest another object altogether which would produce not just a more pleasing product with less waste and more profit, but something which Yosef was able to sell separately for more money. And more often than not, the boy was correct. Till now, Yosef had kept his thoughts about his son to himself, not wanting to ascribe any abilities to the boy which might give Miriam any false hopes, but he could no longer rein in his thoughts about how special Jeshua was.

Yes, he was very different from the other boys in the village. But in the main he was different in the way that he seemed to know things, rather than have to be told them. Miriam and Jeshua would be walking through the fields above Nazareth in order to find herbs or fruits that they needed for the evening meal, and suddenly the boy – not yet thirteen or initiated into Jewish manhood – would talk to her about the meaning of the prayer which men said for the setting of the sun. Or they would be at the well below the town, and Jeshua would talk at length about the source of the pure water which blessed the village, a source from the distant mountains to which neither she, and certainly not Jeshua, had ever traveled. So how did he...could he... possibly have known?

She asked him precisely that question...how he knew so much about this or that, and he shrugged his shoulders, and said that he'd overheard the men of the village talking, and just remembered. But Miriam had never heard the men of the village talking about the source of the water, or other things which Jeshua seemed to know so well.

Increasingly interested in the unusual nature of her son's mind, Miriam would raise the issue with Yosef. She did so again, for the second time in a month, when her husband had just returned from delivering a table to Yizhak, Nazareth's most skilled jewelry maker. Tired, and able to work fewer hours of the day now that he was becoming an elderly man, Yosef finished work early for the evening, and, when Jeshua had gone to bed, she questioned him about the nature of her thoughts concerning their son. Her husband nodded in immediate empathy with what she was saying and told her that there also were times when Jeshua mystified him.

"The other day, I was working with an adze shaping some wood for the back of a bench, and he asked me, *"Father, why do you use an adze, when a chisel awl would give you a cleaner cut and would shape the wood more beautifully?"* At first, I believed that it was a silly question. I've been a carpenter all my adult life, and I know what each tool is used for. So I gave him a quick answer which I knew didn't satisfy him. When I saw him still looking at me, he was frowning; so I asked him what was wrong. He said to me, *"Father, Israel is a land with so few trees that we have to preserve every piece of wood as though it was more precious than gold. If you use a chisel instead of an adze, you will waste less wood and therefore you'll use fewer pieces. Then Yahweh will be happy that fewer of His trees have to be cut down for our needs."*

"I thought the boy was being silly, because despite the implement I used, there would still be the same amount of wood wasted, until I thought about it more deeply, and I realized that he was right...that if I used a chisel awl in the first place, I would be able to undertake the work with greater economy. I tell you, Miriam, I looked at the lad, and shuddered, as though an angel of the Lord had just entered my workshop. And when he'd gone out into the village, I picked up a chisel, and used it on another piece of wood, and I have to tell you that he was right...that the chisel gave a more distinct shape than an adze and it was easier to use, and quicker and I could use a thinner piece of wood because of the finer work, meaning that I'd waste less wood making the furniture. Think about it, Miriam. In the course of a year, that'll mean more income for us. But how did he know? I'm the only carpenter in Nazareth, and he couldn't have learned that from anybody but me. And I hadn't realized it until he told me! Do you think he's touched by the Lord?"

Miriam began to answer, but instead drew back. She, too, had been a girl always observing, always hanging around the adults when her friends were out playing, always asking questions which her parents believed were well in advance of her age. But when she turned 12, she re-discovered the joys of community and friendships, and soon gathered to herself many of the younger girls of the village, and her group soon included some of the boys.

But until the last year of her life in Sephoris, she had found the company of young people her age to be less interesting than the company of adults. It was only in her last year, before she married Yosef, that she'd re-entered the world of young people because the boys had grown more masculine and strong and virile, and she found them intensely attractive; especially Malachai who, in his Initiation year, grew suddenly from a gangling and floppy youth into a tall, muscular and handsome young man.

And it was when Miriam thought of Malachai, about whom she hadn't thought in years, that she flushed crimson, and was forced to sit down or she would collapse. Yosef didn't notice her sudden condition in the dim light of the room; she turned quickly from him and pretended to pick up some linen which she needed to sew. But Miriam could hardly breathe. A revelation had just come to her, and she needed to think through its consequences. In all the many years she'd been married to Yosef, she'd only once or twice allowed her thoughts to reflect on Malachai and the other young men of Sephoris. And she remembered Malachai's face and the youth and beauty of his body in the year of his Initiation...

In just a few days, her own son, her own Jeshua, was about to be Initiated, about to undergo that God-ordained transformation between boyhood and manhood, and he was almost of the age when Miriam and Malachai had lain together and had kissed so passionately and he had touched her in places which had never been touched before or since.

And now her Jeshua was of the age where he, too, would begin to notice girls; where he would soon begin to disappear from the house for entire mornings or afternoons, and would return home and be coy and sullen about where he'd been and who he'd been with. And when she thought about Jeshua indulging in these sorts of things and thinking the thoughts which had consumed her in the year before her marriage to Yosef, she suddenly felt an awful weight of responsibility and dread. Had she brought Jeshua up properly in the eyes of the Lord? Had Yosef given him sufficient tuition in the Word of God so that he would tread the path of righteousness and not be led astray by false gods or deceitful prophets?

While Israel groaned under the oppressive burden of the Roman occupation, there were so many men these days who claimed to be the Messiah, who stood on hilltops and in the centers of towns preaching about the end times and telling gullible men and women that they were the true descendants of King David and the true Messiah. They even blasphemed against the word of the Lord by telling people that their coming had been predicted by Daniel and Zachariah, Isaiah and Jeremiah and all the other prophets of ancient days.

But these days of occupation, while the iron boots of the Romans flattened the countryside and ground their hopes into the dust, while the Imperial Army of Caesar stole crops and animals to feed itself and Israelites went hungry, it was too easy for a boy like Jeshua, a sensitive and intelligent boy, to come under the spell of one of these anointed ones, these false Messiahs, and fall prey to their oily words.

Since he was four or five, Miriam had relied on Yosef to teach Jeshua the history and beliefs of the Jewish people; she for her part had taught the lad all about the different plants and herbs and medicines which grew in the fields around their home, and the way in which Yahweh had invested most of them with some property which benefited mankind. But it was the poisonous ones which caused Jeshua so much confusion. When Miriam warned him about particular plants or berries which could harm a man – even kill him – Jeshua tried very hard but couldn't understand why the Father of the world would put onto the Earth something which could kill hungry people just wanting some food. He could understand why snakes and spiders bit and bees stung if they were threatened, but why would plants need to be given the power to kill men, women and children? What did Yahweh have in mind when He created such things?

As Jeshua grew up into a tall and increasingly interesting boy, Yosef had taken him into the workshop and taught him arts and crafts which would ensure that, when he and Miriam were dead and buried, Jeshua would never want for work or food or shelter, for as a carpenter, he would become one of the most important and respected men in the village to whom everybody turned when things needed to be done.

But soon, this month or next, it would be time to take Jeshua to Jerusalem for his Initiation with the Priests; to test his knowledge; to match his skills in argument against others of his age; and those whom the Chief Priest considered sufficiently ready and knowledgeable would be given the prayer shawl and allowed to wear it into religious services, where he and other boys who passed their initiation, would be blessed. Then, and only then, would Jeshua be counted as one of the men of the community, able to pray with the others and even, please God, lead the prayers.

She had no doubts about Jeshua's knowledge or ability, or that he would become an Initiate, a Son of the Commandments, but what caused her sudden shock was that her son was almost the same age as the youth she had first loved and would have married, had not the Priest knocked on her father's door, and decided the rest of her life for her.

"Are you ill, mother?" Jeshua asked, coming into the house and seeing his mother staring strangely at a blank wall.

It brought her back to the present, and she looked at her lovely son in surprise; she hadn't heard him enter the house. She had seen him every day of her life, many times each day, and knew his face and body better than any sight she looked at; but now she looked at him in the gentleness of the early afternoon light, and she saw that her little boy was growing into a fine young man; his body was lean and muscular; he was growing taller by the day; and his face was...

"Mother? Shall I fetch father? Are you alright? Your face is as white as ash. Do you need a cup of wine?" Jeshua looked at his mother, who sat there, staring at him, seeming as though she'd just seen some evil spirit enter the room. It forced Jeshua to look around, to ensure that everything was alright.

Miriam stood, although her legs were a big shaky, and walked over to her son. "I'm fine. Don't worry," she said. But she was staring at him as though she had never seen him before, as though he were a stranger, or somebody who had been long lost, and then suddenly found. She put her hand up to his cheek, and stroked him, pulling him towards her and kissing him. Suddenly she felt warm and salty tears running down her face. Jeshua pulled away when he realized that she was sobbing.

"Please let me call father," he begged.

But she smiled, and shook her head, saying, "No, it's nothing. For a moment, in the light, you looked like somebody I knew many years ago. It made me feel both sad and happy."

She held his hand, and walked with him to the kitchen table, where he helped her prepare the bread which they would eat for the evening meal.

Jerusalem, Two months later

More than the noise from the hordes of men and women walking the crowded streets; more than the stench of dead animals and filth wherever they walked; more than the tawdriness sitting beside the magnificence of Jerusalem, more than almost anything, Miriam most hated the Sadducee Priests. There were rarely any priests, only rabbis, in the two Israelite towns where she had lived in her life, and they were such small towns compared to Jerusalem that living in them was almost the same as living in the heart of the countryside. In just a few steps, she could be in a field on beside a clean and flowing river; but in Jerusalem, built high on a holy mountain, there seemed to be streets and houses and huge buildings everywhere.

But she had been to Egypt and seen the endless deserts, the Pyramids and the Sphinxes. She'd crossed the vastness of the River Nile in flood; so it wasn't the size of the buildings which made her feel anxious and apprehensive. No, it was the way in which the Priests of the Temple walked around the streets followed by their entourage of sycophants, treating the ordinary people as though they were slaves, not citizens. A trumpeter preceded them and behind him came the Levites banging drums and cymbals; they were proceeded and followed by Temple guards who ensured that the priests' way was clear by pushing onlookers out of the way; then the priests walked along the road, ignoring the people as though they didn't exist, talking and gesticulating as if they owned the entire city; and then to ensure their safety, more guards followed. Were it not for their priestly garb, they could have been officers in the Roman army.

Miriam hated their rich garments laden with priceless gems and jewels and gold, when the rest of Israel was struggling to find money to buy food; she hated the way in which members of the tribe of Levites, their acolytes, rang their silly bells and banged their ridiculous cymbals ahead of them, as though these Sadducees weren't priests at all, but were some dwellers in heaven come to earth; but most of all, beyond anything else, she hated the way in which the Priests looked at her with such unutterable contempt as though she and her family were nothing more than the dung of animals on the bottom of their sandals. A thousand years ago, when King Solomon built his Temple, his priests would have been little more than servants to the needs of the people; today, they were as arrogant as a Roman Prefect, as haughty as princes in the King's palace.

But now wasn't the time for such thoughts. Jeshua was here to compete with other boys his age to see which of them would be granted the prayer shawl and would be initiated into the ranks of Jewish men, and which would be sent back to their homes in disgrace to practice for another year. Few boys were rejected, but if a boy showed a particular promise and learning, then he would be taken up and might be given a preferential post; not training for the priesthood, of course, because that was reserved for those born of the tribe of the Levites, but working within the Temple would mean that Jeshua would never be hungry or want for anything.

Despite her contempt for the Priests, she hoped that Jeshua's life would be made easy if he worked in the Temple. And maybe...just maybe...he might be able to change the way in which the Temple was run and make it better for the people of Israel. She'd certainly spoken to him at length about what was wrong with the Priesthood.

Every night and morning for the past month, Yosef had been questioning Jeshua on different aspects of the events in the Books of Moses and the very heart of the meaning of the Torah. The boy astounded his father with his knowledge not just of the history and beliefs of his people, but of his deeper understanding of the wisdom which was contained within the walls of the Jewish faith. Not only did he know the words of the prophets such as Isaiah, Ezekiel, Jeremiah and Elijah, because most Jews could repeat them from a lifetime of hearing them in the Synagogues, but Jeshua seemed to be able to cast his mind into their minds, and understand deeply the reasons they'd written those words so long ago, in times when the Jewish people had strayed.

Certain that his son would acquit himself as well as any other...far better than most...Yosef delivered Jeshua to the steps of the Temple where he was met by a Levite who summarily dismissed Miriam and then escorted the father and son up the steps. But his mother Miriam continued to follow in their path.

The Levite turned and looked contemptuously at Miriam. "Women are not allowed through this entrance," he said gruffly. Miriam nodded and walked to the upper part of the surroundings, where there was a ramp specially built for women to use in order to enter the women's section of the Temple during the times of prayer. But as she ascended in the hot sun, she noticed that the huge wooden doors were closed and locked, and that she was the only woman who was walking on the ramp. And suddenly she felt embarrassed because when she turned to walk back down, she saw that a number of the Temple guards were looking at her and grinning. One was pointing and talking about her mistake to his companion.

Suddenly furious at being the butt of their demeaning conversation, Miriam determined to go down and berate them. But she looked over at Yosef and saw him gently shake his head; she realized that such a scene might count against Jeshua's Initiation Ceremony, and so she looked deferentially towards the ground, and returned to the level of the courtyard in front of the Temple. She watched as Yosef and her son were ushered inside by one of the Levites.

Alone underneath the hot sun, she continued to descend the ramp and walked quickly away from the Temple grounds into the anonymity of the surrounding streets. But Miriam realized that she was just trying to disappear, to become invisible both to the awesome majesty of the Temple, and to the ridicule of the guards. Yet her son, her only son, was at this very moment undergoing the most important transition of his life, and she was excluded by laws which she would never understand. In mounting anger, she walked back to the lodging house where they were staying, and waited in rising anger and frustration for her husband and her son to return.

+

Yosef put his arm around Jeshua's shoulders and comforted him. As he walked into the vast antechamber, memories came flooding back to him. Even the five decades which had elapsed since his own Initiation had done nothing to diminish the awe which overcame him as he walked into the immense area of the Temple's inner sanctum; a dark and echoing space full of mysterious corners and unfathomable forests of marble columns, the overwhelming darkness punctuated by the pools of brightly illumined light from candles and oil lamps which hung from hooks high up in the ceiling. Everywhere was the smell of sandalwood and other exotic incense burning, the smoke filling the room and causing the beams of light from the candles and lamps to be clearly visible.

Then, as now, it was the biggest building into which he'd ever entered. He remembered its dimensions from when he'd been

Initiated, and from the few occasions he'd visited Jerusalem for the Passover festivals, or Shavuot, the Festival of the booths. But because he and Miriam lived their lives in normal sized houses, he forgot just how big the Temple building was.

Of course, many of the Egyptian temples had been huge but being Jews, and because only Pharaonic Priests and their acolytes were admitted, he had only ever seen them from the outside. Like the Pyramids, they were frightening and impressive in their size... but being inside a vast building made him realize just how small and insignificant human beings were.

Yosef and his son walked past the massive pair of stone statues depicting the lions which symbolized the tribe of Judah, placed on either side of the steps which led upwards to the level of the ark of the Holy Covenant within the inner temple, an area from which all except the High Priest, were banned. As though it was yesterday, Yosef was again thrown back to his boyhood, remembering the moment he had walked into these very Temple precincts and been given into the hands of the Priests for his Initiation. But unlike his memory of that traumatic day, his son Jeshua seemed to be showing no fear either of his surroundings, or of the coming test of his manhood.

"Were you nervous when you came here for your Initiation, father?" Jeshua asked, as though he were reading Yosef's thoughts.

"Yes. Very. I was quivering in fear beforehand and from the time I said goodbye to my father and went alone into the Temple. I remember clearly as I walked on my own, just how scared I was, and I remained frightened during every moment I was there alone."

Yosef looked down at his son in sudden concern, worried that his words might have made the boy even more frightened. But the look on his face was that of a person staring into the glory of a sunset. It was almost as though Jeshua hadn't heard Yosef's words.

"I don't know how I managed to pass my Initiation," he said honestly. Not that he usually told lies, but somehow he couldn't bring himself to utter even the smallest falsehood, nor even an exaggeration, in the House of the Lord.

"I feel no fear," said Jeshua. "It's so quiet and safe in here. In my Father's house."

Yosef stopped walking forward when he saw half a dozen priests, dressed in their prayer shawls and with their large tefillin worn in the middle of their foreheads above their eyes. Proudly, ostentatiously and arrogantly, they walked towards Yosef and Jeshua from within the darkened recesses of the huge building.

"You're late. You should have been here shortly after the morning prayers. The other boys are already gathered, and are being examined," said the taller and haughtiest of the group, his tallit sweeping the ground as he walked.

Yosef was about to apologize, when Jeshua said quietly, "Why are your tefillin on your head so large? My father and all the other men of my village wear tefillin only when they pray in the morning and remove them when they leave their homes. Why do you wear yours during the day?"

Affronted, the Chief Priest looked in sudden displeasure at Jeshua. "You are not here to question me, child, but for me to question you. This is your initiation, a time when we priests will decide whether you are fit and knowledgeable to be counted as a man within our community. Now leave your father and go into the Lord's house quickly."

Jeshua didn't move. Instead, he looked quizzically at the Priest, and asked quietly, "If I'm not permitted to ask questions of you, but only to answer your questions, then you will know much about me, and I will know nothing about you. How can this be God's will? If the Almighty seeks to make me one of the Community, surely I must know as much of you as you will learn of me."

The priests were taken aback by the impertinence of the boy, and one stepped forward and clipped him across the back of the head. "Enough of this insolence. Another word and I'll send you back to your village and forbid you entry into the Temple for a further year."

Immediately, Jeshua said, "Is it your right to forbid me entry to my Father's Temple? Surely only Yahweh can grant that right. We are all his servants, even those who wear such clothes as you're wearing."

Yosef bent down and hissed in Jeshua's ear, "Quiet, you silly boy. Don't insult the Priests or they'll send you away. Now go with them and stop these rude remarks; give simple answers to their questions and don't show off."

He stood and said to the Chief Priest, "My son is very clever and sometimes forgets who he is and where he is from. If he has caused you offence, I apologize for him. I beg you to overlook his rudeness. He is nervous and overwhelmed by the magnificence of the Temple and its priests, as well as the events of the day. We are from a small village, and not used to..."

"Then let there be no more such remarks. Now, Jeshua, go with Nahum the Scribe and he will take you to where the other Initiates are already being examined. And Jeshua, no more of these impertinences or we will send you straight back to your home and forbid you entry here until you learn to behave with respect to us. That means that you will not be considered as a man in your village and you won't be able to participate in the ceremonies which honor God Almighty. You will be ridiculed by the other young boys and girls will not want to marry you. Is what I've said to you completely understood, Jeshua?"

Jeshua looked at his father and realized that any riposte would be dealt with most severely. So he remained silent and walked with Nahum into the Outer Sanctum. As they walked through the huge doors made of cedar and inlaid with bronze, Jeshua saw about twenty or so young men, all seated on cushions on the floor, listening to a sermon from another priest. Nahum directed Jeshua to a cushion on the outer periphery of the group. The boy sat and listened to the Priest talking about the Prophet Elijah and his fight with the Phoenician whore and adulteress Jezebel, who he said was the most evil woman ever to have lived. As the priest excoriated the wife of King Ahab, Jeshua shook his head slowly to himself. Such hatred, such intolerance, he thought.

But the priest had noticed the boy at the back of the group, the newcomer; instead of staring up at him in wonder and admiration as all the others, this boy was looking down at the floor and showing signs of disagreement.

"You! The boy sitting at the back of the others. You boy, stand up," ordered the priest, pointing to Jeshua. "What's your name?"

He stood, and said, "I am Jeshua, son of Yosef, a descendant of King David, of the village of Nazareth."

The priest fixed his eyes on the lad, like a snake judging his strike. "Master! You will call me Master. Now, why were you shaking your head when I was talking about the evil of Jezebel?"

"Master, you are filled with such hatred towards Jezebel; but surely we should forgive her for her iniquities. The prophets of old, such as Elijah and Elisha and Isaiah have filled our minds with hatred and vengeance for those who oppose the way of Yahweh; but my knowledge of Yahweh is that He is a loving and compassionate God and that as His children, we bask in the glory of His light. If that is the case, and as Jezebel became a princess of Israel, surely Yahweh would have looked on her in understanding. And even though she tried to introduce idols into the Temple, she failed and her people didn't turn away from their love of God. Indeed, because of her actions, we have become closer to understanding the centrality of the Prophets Elijah and Elisha to our history, and isn't it said that Elijah of blessed memory is almost as important as our Father Moses the Lawgiver. Without Elijah's fight against Jezebel, without Yahweh testing him and Israel so thoroughly, would we be so great as a people today? So while I respect what you say, Master, couldn't we take the view that Jezebel was one of God's children, sent by Him to test us, and because of her failure to introduce false idols into Israel, she actually strengthened us, and..."

"Silence, you impertinent child," screamed the priest. "Silence, I say! How dare you interrupt me with your childish and stupid interpretations? You have no right to express your opinions here. You're here to learn, not to lecture me with the wisdom taught to you by your village rabbi. You're just repeating his words and not understanding what you're saying."

"Master," said Jeshua undaunted, "I thought I was here to show you how much I'd learned of our Bible, our customs and our Laws and hence prove that I have the right to participate in the community of men. I was simply trying to explain the ministry of Elijah from a different perspective."

"You are here to be examined, boy. You are here to pass the test which will tell us whether you have learned the correct interpretation of the word of God. You are not here to debate with the Master of that word, a Priest of the Temple. You will sit and remain silent until I decide that you may speak. One more word out of your mouth without my permission, and you will be returned to your village," the priest said, spittle flying over the other boys in his fury.

Jeshua nodded and looked down at the floor. But other lads in the congregation had been thinking about what Jeshua had said, and there were mumblings amongst them. None understood fully his argument, but what they did understand made good sense.

"Silence," shouted the Master of the Initiates. "You are here to listen, not to speak. Never in all my years have I had so much insolence from boys who have come here to be initiated. Now be quiet, and I shall continue with the lesson on the evil of Jezebel and the way in which Yahweh helped Elijah and Elisha to destroy her." The master looked piercingly at Jeshua, and continued, "Just as Yahweh will destroy all those who stand against Him."

Jeshua stood in the shadow of the column waiting in trepidation for the return of his father. From the fierceness and position of the noonday sun, he still had several hours to wait, and he felt a burning shame and humiliation at his treatment by the Master of the Initiates. Since his first scalding, Jeshua had felt certain he had been both quiet and respectful, yet something he'd done – a glance or a quizzical look – had infuriated the Master yet again, and he'd been ejected from the Temple, and forced to remain outside. The boy still didn't know what further offence he'd committed, but the result of what he'd done had without doubt damaged Jeshua's future prospects in his village, in his possibilities of marriage, and most especially in his ability to worship Yahweh.

Utterly downhearted, Jeshua tried to work out what his next course of action could be; should he confess everything to his father, who would undoubtedly be horrified that his manhood initiation would be delayed at least a year and possibly more? If he did that, he would risk a severe beating. Should he run away into the desert like the Prophet Elijah, hopefully to be fed meat and bread by ravens sent by Yahweh, but more likely to be eaten by lions or bitten by a snake? But that would horrify his mother and that was something Jeshua couldn't bear to think about. Should he return to the Temple and beg the Master of the Initiates to forgive him? But forgive him for what? What had he done that had infuriated the Master so much that he'd been expelled?

Deep in reflection, Jeshua was on the brink of weeping, when he felt a hand on his shoulder. In shock, he turned around and saw a Sadducee Priest standing and looking down at him. Even though his tallit covered his head and the fringe shaded his forehead, Jeshua could tell that the old man had kindly eyes and was smiling.

"So you've been expelled, have you?" he asked.

Jeshua nodded, and tears began to fall down his young cheeks.

"Many years ago, a Priest in this very Temple made me cry as well. I vowed that I'd never let it happen, ever again, to another boy. What's your name?"

"I am Jeshua, son of Yosef of Nazareth."

"Well, Jeshua, like you, I was expelled when I undertook my initiation. I had a Master just like yours, who wanted to tell us boys how much he knew instead of listening to what we'd learned. Is that the problem?" he asked.

Jeshua nodded, and said softly, "The master was so intent on teaching us boys, and all I tried to do was to discuss the lesson with him, like I do with my father and the other adults from the synagogue at home. I thought that the purpose of being here was to determine how much I knew so that I could be initiated into the Covenant with Yahweh."

The old man laid his hand on Jeshua's head, and said softly, "Ah, beloved boy. Honest and simple. But that's the problem with the Temple. We priests are so far removed from the people that we forget our duty to Yahweh is to act as pathways to God. Some of us forget that and think that we are God."

"But you're a Priest," said Jeshua, drying his eyes with the back of his hand. "Why are you saying this?"

"I'm the Chief Priest," said the man. "My name is Annas, son of Seth." He took the cowl of the prayer shawl off his head and put it around his shoulders. Jeshua was surprised, for the man had looked ancient with it over his head and in the shadow, but now he could see that he wasn't as old as he had thought, but more like the age of his mother Miriam.

"I overheard what the Master of the Initiates did to you. I was very surprised that he told you to leave the group. Perhaps you shouldn't have asked such difficult questions, but on the other hand, it's our job to find out how much of the Jewish Law and Customs and History you know, and shutting you up isn't a good way of finding out," he said. "It's our job to decide which of the boys of Israel know enough about our religion to be entitled to put on the tefillin every morning and night, and to say prayers with the other men of the Assembly. Yet when you boys come here at great expense, and from all over the country, we Priests act as though you're here to listen to nothing but sermons and speeches from us, instead of the other way around."

Annas shook his head in sadness and put his hand on Jeshua's head again, and then hugged him around his shoulders. As though to himself, he said softly, "It's very hot out here. Why not come with me and we'll go and get some pomegranate juice from the merchants over there," he said, nodding towards the area of the Temple forecourt where sacrifices and candles and drinks for visitors were being sold, and where there were men who changed money for travelers from outside of Jerusalem.

"But I have no money," said Jeshua.

Annas smiled, and said softly, "Don't worry. I'm the Chief Priest and they pay me to allow them to have their stalls in the Temple grounds. I'm sure they'll gladly give us some cake and fruit and drink. They make money out of me, and I'm sure they won't mind if I take advantage of them."

Jeshua was surprised. "Why is Yahweh's Temple used to make money?" he asked simply.

Annas smiled. "Yahweh never objected to his chosen people profiting by our relationship with Him. Priests have to live, just like boys from the village of Nazareth," he said softly.

They walked towards the merchants, but Jeshua couldn't understand why Annas was being so kind to him, whereas the other priests had treated him so horribly. He asked why it was.

"I was sitting up there," he said, pointing to rooms in an upper gallery above the courtyard. I watched all the boys enter for their Initiation Ceremony. I like to see if I can guess, just by looking and the way they walk and conduct themselves, which one will shine like a sun above the others. I saw you and the way you walked with your father, and I had a feeling that you would be a special young man.

"So I followed you down here, and I've been observing you while you were in with the Master of the Initiates. And I saw myself in you," he said. "I too had a thousand questions I wanted to ask, but the Initiate Master who examined me all those years ago was so fierce and terrifying that I was rude to him. It was to overcome my own fear. And I asked him too many questions, and he ordered me to leave. Had my father not been so important, I still wouldn't be initiated," he said, and laughed. "And now I'm the Chief Priest, and all the other priests are answerable to me."

They drank pomegranate juice, and Jeshua thought it was the most delicious thing he'd ever tasted.

"I want you to sit with me in the outer Temple forecourt. I want to discuss what it's like to be a child in a village in Israel. You see, Jeshua of Nazareth, I've been associated all my life with Jerusalem, and I've hardly ever been outside of the city borders. I know the names of the other villages and the cities, but I've never been to them, and my work in the Temple has kept me so busy that I would like to talk about the sorts of things you do," he told the boy as they walked back to the forecourt. "To know what it's like to be an ordinary Israelite."

Some of the other Priests, including Nahum, had come out from different enclosures when they saw Annas walking towards them. He was so powerful that they knew it was always better to be close to him than far away, wondering what he was thinking, saying or doing.

He sat down on a wooden stool in the cool of the shade, and invited Jeshua to sit at his feet. Other priests came and gathered around them, wondering if a lesson or a sermon was in the offing. What they couldn't understand was why a man as important and powerful as Annas was spending his time with a country boy who was obviously a failed initiate.

"So tell me, Jeshua, about the village in which you live."

The boy smiled, and said, "I live in Nazareth with my father Yosef and my mother Miriam. Miriam is father's second wife, his first, Melcha died in the month of Tammuz fourteen years ago. My father is a carpenter and a man of God."

"But tell me about the village. How many people live there, what do they do, how close are they to Yahweh?" he asked.

"Nazareth is out of the sight of the Romans, and so our life is peaceful. We are high in the hills and the air and water are very sweet. There are a few hundred people who live in the village and yes, they are all close to Yahweh."

"And are you close to Yahweh, Jeshua?" asked Annas.

The boy didn't answer at first, and the other priests looked quizzically at him. Surely he should have been taught by his village priests or his father what the correct answer was to be given.

"I don't know, Annas. When I'm in Nazareth and I'm alone in the fields, and I look up at the sky and I can see forever, then I'm close to Yahweh. I can see his face in the clouds and I know that He's looking down at me. I can feel His presence breathing into my body. I pick up a flower and look at it carefully and I can see patterns in it which couldn't have just happened without the creator of all things having decided that this is the way the pattern will look.

"But then I come to Beth Lechem or Jerusalem and I see the Temple being used no better than the sort of monthly market we have in Nazareth, then I can't understand how Yahweh can permit this to happen. How can this be a place for trading and buying and selling, when it's supposed to be the House of the Lord Yahweh?" he asked.

Nahum the Priest, infuriated by the impertinence, snapped, "Silence, boy, for you are in the presence of..." But a look from Annas made him stop talking and look red-faced at the ground.

Annas said, "Jeshua, our father Moses brought us out of the Land of Egypt so that we could be free people and no longer slaves to the Pharaoh. Freedom of a people means that they can build their own land, their own Temple and worship God in their own way."

Jeshua interrupted, "But when Moses came down from Mount Sinai carrying the first tablets of the Law God gave him, he saw that the Israelites had turned away from the sight of God, and had melted down their jewelry to create a golden calf in order to worship a false idol. Isn't what you're doing here, Annas, just the same. Aren't you worshipping a false god by making money from traders and merchants? What's the difference between one and the other?"

The other priests looked at Annas in amazement. Surely he was going to thrash the boy, kick him out of the temple, forbid him ever again to darken the portals. But instead, he smiled indulgently, and looked up at the priests, and said, "This boy asks questions which need to be answered. Does anybody here know the answers?"

After the way in which Annas had treated Nahum, none of the other Priests was sufficiently confident to say anything. Nobody understood this extraordinary relationship which their leader seemed to have with the lad, who was not just a prospective Initiate, but not even from Jerusalem. So Annas said, "Jeshua, have you ever heard of a King called Melchizedek? He is mentioned in the Book of Genesis in our Holy Bible. Melchizedek was the King of Salem. Some even think that by the name of this ruler's kingdom, Yahweh was referring us to His holy city of Jerusalem. Anyway, Melchizedek brought out bread and wine to our father Abraham after he won the spectacular victory over the four kings who had besieged Sodom and Gomorrah and taken Abraham's nephew Lot a prisoner. Because of Melchizedek's kindness and because he was a priest, Abraham gave him a tithe of a tenth of the bounty he won in battle. We believe that Melchizedek is part of the continuous line of priests from whose loins came our own King David. There are even some who speak of Melchizedek as being one and the same as Shem, the son of our father Noah.

"You see, my boy, the very fact that the patriarch of our religion, Abraham, gave the priest Melchizedek a tithe means that from that moment onwards, all priests were entitled to receive payment for their role in serving Yahweh and the people of Israel. Do you understand?"

Jeshua nodded slowly. But then he shook his head. "But it's not the same thing, Annas. Of course we must all be paid for the work we do, or how would we live. But that isn't the same as making the Temple of the Lord unclean by selling food and drinks and changing money, is it? This holy place is like a market, a bazaar where people come to enjoy themselves. Is that why God put His Temple, his holy house here on Mount Moriah where Abraham nearly killed his only son as a sacrifice? Surely our daily lives must remain outside the walls of the Temple, and when we come inside the grounds, into the place where Yahweh is, we must be pure in our minds and our hearts, and we can't be pure when our thoughts are all about how much we can earn or how much we can enjoy ourselves."

The lad looked at the priests surrounding Annas and became frightened. Unlike Annas, who was smiling indulgently and who obviously enjoyed seeing a young version of himself reflected in Jeshua's innocent questions, the other priests were increasingly furious at the boy's impertinence, presumption and rashness. And they were amazed at the license which Annas was allowing him. Sensing their growing discontent, Annas looked up at the gathering, and said softly, "How can we Priests act as intermediaries between God and the Children of Israel unless we know what the Children of Israel are thinking and saying. This child, for all his naivety, is the voice of the people. If we are to be both leaders of Israel and servants of the Lord God, then Jeshua's is a voice we must listen to. For be assured, brother priests, that if we don't listen to him, others will. In these dangerous times, when the Romans are fomenting hatred and oppression, the Children of Israel look to us to help them. We are their Priests and we must give them answers. If we fail, then they will look to the Pharisees and if they're still not satisfied with those answers, they'll look towards the Zealots or the Essenes who all claim that they have the answer to our people's suffering. And if that happens, if they turn away from the Temple, then where will we Priests be next year or the year after?"

CHAPTER SEVEN

Qumran, on the shores of the Dead Sea 15 CE, the third year of the reign of the Emperor Tiberius

It was the silence which overwhelmed them as they descended deeper and deeper into the unknowable. The silence and the peace and the certainty of where they were! As though the familiar land of Israel, one they had known all their lives suddenly deserted them and they were stepping down into another world, a nether world, *Gehenna*, away from people, away from animals, away from anything which lived and breathed. And as they walked down and down along the narrow, rocky track, descending into a vast and limitless valley, a sense of serenity settled on them. They were cut away from the worries of the world, excised and removed from the problems which pressed in upon them.

Yet it was only the surrounding world which changed. The serenity which they experienced as they walked away from Jerusalem slowly ebbed as each footstep took them lower and lower into the Valley, as though they were now descending into *Hell* itself. Within themselves, there grew a feeling of foreboding, a sense of menace as the land became increasingly unfamiliar, removed from the creation of God which they had known all their lives. The deeper and lower they went, the more the feeling of imminent peril grew. There was no life in the place, no green grass of the fields, or the tinted leaves of berry bushes or the vibrant blush of fruit trees. It was as if Yahweh and all which He had created, was absent, as if the Angel of Death had agreed with the Almighty that what was above, was God's domain, and all which lay below belonged to he who had created *Gehenna*.

Sensing her concerns and dismissing his own, Jeshua put down his staff, and walked back up the hill to where his mother Miriam had stopped walking, and was surveying the land ahead, standing still, her face drawn with the events of the recent past and wondering about where she was going. She had been observing the yawning fissure in the earth's surface for some time, as though she was frightened of descending into undefined and menacing territory.

Many years earlier, when Jeshua had just been born, Miriam and his father Yosef, may God rest his blessed and eternal soul, had trodden unfamiliar ground all the way to Egypt. He was a baby, and didn't remember a thing, but it was part of the family's stories told at night after the work of the day was done.

But that was nearly twenty years earlier, and Miriam had been a young and vigorous woman. Today, as Jeshua walked back up the steep path towards where his mother was standing, he could see clearly how she had aged in the past few years. Since Yosef had been taken sick and slowly became increasingly incapacitated, Miriam's vigor seemed to evaporate like the morning dew in Spring. Though there was still fire in her eyes, she was visibly older, especially so since her beloved Yosef had gone to his eternal rest and was safe in the bosom of the Almighty.

As Jeshua climbed towards her, he could still see aspects of the young woman who he loved so much when he was growing up. Now she was a widow, he loved her even more, for it was his responsibility to protect her. And she wasn't like the widows and old women of his home in Nazareth. Unlike them, Miriam was still youthful and sprightly, despite the grey which suffused her hair.

The old women of Nazareth seemed to just give in to senility. Miriam didn't, and still maintained her appearance, washing her hair weekly in the brook beside her house. The old women of the town seemed old before their time, spent from a lifetime of struggle, grey as the timeless sun bleached their hair of color, and stooped like gnarled pieces of timber. They walked supported by wooden staff, stooped as though they were carrying the weight of the world on their shoulders. So different from Miriam. She was only 17 years older than him, and yet she seemed to have retained much of the vigor of her youth. He was so proud of her.

Jeshua looked at his mother in love and pity, and was sad that a look of concern had suddenly appeared on her face as she looked down into the valley, and the heaviness and smells of the air started to cause her concerns. Since the death of Yosef the previous year, all spirit and joy seemed to have left her body. Life had been drained from her being by the harshness and emptiness of the life she'd lived since Yosef had been laid in the ground, wrapped in his *tallit*, and Jeshua had said the prayers of the dead for him every morning, and every night for an entire year.

Upon his death, Jeshua had taken over his role as the carpenter to the village and had succeeded in the transition. But as he grew in stature and confidence, Miriam had declined in both her health and her joy. She was often seen walking along the road, mumbling to herself as though still talking with Yosef. She would set places at the table for three, not two. Yosef's other children, all except James, had their own families, and never came to visit.

Once they ended the prescribed mourning period for their father, they seemed to turn their backs on his other family, leaving Miriam even more isolated both from Yosef and the wider community. Jeshua had gone to the house of each of them and berated them for their callous indifference towards his mother, but they didn't care. They merely said that their father had chosen Miriam as a wife, and that they had no true relationship towards her. It was only the youngest of Yosef's sons, James, who continued to visit and maintain his relationship with a woman he had grown to love and admire as the helpmate of his father.

But the family's disdain continued to hurt Jeshua and in growing concern for his mother's well-being he called Yosef's other children to his mother's house. Still they repeated their same story, all except James, telling Jeshua in front of Miriam that she and Jeshua had stolen their inheritance. In pity, Jeshua had turned his back on them. Only James had joined him in trying to cheer Miriam away from her melancholy.

And it was James who told Jeshua of a community of good people he had heard about from a visiting preacher. They lived by the shores of the Dead Sea to the East of Jerusalem.

From the description which his half-brother gave, the spiritual values and the peace and quiet of the location sounded precisely what Miriam needed. So he told her that he would accompany her there, and she should stay with the community in the tranquility it offered for as long as she wanted...months even. When she was ready to return, she should send word to him and he would come back and get her.

Yet now that they had left Jerusalem and were walking down the steep path from the City of David towards the Dead Sea, he could tell for certain that Miriam was beginning to doubt her agreement. Somehow, she'd envisaged that the area into which she was traveling would be the same as the land around Nazareth and Sephoris, full of trees and bushes and fields. But the more they descended, the more the place frightened her, for in her mind, it was Gehenna, the Valley of the sons of Hinnon, where in ancient days people had sacrificed babies and worshipped the evil pagan God Moloch, a place which smelled perpetually of burning flesh. It was where the damned had suffered terrible tortures in hot and hideous conditions.

He walked back up the path to where she was standing, and asked, "Mother, what's wrong?"

"This place. It's evil. I can feel it. I can feel the accursed in the air. They speak to me on the wind. I can hear their moaning."

He put his arm on her shoulder, and said gently, "Their voices are nothing more than the wind in the rocks, and the smell is not the spirit of the dead, but brimstone, the same burning yellow stone which God sent down from the sky to destroy the evil people of Sodom and Gomorrah, cities which were on the edge of the sea below. It's the yellow rock which surrounds the edges of the Dead Sea. We were told about it being in the air. But you'll get used to the smell very soon, and then it will improve your health and your breathing. The Essene preacher spoke of it, and told James how in the beginning, it was offensive, but when the nose became used to it, it improved health and wellness."

She nodded, but still refused to step forward. "There are no trees. Where is the grass? The flowers? I see nothing here, Jeshua. How can such a large community as a thousand souls live down here if there's no grass? Where do they get their food, their water?"

"Come, mother," he said. "Trust me and trust the preacher who told James about the Essenes and about Qumran. He told him that we'd have these doubts as we descended from Jerusalem. We have to move on, because we must get to the bottom of the valley by nightfall. We can't sleep out on the rocks. It's another three or four hours walk."

Reluctantly, Miriam nodded, and followed her son downwards, ever downwards, into the depths of the valley.

It was nightfall, and the pathway was already difficult to follow, by the time the ground leveled out and they realized that they were on the valley floor. Jeshua decided that it was too dangerous for them to continue, and so he gathered some driftwood and dried grasses, and with his flints lit a small fire. It gave Miriam comfort, illuminated their dark locale, and enabled Jeshua to warm the already-stale bread which they'd purchased three days earlier. Miriam opened the bag of lentils, olives and dried meat and knowing that their journey was nearing its end, they ate less sparingly than at other times during their long walk.

As the desert night began to grow sharply colder, Miriam pulled the sheepskin tighter around her and wondered if she would ever again ascend out of this Valley of Death into the blessed light of God's nation. She had agreed to travel to the Essene community in Qumran persuaded by Jeshua that her mind and spirit and body needed to be instilled with the pure essence of Yahweh, and from what the Essene priest had told his step-brother, the community beside the shores of the Dead Sea was a place where people walked in the footsteps of the ancient prophets.

Miriam lay awake, looking up at the stars and listening to her son's gentle breathing. The sky above Nazareth was huge with countless stars in the firmament, but the night sky above the desert was somehow infinitely larger and the points of light were so much more brilliant. It was much hotter here during the day, yet far colder at night. From time to time, she saw a shooting star and said the traditional blessing. They said that shooting stars were the tears of Yahweh when He looked down and saw the plight of his children Israel under the iron boots of the Romans. Yet Miriam knew that this was nonsense, because Yahweh was immeasurable and all-powerful and if He had wanted to put an end to His people's suffering, he could have done so easily by driving the Romans from the land which He had given to them. So why hadn't He? Why did He allow His people to be so badly hurt, their spirits crushed, their strength drained? Why did He allow the Sadducees to rule the Temple as though it was their own Palace and they were kings and emperors, when the Temple had been built by King Solomon as a house of worship of Yahweh for all the Jewish people?

She sighed. There were so many questions which needed to be answered. In her life with Yosef, she had always asked him to help her understand the world around her, and he'd done his best. Then when he'd died she relied on Jeshua, whose insights were more spiritual, more profound, but lacking Yosef's understanding of the world around them. She'd asked Yosef's other children but had been firmly put in her place that she was now a widow and no longer held the status of being their father's wife, so all except James had turned their backs on her.

Dear James! Such a kind and honest and decent man, now with a beautiful family of his own. A friend to Jeshua even though he was many years older, and now a friend to Miriam in her loneliness. James would often buy food and candles and bread for his own family, but always bring around some extra for Miriam. Sometimes, he would stay at her house for dinner before returning to his wife and children. He and Jeshua and Miriam were as close to each other as a divided family could be, and to his great credit, James rejected the pressure put on him by his brothers and sisters to turn his back on Miriam.

Perhaps this was the time, now that Miriam was going to the Essenes to recover her spirit. Perhaps she would never return to her home. If only, like the prophets and the seers, she could foretell the future.

But she knew that ultimately, James must succumb to the pressure and side with his siblings against her, and an attempt would be made to drive Miriam and Jeshua from Nazareth. Where could they move to? Sephoris was no longer an option, having been taken over by the Romans as the center of their base in Galilee. Her own mother and father had died long before the theft of their town, which was a mercy for their hearts would have been broken had they seen the reality. Since their deaths, her own siblings had scattered throughout Judea and she'd not heard from any of her sisters in two years.

So if Yosef's children insisted on her removal from the family home, where could she go? Who would look after her? Jeshua was a good and wonderful son, but since Yosef had died, their income had declined dramatically. Jeshua was a good carpenter, but instead of following his father's business methods, and seeking opportunities to build furniture, Jeshua was more inclined to wait for people to request work of him, or to do favors for people, to repair widow's chairs or tables without charging them, or to make furniture for the synagogue without earning a profit. Yes, he was beloved by the people of Nazareth, but they were taking advantage of him, and the family was suffering.

She closed her eyes and tried to think of nothing. Tomorrow would be another day and there was a long walk on the western shore of the Dead Sea, south towards Qumran.

The community was some distance from the Dead Sea, yet through the heat haze on the horizon, it looked as though everything was a part of everything else. There seemed to be no boundary to divide the land from the sky and the sky from the sea. All fused into one burning yellow-white jumble, broiled by the sun, heat haze rising like dizzying sprites from the blistered rocks as though some ethereal being was dancing in the landscape. And the very shores of the sea itself were painted as though by some demonic hand in stripes of yellow brimstone and bleached whites as though the rocks were the bones of animals left to rot in the sun. And within the dead hand of the land, some evil spirit had placed men, women and children enslaved and captured within the distant surrounding walls of the mountains.

As they walked southwards on the Western side of the Dead Sea, the sun rose over the Mountains of Moab which made up the Eastern shores, and even though it was early in the morning, its brightness and intensity began to frighten away the mists. The closer they walked, the more obvious became the dwelling places of the Qumran community, the Ir Hamellah, the City of Salt. It was some distance from the Dead Sea, but there were cultivated fields between the city and the water and Jeshua and Miriam could see people working within them. Fields, yes, but not the green fields of Israel, not the lush orchards of Nazareth, with their plentiful olive and fig and orange trees; these fields were dry and dusty and salty. Only God knew how crops could grow in such a setting.

Also visible were people walking around the large city. Some were on rooftops, some were tending to crops grown in the nearby wadi, some were sitting outdoors at tables in the shade of huge palm and date trees, and others still were tending herds of goat, sheep and oxen. It was a lively, busy community, but the thing which was most impressive, and which made it so utterly different from any city to which he'd ever been, was that there were only two roads...the one on which they were traveling towards it, and the one on the far side which went south, further into the Negev Desert and on towards the Gulf and the town of Eilat where King Solomon had found precious minerals in ancient times, and extracted metals. It was a part of Israel that few people ever saw; it made Jeshua feel closer to God; it made Miriam feel trapped.

Their approach was noticed first by men in the fields, who straightened from tending the crops and leaned on their hoes or shovels, glad of the break in routine. The inhabitants of the community wondered who these strangers could possibly be. Nobody came unannounced to the Essene congregation by the Dead Sea. The only people who ever passed by were traders with the city of Eilat far away, or visitors to wanted to take the precious waters of the oasis of Ein Gedi to the south. Perhaps this man and this older woman were passing through.

Yet the Master had made no mention in this morning's Gathering of any strangers or visitors. They were dressed like poor Jews, and not like Roman's visiting the provincial parts of the Empire, rich visitors touring the provinces to see if they could buy curiosities which they'd take home and sell for a fortune in their marketplaces.

As they came nearer, it was obvious that man was young and strong looking; probably the son of the woman. But that was all they could tell. As the workers in the field studied the newcomers, a bell rang, a signal from the Master of the Fields that work had to continue, regardless of the interest shown in the arrivals.

Jeshua and Miriam were within shouting distance of the houses and dwelling places of Ir Hammeleh when four men walked out to greet them on the road. All of the men wore crude garments made of woven hessian. Around their heads were bands of cloth of different colors. Unlike the Priests of Jerusalem, he couldn't tell the difference between the rank of one and the other from their clothes, or any ornaments which they wore. In Jerusalem, priests of the highest rank wore turbans and hats of metal and cloth of the finest gold; here, the men merely wore coverings to protect their heads from the fierce sun.

Out of respect, Jeshua and Miriam stopped walking any closer to the city and waited for the leaders to come to them. As they neared, Jeshua saw that their faces and hands were as brown as old leather, the effect of the harsh climate and the intense sun. Three of the men stopped, and the man who was obviously the leader of the community came forward.

"In the name of Yahweh the Almighty, Blessings be upon you," the leader said. "We have brought sweet water, dates and figs to sustain you after your journey and before you accept our hospitality."

Jeshua bowed and held out his cupped hands. In the tradition of desert dwellers, the leader was joined by the others, who tipped the fruit into Jeshua's hands. Jeshua turned and gave his mother the fruit, then ate some dates and figs himself. Water was given, and first Miriam, and then Jeshua drank greedily from the flask.

When the blessings and thanks had been given and traditions observed and the rituals accomplished, Jeshua said, "My mother and I thank you and your brethren for your generosity. What we carry with us, we beg you to share. My home is your home, my hearth your hearth, my goods are your goods. May we meet and depart in peace and may our words bring you joy and understanding. Yahweh looks upon us and smiles."

The four community leaders said, "Amen, Selah. Measure and reflect upon what has been said."

Confident that the young man and the middle-aged woman were Jewish and genuine travelers, the community leader said, "I am Gideon ben Manasseh. I am the leader of the community of Ir Hammeleh. We don't often get wanderers approaching our city without our having been forewarned of their arrival."

"I am Jeshua ben Yosef of the village of Nazareth. I accompany my mother Miriam bat Joachim, born of Sephoris but whom married Yosef of Nazareth who has died recently and for whom the mourning period has now come to an end. We have journeyed to your community in order for my mother to seek understanding, repose and safety. She is possessed of many frightening dreams and needs the love of a community such as yours to mend her."

Gideon looked at Miriam and nodded. He was a man in his late sixties who had lived for his entire life in the Qumran community. He had never known any other life, and would look forward to Miriam telling him about her experiences during the day when the community was working, and he was no longer in the scriptorium. He looked at Jeshua, and studied his face.

"And you, Jeshua ben Yosef. Will you be staying with us?"

Jeshua smiled and shook his head. "With your permission, I will rest for a few days, and then return to Nazareth. I have work which I must finish. I am a carpenter."

Gideon ben Manasseh said softly, "I think you will stay with us longer than a few days, Jeshua. I see from your eyes that you are a soul who seeks the answer to many questions. Perhaps you will find the answer in the peace and tranquility of the desert which surrounds us, or in the writings of the Teacher of Righteousness, from whom we take our understanding. We do not know each other, Jeshua, but I think that you will remain with you mother, and that once you breathe in the peace and joy of our community, you will not leave. But enough! You must be tired from your walk. Come with us, and be welcomed into the Community. Join us for prayers and then for our evening meal."

They turned, and Jeshua and Miriam followed the four leaders. One of them, who introduced himself as Yoram, asked "Do you have any meat or any other flesh with you. We only eat fruits and vegetables. We cannot permit the flesh of animals to be brought into our city."

"My half-brother, who was visited by one of your members, an Essene priest who visited Nazareth some weeks ago and who came to buy medicines, and spoke about your prohibition on eating the flesh of animals. We have consumed meat on our journey to sustain us, but we left what remained on a rock far distant from here so that the birds and animals could consume it. Now we carry no meat with us. Only bread and lentils and some desert fruits we gathered on the journey from Jerusalem."

Gideon turned, and asked, "And did this Essene Priest also tell your brother the rules of our community?"

"He said that they were a secret and told only within the community to those who were initiates. He said that until we were initiates, they could not be told to us," said Miriam. "This priest came to purchase the juice of the pomegranate, which cannot be grown in your soils, because it was the only thing which cured the worms which grow inside a man's body. He told my step-son that one of your members was faint and wasting with this worm. I pray that the pomegranate juice helped him."

Yoram smiled and nodded. "He was talking about Shoshanna, one of our sisters. And yes, she drank deeply of the pomegranate juice for a week, and the worm was expelled from her body. She is now well restored."

Gideon remained silent as they walked towards the cluster of sand-colored buildings. Each was rectangular and there were streets running between them. There was none of the vast and glorious architecture of Jerusalem, with its immense temple and palaces and huge towers built above the walls which looked like fingers pointing towards the sky. Instead, the city of Ir Hammeleh looked like the wooden blocks which children played with and from which they built imaginary buildings and structures. Some of the buildings in the city were long and low, others smaller and less squat with gaps in the wall where Jeshua could see dozens of men who were seated at long tables, and writing with bird quills on long scrolls of vellum, occasionally dipping their quills into bronze ink wells.

In other buildings, there was smoke coming from the roofs, which he assumed was where the community food was prepared. And still other buildings, by far the vast majority, seemed unoccupied. These, he assumed, were where the community members slept.

As they entered the outer streets of the city, what struck Miriam most noticeably was the absence of noise. In her own village of Nazareth, the moment they neared the outer precincts from the surrounding fields, the voices of the people were immediately noticeable; children crying, mothers shouting, fathers demanding, grandparents snoring. Yet in Ir Hammeleh, there was no noise. It was as though the city was completely empty, yet everywhere she could see people. Walking with their heads bowed towards the earth, sitting inside or outside of their houses, congregating around long tables, writing with quills on parchments; but all in total silence. The only sound which could occasionally be heard was the distant scream of a bird in the distant wadi.

Gideon walked towards a large low building, and motioned Miriam to enter. Softly, he said, "It is the sleeping quarters of the women. Your son will be on the other side of the community buildings, in the sleeping quarters of the men. You will meet tonight when the bell rings to call everybody to prayer and for the evening meal. Because you are strangers, you will sit at a separate table from the rest of the community. You will be served your food. Members of our community serve themselves, but you are honored guests, and so it will be our privilege to serve you. You will join us for the community prayer, but when we separate and go into our Prayer House, you will not follow, for until you are a member, there are things which are forbidden for you to know. Instead, you may walk around the city, or walk to the shores of the Sea. But do not enter the sea, nor touch the water with your hands," he warned.

"Why not?" asked Jeshua. "Is it sacred?"

"No," smiled Gideon. "The water is not like the water which we find in rivers or springs in the world above, where you live. This water is full of noxious things, and no living thing has ever been seen within it, which is why it is called dead. There are no fish and no plants in the Salt Sea such as you find in other seas. And if you swallow this water, or it gets into your nose or your eyes, then they will swell up and you will become very ill. Some years ago, one of our members was walking beside the Sea and he slipped on the bank. He fell in, and his head went below the surface. His face swelled up, and he was blind for weeks. He could barely breathe. He was lucky to live. Truly, it is the sea of the damned," said Gideon. "Our texts tell us that in the time of Abraham our Father, this was a pure and pristine sea of the finest water, but the cities of Sodom and Gomorrah turned their backs on the Lord and entertained evil ways. When Yahweh punished them by destroying them with fire and brimstone, the water absorbed all their sins and it is now deadly to the touch of mankind. We respect and fear this Sea, this Dead Sea, as a sign to all Jews of what will happen to us when we walk outside of the gaze of the Lord."

+

Miriam enjoyed the company of the other community members she met in the House of Women. Some had been members of the Community for their entire lives, and had never ventured beyond the confines of the Dead Sea. These were the women who begged her to answer their questions about Jerusalem and the Romans and life in Israel, and everything else.

Other women, with whom she had much more in common, had joined their husbands late in their lives, when the men had elected to become Essenes and live a contemplative and spiritual life in the desert. Some of their husbands had held high positions in large cities; others had become disillusioned with life under the Romans; others still had believed that the growing immorality in the Kingdom of Israel, in part under Herod

Antipas and in part under the Roman Prefect who had replaced Herod's incompetent brother Archelaus in Judea, both in its capital Caesaria and in holy Jerusalem, had become too much for the pious of Israel to bear, and so many had retreated into the safety of the desert. But it was the Sadducee priests and their Levite assistants in the holy Temple of Solomon, perverted by the evil King Herod, who the Essenes hated the very most. They could barely whisper their name.

When she first arrived in the House of Women, she had sat on the simple bunk allotted to her and wondered what she was doing here. The huge room was as sparse and ordinary as any she'd seen. Yes, it was very clean, having been swept just that morning to remove the ubiquitous dust and desert sand which was everywhere; but it was completely devoid of any comforts of humanity. Unlike her home, where the shelves and wall niches held those ornaments and objects which were precious to her – things with which she'd grown up as a child, things given to her for her wedding and the birth of Jeshua – this house had no place for such items. It was just rock walls and a ceiling made of the leaves of the palm trees.

The sparseness had depressed her, and she lay on her bunk waiting for something to happen. And when a bell rang and there was much movement outside, Miriam wondered what sort of a reception she would be given. As women of the community silently walked in, they looked at her, smiled, but went about their business as though she didn't exist. Miriam smiled back, hoping that her gesture of friendship might encourage somebody to come over and greet her; but they simply went to their bunks, sat down, and remained silent. It was both extraordinary and unnerving. Miriam decided to leave the community as soon as her body was fully rested.

But it all changed when an older woman walked in, and every woman in the room, including Miriam, stood. The woman closed the door and stood in silence. Then she said, "Blessed are you, O Lord, our God, King and Maker of the Universe, who has brought this day to a close and enabled us to thrive and endure the vicissitudes which plague your land of Israel. Keep us safe, Lord God, from the evil ones in Jerusalem and other parts of Your realm. May the Evil One, cursed by he, remain blinded to our community. Lord God, maker and giver of all things, we thank you for enabling us to work today for the benefit of the community, our friends and ourselves. If any have been slothful in their work, resentful at any of the tasks they have been given, or churlish in sharing their gifts with those of the community who are less able, then I pray that you forgive them, and show them how to improve themselves tomorrow. If any have worked hard and shared their bounty selflessly with others, then I pray that you will smile just as willingly on others who do not share their capacity. And may tomorrow be a better and more rewarding day for us and our community than was today. Amen. Selah."

Everybody, including Miriam, replied 'Amen, Selah.'

Then the older woman turned in Miriam's direction, and said, "And I welcome a guest and a visitor to our community. She is a Sister in Yahweh, and as such you will love her as you love your sisters. You will help her because our ways are strange. You will guide her, for even though our community is our safety, beyond our community is great danger. And you will befriend her, for in friendship is the bond which unites us all."

The woman walked over to Miriam, and kissed her on the cheeks. "I am Sharai. I am the leader of the women of our community of Essenes. May I be permitted to know your name?"

"I am Miriam bat Joachim. I have traveled here with my son, Jeshua. I was born in Sephoris but married Yosef of Nazareth who died recently, and so I have come here to refresh my spirits."

"Miriam, you are beloved and welcome," said Sharai.

The moment she said it, all the other women gathered around Miriam, and kissed her in greeting and friendship. Two of the younger ones, women in their late teens or early 20's, told her that they would be her guide to both the community, its rules, its prohibitions and the surrounding area. They explained that although there were things which could not be told to her, there were many things which could be shared. They took her by the hand, and led her to other, older women and introduced her. By the time Miriam had met more than seventy, she shook her head and burst out laughing.

"Stop! Please stop! No more. I can't meet anybody else. In my village of Nazareth, I knew far fewer women, and I only met a handful each day. This is all too much," she said, sitting on another woman's bunk. Sharai came over, sat beside her and put her arm around her. "Miriam, we are a community. For the time that you'll be here with us, these are your sisters. You will have to get to know them. For they, like you, will still be here tomorrow."

She turned to the two younger women, "Ruth, Esther, enough now. If Sister Miriam is feeling strong enough, take her outside and show her where the Eating Hall and the Prayer Hall are; then take her to the shores of the Sea and explain the dangers of going to close to its edge. When you return, you will wash your bodies and then we will go to Prayers for the Eternal One; after that, we will eat and then return here, where we will learn more about you, Miriam, and how you came to arrive at our community."

All she wanted to do was to sleep, but by the time they had walked around the encampment, gone to the Dead Sea, climbed onto the limestone rocks and looked at the dozens of caves where the majority of the community slept at night, it was time for their communal dinner. And Miriam had to admit that she was starving. The last time she'd eaten properly was in the morning when they'd wakened at the foot of the steep pathway down from Jerusalem. When they'd arrived, she'd had a little fruit and water which Gideon ben Manasseh had given them before they entered the community, but after walking for so long, and so far, she now realized that her body needed food badly.

Miriam and the other women entered the Eating Hall from the southern door, just as men were entering from the north. They sat at separate long tables, and it was obvious from the quiet in the room that food was taken without any conversation. Miriam took a wooden bowl and a spoon from the serving table and helped herself to a bowl full of uncooked fruits and vegetables and bread. She turned to Esther with a quizzical expression on her face.

"Our Rule doesn't allow us to adulterate food. As God provides it for us, so we eat it. We make bread from grains, but all our fruits and vegetables are uncooked. You'll soon get used to it," Esther whispered.

She could see large and succulent pieces of many different kinds of vegetable and leaves, but what she really craved was meat. Only once a week, and usually at the beginning of the Sabbath, did she and her family eat meat, but having been without the taste of chicken or sheep or cow for weeks now, only having eaten dried meat of the consistency of leather, her mouth and tongue craved its warmth and tasty juices badly. But the freshly baked bread smelled delicious. She picked up a thick square of it and followed Esther who was returning to her seat.

They sat in silence, and Miriam waited for her cue before picking up her spoon and beginning to eat. When all the community had taken their food and was seated, Gideon stood at the head of the table and walked to an elevated rostrum. He stood up and placed a scroll onto the table. Turning the ends of the scroll until the parchment was at the correct place, he looked up, and said in a sonorous voice, "Blessed are you Yahweh, our God, who has enabled us this day to meet in peace and harmony, away from the sight of the Sons of Darkness and the men of perdition. Blessed are you Yahweh, who has provided for us this food that we may sustain ourselves to work in Your sight and to worship Your Holy name. Amen, Selah."

Gideon looked up, and smiled at the community. "Eat friends, and be healthy. And I am delighted in the arrival of two new guests who are welcome in our community. Miriam and her son Jeshua from the village of Nazareth. They are here to find peace and comfort and an end to their suffering. Welcome, Miriam. Welcome Jeshua."

Everybody turned and looked, smiling at the newcomers. In embarrassment, Miriam smiled back, and looked down at her bowl, but then glanced up to see whether Jeshua was embarrassed. He appeared not to be, and was beaming a smile back at all those who welcomed him.

Gideon continued, "Our Community Rule, the work of our great Master, the Teacher of Righteousness, may Yahweh bless his immortal soul, is the glue which binds us together. Because we have two strangers eating with us, I shall not begin with the Secret Precepts as left to us by our master, the Teacher of Righteousness until our guests depart from the presence of us, the Righteous Ones, and they return to their lodgings. Instead, I shall read to you from the Rule."

He cleared his voice and moved the scroll to the left until he found the part which he was looking for.

"For according to his abilities, and according to his insight he shall be admitted to the Community. In this way both his love and his hatred shall be manifest, and all shall know him as one of the Chosen ones. But be warned, for there are voices which will try to seduce you, and for this reason, no man shall argue or quarrel with the men of perdition. He shall keep his council in secrecy in the midst of the men of deceit and admonish with knowledge, truth and righteous commandment those of chosen conduct, each according to his spiritual quality and according to the norm of time. He shall guide them with knowledge and instruct them in the mysteries of wonder and truth in the midst of the members of the community, so that they shall behave decently with one another in all that has been revealed to them. That is the time for studying the Torah, the clearing of the path of truth and law, in the wilderness. He shall instruct them to do all that is required at that time, and to separate from all those who have not turned aside from all deceit.

These are the norms of conduct for the Master in those times with respect to his loving and to his everlasting hating of the men of perdition in a spirit of secrecy. He shall leave to them property and wealth and earnings like a

slave to his lord, and he shall show them true humility before the one who
rules over him. He shall be zealous concerning the Law and be prepared for
the Day of Revenge.

He shall perform the will Yahweh in all his deeds and in all strength as
Yahweh has commanded. He shall freely delight in all that befalls him, and
shall desire nothing except God's will..."

Gideon looked up from the scroll, and said softly, "Brothers and sisters in Yahweh, the Men of Perdition, the Sons of Darkness, are our enemies. Many who live outside of our community believe that Rome and the Romans are the true enemies of the Sons of Israel. But believe me when I say to you that the true enemy is sitting up there..." He pointed to the West, towards Jerusalem..."and is dressed in the raiment of Priests and acolytes, in rich brocades and gold turbans and wearing the Urim and the Thummim, the lights of perfection, the revelation and the truth, and they soak up the very lifeblood of the Jewish people and create a barrier between Yahweh and His chosen ones. Yes, the Romans are evil and must leave our nation; but we have been conquered many times before and have always prevailed. In our past, we have felt the boot of the Egyptians, the Assyrians, the Babylonians, the Greeks and now the Romans. Great empires come and go. Only we who have been blessed by Yahweh as His people remain to live in the fulfilment of His word. So it is not they, the mighty conquerors with their swords and chariots who are the enemy of the Jewish people. It is those who infest the Temple on the hill of Jerusalem and who falsify the God of we Jews, these false sages who sit atop the mountain like vultures in their nest, my children, who are the Sons of Darkness, the men of perdition, the evil ones who have captured Israel and become prostitutes in the eyes of Yahweh.

"Rome will always be Rome, just as before Rome our forefathers were told that Greece and Assyria and Babylon and Egypt would be the rulers of the world for all time. But what has happened to these great empires? They are dust in the desert, forgotten and now mere remnants of what they once were. Where are their great armies, their weapons, their mighty ships and fighting machines? Gone. All gone. And after Rome, some other great nation will rise up and will tread on the sacred ground of Israel with their iron boots and their chariot wheels. But these are conquerors of land and buildings...not conquerors of the soul of a people. Nobody can conquer Yahweh or His chosen ones. Nobody, my beloved brothers and sisters in the eyes of the Lord. Yet today, the Children of Israel are in the thrall of the Sadducees and Levites and priests who control the damnable and false buildings which replaced the blessed Temple of our King Solomon, built by the evil King Herod, and now nothing more than a house of whores and thieves, of men who blaspheme in the name of the Lord by trading their merchandise on the grounds of Solomon's holy temple..."

Jeshua looked at Gideon in astonishment. His mind flew back six years to Jerusalem, to the Temple, to the time of his initiation, when he argued with Annas, the Chief Priest about the very things which Gideon was now saying. At the time, and ever since, he'd thought that he was the only person in all of Israel who thought these things. Now he realized that others too, others in this very community, believed precisely what he believed.

He shook his head in wonder. For years...for much of his life...he'd thought himself so different from those around him that he believed he was suffering from some affliction of the mind. But now, suddenly, purely by chance, he had entered into a realm where men seemed to think the same thoughts as he thought. Could he have found his true home? Could this be where the rest of his life should be spent?

CHAPTER EIGHT

Thirteen years later 28 CE, the fourteenth year of the reign of the Emperor Tiberius

The decision was the hardest she had ever had to make, yet for the sake of her son, and at the behest of Yahweh, she knew that she had no alternative. She would miss her many sisters and brothers in the community. She knew that when she put her foot on the path, a path she hadn't trodden in thirteen years, a path which led up to Jerusalem, she would no longer be protected by the cocoon of her sanctuary. And she knew that she and Jeshua would be prey to the evils against which he had preached about for so many years. But she also knew that it was the only decision she could make.

For eleven years, Miriam had been a sister of the community. She had seen her brilliant young son rise from young neophyte, a visiting guest of the community, to becoming leader of the Essenes sect on the shores of the Dead Sea, the youngest leader in the Sect's two hundred-year history. His learning, knowledge, and virtuous nature had attracted people of the community to gather around him whenever he wasn't working, and to men like Gideon and his successors, his innate gifts made him into a natural leader.

Miriam herself had also gained in status, for she was now the Leader of the Women of the Community. And her rank was not because her son was the most important man of the community, because no one person was more elevated than another, but she had gained the status in her own right. It was she who welcomed the new members, showed them around the community, prayed with them in the earliest of their days, taught them the most secret mysteries of the Rule, and prostrated herself beside them when they became initiates.

Wherever she went, Miriam was admired, welcomed, sought after and respected. The community now numbered over two thousand souls, far bigger than most of the villages and towns of Israel. Yet unlike those towns where there was jealousy and rivalry, avarice and greed, theft and insecurity, Ir Hamellah at Qumran was run as the purest of pure communities. There was no hierarchy, no government. Her status as Leader of the Women, and Jeshua's status as the Leader of the entire community gained them no special favors or privileges; indeed, it was a burden that most members of the community were happy to see another shoulder. But because they were the two around whom the Community coalesced, they had been chosen, like the Children of Israel were chosen by Yahweh, and they had accepted their responsibilities.

Since his accession, he had slowly and cautiously introduced the importance of one of the religion's ancient forefathers, Melchizedek, King of Salem, into the community's worship. Melchizedek, the priest king who had given comfort to Father Abraham. The community scribes were now completing a scroll in Melchizedek's honor, and including his story in other more ancient scrolls.

Jeshua was very keen for the Community to involve itself more in the history of the Jewish people, especially in understanding the ideas and injunctions of the Prophets Isaiah and Jeremiah. When Jeshua had first arrived, it seemed as though the Community had been created to worship the words, and show reverence for the beloved Teacher of Righteousness who, it was said according to their laws, had returned to Yahweh a hundred years earlier, and whose words, deeds and thoughts were still the lifeblood of the Community.

But it was Melchizedek who inspired Jeshua the most, for it was he, the ancient and great King of Salem, who had created the bond between Yahweh, the Kings who ruled Israel, and the Priests in the Temple. And it was through the descendants of Melchizedek, according to King David's Psalm, that a golden age would be ushered.

Miriam worried sometimes about her beloved son. He was so consumed by anger and distress that the Temple of Yahweh in Jerusalem had been appropriated and prostituted by the wicked Priests, the hated Sadducees and the stiff-necked unbending legalistic Pharisees, that sometimes she thought demons might have taken over his mind.

But in all of the peace and harmony of the Community, there was one issue which Jeshua had initiated which was causing distress and dispute. Despite opposition from those who had lived in the community much longer, Jeshua was intent on spreading the words of the Community around Israel to other communities. He encouraged the scribes to copy more and even more of the Community's holiest books, so that these other communities would have the texts and scrolls that would enable them to flourish in different parts of Israel. And ultimately, she knew, her son wanted to spread the ideas of the Essenes throughout the whole of Israel, so that the people would once again return to the clear path of righteousness, and leave the rutted route which led to the prostitutes of the Temple and the constraints of the Pharisees.

Miriam had spent the past many years in the joy of watching her wonderful son grow from being an astounding and brilliant young boy in Nazareth, into a beloved leader of the thousands in Qumran. His gentle, compassionate, yet determined way of dealing with both the Sect's members and the philosophy of the Community, had spread far and wide throughout Israel, and had created a large number of additional followers. Now, because the community had grown to the limits of its ability to accept, feed and house any more acolytes, it was having to turn aspirants away...which was why Jeshua was encouraging the establishment of other communities. Israel was becoming more and more violent and dangerous, with the Romans tightening their grip on every aspect of Israelite life, the Zealots determined to kill the occupiers and drive them from the Holy Land, and the Pharisees spending their time searching the Books of Moses for words instead of ways to behave compassionately.

Worst of all, though, were the Sadducees, working hand in hand with the occupiers to pervert the Temple into a source of wealth for their fabulous lifestyles, and licking the boots of the lackey King Herod Antipas, the Tetrach of Galilee. This evil monarch had unlawfully married his own half-brother's wife, Herodias, a woman who was now perverting his mind with wickedness.

But in Miriam's Community, protected and protecting, everything was good. Miriam was never lonely, for she was constantly in the company of other women, and from time to time, when the community came together as a whole, she enjoyed talking with the men. Whenever she thought of how her life could have been, perhaps as a satisfied wife of her first love Malachai with lots of children running around her large house overlooking the sea, her body ached for the touch of a man's hand, for his lips upon her lips. But those bodily feelings soon went away when she heard the all-too familiar words, *"Sister Miriam, forgive me interrupting your thoughts, but I need your advice..."*

And she was now getting to a stage in her life when she would soon die and return to the bosom of Yahweh and so men and the physical needs they could satisfy were less and less pressing for her. But she still needed to take long walks at the end of the day along the shores of the Dead Sea in order to stop her mind from roaming into places where she knew that Yahweh wouldn't want it to dwell. She had been such a passionate girl, her mind always racing into thoughts which would have alarmed her parents, and when she grew into womanhood and married Yosef, she'd sublimated these thoughts to be a good and loving and loyal wife. And now she'd turned into a venerable woman, these thoughts were disturbing her, which is why she walked often by the shores of the sea.

And then came the day when her settled and peaceful life changed forever. It was on one brilliant and blistering summer's day. The temperature had become unbearable by the middle of the morning; the ground too hot to walk upon, even in sandals, and the rocks and buildings themselves were too searing to the touch. The insides of their houses were airless, but the summer sun made it impossible for them to go outside. So they had prayed and suffered and returned to their homes as the date groves and planted areas were impossible to walk through. But the day passed in laziness and as the sun sank into the western sky, the heat slowly left the air, and Miriam knew that she had to leave the community buildings and walk outside.

She worried about her son. Miriam had long known that Jeshua's mind was somewhere else, but had ascribed it to the responsibilities he suffered as leader of the Community. What she hadn't realized was the enormity of the changes that she, and Jeshua, would now have to accept. It was during her long walk from the Community along the shore that everything changed. Exhausted from the long and enervating day, she knew that she had to walk a long distance if she was going to be able to sleep that night, and she also needed solitude for her mind to think over the many problems which had visited her.

Miriam walked from the community compound and beyond the dining hall, the scriptorium and the scribe's preparation rooms, and the kitchens, and along the pathway of the date palms towards the Dead Sea. Turning right in the direction of Ein Gedi and Eilat, distant places she had only heard about, she walked in the late afternoon, breathing in the sulphurous air to which she was now so accustomed. As she walked to her favorite spot, a promontory which was like a finger into the sea, Miriam spotted a tall man wearing a prayer shawl over his long robes, standing just before the promontory on the putrid and slimy banks of the sea, his shadow in the falling sun pointing like an accusing finger across the waters eastwards towards the Mountains of Moab. In the sea were huge blocks of salt floating in the acrid and poisonous water. On the banks, between the water and the mud, was a white and yellow scum which could not be touched, because if it accidentally reached the eyes or the nose, it would cause terrible pain and suffering.

Miriam walked over to where the man was standing. As the desert air cooled with the descent of the sun into the West and shadows becoming more distinct, she saw him staring into the darkening folds of the distant mountains. She approached, her heart nearly stopped, because the light from the setting Western sun was surrounding the man's body, and it looked as though he was golden and on fire. Her mind flew to the story of Elijah who had been taken up by Yahweh in a fiery chariot before the Almighty had destroyed the evil Jezebel.

Her heart in her mouth, flushed with fear and apprehension at the nearness of the Almighty, Miriam stood ten paces away from Jeshua, and remained silent. The man was her son, Jeshua.

"You are welcome here, Mother," he said. "How...?"

"Your shadow joined mine in the salt sea. I saw a man, but in my heart, I knew it was you, because anybody else would have made their presence known. Only a mother would understand her son's need for peace and solitude."

She loved his melodic voice, which had the power to soothe and inflame the passions all at the same time. She was his mother, yet she was unlike any other mother she knew; for their ages were not all that different. There was only fifteen years which separated them, and Jeshua's knowledge, wisdom and brilliance made those fifteen years completely unimportant. It was as though they were brother and older sister, or the very best and closest of friends.

Miriam didn't know whether to say something, whether to disturb her son in the presence of the Almighty. Sensing her discomfort, Jeshua said, "I have come to a decision, Mother. I have spoken with the Lord, and Yahweh has guided me. He has told me what I must do. He has built the path beneath my feet, and now I must take the first step."

Her throat dried as she waited to know the details of the mission which Yahweh had given to her son.

"I know you are happy here, Mother", he said softly, "but if the Almighty gave me a task, who are we to put our own happiness, our safety, before the demands of our Lord?"

"What did Yahweh say to you, Jeshua?"

He remained silent for a long and uncomfortable moment. She was silhouetted like a burning candle in the late afternoon sun and the stifling air, but she dare not move a muscle, for that might disturb his thoughts. Jeshua hadn't even turned and looked at her since he'd acknowledged her presence, yet she knew that they were joined together. Whenever they met in the community, he always came over and smiled and kissed her. Yet standing in the presence of the Lord on the shores of the Dead Sea, Miriam was beginning to feel as though she was an intruder between her son and their God.

Slowly, softly so that she had to strain to hear his words, Jeshua said, "Yahweh has told me that I must leave this place. He has told me that I may take you with me if you are willing to undertake the journey. Yahweh has told me to take the word of the Community and spread it far and wide. Like Moses, I must take our commandments, our laws, our knowledge and our wisdom, and make the people of Israel see the error of their ways. Like Isaiah, I have said to Yahweh, *'Here I am, send me.'* I am a Moses come back to his people; as he brought the word of the Lord down from the mountain called Sinai, I bring the words of this blessed community and give it as a remedy, an antidote to the poisonous filth which is preached by the Sadducees and the Pharisees. I have come to save my people.

"The people of Israel are breaking the sacred covenant which Abraham made with God. Yahweh stayed Abraham's hand just before he sacrificed Isaac on Mount Moriah and God ordered Solomon to build his Temple there when our people returned from our exile in Egypt. But the very place where Yahweh spared the life of Isaac, and through him breathed life into Israel, has become a bed of thievery and unholy rituals. It is a place where harlots and moneychangers and merchants are prostituting God's home and God's words. It has become a house of commerce and is no longer a House of Prayer.

"By following the dictates of the Sadducee priests in Yahweh's Temple, the people of Israel are transgressing against the word of the Lord. The Almighty has ordered me to go out of the Community and into Israel and cast out the devils. He has said that it is my mission to go forth into the Land of Israel and preach the laws of our Community so that the People of Israel will again return to the right hand of God and will be cleansed. The Community Elders will try to prevent me, because we are sworn to secrecy, which is why we must leave now, and tell nobody where we are going, or what we are going to do."

He turned around, and Miriam saw his face illuminated by the golden glow of the late afternoon sun as it sank into the Western sky. Her knees were weak as she looked into his eyes and gazed upon his face. It was totally serene, more peaceful than she'd ever seen her son before. Gone was the look of anguish which he carried as he pondered the great thoughts which were always in his mind; gone was the pained expression as he dealt with the trauma of everybody's problems in the Community; and gone was the fear of being unworthy to Yahweh, which she could always detect followed his every waking breath.

Suddenly her son was a man of God, truly a man who was as one with Yahweh. Here was a disciple, a Prophet, a man who would walk the pathways of Jewish history with Moses and Aaron, with Elijah and Elisha, with Isaiah and Ezekiel and all the other great men whose words were inspired by God Himself.

Suddenly, her son looked up into the heavens, into the setting rays of the sun. Neither he, nor his eyes were anywhere on earth, but he was in the infinity of Yahweh. Slowly, without any understanding of where he was, or even of the presence of his mother as his witness,

Jeshua lifted his arms casting a shadow over the Dead Sea, and in a dark and stentorian voice said, through himself, but to the people of Israel, "A thousand years ago, Yahweh told Father Moses his name and ordered him to take the children of Israel into the land which he swore to them would be theirs forever. He said that His name was **'I am that who I am.'** Then Jezebel threatened Yahweh's Holiness, and Elijah was told by God to cleanse the land of idols. Now Yahweh has told me *'I am that who I am'*. My Father has ordered me to go to the People of Israel and tell them that Yahweh has said this, and that He has sent me to make them repent of their ways. Yahweh has told me to rebuild His Temple in Jerusalem and others in Galilee and throughout the land, to save the people from the evil of the Temple of harlots and money changers, and to preach the word of the Lord. My Father has told me that he will open the people's eyes and they will follow me and the Community I lead."

She looked at her son and in his place, she saw the figure of ancient Moses on the windy peak of Mount Sinai; but this figure transformed itself suddenly and miraculously into the body of Elijah, which, in the sulphurous and sickly fumes of the Dead Sea, slowly began to burn as it rose upwards in a fiery chariot, arms outstretched to be received by Yahweh as it ascended to the heavens. And just before her eyes became dark, she saw the face of the Prophet Isaiah, who chastised Jerusalem for her unfaithfulness and told them how to return to the Face of the Lord.

Suddenly it became pitch black, and Miriam fell to her knees in a faint.

+

Miriam had not walked along this road in many years, not since she and Jeshua had descended from Jerusalem in order for her to find peace. Both she and Jeshua had found peace, contentment and fellowship in the Community, and now she was ascending the steep pathway back to Jerusalem, back into the life she'd once led. It was a life to which, living in the peace and the love of the community, she'd hoped never to return.

She and her son were climbing from the depths of the Dead Sea, back into the land of ordinary people, where rancour, ill-discipline, argument and discord were the currency of the day. Her heart was beating, not with the exertion of the journey, but in fear of what she would encounter. For the past many years...Miriam had almost lost count of how long she'd stayed in the community...her life had been ordered, regulated, restrained and trouble-free.

And now she was returning to uncertainty and danger. Yet she knew that she had to follow her son back up into the troubled world of Israel, the world of Roman Judea and of the corruption by Roman gods in the land of Yahweh. For God had ordered her own son, her own Jeshua, to rid the Holy Temple of Solomon of its prostitution and despoliation by the followers of the evil Herod, the Sadducee Priests, who used the love of the Children of Israel for their Yahweh in order to corrupt and pervert the Temple for the sake of shekels.

She walked with difficulty, but as she watched Jeshua climb the steep track, bounding from one rock to another, she knew that Yahweh was lifting his spirit, lightening his footsteps and carrying him upwards. Tired, hot and barely able to breathe in the oppressive air she knew that she was tarrying, and worried that her son would be disappointed in her.

But Jeshua turned from time to time and saw his poor mother struggling and he returned to help her; but she knew in her heart that despite her son's goodness, even he would find her delays an inconvenience, so anxious was he to scale the track into the Judean wilderness and begin the mission which Yahweh had ordained for him. Once they had fully ascended, it would be two or three days before he would see the buildings of King David's city of Jerusalem.

Jerusalem! The City of Peace; the City of God; the City of Inheritance. The City which was the capital of King Melchizedek, the King of Salem, the King of Justice, the priest king who had given bread and wine to blessed Father Abraham when he returned from his victory over the four kings.

They had left the shores of the Dead Sea in a dreadful hurry, simply packing up their belongings into small packs which they carried on their backs. All they had taken from the community were skins full of fresh water and food for the journey, and bid people goodbye, telling them that they would return one day.

In amazement, despair and sorrow, the Community had turned out to bid them farewell, calling after them for explanations. But Jeshua had merely blessed them, and told them that sooner or later, they would hear of him and his mother, and then they would understand. As they left the compound, Jeshua had turned to one of the Elders, Eliakim, whose name meant 'God rises' and said to him that the mantle of the leader of the Community was placed on his shoulders, and he must love all men and women and children equally, and teach them the Word of God as well as the words of the Teacher of Righteousness.

Miriam hadn't looked back towards the Community even once, remembering what had happened to Lot's wife as they fled from Sodom on the shores of the Dead Sea a thousand years earlier, and now she was so far away that the Community was completely out of sight and they were nearing the top of the pathway which led out of the depression in the skin of the earth and into the Judean Desert, and then further on to the uplands on which Jerusalem had been built. From the very depths of God's realm to the very heights of His domain, just below the level of the sky!

Miriam could fully comprehend the lightness of step which had entered into Jeshua's body. He had come to the Community as a healthy young man and had stayed because there he found peace and tranquility. But because he was such a natural leader of people, he was soon made into an Elder despite his youth, and then when Zimri had suddenly died two years after their arrival, Jeshua had been unanimously elected the Community's leader. He did not want the position; he knew the stresses that had brought an early death to the beloved Zimri, but accolades and pleading by his brethren had forced it upon him, and since he'd been the Leader, the Community had grown and spread and new prayers had been said and books written and scribes commissioned and much more.

But with the authority he had accepted, an awful weight of responsibility had been thrust upon Jeshua's shoulders, and he had aged and grown visibly weary. But that was then. Now, suddenly, having heard the voice of Yahweh, her son had returned to the youthfulness which Miriam had always loved, and as she looked up to where he was climbing in front of her, she was shocked when she saw Jeshua suddenly disappear as though taken up by Yahweh. He had reached the top of the pathway and was now standing out of her sight on the level reaches of the Judean Desert. She smiled at her sudden isolation, pleased to be completely alone in the wilderness. She looked over into the East at the wondrous Mountains of Moab in the far distance, and then upwards to the edge of the escarpment which was the great scar in the Land of Israel from the north to the south, and which led from the Sea of Galilee to the Dead Sea and then beyond to Eilat and the end of the earth. She wasn't afraid of her isolation, because she knew that her son was just a call away. But for a moment, she sat on a rock, and breathed in the fresh air and felt the burning sun on her naked face. She hadn't smelled air like this since she'd descended into the sulphurous fumes of the Dead Sea. It was sweet, fresh, clean air...air which smelled of desert flowers and petals and pollens. Everything at the bottom of the earth where she'd lived smelt of death and decay. Even the figs and palms and dates which grew in abundance barely had a fragrance about them which was able to ward off the stench of the Dead Sea. They even tasted sulphurous and sharp.

And now Miriam realized how much she had missed the purity of the Land of Israel, of the crops and the flowers and the smell of roasted meats which rose from the kitchen fires and the aroma of freshly baked bread which filled the house every morning she had risen from her bed as a child.

To her embarrassment, Miriam found her eyes full of tears. And as she sat on the rock, she felt herself crying; crying for the joys and memories of her youth, for her long forgotten lover, Malachai, the boy whom she had once wanted to marry; crying for dead husband, for the friends and family she hadn't seen in all these years; and crying for the loss of the tranquility and security which the Community had offered her.

What was her life going to be now that she was re-entering the Land of Israel? What dangers would she have to face? Who would oppose them and try to end their mission? Would it be the Priests of the Temple, or the Romans, or the Pharisees or the Zealots or the Temple merchants whose livelihoods Jeshua was intent upon ending? Could it be this new band of evil men who carried a hideous dagger, men who called themselves the Sicarii after the small daggers, or Sicæ, which they concealed under their cloaks, and whose mission it was to assassinate the friends of the Romans.

Many new members had joined her Essene community in recent years because of the evil of the Sicarii. These men would walk with a group of worshippers going to the Temple, or stand beside one of the Priests who was friendly to the Romans, and then pull out the dagger and stab him to death. As the crowd gathered, the murderer would wail and moan and cry out in anguish as though he was a mourner, and by doing so would escape unsuspected into the crowd. But by being murderers of both the Romans, and the Jewish friends of the Romans, they were bringing even more destruction and evil to the land of Israel and its long-suffering peoples.

Danger in the upper lands of Israel could come to them from all of these groups, or none. It could be a new group of fanatics who had suddenly arisen in opposition to the Romans, some group who, because of her separation these many years, she had not yet heard. Or things could go well, and her son would be listened to and beloved by the People of Israel, just as he had been adored by the people of the Community. There was so much she didn't know, so much she needed to know to stop her worrying. And what most terrified her was that even treading the pathway of spreading love and life and Yahweh's understanding of His peoples, could bring death and destruction upon her son's head. The Romans might hate him for bringing a message which their Caesar would not admire, the Priests in the Temple might report him to the Romans as a trouble-maker, the Pharisees might hate him because he opposed their rigid interpretation of the Jewish laws, and the people of Israel might hate him because his message to them was to put their faith in Yahweh, and not to lift up their arms in anger.

"Mother, are you alright?"

Just hearing his voice brought her happier spirits back into her mind. How could things go so wrong when she was following in her son's footsteps. Like a brother, like a father, like a husband, Miriam had total faith and love for Jeshua. She looked up and dried her eyes. She nodded and stood, continuing her ascent. She soon joined him, and as they both stood on the level surface, with the descent behind them and the path through the wilderness in front of them, Jeshua encouraged his mother to bow her head, and give thanks to Yahweh that He had seen fit to bring them this far in safety.

"Blessed are You, Oh Lord our God, who had shown us the path and set our feet on the road to the redemption of Your People, Israel. Blessed are You, Yahweh, who has breathed Your words into my ear and made me the instrument of Your Will."

Miriam said "Amen", and they continued walking. Walking across the dry and desiccating desert in the direction of Jerusalem, the City of God, the City of Inheritance, the City of Peace.

CHAPTER NINE

Caesarea Maritima, on the coast of the Mediterranean Sea 28 CE, the fourteenth year of the reign of the Emperor Tiberius; the second year of the Prefecture of Pontius Pilate

Where once he had known delight, today he knew only despair; where once he had walked by the shores of his domain, today he lay on a couch and pushed pomegranate seeds around a plate to see what patterns he could make.

When he first came to this benighted land, surrounded by his troops, carrying scrolls of appointment and the insignia of office, he had been the center of the world. The Jews had come out of their houses in their thousands, just for the honor of looking at the face of the man who would be their ruler; and as they gazed and looked upon the face of Rome, they realized that this man, this Pontius Pilate, owner of an ancient and noble name, was a lord as was no other.

Things had been so different when he'd first arrived. As soon as he'd made Herod's old Palace his own, he'd ridden on a horse through the spuming surf, walked to the tops of hills to survey his realm and barked orders at shopkeepers and tradesmen who had scurried and run in fear of his majesty. He'd instructed that a role of prisoners not sentenced by the Sanhedrin, the court of the Temple, be brought to him, and almost at random, he'd selected ten serious miscreants to be crucified and ten minor criminals to be set free. He'd ordered the High Priest to be brought to him from Jerusalem to pay him obeisance, he'd met with all of Judea's senior military men, he'd allowed tributes from nearby Princes and rulers and tyrants to be paid to him...all had come to him and genuflected before him. All were humbled before Rome.

And to show everybody, Jew and Roman alike, that he was the most important man in the land, he'd also ordered his own troops to fetch him whatever it was that his heart desired, whether he desired it or not.

But that was when he'd first arrived. In the years since then, what he'd said would happen, failed to happen, little but commands had come from Rome, and his assurances that he had the ear of Caesar turned out to be an overstatement bordering on hyperbole. As those around him who expected much became disillusioned, his orders had been shown to be hollow, his voice rarely heard beyond the Palace gates and whenever he rode through a town or village, not even children came out to look at the dust from his horses' hooves. Where there had been fear, now there was complaisance; where there had been respect, now there was disdain. The more he shouted his orders, the less they were obeyed to the letter. The more he punished, the less he was noticed. People only attended him when he ordered them to, and his Captains found excuses not to attend strategy meetings which he called.

From time to time, he had ridden into a village or a town like the avenging Furies, like Megaera the jealous one, like Tisiphone, the blood avenger and especially like Alecto, who was unceasing in pursuit, but he now knew that his commanders extorted tributes from the town's leaders to warn them in advance of such an attack, and the streets were emptied when he bore down. He'd severely disciplined a couple of infantrymen and sent others to Rome for trial, just to make an example, but it was all useless. So he'd settled down to staying in his palace and enjoying the waters of the Sea, the women who were supplied to him, and the occasional tribute from some noble who was traversing from the East to the West.

And today was no different from any previous day, because he felt just as bored and listless, just as burdened by problems as always, a figure of ridicule to his own men, hated by the Jews and now hating them.

He'd been warned about Judea when he was in Rome to secure the appointment. Those who were close to Tiberius and Sejanus, the head of his Prætorian Guard – but could anybody be said to be close to Tiberius? – told him to purchase another province; somewhere in North Africa perhaps, or in Gaul or Lusitania. Anywhere, they urged, rather than Judea with its wild men and invisible and incomprehensible God and its insane priests and especially its harsh and unforgiving landscape.

And when he listened to people speak of Judea, he ran urgently back to the Imperial Palace to beg another audience with Sejanus. He'd tried; oh, how he'd tried to change the location that his money had purchased. But now that Tiberius was permanently on the isle of Capri and no longer in charge of the affairs of Rome, the petition he'd handed over was already read, agreed to, the money pocketed by Sejanus, and all was set for his Prefecture. The deal was done. The dye was cast. His future was both assured and unsettled at the same time. And all he could do was to try to make the best of it.

He'd tried to see Sejanus to beg him to change his mind, but the Palace doors were closed to him. Now that the decision had been taken it was too late, and so Pilate determined that he and his wife Claudia Procola would spend five years in the province where he'd work hard to make their fortune, and return to Rome to negotiate another position, possibly as Procurator of an entire nation like Hispania Tarraconensis.

When the family had first arrived in Judea, they had born hope in their hearts, but the primitiveness of the buildings in which people lived, the plainness of the food, the lack of civilization, of theatre and gladiators reminded them that they were at the very furthest reaches of the Empire. Look to the West and everything was rich and vibrant, the center of the world; look to the East and there was nothing but baked earth, emptiness, desert, hostility and ignorance. And in Judea, Pilate's unhappy feet straddled the East and the West.

What a mistake it had been to buy this office! But what else could he have done. As a man born into a lowly Equestrian family rank and despite the antiquity and authority of the Pontian family from which he drew his ancestry and his name, none of his predecessors had risen to any great height in Rome or one of its provinces. So he would by rights have spent the rest of his life in minor duties and earning barely enough to purchase a slave or two; maybe he could have purchased some trading rights within the Port of Ostia, or taxation rights on imported wine from some recently conquered nation. Nothing, though, would have made his fortune.

Which was why he'd invested in his future, borrowing to buy the Prefecture of the only province available, the part of the empire which nobody else was willing to purchase. For he'd worked it out that he could use the taxes raised from the people to pay back his debt and within five years have made his name to come to the attention to the Emperor. Then five years later, he could have made enough money to trade that province for a larger one so that within ten or so years of his initial borrowing, he'd be able to return to Rome as an exalted provincial governor; maybe to become a Censor; maybe even a Senator! And one day perhaps even rise to the rank of Consul. But who knew what would happen when Tiberius finally joined his ancestors? Though he wasn't of noble rank, could Sejanus manipulate his path to become Emperor? That could only mean good things for Pilate now that he'd already lined Sejanus' pockets with money?

He pushed the pomegranate seeds into a circle, the plump fruit swimming in its blood red juice. What was he going to do today? He was surrounded by three thousand men at arms, but what joy was there in going on another patrol or more maneuvers? He could ride to Jerusalem and demand to have interviews with the High Priest in the Roman garrison, but the man would use elevated language, and quote from his tribes holy writings to prove him wrong, and that would leave him angry and frustrated.

He could take Claudia Procola to Syria but there was no Legate to see, for he was kept in Rome by Tiberius because he had this crazed idea of centralizing the government. Yet when the Legate visited Syria on one of his inspections, he had shown an intense interest in how Pilate was managing the province, especially how more taxes could be extracted from the Judeans. Even if he was visiting the Legation, the Legate in Syria would only demand to know the purpose of his visit, and then how would he answer? Boredom? Hardly the thing to say to one's superiors, even if they were only there for a month a year.

So Pilate simply pushed the seeds of the pomegranate around his plate, and pondered his life.

She watched him with a mixture of contempt and bemusement as he fiddled with the fruit on his plate. Were she watching anybody else, she would have assumed that a Prefect, or any governor, pushing pomegranate seeds around in such studied concentration would have been working out some tactical attack strategy for some future thrilling maneuver of his army, a way of causing despair in the enemy's ranks when the disposition of the battlefield suddenly changed and the opposing forces realized that it was about to be crushed under the heel of Rome.

But she knew her husband too well, well enough to convince her that his mind wasn't fixed on battles and glory and the defeat of enemies which might bring him esteem in Rome; no, his mind was fully engaged in the creatively exhausting maneuvers of making patterns on his plate by pushing around the seeds of a pomegranate.

As Prefect, he had so much to do, yet during the past year, his mind had wandered into the fields of trivial activity; doing things for the sake of doing things so that if people saw him, they'd think that he was busy doing important things. He would furiously push scrolls around, pretend to digest their contents, order people to do unnecessary things just to get them out of his presence; but in reality, he'd spend all day deciding what to wear to the evening's banquet in honor of some provincial nonentity.

Yet when it came to really important things, those details of his administration which could become a matter of life and death, issues which could line their pockets so that they could return to Rome and civilization, he didn't have the attention to govern the lands which had been entrusted into his control by Sejanus, the second most powerful man in the world. She had managed to prevent damaging secret reports about him from being sent to the Senate, but how long she'd be able to do so, she simply didn't know. The forces were militating around him. And the dark and conspiratorial whispers were no longer confined to hidden corners or night time corridors; instead people were openly contemptuous of him, of his vacillation, his lack of organization, his cruelty, and his despotic commands which were usually reversed the following day, or were nullified when some underling referred the Prefect's instructions to a Centurion for verification.

Nothing was being done by Pilate to bring order to the chaos which was Judea. Claudia Procola had begun her husband's Prefecture by advising him on what she would do, were she Prefect. He'd contemptuously told her that Roman Matrons did not now, nor would they ever, govern the Empire and that she should concentrate her mind and effort into ensuring that the banquets he ordered were provisioned with good food, wine and guests; that she should look the part of a beautiful Roman matron from the moment she rose in the morning to the time she went to bed at night, so that the provincial women, who dressed in crude cloths and colorless unfashionable gowns, should know what a real woman looked like.

But within months of his arrival, the daily briefings he should have received from his field commanders were being given by men of lower rank, the Priests of the Temple in Jerusalem rarely came to pay him respect, and not a word had been heard from his commander, the Syrian Legate. It was as though the chain of command which joined Rome to her provinces had suddenly broken to the south of Damascus, and Judea no longer existed in the sight of Sejanus and Tiberius. And that, more than anything, was a real concern. Underlings could be sent back to Rome in chains; insubordinate Jews could be crucified; but when the Syrian Legate became irritated by how one of the provinces under his command was being run, well, that was a potential death sentence. Return to Rome in disgrace wasn't an option. He would never be able to repay the debt, and he'd never be able to buy another post. So cutting his wrists was his only honorable path forward unless he made a success of his Judean exile.

Unconcerned about her husband's thoughts of suicide, divorce, thought Claudia Procola, was the only option left to her. For the past two years, since they'd come to this hideous place beyond the sight of Rome and its gods, she had shouted at him, threatened him, ridiculed him in public, begged and entreated him in the privacy of their bed chamber. She'd even stooped to servicing his body as though she were an 18-year old in the hope that sex might awaken his interest in his career. But it was all to no avail. Nothing she could do to or for him would shift the lethargy which had conquered him since he'd farewelled the Legate, crossed the lands from Syria into Judea and come face to face with his reality.

When she'd married him ten years earlier, against the wishes of her parents, she told them that she could see great things in him. But like a guttering candle, the winds of challenge, of politics, and of his crushing inability to be a true Roman nobleman had blown out the flame, and now he was nothing more than a shell, an empty husk who barked orders, drank too much, fussed over trivia and drained her of the will to continue.

Quite why he'd taken such a dislike to Judea, Claudia Procola couldn't understand. Yes, it was nothing like Rome or the Roman countryside; it was a desert land of harsh rocks and an even harsher sun. But some of the people were intelligent and even diverting. It was a shame that old man Hillel had died the previous year. She'd heard his name mentioned everywhere she went, and so she commanded him to come to an audience in Jerusalem when she first went there. She was interested in his quarrel with the other Priest. The old man had been the very opposite of the arrogant priests she'd met in the Temple of Jerusalem. He'd been kindly and generous and understanding, with a wicked twinkle in his eye. And he took great and malicious delight in telling her about the man he most disliked and quarreled with all the while, somebody called Shammai. When Hillel had presented himself, she'd expected him to fall down and kiss her feet; after all, she was the most important woman in Judea. Yet he'd treated her like an old friend and set about advising her about his religion.

She'd discussed with him Rome's conquering of his land, and he'd seemed quite bemused by her words. He said something which she'd remembered ever since, and it still struck her as an extraordinary insight into how she should treat with the world. She told him that eventually he and the other Jews would have to give up their fight against Rome and bow to the Roman will. Then, she said, Rome would be Judea's greatest ally and all would be well. But he'd looked at her for a long and embarrassing moment, before he said: "Lady, to understand the Jews, you must first know the very foundation of us as people, and of our relationship with our Lord God. If I am not for myself, who is for me? And when I am only for myself, what am I? And if not now, when."

She tried to understand what he'd said, but the philosophy eluded her. Her face showed her confusion, and she asked him to explain what he meant. He'd smiled, and told her that only when she understood his meaning, in her heart and not by instruction, would she understand the Jewish people.

She'd wanted to see him again to continue their discussion, but he'd died the previous year. Maybe she'd talk with his arch enemy, Shammai.

Suddenly her husband pushed the plate away. It clattered to the floor, and he stood from his couch, as though fixed on doing something. He turned and walked towards the doorway in which she stood. When he noticed her, he said, "Claudia Procola, you're up early."

"Early? It's half way through the morning. So what is my husband, the revered Prefect of Judea, intent on doing this morning? Or is punishing pomegranate seeds enough to occupy you?"

Furious, he snapped, "Have a care Lady, and remember to whom you speak."

He pushed past her and disappeared into the vast palace built by King Herod the Great in honor of the Emperor Augustus. She saw that the guards were looking at her and noted the contempt in which they held her. Her! A Roman matron, judged to be contemptible because she was the wife of a man who was being ridiculed openly by his men, and disrespected by the population he was supposed to govern. Suddenly furious, she wheeled round and determined to confront her husband.

She soon caught up with him. He was already outside the Palace precincts, walking quickly beyond the Hippodrome towards the enormous harbor.

"Husband," she called, the morning breeze carrying her words. In surprise, Pontius Pilate turned around and looked towards her.

"You follow me? Why?" he asked.

"I asked what you will be doing today. Other Prefects and Procurators of other Roman provinces work from morning until late at night in the service of the Emperor. Yet judging by your efforts, Judea seems to be the only province in the empire of Rome which doesn't require such government. Why not sell your commission from Sejanus to somebody who knows how to profit, retire to some farm in Gaul and spend the rest of your life raising geese?"

At the mention of Sejanus' name, Pilate spat, "Silence fool! Do you want the walls to come crashing down upon our heads?"

Claudia Procola shrugged. "Well, at least that would provide some amusement in this place. It's as exciting here as a Greek necropolis."

"What do you expect of me, Claudia? I'm doing the best I can."

"And your best is any other governor's worst. Govern, for the sake of the gods," she hissed. "Do something. Don't just lie around. Rule the country. Make a fortune like you promised."

"But there's nothing here to make a man's fortune. It's a land full of hatred and rivalries. The Jews pay their taxes only when there's a sword at their necks; if I try to introduce any Roman banners or statues into their towns and cities, I'm faced with a revolt; the Priests hate everybody and everybody hates the priests. It's terrible. If only I'd chosen somewhere like Cyprus or Thracia, where I could control the inhabitants and make a fortune from fishing or olives or wine. But these damnable Jews won't...don't...they just....oh, it's useless."

"Fool!" she shouted. The soldiers who manned the distant walls looked around sharply at the sudden commotion. "Fool! If only you'd listen to me, you and I could make our fortune from this very place. It's ripe for plucking, like a red apple. The Jews are always fighting among each other. So control them with the troops you've got. Teach them the hard lesson that Rome is their master and if they don't pay taxes we'll squeeze them until their blood runs in the streets and they beg you to let them fill your coffers. Their priests refuse to allow a statue of the God Augustus into their temple? So crucify a few priests and you'd be amazed at how easily the statue will be accommodated."

He looked at her in amazement. "And just what do you think I've been doing during the past two years of my Prefecture? Do you think I didn't do all of these things when I first rode into Judea at the head of a legion of my men? Are you so stupid? Everything I and my commanders have tried has worked for a week or two or three, and then the Jews disappear into the hills, or the Zealots kill a dozen or so of my men, or the Priests fawn and ingratiate themselves and find all sorts of ways of undermining my authority. Judea isn't a land, but a bog, and every time I try to control it, I sink lower and lower. I'm drowning in a swamp and neither I nor my commanders know how to extricate ourselves."

She sneered at him, openly contemptuous. "Then drain the swamp, you fool. Petition the Legate in Syria for more men and tread these barbarians into the ground. Stamp your authority on them.

Break a few necks, make children into orphans and then send them as slaves to Rome; sack their treasuries and destroy their temples. Just do something! Was this how Julius Caesar spoke when he faced the wild men of Germania, or was this what Augustus Caesar said when he faced the wrath of Marcus Antonius? Was this how any of the other heroes of Rome acted when they faced opposition?

"Of course it wasn't. They would never have pushed pomegranate seeds around a plate. They'd have gathered a force of men around them, and brought hell and horror to those who opposed them. They'd have torn down the Temple buildings and thrown the priest's bodies into the street to be the carrion for vultures. They'd have crucified a thousand men, women and children along the road from the sea to Jerusalem.

"How do you think Rome got to be the ruler of the world? Not with men like you who cry and whimper that it's all too difficult. No, real men face their enemies, use overwhelming force and crush opposition so that it dares never show Rome its face again. If you were any kind of a man, Pontius Pilate, you'd be leading 3000 troops into Jerusalem and show them who is in command of Judea."

She turned and walked back into the Palace once occupied by King Herod, the King of the Jews, leaving her husband to sigh and contemplate how he could divorce his wife without affecting his political future when he returned to Rome.

CHAPTER TEN

Jerusalem, in the Roman province of Judea 28 CE, the fourteenth year of the reign of the Emperor Tiberius

Joseph bar Kayafa, High Priest of Jerusalem, flicked away a fat and lazy fly which had just landed imperiously on some of the scrolls on his desk. The insect, black and bloated from feasting on rotting summer meats left in the refuse heap on the outskirts of the city, rose to the ceiling the moment the priest's hands approached, buzzed around the smoky oil lamp, and then settled upside down on one of the wooden beams. Joseph had lost count of the number of times his thoughts had been interrupted by the annoyance of flies and midges and other irritating insects while he was trying to deal with all of his increasingly urgent business.

It was a fiercely hot day, and although the drawn shades kept the blistering rays of the sun from entering his room, nothing could restrain the enervating heat from draining all the energy he had left. Beneath his robes of office, his golden turban and his prayer shawl, his body was prickling in the airless cauldron in which he sat and tried to work. But he had papers to write, orders to give, arrangements to make and nothing must distract him. More than ever, the future of God's people was in his hands, and his alone.

These were troubled times. Since the city was conquered and taken from the Jebusites by King David a thousand years earlier, Jerusalem had always been fraught, but during the past few weeks, it was as though the very fabric of the city was like the skin of a drum. For reasons known only to the Almighty One, Blessed be He, some manic musician was pulling the drumskin tighter and tighter to see what would happen when it fractured. He and his fellow priests were used to the normal tides of emotion which flowed through the streets of Solomon's city and knew how to deal with them. They were accustomed to the constant rows between their Sadducee brethren and the Pharisees, between the Zealots and those who wanted to live in peace with the Romans, between those who wanted to worship the gods of other peoples and those who demanded that the Temple remain true to Yahweh.

His situation as High Priest was to ensure that Yahweh remained for all time the God of the Jews, that He was worshipped in the Temple, and that the Romans were accommodated as best as possible so that they didn't interfere too much. He'd heard of the end result of other revolts in distant parts of the empire of Rome, and the way in which the Legions had crushed the people into servitude and submission. When a region of the Empire revolted, thousands were killed and thousands more sent into slavery in distant parts of the Roman world. So his was a fine balancing act, but if he plied the road between the imperial Romans and the intemperate Jews, acting as the water which doused both fires, then perhaps, just perhaps, he could lower the temperature and peace could be maintained.

But the heat in his office was already so great that he might have to evacuate and find some shaded area of the Temple to set up his desk and do his work where there was a breath of wind. It wasn't even the height of summer, and already the thick air burnt the skin whenever he stepped outside.

Joseph picked up another scroll to see what his spies in Caesarea had to report. For the past two years, ever since the new Prefect's first flurry of imperialistic hubris of wandering the length and breadth of the land, ordering this and that, Pilate had seemed to have become a self-confined denizen of his Palace, letting his Centurions and Legionaries trample the Israelites under their heels, rarely showing his face. Indeed, the only good thing about Roman rule was that even though the conquerors were hated by the Jews, Pilate seldom interfered with the way in which the worship of Yahweh was undertaken. Only once had he insisted upon carrying a statue of Tiberius through the gates of Jerusalem, and the outcry had been so great, he'd relented and left the statue outside the walls.

But now, according to bar Kayafa's spy, things in Caesarea were beginning to bubble, and Pilate had been making noises about riding to Jerusalem and making his presence felt. Joseph shook his head in bemusement as he read the spy's report, wondering why there had been the sudden change in attitude.

He picked up another scroll, and saw that it was addressed to him. The writing wasn't Koine or Hebrew, but Latin. Joseph noted with concern that the scribe had written his name as "Joseph son of Caiaphas, High Priest of Judea, son-in-law by marriage of Annas, former High Priest of Judea." He disliked the way in which his proud name was rendered into Greek or Latin. When he was a child growing up in his parent's home, his mother and father had burdened him with nicknames and endearments. As High Priest, he deserved respect as the bearer of a great name, one which should be used by all who met him, be they Greek, Roman, Egyptian or Israelite.

He broke the wax seal and read the three paragraphs of the scroll quickly. Pilate, it seemed, would be visiting Jerusalem in the following week, and ordered Joseph Caiaphas and his most senior priests of the Temple to present themselves to pay tribute to the Prefect, and to explain to him why the men and women of Jerusalem continued to refuse to place a marble bust of the Emperor Tiberius in their homes.

This time it wasn't the heat which made Joseph's skin prickle, but a feeling that the sleeping beast was stirring in his lair, and was about to cause trouble in the land. What had awakened Pilate? Why, after almost two years, had he suddenly decided to confront the people? They paid taxes, supplied the Army with food, gave tribute, housed the Centurions when on maneuvers, and rarely these days rose up in violent confrontation. Only the cursed Zealots, who hid in the hills and rained down rocks and arrows and spears on passing Roman patrols, caused problems for Joseph, and the Romans dealt with these Jews very harshly.

So what had caused Pilate to turn his head from his pleasures and indolence, his life as a rich and fat provincial governor, and look towards Jerusalem? Joseph again picked up his spy's scroll and re-read it, but there was no clue from the man as to the cause of the sudden disruption. But in his heart, Joseph knew of the reason. It was Claudia Procola, Pilate's wife, whose bony and grasping fingers were prodding him into action. Joseph had always recognized her as the source of power in the Prefect's family, an ambitious woman who saw herself as far more important than birth had made her. Like a vixen, her small and intense eyes saw everything, and when she and

Joseph had first met, he had the uncomfortable feeling that Rome's government would be delivered out of the bedroom and not from the throne.

He picked up a cloth, removed his turban and wiped his forehead, his scalp and the back of his neck. He was sweating profusely, and it wasn't just through the heat of the room. But this was just one of today's problems. There were other scrolls which had to be read before his official duties as High Priest began.

Joseph tore the wax seal from another, this one from a spy in Jericho, reporting on the disposition of a Roman raid into the surrounding hills, the crucifixion of three Zealots who had been injured during the fighting and been captured, and the rising anger of people towards the Priesthood in Jerusalem that their prayers for Yahweh's intervention were still not answered.

The spy noted that several travelers and strangers had arrived in Jericho and sought lodgings. He'd tried to find out from whence they had come, but only in the case of a son and his mother had he been successful. Joseph was surprised to read that the son, one Jeshua ben Joseph from Nazareth and his mother Miriam bat Joachim, born of Sephoris, had traveled to Jericho from the community of Essenes on the shores of the Salt Sea. It was odd; members of the heretical Essene community rarely left their homes, and on the occasions they did, only rarely did they admit to being who they were. The rules of secrecy would have prevented this Jeshua from telling others who he was.

Before he stood and left his suffocating room, Joseph bar Kayafa thought for a moment. Then he picked up a stylus and wrote back to the spy. He wanted this man and woman followed and their actions and conversations reported back to him. There was something about... or maybe it was the heat.

When the day was done, when the final prayers were said, when the smoke from the sacrifices had wafted away over the rooftops, and when the sun finally had settled into the West, Joseph and his father-in-law Annas, sat sipping goblets of wine and pondering the future. He loved his elderly father-in-law dearly and found great relief in listening to his counsel. Still bitter that he had been deposed all those years ago by the Procurator Valerius Gratus and succeeded by an idiot called Simon ben Camithus who had lasted only a year as High Priest, Annas was pleased that his son-in-law continued to seek his advice.

They had discussed the sudden desire of Pilate to intervene in the affairs of Jerusalem, and now had a path upon which he could tread; then they'd talked about how to quell the anger of the Zealots to prevent disaster, but the problem was still unresolved. And finally, they'd settled down to drink wine and talk about events which weren't as pressing.

"Tell me, Father-in-law Annas, why would a member of the Essenes make his presence known when he left the community and wandered around the Land of Israel?" Joseph asked.

Annas looked at him in amazement. "He wouldn't. The rules of that heretical community prevent them from mixing with the rest of Israel, and if they're forced to leave, they must travel in secret and maintain their mystery at all costs."

Joseph picked up the scroll from his Jericho spy, and handed it to his father-in-law. The old priest read it quickly, frowned when he scanned the last part of the report and re-read it. He rolled up the scroll and handed it back to Joseph. But instead of commenting, he looked up at the ceiling, and closed his eyes. Joseph knew his father-in-law well enough to remain silent.

After an agonizing time, Annas looked over towards Joseph and said softly, "I know this man. Twenty years ago he came to Jerusalem for his ceremony of Initiation. The child was brilliant; extraordinary; and there was something of the mystic in him. He was far too intelligent and knowledgeable for the idiot priest who was in charge of teaching the Initiates. So he was ejected because he dared to ask questions. He and I sat in the courtyard just below here. I'll never forget our conversation. He was astounding. He questioned me about how Yahweh could have allowed money changers and sellers into the Temple precincts. Other priests who were listening wanted me to cuff his ears, but I could see the light of the Lord in his eyes, and I answered him without artifice, without guile. I spoke to him in a simply and in a straightforward manner, not patronizing, but in an order for him to understand fully the meaning of the Temple to the life of Israel. I remember that even though he was only a child, it was like talking to a man.

"I often wondered what had happened to him. So he joined the community of Essenes, did he? It doesn't surprise me. As a boy, he needed to look into his heart before he became a man; before he could look outwards at the rest of Israel. So for twenty years he's prepared for this moment," Annas said, but then withdrew into his thoughts.

"What moment?" asked Joseph.

Annas looked at his brilliant son-in-law and smiled. "I don't know. For some reason, he has determined that this is the time to climb out of the depths and ascend into God's light. Yahweh has ordained a purpose for this man. We must wait to see what that purpose might be."

Now it was Joseph bar Kayafa's turn to remain silent and think deeply about his father-in-law's words. Annas, regardless of his gentleness, goodness and reverence for Yahweh, rarely thought beyond the walls of the Temple. Yet Joseph had been able to remain in his position as High Priest during these ten turbulent years because he viewed Israel as a part of the Roman empire and had done everything in his power to reach an accommodation with the authorities, to try to blend the requirements of his God-given task as High Priest with his obligations to those who now controlled the province of Israel.

Yes, it had gained him many enemies, especially among the Zealots who wanted nothing more than to see the last Roman soldier carried home, dead, on a litter, but that wasn't the way of the world. In their naivety, they thought that defeating the Roman legions in Israel would force the Empire to withdraw. Yet they didn't seem to understand that Rome couldn't tolerate defeat because the moment a defeat of it's army went unpunished with a full measure of retribution against the colony, the Senate would order every available legion to travel to the land and decimate it. It was Rome's way of keeping its other colonies in order. Once it was known in Egypt, in Lusitania, in Germania and in Gaul that Rome could be defeated, then it was the end of the Roman empire. Which is why a province which rose to fight Rome, would be decimated.

And now this Essene, this Jeshua ben Joseph of Nazareth and his mother Miriam bat Joachim of Sephoris, were wandering the land. Why, he wondered? What were they doing? What was their reason for leaving the Essenes on the shores of the Salt Sea and coming to

Jericho? Was it to put the community behind them and become normal Israelites again? Or were the Essenes becoming like the Zealots and planning a move against Rome? And if that was the case, would they also plot against the Sadducees in the Temple, for the destruction of the priestly hierarchy was the Essene's ultimate goal.

"What thoughts are going through your head, son-in-law?" asked Annas. "Why would an Essene openly admit to being who he is?" "It isn't a crime to be an Essene," replied Annas. "Not a crime in Israel," said Joseph, "but by their own rules, they are now unable to return to their community. They've disclosed the secret of who they are. They've cut themselves off. Unless they return to our community and worship in the Temple, they'll have no society, no village, no friends."

Annas thought deeply, stroking his beard. He sipped his wine and nodded slowly. "Then maybe this is the time to seek them out and listen to what they're saying."

CHAPTER ELEVEN

Jericho City, in the desert of the Roman Province of Iudea 28 CE, the fourteenth year of the reign of the Emperor Tiberius

Even though she had spent four weeks in Jericho, eating meats and cheeses she hadn't tasted in years, and being served by the women of the inn instead of her serving herself and her sisters, Miriam still found that she thought and acted like an Essene. When she was asked a question, even one as simple as "How did you sleep last night?" by one of the other guests at the inn, she answered immediately and without thought, "The Oneness, Blessed be He, gave my soul good rest for its return after my death."

She found difficulty in giving a straightforward answer. Could she say that she'd slept well without disclosing some deeply hidden rule and thereby negating her obligations to the Community?

Her son, Jeshua, constantly surprised her by happily discussing his life as an Essene by the shores of the Salt Sea; he would tell people of the Rules of the Community, of their beliefs and the philosophies which drove them forward, and where he now realized that they were going wrong by keeping their greatest gift, a true understanding of Yahweh's requirements of His people, all to themselves. And people listened to the brilliant young man, were seduced by his dark burning brown eyes and his handsome leathery skin, by his gentle smile and willingness to open his heart even to the most trying of questioners.

But the further he delved into the mysteries of the Essene community which he had once sworn solemnly in the name and grace of Yahweh to keep secret, the more Miriam worried about his eternal soul. How could he break so compelling an oath to God Himself as he was now doing, without risking damnation and a lifetime in Gehenna?

Yet when Miriam had confronted him, he'd smiled, and put his arm around her, and said simply, "The oath we swore was made by Man. It was the Teacher of Righteousness who created this rule. God, my father, when I was with Him beside the edge of the Salt Sea, has told me that I am not bound by it. Understand, Mother, that it was made to protect an institution created by Man. But I have spoken with our Lord Yahweh, *I am who I am*, in the desert, and He protects me. He tells me that although righteous, the men and women of the community are wrong to have kept His words only for themselves. Yahweh told me that it is my responsibility to take His words, His thoughts, His instructions, and make them known throughout the length and breadth of Israel. We are being suffocated by too many forces, mother," he had said. "The Romans are stifling us, but we will never be so powerful as to defeat them, and so we must find a way to accommodate their requirements.

"We Jews must keep for ourselves that which Yahweh gave to us, and we must render to Caesar that which Caesar has conquered. The Zealots are stifling us by causing more Legions to flood into Israel to quell their uprising; the Sadducee priests are stifling us by their degradation of the Holy of Holies and their prostitution of Solomon's Temple, Yahweh's home; and the Pharisees are stifling the people of Israel by their insistence on the rule of law instead of the rule of God. And from what the people of Jericho have told me, there are now many men, wearing loincloths and ashes, who call themselves Messiah, the anointed ones, who claim to be a Joshua or Elijah come to save the people of Israel; they wander in the desert and scream at the sun and the moon and the stars.

"But Yahweh has opened my ears and silenced my eyes to this discord, and He has told me to spread the words of the Community Rule far and wide; from Jericho it will spread to Jerusalem, then Yaffo, then Sephoris, and then beyond Israel to Tyre and Sidon and Egypt, to Cappadocia and Athens and Cyprus and even to Rome itself. Soon, the whole world will know about the wonders of the one true God and His plan for mankind."

In earlier days, she would have been frightened of the way in which his eyes seemed to see through her, to see beyond her and stare into the infinity of Yahweh's domain. But she had become so used to her son's ethereal presence, to actually see the light of God within him, that she knew now with total confidence and assurance, that when he spoke, he did, indeed, speak with the mouth and words of the Almighty One, Blessed be He. She had often wondered to herself whether Jeshua was a prophet like those from the old days, Isaiah, Jeremiah, Elijah and the others. But how could her son, even her beloved Jeshua, be a prophet? She had remembered everything about him when he'd suckled her at her breast, cleaned him when he was a baby, nurtured him when he was a little boy, soothed his tears when other children in Nazareth had been rough with him, and watched him grow into a youth and then a man who'd outgrown all the others of her village and astounded the Priests of the Temple in Jerusalem.

And hadn't Isaiah and Jeremiah and Elijah been born of a woman, suckled at the breast and cried as babies, and grown into leaders of Israel, talking one to one with Yahweh? So if these ancient prophets could have heard the voice of God, why not her son? Why not Jeshua?

It was a hot day, hot even for the blistering summer months. Not a cloud in the sky muted the burning rays, and the trees and crops in the fields at the bottom of the hill seemed to shrug in despair of relief. Jeshua and his mother sat in the shade of Jericho's massive stone walls, protected from the fiery sky and listened to the silence, broken only by the hysterical buzzing of insects and the occasional scream of a bird looking for prey deep in the valley.

It surprised her when Jeshua said, "We must leave Jericho tomorrow morning, early, before the sun is too high in the heavens."

"Where are we going, Jeshua?" "Jerusalem." He said it with a finality which surprised her. There was no room for her to question his decision, nor did he say it as though knowing it would come as a surprise to her. It was the destination which had been his goal ever since they'd left the shores of the Salt Sea.

Yet the very name of the city sent shivers through her. As though it was a deadly destiny and he, her own beloved son, was heading towards some sort of confrontation with a demon within himself, from which she could offer no protection. It wasn't the Romans who terrified her, nor the Temple Sadducees, nor the Pharisees nor the Zealots, nor the throngs of people who crowded the marketplaces, nor the fights which regularly broke out leaving people broken and dead in the streets. Nor was it the Sicarii who stabbed people they accused of collaborating with the Romans and left them dying in the streets. No, it was none of these which frightened her for she knew that Jeshua could protect himself from all and any of these. It was her son who terrified her, for who would protect him against himself?

They used up the last of the money they had in their pockets to pay for their accommodation and food in the inn, and prepared themselves to tread the road to Jerusalem, normally a day's walk. But although they'd rested in Jericho for many days, he knew that Miriam was still exhausted from the journey from the Dead Sea up to the heights of Jericho. Exhausted in body, and in spirit, for the further they'd traveled from the community at Qumran, the more worried and nervous she'd become. So on the journey, Jeshua would force Miriam to rest at an inn or by the roadside overnight, so that she didn't exhaust herself for their arrival in Jerusalem.

Warily, she asked him, "Son, we have no money left. How will we buy food or pay for accommodation?"

He smiled, and told her that he was a carpenter, and that he would be paid for work he would do along the way. When she pointed out that he had no tools, he held up his hands, and said gently, "These are the only tools I need; those provided by God my father. Other tools, like nails and an adze I will borrow."

"Then why do we have to leave this wondrous city? From here, I can gaze east and see the final resting place of our father Moses on Mount Nebo. There are wonderful palaces here in Jericho with great buildings and rich men where there is always work to be done; there are many people in this city to whom you can preach the word of our Community. Why do we have to go to Jerusalem, with its Sadducees and Pharisees and the danger of the Sicarii? Why can't we just remain here?" she asked softly.

He smiled, and said, "King David of blessed memory, anointed by God, chose Jerusalem as the most holy site for the Temple to honor our Lord. Because of his failures as a man, the Almighty refused to allow David, my ancestor, to build his Temple, but demanded this act of David's son Solomon. The purity of the Temple which the wise and blessed Solomon built is renown throughout the generations. When King Herod rebuilt the Temple, he made it into a whore's bedchamber. Yes, it's grand and glorious with its marbles and mosaics of birds and animals; but what is the difference between Herod's Temple and some Roman Palace or Egyptian brothel? Only the Holy of Holies where the Ark of the Covenant once stood is sacred. But where Israelites should stand in awe of the Almighty and worship, there are priest's rooms and offices, shops selling trinkets, money changers, and places to buy animals for sacrifice.

"Is this a place which Yahweh had in mind when he gave the holy tablets of stone to Moses on Mount Sinai? Did God want money to be exchanged or animals to be sold or food to be eaten on His holy ground, in His house? This place must be cleansed if Yahweh our father is to reside in the bosom of His children Israel."

His mother looked at him in horror. "And is this the reason we left our community, our friends, our brothers and sisters, to climb out of the grasp of the Salt Sea into the heat and dust of Jerusalem? To cleanse the Temple?"

Jeshua nodded. "For I cannot truly worship Yahweh knowing that His holy Temple is the site of commerce and trade, of the prostitution of the Priests and the angry disputation of the Pharisees."

Miriam suddenly smiled and put her hand to her son's cheek. It surprised him. He shook his head. "I don't understand," he told her.

"When you were a boy becoming a man, when your father, God rest his soul, and I took you to Jerusalem when you were 13 for your initiation, I waited for you to emerge. You were later than all of the other boys. I was frightened that you'd been detained, and so I went into the Temple. Some of the Sadducee priests shouted at me, and told me that women weren't allowed where I was walking. But I ignored them and told the guards that I was looking for you.

"I eventually found you sitting beside Solomon's Fountain. You were with the High Priest. He had his arm around you, and he brought you over to me. I asked you if you were alright, and you said nothing. Then I asked you why you were delayed, and you said to me *"Did you not know that I would be safe in my Father's house?"*

"I didn't understand when you said that you were in your Father's house, and asked you why you had to be in the Temple. You didn't answer, but the chief priest seemed to understand, and he said to me, *"Take the lad back to your home, mother of Israel. But be prepared to lose him to us forever. For your son is like me when I was his age. When I was a child, I spoke as a child. I understood as a child. I thought as a child. But your son, Miriam of Sephoris, is an Initiate and so now a man of Israel, and when I became a man, I put away childish things. I see my life in a mirror, darkly, and I am face to face with my present and my past. Now I know who I am, just as Jeshua will know who he will be in time. And I predict that he will be a great man, and lead Israel into the paths of righteousness."*

"I have never forgotten those words, Jeshua. They're inscribed on my memory. For years, I watched you grow and was proud of you; but also mystified. For you weren't like the other boys and girls of Nazareth. You were alone, yet you were never lonely. I would watch you sitting at our table, or walking in the fields, and you would be staring into the distance, as though you saw things which were invisible to us and to others.

"Yet I was never worried about you, for I knew that you were always in the company of Yahweh, and that he would guide you through your life. But now, now for the first time, I truly believe that I understand what the old priest meant when he spoke to me all those years ago. You are going to fulfill the destiny which Yahweh has written for you in the Book of Souls. I don't know what that destiny is, or how it will affect you, but I will always be by your side. And may He protect you and keep you safe."

Tears welled up in her eyes, and Jeshua reached out to Miriam, drew her into him and hugged her.

Jerusalem, Capital of Israel The Roman Province of Iudea
28 CE, the fourteenth year of the reign of the Emperor Tiberius

Little had changed since she was last here when her son Jeshua was presented to the Temple for his initiation. It was many years ago, but the sights and smells and noises were fresh in her memory. The streets were still as crowded with men and women, carts and stalls, dust and noise. Perhaps now there were more Roman soldiers in their metal breastplates, their helmets and tunics, their swords and spears. Perhaps there was more fear on people's faces, for when she looked into their eyes, they averted their glances and pretended they were unaware of her presence. Indeed, the closer she and Jeshua walked into the center of Jerusalem, the more she realized that there was no lightness in this place, no humor or ease of being. It was as if, instead of the brilliant deep blue sky of the middle of the day, a black cloud had descended from the heavens and obliterated God's grace.

Only the Roman soldiers looked directly at Miriam and Jeshua, but their suspicious looks made her wonder if they thought that she was about to commit a crime. Unlike in her community of Essenes on the shores of the Dead Sea, nobody in Jerusalem smiled at her as she passed, nor gave her a friendly nod, nor wished her God's blessings on such a beautiful day.

They passed through the Water Gate along Jericho Road, close to the Pool of Siloam, and were soon surrounded by so many people, that there were times her son was lost to her in the crowd. Though tall – taller than most Israelites – she couldn't see him as throngs of people, traders and artisans, citizens and worshippers, priests and guards, Romans and travelers surged around her, separating her from Jeshua. But as she was carried along the roadway, there were moments when the crowd parted and she caught sight of her son's head, his once-black hair, now bleached brown by the sun, clearly visible. He stood tall and straight, unlike many of the Jerusalemites, who were bent from lifetimes of carrying heavy loads on their backs.

She saw him walk off the Jericho Road into a small laneway whose sign in Hebrew read 'Street of the Blessed Nehemiah." Though she had to push her way across the throng, apologizing to people as she traversed the road, she eventually stood by Jeshua, and asked, "Why have you stopped?"

Smiling, he pointed to the sign, and told her, "This is the very spot on which the prince, Nehemiah, and the scribe Ezra, told the people of Jerusalem of the word of the Lord. Nehemiah's name means Yahweh will comfort you, and this is a sign that God's mission has been entrusted to me."

Miriam looked at the sign, and Jeshua could see by her face that she didn't understand. So he told her, "Fifty years after Nebuchadnezzar had destroyed Jerusalem and taken the Israelites into captivity in Babylon, Nehemiah asked the Persian king if he could return and rebuild the walls and the Temple of Solomon. When he returned, he stood on this very spot and spoke to those who had come with him.

"It is written in his book, *'And all the people gathered themselves together as one man into the street that was before the Water Gate; and Ezra the Priest brought the law before the congregation. And he read it to them in the street that was before the Water Gate, and the ears of all the people were attentive unto the book of the law.'"*

Again, he looked at his mother, but it was still apparent that she didn't understand. "It is here, on this very place, that I will gather the people of Israel and open their eyes and ears to what is happening in the Temple," he said, pointing to the nearby walls and towers which housed the Holy of Holies. "Just as Nehemiah rebuilt Jerusalem from the ruins and brought the children of Israel back into the home of the Almighty, so Yahweh has commanded me to open the eyes and ears of His people, and rebuild the Temple in His image and bring them back to the path of goodness and purity."

"But the Temple is built," she said. "I don't understand."

"A building is stone and mortar, timber and nails. But the house of the Lord is built of much sturdier things. I am a carpenter and can build a house which will bring comfort to mankind. But to build a Temple which brings comfort to mankind's soul doesn't require wood and nails, stones and precious metals. This is a Temple which I will build in the minds of mankind, one which will warm their hearts and satisfy their souls. Together with the Children of Israel, I will build a House that will be pleasing in the sight of the Lord."

Miriam, still not understanding, looked uncertain and concerned, so her son explained further.

"Mother, before a temple can be built within a man, there must be a proper temple built here, in David's city. That thing," he said, pointing to the walls of Herod's temple, "Is an abomination in the sight of the Lord. A house can only have one master. Yet the Sadducees and the Levites, the officials and guards of the Temple who subjugate the common people...Yahweh's people...have turned a house of prayer into a source of common business. That is not a Temple, but a house of taxation and of commerce. The priests have built a wall between the Lord my father, and His people, and the only breach in that wall is a door controlled by money lenders, tax gatherers and those who arrogantly believe that they are the voice of God. The Temple must be cleansed of that which is befouling the home of the Father. The traders and the money changers must be removed; the Priests must give up their precious vestments and their offices and their obscene ways. The house must be returned to the people."

Unknown to Jeshua and his mother, a short, dark skinned man who had been waiting at the Water Gate for their arrival into the city was standing on the Jericho Road, listening to their conversation. When he'd heard enough, he said to his companion, "Follow them and report back to me where they go, and who they talk to. I'm going to the Temple to report what I've just heard."

He scurried off, and despite the crush of people which caused difficulty traversing the roads which led to the gates of the Temple, the diminutive spy eventually passed the guards and when he was recognized, was swiftly admitted to the rooms of Joseph bar Kayafa, High Priest of Jerusalem.

Joseph towered over the little man, whose face showed the ravages of cankers and the diseases of a dissolute life, and invited him to sit down. The spy, Malachi of Jaffa, wasn't awed by Joseph who towered over him, his height exaggerate by his turban; nor did his grandiose robes or his sumptuous office overwhelmed him. Nothing in heaven or earth affected Malachi other than bags of money.

"Well?" asked Joseph.

"I followed this man Jeshua the Essene from Jericho to Jerusalem. Of course, had I followed him directly, he would have spotted me, and so I and my assistant sometimes went behind them, and sometimes we'd leave the path and quickly enter the desert so that we could skirt round them and go in front. For there's only one road and it was obvious where they were going..."

Impatient, Joseph waved him on, "Yes, yes, get to the point."

"Well, when he and his mother got to Jerusalem and entered the Jericho Road through the Water Gate not two hours after sunrise, he was passing Nehemiah's street. That's interesting, I thought, for why would he stop at such a place, when everybody was moving towards the Temple, or to the market place. So I was very cautious, but despite the danger of being caught by him, I ensured that I got closer and closer. Then, suddenly, he stopped, as though he'd seen an angel. He looked white and shocked and stared up at the sign. And his mother came up close to him, and I saw them smiling and nodding to each other, as though they were plotting something. Though it was dangerous and difficult, for he's big and he has a vicious countenance, and despite the risk of being seen by him, for he would have beaten me into a pulp, I managed to get closer and closer, so close that I could almost smell his breath, but I made certain that he couldn't see me. It was then that I overheard everything he said. And you're not going to like it, because he mentioned you by name. He said, "The first thing I'm going to do is to make Joseph Kayafa, the evil priest, suffer for what he's doing."

"Suffer? He said he was going to make me suffer? But I don't know this man."

"He knows you, though, Joseph. And he hates you with a vengeance. He swore an oath by the memory of the Prophet Nehemiah that he was going to kill you."

Joseph bar Kayafa sat down on his chair in shock and mystification. "Are you certain that's what this man said? That he called me an evil priest, and that he is going to make me suffer? To kill me?"

Malachi of Jaffa nodded. "Word for word. I heard him as if he was as close to me as you are right now. And he said more. He said that he was going to destroy the Temple, stone by stone. He was going to raise a mob and storm the Inner Sanctum."

"When? When is this going to happen?"

Malachi of Jaffa shrugged. "Tomorrow perhaps. Maybe next week. Maybe in a month. He didn't say, and all I can report back, my friend, is what I heard. But with more men watching him day and night, and with others following his evil mother Miriam, for I'm certain now that she's a witch, I can get a much more accurate understanding of what this man is plotting. Of course, I'll need a lot more money than I've been paid so far, if I'm to employ others and protect you from the evil this person is going to visit upon God's house. Three, four times more men, I'd say. I know and trust a number of good people in this city who'll work for me and keep me informed. And in that way, I'll be able to keep you safe."

Joseph looked hard at the spy. He'd used him on many occasions and the man usually produced good results. But he was also wary of him, because he didn't always walk in the path of the Lord. And he was reputed to pay for the favors of different women in different towns in Israel, some of whom had disappeared and were never seen again.

But Malachi usually had good information, though he was expensive. Joseph often heard of murmurs and rumblings of discontent in the population long before it came to the notice of the Roman authorities, and so he was able to warn the Prefect of Judea of potential problems which could cause an uprising, and that in turn would cause a hideous crackdown on the population with deaths and blood in the streets. Though he hated collaborating with the Romans, unlike the Greek invaders in past centuries, they didn't insist on putting their pagan gods into the Temple to be worshipped; and provided the people were peaceable and respectful, they ruled in cooperation with the local authorities.

The only times when the Romans cracked down on the people was when there was an insurrection, an uprising, or even an assault against the Legions; and then the retribution was merciless. Dozens, sometimes hundreds of citizens would be rounded up and crucified in the most hideous way along the roads into and out of Jerusalem. So Joseph did everything he could to keep peace and ease tensions until the Romans allowed Israel to govern itself as a tribute-paying colony of the Empire.

"I will give you more money; but I will want to know exactly what this man Jeshua is plotting, with whom he's meeting, and what his mother is doing. You say she's a witch. Then bring me proof of her witchcraft. King Saul expelled all witches from the Land of Israel, and..."

Malachi interrupted, "But what about the Witch of En-dor?"

The High Priest nodded. "True. If this woman is a witch, then she will be expelled. I will exile her from God's Holy Land. Now, take this letter and go and see the Temple treasurer. He'll give you what you need," Joseph said to him.

Malachi rose, nodded and opened the door to the office. But as he was leaving, Joseph said curtly, "But don't think that I'm just a prey for your avarice, Malachi of Jaffa. In return for this additional payment, I expect results. You say this man is a ruffian, but he is an Essene, who are known to be peaceable. You say his mother is a witch, yet you bring me no reason to believe you. Be true to me and you'll be rewarded. Lie to me, and it will be your name, not this Jeshua of Nazareth, which I will give to the Roman authorities as a troublemaker."

+

Four streets away, in a narrow alley distant from the shadow of the towers and walls of the Temple, Miriam, mother of Jeshua, stood outside of the entrance to the house, and tried to remember whether or not it was the correct one. She hadn't stood here, nor seen this house since she'd last been in Jerusalem when Jeshua came for his initiation. That was 18 years ago.

She and Yosef had stayed in this house for four days, until they'd returned to Nazareth, and since then, they'd had no contact or communication with Elizabeth, Yosef's kinswoman. Was Elizabeth still alive? Was her husband, the Priest Zachariah still alive? Had their children survived them, and were still here? If not, who now lived in this house?

Jeshua was walking around the grounds of the Temple, and they had planned to meet here later in the day. But Miriam now had the task of knocking on the door...and who knew what would happen then.

She crossed the narrow street, kissed the mezuzah on the top of the right-hand door frame, and diffidently, softly, tapped on the door. Holding her breath, she waited. And waited.

There was no noise from inside the house, and still holding her breath, she tapped again, but louder this time. And then she heard movement from within. The door opened, and an old woman stood there, frowning. "Yes?" she said.

Miriam smiled, hoping that this was her late husband's kinswoman, for she did not recognize her. "Are you Elizabeth?" she asked.

"Who are you?" asked the woman. "What do you want in my house?"

"I am Miriam. Wife of Yosef of Nazareth. If you are Elizabeth, you are my kinswoman."

The old woman looked uncertainly, squinted in the bright morning sun which reflected off the white walls of the houses opposite; and then she beamed a smile. "You've grown old, Miriam," she said. "But so have I. Come in. Rest. I will refresh you. You are welcomed and blessed."

She stepped inside the house. It was no different from what it had been all those years before. A table in the main room, on top of which was an oil lamp, some cloth and sewing needles, was surrounded by four chairs; a stool was in one corner of the room; a cloth partly draped over an archway led through to a small courtyard where Miriam could see a lit oven with clay pots inside and on top to prepare for the evening meal; and in another corner was a staircase which led to the roof, where in the summer months, Elizabeth and Zachariah left the stifling heat of the house to sleep.

"Sit, kinswoman, and tell me of your family. How is my kinsman Yosef? Is he still alive?" she asked.

Miriam told her of his death some years ago, that apart from his son James, she had lost contact with his other children, and that she and her own son Jeshua, were in Jerusalem.

Saddened by news of Yosef's death, she said a quick prayer to Yahweh to protect his immortal soul, and then asked, "And why have you come to this city? Times are not good here, sister. The Romans' iron grip is tightening, and there is talk in the streets that Pontius Pilate will be here tomorrow. And that spells trouble."

"Pontius Pilate?" asked Miriam. Elizabeth looked at her strangely. "You don't know?" "My son and I have lived in seclusion for many years. We aren't aware of what's been happening in Israel or beyond. Who is this Pontius Pilate?" "He's the Roman's overlord, the Prefect of Judea. He has the power of life and death over us." "And is he a good man?"

Elizabeth smiled. "He does very little. It is his wife Claudia Procola who holds the power. They say that she directs his actions, and whomsoever she doesn't like dies the following day by crucifixion."

Miriam listened in horror to her stories of what the Romans were doing, and how they were draining the land and its people of wealth and prosperity through the taxes they demanded.

"But why is it that you don't know these things. I remember when you were here all those years ago that you were clever and inquisitive. Has time dulled your mind and blunted the sharpness of your thoughts?"

And so Miriam told Elizabeth of how the death of Yosef had caused her such grief, and why they had left Nazareth to go and live on the shores of the Dead Sea for so long. Elizabeth's face clouded over in suspicion.

"But that's where the heretics live. The Essenes. Surely you didn't... you haven't..."

"My son Jeshua led the community, but he has now left it and we are traveling around Israel to spread the word of the Teacher of Righteousness, and put Israelites back onto the path of the Lord God," she told her kinswoman.

Surprised, Elizabeth said, "But these things are never discussed beyond their walls! The rules of that community are that no member is allowed to preach outside of the group; that their ideas are secret."

"Yes," said Miriam. "Jeshua knows that. But he says that it is only by following their way to God, will Israel be saved."

"From the Romans?"

She shook her head. "No, from themselves. From the priests of the Temple and the money changers and those selling sacrifices. The Children of Israel have wandered from the path of righteousness, like they did when Father Moses went to the top of Mt. Sinai to receive the word of the Lord, and when he returned, they were worshipping a golden calf.

"My son intends to preach the word of the Essenes and bring them back to the path which Yahweh has ordained for them," Miriam told her. "To cleanse the Temple, and..."

Elizabeth interrupted her, shaking her head. "Miriam, my husband, Zachariah, is a priest in the very Temple which your son seeks to destroy. My son, John, lives in the desert and immerses sinners in holy water to cleanse them of their sins and purify them. I am of the Tribe of Levi, the priestly tribe, and a descendant of Aaron, brother of Moses and he who was the first priest of our people. Your own husband,

Yosef was a descendant of David. Yet you, my kinswoman, and your son, seek to destroy us."

Miriam smiled, and shook her head. "No, sister. My son is not the Angel of Death. He is the redeemer of his people. He has come to shine a light on the dark road trodden by our people. He will lead you and Zachariah and all others back onto the path which God has laid down for us. You and Zachariah and the priests of the Temple have taken the wrong road, and your way is full of rocks and stumbling blocks. Yet my beloved Jeshua, my son, has been sent to save you from your own trail of destruction, to lead you back onto the path ordained by our Lord to Moses when he led the Children of Israel out of the bondage of Egypt."

"You make him sound as though he has been anointed with holy oil, another Elijah come to earth in a fiery chariot. But is Jeshua anything more than all of these other messiahs who travel the roads and highways in Israel telling the people that only through them will they achieve salvation in the eyes of the Lord. The Romans have crucified many such self-proclaimed messiahs in the past month, calling them rabble-rousers and trouble-makers. Your son Jeshua will suffer the same fate unless he's very careful," Elizabeth told her. "You mourned the death of your husband, but you will doubly mourn when you watch your son die of agony, his wrists and ankles nailed to a wooden cross."

Miriam blanched white at the thought, but insisted, "No! My son is not like these false messiahs. They are either mad, or telling the people lies that they want to hear in order to grow rich. But my Jeshua preaches the words of the Teacher of Righteousness, the founder of our Community. He said, *"The heavens and the earth will obey His messiah. Take strength in His service, you who seek the Lord. Over the meek will his spirit hover and the faithful will he restore by his power. He will release the captives, make the blind see, and raise up the downtrodden."*

"But this is what these false messiahs preach," insisted Elizabeth. "This is why they cause trouble. For they're seducing good and honest men and women away from the Temples and the synagogues. And when they preach words which say that the Romans will be defeated and expelled from our land, spies in the gathering report these words to the authorities, and then they're arrested and tried and crucified. Crucifixion is a hideous death, Miriam. Is this what you want for Jeshua? Is it, Miriam? I have comforted mothers who the Romans forced to watch their sons suffer the excruciating pain of nails being driven through their hands and feet to secure them to the cross beams; and to see the life slowly ebb away from them. Sometimes it takes days for men to die like this.

"Is this the fate you want for your son, kinswoman? Because if it's not, then I beg you to return to your community at Qumran and live your life outside of the sight of Rome. For these are perilous times, and only by obeying the laws of the land, can we all survive. Israel can't risk more of these rabble rousers, kinswoman. There's talk of the Romans ordering the Legion XII Fulminata to come south from Syria to quell the voices of dissent in Israel. If that happens, then God Almighty help us all, because they're notorious for killing innocents along the way, raping the women and sending entire populations to the godless North as slaves," said Elizabeth.

But Miriam shook her head gently and smiled, "Dearest kinswoman... sister...you worry about the future, but Jeshua is here for the present moment. And once he has preached and led the people back onto the path of the Lord, then no Roman army will be able to defeat us. Just as Yahweh stopped the sun in its path at Gibeon when Joshua was fighting the Amorites, so He will stop the Roman arrows and spears in their flight through the air. The arrows and spears will stop mid-flight and fall harmlessly to the ground, and the Army of the Lord will triumph. The Romans will be expelled; the Temple will be cleansed, and all will be ready for the return of the days of the righteous."

Elizabeth looked at her in silence, and shook her head. She was suddenly suffused in sorrow, not for the present, but for the future.

Jerusalem, Capital of Israel, The Roman Province of Judea
28 CE, The second year of the Prefecture of Pontius Pilate

Now that he was in sight of Jerusalem he began to feel safe again. Pontius Pilate opened the curtains of his litter, which hid him from any onlooker, and gazed up at the city on the hill. At least here he would be surrounded by good, honest Romans. The journey from the coast where he lived in Caesarea Maritima to the mountain city of Jerusalem had taken three days, enabling him to visit some of his men's encampments along the road, and to sit around the camp's fires and eat and drink with them, listen to their stories, find out about what was truly happening in the province where he was Prefect, yet from which he felt distant and removed.

Best of all, of course, was that he was away from his wife, Claudia Procola, and the intrigues and back-stabbing in his household. He loved being with the Army and missed his days when he'd served with distinction in North Africa and Spain. He'd only left the Army because as an Equestrian his place wasn't in the military, but building up his reputation and career as a Roman office bearer. He'd made good money looting while he was in the Army, and when he'd returned to Rome, he knew he'd have to use much of it to buy his way into an Office. Which is what had happened. And not only all of the money he'd made in the army, but he'd had to borrow from money-lenders on the assumption that the office he purchased from Sejanus, Emperor Tiberius' right hand, would return good rewards.

But it hadn't. He spent all of the money he was able to raise in paying back the interest on his loan. Which is why he wasn't able to afford to do the things which would pleasure his wife, or put down sufficient money to purchase his next office; and that meant going back to the money lenders who, because he sometimes had to default on paying that month's interest, would now charge him a higher rate of interest.

But now the journey was over, and Jerusalem was in sight, he realized why he hated this land so much. It wasn't just the lack of funds, nor the interminable heat nor the insects, but the very structure of the land itself. He hated the roads, rutted, dusty and crooked, often traversing valleys making him prey to armed Zealots who might be hiding in the hills, ready to rain down rocks and spears and arrows. Although armed men surrounded him in the front of his litter as well as in the rear, he knew that an attack by these madmen could decimate his protection. There was a Centurion and his Century of 80 men in the front, and another Centurion and his men in the rear, but a couple of hundred Zealots high in the hills above them would make short work of his troops with their advantage of raining down missiles.

And it wasn't just the roads; he also hated the countryside, dry and lifeless, barren and full of scrub; gnarled stunted trees, and fields which were full of rocks and boulders making any crops almost impossible to harvest easily; trees which produced small and bitter fruits, and sheep and cattle which foraged for whatever stalks they could find in the dry and dusty ground; olive trees which produced bitter fruit; streams and dried up river beds instead of the mighty flowing waterways of Italy, like the Tiber, the Po or the Arno.

He hated the silly little villages with their ridiculous houses, most built perilously on the sides of hills. Unplanned, rudely formed with no magnificent forums or amphitheaters, no libraries or Temples or public baths or basilicas or shops or triumphal archways. The only public buildings seemed to be these small, square prayer houses the Jews called Synagogues where the men gathered to pray and the women seemed to be forced into a separate part of the building.

But most of all, he hated the people. Such ignorant peasants, without even a modicum of sophistication or culture. No plays or musical performances, dancing or gladiatorial contests. And only one god. Just one deity they called Yahweh to whom to pray. A god who the priests said looked after everybody and everything.

Yet no wonder the crops failed so often in this benighted place if they didn't pray to the Goddess Ceres; and was it any wonder that the Roman armies had marched so easily into the capital cities because the people didn't sacrifice to Jupiter, mightiest of all the gods who controlled the weather, law, order and strength; or to Mars the god of war and his consort Bellonia, goddess of conquest and its aftermath, peace.

Would these ignorant peasants never learn that unless one sacrificed and prayed to these and the other gods, unless households had niches in their walls with the god's idol to protect them, then they were prey to disasters and the vicissitudes of the gods?

Pontius Pilate's own particular household deities were Juno, consort of Jupiter and Queen of the gods, Minerva the goddess of wisdom, Venus the goddess of love, and Vesta, goddess of the hearth and protector of homes. Every morning and every night, he put food and drink at the feet of these gods' idols; every day he prayed to them for wisdom and good fortune. And just look at how these gods had been instrumental in his rise to fame and power. From such humble Equestrian origins, he had risen to be the third-most powerful man in Rome's most eastern provinces of the empire.

But his favorite god was recently introduced into Rome from Persia. It was their god Mitra, which the Romans called Mithras. He'd first become an initiate when he'd moved into Rome, and was captivated by the god. The worshippers met underground in cellars and enjoyed a ritual meal, united by a secret handshake. Their faith in Mithras taught them that hundreds of years ago, in the early days of Rome, three wise men in Persia heard of the baby Mithras as a savior who was a god, and brought him gifts of gold, myrrh and frankincense. The baby god was born on the day of the Winter solstice, Sol Invictus. He traveled the land as a boy inflaming peoples' minds with the wonder of his words, but through jealousy, he was shunned. He was asked to slay a huge white bull, which he did; the bull's blood fell to earth and became everything which mankind eats. Mithras then assembled twelve followers who carried his words forward, words he taught them at a last supper before he died on the spring equinox. His spirit ascended into heaven, leaving only his body which was buried in a rock cave. Mithras was the favorite god of Roman soldiers and they regularly went below the ground into caves and cellars and feasted in his worship.

Pilate had even brought an idol of the god which he kept in his private apartments. It was one of his few comforts, and something which he did in private away from the sneering eyes of his wife. And he knew that he was ridiculed by her and by his senior captains, just as he'd been ridiculed when he'd accepted this Prefecture.

He wasn't a fool. He knew that other governors sneered at him, as did Senators, for accepting the appointment of Judea from Sejanus, head of the Praetorian Guard, friend and counsellor to the Emperor Tiberius. But Pilate was only a Knight, and the appointment would mean his elevation to a higher position, even if that position was one which few others would take. It had cost him plenty, but he was informed by Sejanus that the rewards would make him a very rich man. And Sejanus told him that two years in the barren East would enable him to purchase the Prefecture of a much larger and more prestigious province, or even a Procuratorship or a Governorship of somewhere; or who knew...he might even, one day, be in charge of a country like Britain or Gaul.

But no matter how often he reminded his wife of Sejanus' words, Claudia Procola continued to ridicule him every single day. Her ridicule was always the same; not keeping sufficient money from taxes he collected in Judea, instead sending most of it to the Emperor's treasury in Rome. But she didn't understand how much Rome demanded, and how difficult it was to extract money from these barbarians. His revenue by taxation was less than half that levied by other Prefects in other Provinces of a similar size and population. His tax gatherers were attacked, robbed and murdered, despite his meting out severe retribution on the civilian population every time it happened. Yet the Zealots didn't mind how many citizens were strangled, decimated or crucified; they kept on robbing him.

Even his predecessor, Valerius Gratus had failed raise taxes from these barbarians. And Gratus hadn't become wealthy from his time in Judea; yet, somehow recently he'd made, or managed to borrow enough money to purchase an appointment to the new Province of Dalmatia, which promised to be a very good reward for his hard work.

Gratus had not been a good Prefect of Judea, and his term had been marred by civil dissent and many crucifixions. Yet perhaps the greatest legacy he'd left to Pilate was to get rid of the anti-Roman, troublemaking and stiff-backed High Priests from the Temple. Finally, Gratus had found, and installed the right man for the job. The previous appointments, one after the other, had immediately reacted against him by contradicting his orders, and so he'd dismissed them and looked around the priestly hierarchy for a man he could trust. Finally, he settled on the installation of a man called Joseph Caiaphas.

This High Priest was a good and trustworthy man in charge of the Jews with whom Pontius Pilate could do business, and on whom he could rely. Caiaphas regularly informed him of problems which were beginning to foment in the villages and towns of Judea; and he would quickly send in a detachment of the Army to arrest the trouble-makers. And to teach them a lesson, he'd imprison them or even sometimes arrange for their crucifixion if they were uttering treason against the Emperor or the State.

He had sent a messenger ahead to inform Caiaphas of his arrival, and ordered him to come to him after sunrise tomorrow in Herod's Palace, where he stayed when he was in Jerusalem. Or should he meet him in the Antonia Fortress, a more austere military building, and one which spoke more of his power as Prefect of Judea than did Herod's Palace with its rich furnishings and gold and silver ornaments scattered around everywhere. He was safer in the Antonia Fortress, with its 600 soldiers, and its colonnades overlooking the Temple and all that went on in that stinking place with its animal sacrifices and hordes of people. Or should he order Caiaphas to remain in the Temple, and Pilate would hold court within the most holy place of the Jews; that would cause great anger and resentment among the Jewish people. There would probably be an uprising, and then Pilate would order his troops to put it down mercilessly. That would show Rome he was a fearless and merciless Prefect and bring him to the attention of the Senate.

But it could also cause him problems, because Tiberius and the Senate didn't like disharmony and discord in their provinces; it often disrupted the collection of taxes, and he could be the subject of criticism for the tensions during his rule. Being Rome's servant, where all the decisions were his, was onerous and dangerous. One wrong decision in such an uncivilized place as Judea could cause a massive uprising; then the Legions in Syria would have to come south to quell it; and he would be hauled before the Senate in Rome to explain himself and his decisions. And wouldn't Claudia Procola just love to see him humiliated before the people and the Senate. She would divorce him and spend the rest of her days telling all of Roman society about how useless he was as a man, and an official of the Empire.

So he decided to be safe and order Caiaphas to attend on him where he normally resided when he came to Jerusalem for the major Jewish holidays; he would see him in the throne room of Herod's Palace after he'd broken the night's fast. Yes, that was the best decision.

The Villa of Tiberius Julius Caesar, the Island of Capri 28 CE

Although he was born Tiberius Claudius Nero, and was happy with this name when he was a soldier, General and leader of the Army, since becoming Emperor all those years ago he was now styled on coins, plinths and tablets as *Tiberius Caesar Divi Augusti filius Augustus*, a title as unwieldy, inconvenient and grandiose as many of the buildings in Rome.

He was happy in his villa on the Isle of Capri. He was 68, a venerable age, and wanted to relax at this stage in his life after a long and successful career. And what better place to retire from the corrupting, malicious and festering miasma which was Rome. Though still Emperor, he needed the quiet and peace of his island. There was the warmth of the sun, which pleased his old bones and his skin; the air perfumed with the profusion of flowers and the scent of blossom trees which grew in his gardens and the surrounding hills, so different from the stench which pervaded Rome with its stinking sewers full of human waste and the pestilential Tiber, full of dead human beings.

He was happy here on Capri, especially as he had so many little boys and girls who the local peasants sent to pleasure him in the hope of their family's advancement; he delighted every day with the new batch of disgraceful drawings and sketches and paintings of prostitutes engaged in unnatural acts with men, women and beasts of burden, brought to him regularly from Rome and created by artists to excite him in his solitude; but most of all, he was happy that he didn't have to deal with the governance of Rome and the Empire, and could leave that safely in the hands of Sejanus. Or so he had once thought when he left Rome for the last time for self-imposed exile on Capri.

For as the sun shone on his face, as he relaxed on his patio lying full length with just a light gown on his body on the cushion-covered *lectus tricliniaris*, he remembered yesterday's scrolls, sent to him by the Amanuensis of the Senate. Rolling onto his left side, he picked it up again from the side table, and re-read it.

On its own, what the secretary had written wasn't all that worrying, the daily deliberations, the condemnations, the laws passed, and especially great praise for the way in which his appointed nominee was governing in his stead; but read in combination with secret scrolls he'd received from his spies in the Capitol and in the Imperial Palace, where Sejanus had taken up residence, and it pointed to a very worrying situation.

Tiberius had trusted Sejanus ever since he'd been appointed Emperor in place of his adoptive father Augustus. Together, the new Emperor and the Commander of the Praetorian Guard had ruled the Empire, Tiberius overtly, and Sejanus covertly, whispering advice into his ears. And it had been a good partnership, until the mysterious death of Tiberius' son Drusus. After that, with no clear Julian family successor, Sejanus became indispensable. Tiberius even dubbed him *Socius Laborum*, though describing somebody whose family were mere Equestrians from Etruria as a partner in the labors of the Emperor, caused many Senators to become apoplectic.

Yet his elevation had not proceeded as Tiberius had hoped. With the loyalty of 9000 Praetorian Guards at his disposal, Sejanus soon became an official of the Palace to be feared, rather than consulted. Of course, Tiberius knew and understood the reaction Senators and noblemen had towards his second-in-command, but with his sons dead, and with his mother Livia ensuring that Sejanus never overstepped his powers, the Empire was ruled successfully.

But after Drusus' death, and despite his mother's urgings, Tiberius didn't want to anoint a successor, and followed Sejanus' advice to take a long break from Rome, and go and spend a lot of time in his villa in Campania; but he soon tired of this, and wanted to be away from the mainland altogether; so Sejanus persuaded him to go to a delightful villa on the Island of Capri, where he'd been in residence for the past year and a half. It was an excellent choice. It was close enough to Naples so that young prostitutes could be brought over for orgies, but far enough from Rome so that his sexual desires could be kept discrete, especially from his mother Livia.

And since he'd been so far distant from Rome, during the past two years, he'd led a much more relaxed and pleasant life. But things were now starting to change. He'd had a number of reports from his palace spies that Sejanus was beginning to act like a tyrant. And stealing from him. The agreement they had come to when Sejanus persuaded him to leave Rome, was that when he sold a Governorship or a Prefecture, he would share the proceeds with Tiberius. But word had reached him from his spies that two recent Prefects had been appointed, and no money had been forthcoming from Sejanus.

And it wasn't only the money. According to other of his spies, Livia, who was ensuring that Sejanus' powers were held in check, was old and increasingly weak. She was reported as being seen walking along corridors in the middle of the day but as if asleep, talking to people who weren't there, arguing with specters, threatening shades, pleading with her husband, long dead.

And she was taking more often to her bed for long periods; not that Tiberius minded if the murderous poisonous old harridan died and nobody was willing to pay Charon to ferry her across the River Styx to her eternal rest. For all Tiberius cared, his mother could rot in the ground, unloved and unmourned for all eternity. He even delighted in the thought that she'd be incarcerated in the ground, but because nobody would put coins in her dead eyes to pay the ferryman, all she could do was to sit in her earthen tomb and look across the river, see her family play and frolic in the fields of Elysium, and scream in eternal torment that but for a few coins, she was prevented from joining them.

But the old devil was still alive, and Livia's growing incapacity was a problem, because it meant that her descent into senility allowed Sejanus and his confidantes actively to plot and scheme to take control of Rome when Livia died. Tiberius' spies had copied a list of Senators' names Sejanus had drawn up, men who would immediately be arrested for treason and put on trial when he attempted his coup.

And there were many Equestrians of the city who were loyal to the House of Julian who were also to be arrested and tried. Of course, they'd be offered the right of death by suicide, instead of a trial and public execution; but knowing Sejanus, many of the suicides would be assisted...somebody holding the man down while another poured poison down his throat.

The situation was becoming serious. Perhaps Tiberius should return to Rome with an armed guard; but that could mean open warfare on the streets between a legion of men loyal to Tiberius, and the 9000 men of the Praetorian guard who would be loyal to Sejanus.

Not that he was concerned about open warfare; Tiberius was, after all, one of the greatest military commanders in the annals of Rome. Should he want to, he could rally an army, say one stationed in Gaul, order its return, put on his armor, and lead his men into the middle of Rome. Any Praetorian Guard who didn't immediately step across the line to side with his Emperor would be executed.

But nothing in his life was simple, for blood on the streets would cause mayhem and civil disquiet among the populace, which could cause the Senate to do something drastic. He didn't know what, but now that he'd erred by putting Sejanus in charge of Rome and the Empire, even he, even Tiberius, Emperor and God, could be victim of strangulation or poisoning...or his throat might be cut one night...or...

The first thing he had to do was to arrange for his nephew, Gaius Julius Caesar Germanicus, whom his troops called Little Boots, to go and stay under the protection of his grandmother Antonia. Though only 16, it was imperative to protect the boy, because if Sejanus was planning a purge to gain power, then little Caligula would be one of the first to be murdered.

What a disaster, and all because of Sejanus' desire to be married into the Julian family, which Tiberius had refused. Was there no end to the man's quest for power? In the beginning of Tiberius' reign, they had been like brothers; the Emperor had relied on Sejanus' skill and craft and knowledge of people, as well as his extensive network of spies, to tell him who he should support, and which potential enemy he should reward with a job in the distant part of the Empire. But latterly, when Sejanus kept telling him that he needed rest and to be away from the rat's nest of the Senate and the capital, suddenly, Sejanus thought that he was Emperor.

Perhaps Tiberius should return to Rome? Or should he do nothing, tell Sejanus he could do what he wanted, provided Tiberius was allowed to live out the rest of his life in Capri and let Rome plummet into the miasma which was of her own making?

Tiberius closed his eyes and smiled at the thought of the chaos which would ensue; of the Senators and Consuls, the Equestrians and merchants and their disgusting wives and sniveling children who he could see in his mind running, screaming through the streets of Rome pursued by drunken and crazed guards, bloody swords in hand, chasing them and stabbing them; the streets running in blood, the pristine white marble of the temples splattered with the gore of the dead and dying.

A distant sound caused him to open his eyes. Pleasant as the image was, Tiberius was the son of the heir to Julius, the Emperor Augustus and the Empress Livia. And if he sorted out this problem with Sejanus, then Tiberius' name would go down in the annals as Rome's greatest military commander and a man still beloved by all of the Armies, all over the Empire. Though he would love to wreak revenge and unleash the Shades of Hades on the pampered and incompetent Senate and their lackeys, he would not allow Sejanus to become the next Emperor. Family and blood was more important talent and ambition.

Leave Sejanus in charge, and rule would be given to an unknown provincial family with no history in government. Then what would become of the Empire? So many difficulties. Problems in Britannia, Germania, Gaul and especially in that hideous eastern province of Judea. He'd received word that the Prefect appointed by Sejanus, some nonentity from the Pontian family, was being controlled in everything he did by his shrew of a wife; and that the flow of taxes had dried up like a stream in summer. There were problems with the fanatics in the countryside, and reports had come to him that there were dozens of religious maniacs wandering around the country telling the populace not to pay taxes or to obey the laws of Rome, because some god or other was about to come to earth and he would rule the world.

Well, Tiberius ruled the world, not some minor deity in some far-away corner of the Empire, and the world's ruler would send a command to Sejanus to deal with it immediately, or he'd...he'd...and as he was pondering what he'd do, two little children from the local village, a lovely little boy with black hair and sapphire-colored eyes, and a sweet little girl whose brown hair was lightened to blond by the sun, came wandering over the patio towards him, in the care and protection of their mother. The mother was smiling as she held their nervous hands, nodding and bowing in fear and reverence as the three walked across the patio towards where Tiberius was sitting.

And the mother bowed deeply one last time, released the hands of her children, whispered some message of encouragement into their ears, turned, and walked swiftly away, leaving her children in the Emperor's care.

Jerusalem, Capital of Israel

As the two children walked towards the encouraging face and the open arms of the Emperor Tiberius on the Island of Capri, two people, an older woman and a young, tall and lean man, walked towards the twenty or so tents in the courtyard that lay in front of a large single-story building made of white Jerusalem stone. Though dusk was about to fall, the young man could see that candles had already been lit in the large building, and that many people were already inside. As so many of the buildings of Jerusalem, constructed of the rocks on which Jerusalem was built, as the sun sank into the Western Sea, its last rays made the white stone seem to burn with a pink glowing intensity.

Jeshua stopped walking and waited a moment for his mother Miriam to descend from the road which ran between nearby Bethlehem and Jerusalem, onto the path which led to the caravanserai. It was unusual for such a building, created to service the needs of the many caravans of camel traders who traversed from north to south, east to west across the King's Highway, to have been situated so close to two cities. These resting places, which looked after the animals, and the requirements, both food, rest and personal services of the traders, were normally located far from a city. Caravanserai in cities were located close to one of the gates in the walls; or if cities were more than a few days travel apart, the caravanserai would be placed so that camels, donkeys or mules and their owners would have not have to travel more than fifteen miles, or a day's journey, before finding a place where there was wood for a fire, straw and water for the beasts, and to meet the needs of the men of the caravan. And somewhere safe for the produce they were transporting, protected from marauding gangs of thieves and Bedouin tribesmen. But the Romans had closed the caravanserai in both Bethlehem and Jerusalem because there had been too many disturbances, and so they ordered them to be built outside of the town.

Which was why Jeshua and his mother had left Jerusalem and walked the three miles in the direction of Bethlehem. Elizabeth, their kinswoman, would not give them shelter because she was frightened that when her husband Zachariah, a priest in the Temple, found out that Jeshua had led the Essenes, whom her husband despised as heretics, there would be trouble.

So Miriam told her kinswoman that she and her son would find lodgings in Jerusalem. But it hadn't been possible; all the lodging houses and inns they went to were either full, or unwilling to take strangers who weren't traders. It was the time approaching Passover, and so most of the lodgings were full of worshippers. They were advised to leave the city and try their fortune in a nearby caravanserai. If there were no lodgings, then there would always be a tent in which they could sleep and shelter in.

They walked through the encampment of tents, used by the men of the caravan who couldn't afford to purchase a room for the night, towards the front door of the building. From inside they could hear the noise of men talking in a multitude of different languages. Some people were laughing, some shouting, and there was even a man singing. Jeshua listened carefully and thought he could recognize it as a refrain which sounded as though it came from Africa; possibly even from Egypt. But it had been so long since he'd heard the Egyptian tongue that the words made no sense to him.

He reached for the door's handle, but Miriam restrained him. "Should I go inside? I'm a woman, and there are no women's voices in there. Maybe I should wait here while you see if there is a place for us to sleep," she said.

Jeshua smiled, and kissed her on her forehead. "Mother. You are with me and I am with God. We are in His care and protection. You need have no fear."

He pushed open the door and he and Miriam stood on the threshold. It was a large room with many people inside sitting at tables. Flagons of wine and ale were on the table, as well as bowls of lamb, fruits, figs, olives and bread. And there was the smell of a dish of mutton stew bubbling in a cauldron over a large fire in the back of the room.

As they remained standing inside the door's frame, the room slowly sank into silence; the laughter and shouting disappeared, as all eyes turned towards the strangers who were about to make their entrance. Strangers weren't welcome in any place in Jerusalem or other cities of Israel in these days. A caravanserai was different, of course, because it catered to caravanners who traveled vast distances from East and West and North and South. But every caravan which ended its day's journey in the courtyard had men and boys whose dress spoke eloquently of their trade and their purpose for being there. But these strangers, this young man and this old woman, were dressed like villagers and came with no animals or goods. Just a walking staff and a cloth bag holding their meager possessions.

The owner of the caravanserai looked up from the cooking area and turned to see why his room had suddenly become quiet. He saw the man and woman at the door and knew trouble when he saw it. These strangers weren't with a caravan and didn't have the look of workers.

"What do you want?" he shouted across the room. "Why have you come here?"

Jeshua said, "We seek shelter for the night. And for the rest of the week if you have it. My mother and I have come from Jerusalem, where there is no lodging."

But the owner, Matthew, wasn't moved. "This place is for travelers. Be on your way."

"We are travelers," said Jeshua. "I have come from the shores of the Salt Sea. All we require, my mother and I, is a place to sleep. We ask nothing more."

"There's no room," said Matthew. "Now be off with you. I want no trouble here, nor people who don't belong."

The crowd in the inn were fascinated by the interchange, and waited for the young man to do or say something. Would he offer money? Would he make a demand? Would he threaten to bring the Romans back with him? Or would he just turn and leave?

But Jeshua smiled at the caravanserai's owner, and said softly, "Did not the Prophet Ezekiel say to welcome a man if he does not oppress anyone? Especially a man who gives his bread to the hungry and covers the naked with clothing. I have given food to the hungry and clothed those who had none. If the Prophet Ezekiel were to come to your door, would you turn him away, as you would my mother and me?"

Suddenly Matthew was uncomfortable, all eyes upon him. He said, "No, but you're not the Prophet Ezekiel, and I want no trouble. Who are you?"

"I am who I am. You do not know me, my brother, but one day, you will. We are both children of the Father, yet we are become strangers in a strange land, a land which is our home. As brothers, should we not proffer our hand to help those in need, to lift the downtrodden, feed the hungry and clothe the naked?"

And then a voice from the back of the room shouted, "I have room in my tent, stranger. You and your mother can share my floor. And I have blankets to keep you warm. Give me half of what I've given this thief of a landlord, and we'll all be happy."

Everybody in the room laughed. Knowing that the feeling in the caravanserai was turning against him, Matthew said, "Well, if that idiot is willing to let you lay in his tent, then I suppose you can stay. I pray he won't wake up tomorrow dead, with his throat cut. And if you have money you can buy food and drink. I don't apologize for what I said to you before, because these days with the Romans and the Zealots, a man has to be very cautious. So enter, sit and I'll sell you food. And Nathanael back there has offered you his tent to sleep in. But no matter about his generosity, I'm still going to charge you for the room and breathing my air."

"The air, brother? How much does God the Father charge you for the air you breathe?" Jeshua asked.

The men in the inn burst out laughing. All eyes turned towards Matthew, waiting for his response, but even he smiled. Over the hubbub, he shouted, "Come in. Enter. Sit and I'll give you food and drink."

The entire community cheered, and Jeshua and his mother walked between the narrow aisles in the inn until three men made room for them at their table to sit down. Matthew came with two bowls of mutton stew. Miriam thanked him, and searched among their possessions for their two spoons, watched closely by their neighbors. After saying his prayer thanking the Father for the blessings of food, drink and shelter, Jeshua and Miriam ate greedily; they hadn't had food since the previous night in Jericho, and hadn't eaten more than bread and olives in more than two days. The food was plentiful, tasty and nourishing. When they'd satisfied their hunger, one of the men sitting nearby, who had waited patiently until Jeshua had said a thanksgiving prayer after their food, asked, "From which city to you come? Which is your tribe? Where are you traveling?"

It was Miriam who answered, to the surprise of the man, and those around him. Women did not usually speak when in the company of men, but women who were of the Essene community obeyed no such rules, and were accorded equal status, except in the leadership of prayers when the Community came together.

"We are Israelites of the Tribe of Judah," she said. "I was born in Sephoris and my son Jeshua was born in Bethlehem, but spent his childhood years in Nazareth. We have come to Jerusalem."

"And why are you here?" the man asked.

Jeshua began to speak. And Miriam saw, as she'd seen many times in the Essene community in Qumran that when he spoke, quietly at first, but then with increasing vigor, people stopped what they were doing and listened to every word. There was something, some inner quality about her son, which drew people to him and made them listen to his every utterance. Unlike many priests or other holy men who were overbearing and affected and often shouted and demanded that their audience listen, her son always spoke quietly and with such sincerity that people naturally wanted to listen to him. She'd been told by many people in her community of Qumran that listening to him was like listening to a mother sing to her baby. But Miriam thought that it was as if the Prophet Elijah or the Prophet Ezekiel had returned to this world to walk again among their people and preach the word of God.

"We are come to Jerusalem, friends, because this is the house of my Father, and it is right for a son to live in his father's house," he told them.

"Your father lives in Jerusalem? Then why are you seeking lodgings here?" asked Matthew.

Jeshua smiled. "My father is Yahweh. His house is the Temple."

Many men in the room laughed. "You're the son of Yahweh? Of God?" shouted Matthew.

"I am the son of a man. Yet Yahweh is my father for He is father to all men. I am here to cleanse His house which is being defiled and must be purified," Jeshua told them.

But the moment he said it, the very temperament in the room seemed to change. Miriam immediately became wary, for she was looking at Matthew and suddenly his good humor disappeared, and he looked angry. She'd seen that look on a face before. It was the look on her kinswoman's face, Elizabeth, when she told her that Jeshua and she were Essenes.

"If you're talking about the Romans, stranger, then you will say no more while you are under my roof. Men have been crucified for saying less than you've said. Destroy yourself if that's your desire just like these madmen wandering around the desert saying that they're Elijah returned to earth who have come to save mankind; but remember this, the Romans punish by decimation. By saying the things you've said tonight you've put us all in danger. If there's a spy in this room, then the Romans will descend on us like a plague of locust; they'll take ten good men from here for just one of you, and crucify you all as an example. So hold your tongue and say no more of these things," Matthew told him.

"My son," said Miriam, "isn't talking about the Romans, Sir. He speaks of the Priests and the money-changers, those who sell sacrificial animals and food and drink in the courtyards of the Temple. In the very place where Yahweh should be worshipped, the priests force Israelites to engage in trade and money. It is the wrong thing to do in Yahweh's house. That's all my son means."

"That might be what he means, lady, but he has to be careful in what he says. These are dangerous times, and such talk can bring disaster with it," Matthew said.

Men in the inn nodded in agreement, but Nathanael, who had offered to share his tent with Jeshua and Miriam, said, "The man wasn't speaking against the Romans, Matthew. He was only saying that it's the Priests themselves who are defiling the Temple. How many of us here have said that we're not happy when we go to the Temple to pray, and we can't even walk across the courtyard without some shopkeeper assaulting us and demanding that we buy holy oil or animal sacrifices or blood offerings?"

Many around him nodded in agreement.

"Or we're forced to give donations to the Priesthood? Or spend our hard-earned money to pay for vestments for the Levites?" said another man sitting nearby. Suddenly many of the men in the inn were nodding in agreement, and expressing their anger at what was happening in the Temple.

"Well," shouted Matthew, "I like the Sadducees and the Pharisees because I'm a publican, and they consider publicans, like tax collectors, to be the scum of the earth, and that means that I don't have to pay a tithe to the Temple. More money in my pocket."

Nathanael stood from the opposite side of the inn, and walked around the tables until he was standing close to where Jeshua and his mother were seated.

"You've traveled a distance and you must be tired. I will escort you to my tent. I have to rise early and walk into Jerusalem, so we all need to sleep."

Jeshua took the last of the coins from his pocket and put them into the hands of Matthew, thanking him for his food and hospitality. They all bade goodnight to the other men in the inn and when outside, Miriam felt the sudden biting cold of a Judean night, wrapping her clothes more tightly around her. She was used to blisteringly hot days and freezing cold nights in the Negev Desert where the community of Qumran had built their village, and so she looked forward to the blanket which this man had offered them.

They entered his tent on the opposite side of the courtyard. It was a large structure, enough for the three of them to sleep comfortably. The man's possessions were on the floor near to where he had determined that he would sleep during that night.

They all sat, cross-legged on the floor, and the man said, "I am Bartholomew Nathanael of the tribe of Judah, the same tribe as you.

As my first name tells you, I am the son of Talmai and I come from the town of Cana in Galilee.

Jeshua nodded in acknowledgement. "Tell me, brother, are you acquainted with the history of our tribe?"

"As much as any of us," Nathanael answered.

"Then you would know," said Jeshua, "that in ancient times, another man with the same name as your father was the King of Geshur. And he had a daughter whose name was Maacah. And Maacha became the wife of King David, who was our ancestor. And she became the mother of Absalom. So we are brothers of our Father Yahweh, and we are brothers in blood through the Royal line of the greatest King of the Jews, the man who conquered the Jebusites and took possession of Jerusalem."

Nathanael laughed and turned to Miriam. "Your son, lady, is a great teller of stories who speaks of events which happened a thousand years ago. I am a humble man who owns a single camel, on whose back is my world, yet he tells me that I am of royal blood. I travel from city to city with other camel owners buying merchandise in one and selling in the other, and with the little money I keep, I can afford to pay for my lodgings and food, and continue to travel. If I'm of royal blood, then why am I not living in a palace, instead of this tent?"

Miriam said, "But here you have all that you need. What more can a man want, than to walk in the light of God?"

"Some more money would be welcomed," said Nathanael. "If I'm in Babylon and I buy some spices I can look forward to a profit. But what if, by the time I travel to Gaza, another caravan has just been there selling spices and I can't sell mine to anybody? Then I don't eat. What good is the light of God to me then? My days and nights will be in darkness until I find somebody who'll buy my goods."

Jeshua shook his head, and said softly, "Brother Nathanael, we come into this world with nothing, and we leave with nothing. But if we have food and clothing, that's all we need and we should be content. Many want to be rich, but this leads them into temptation, into a trap and into harmful desires which cause good men and women to descend into a life of ruin and destruction. Money, my brother, is of use when we want to buy goods. Beyond that, it has no value. But the love of money is the cause of all evil. Because so many crave money, they leave the path of faith and pierce their flesh with the arrows of desire. God will provide, even when you believe that you are traveling in the darkness of despair."

Nathanael listened carefully, not just to Jeshua's words, but to the way in which he spoke. It was as if a sudden peace and calm had descended upon his tent.

"And you, Jeshua of Nazareth. What do you do?" he asked. "I am a carpenter." "Then you carry your trade with you. You are fortunate. You don't have to travel from town to town to make money. Is that why you've come to Jerusalem? To build something in the Temple?"

Jeshua thought for a moment before answering. "I am come here to knock down and then to rebuild."

Nathanael looked at him curiously. Miriam looked down at the blanket on which they were sitting, worried about what her son was about to say.

"Understand, Bartholomew Nathanael of Gaza, of the Tribe of Judah, that the Temple in Jerusalem has become corrupted by priests and their acolytes, by sellers of ornaments and witch's spells, by money changers and merchants. It is not a house of God. It is a house of pleasure where whores seek to mislead good men from the path of righteousness and divert women from prayer into prostitution. I will destroy the corruption which pervades my father's house, and within three days I will have rebuilt it in the way which Yahweh wishes."

Nathanael burst out laughing. "Three days? It took Herod fifty years, and he had a thousand slaves to do it."

Jeshua smiled, and said quietly, "Brother. A Temple is nothing more than a building. That which is evil will be destroyed, and within three days will rise again. Breath will be breathed into the fallen stones, and they will be risen up, as if from the grave, and with the hand of God, my Father, a new Temple will be built. And this Temple will be a sanctuary for all mankind."

Jerusalem, Capital of Israel

Pontius Pilate, Prefect of the Roman province of Judea, slowly surveyed those in the room looking right to left and left to right, saying nothing, but staring into the eyes of the men and women who were holding their breath in rapt attention. He'd seen Sejanus do this when addressing the Senate as Tiberius' second in command of the Empire, standing there, surrounded by the most important men in the world. Any other than a Julian or an Augustus would have been terrified, but it was then that Pontius truly understood the importance of silence over bombast. Sejanus waited a long time before addressing the Senators, and when he did, a nervousness had spread through the minds of the many there, and he had their complete attention.

A leader's silence made men worry as they sat there, wondering what he might say or do next, whereas shouting and blustering reduced the authority of those who purported to be in command. And he'd learned the lesson of Sejanus well. Pilate remained silent, while many in the audience squirmed in their seats, wondering if the awesome might of Rome was about to descend on their heads.

He felt a sudden and unexpected stirring in his groin. Unexpected? No, it happened every time he sat on the throne of the dead, diseased and unlamented King Herod in his ostentatious palace in Jerusalem. Unlike in Caesarea where he was dominated by his hideous wife Claudia Procola, here he was the King. This was his domain, and these were his subjects.

This is why he'd spent all that money with Sejanus in order to secure a province to govern! This was the power which his money had bought. The power to travel like a king from town to town in Judea, to have crowds come out to stare in awe at his majesty and the authority which his personal guard afforded him. And this was just the beginning, because once he'd extracted more money from these Jews, he'd have enough to buy a province closer to the heart of Rome. And from there, with his guile and ability to build a fortune, he would eventually return to the center of the world and maybe, just maybe, with the right friends and enough money, he'd become a consul. Because then he'd be untouchable, and he could pay a poisoner to dispatch his wife to the nether world of Hades; or have her stabbed and push her body into the Tiber, to disappear forever under its pestilential surface and eventually be carried out to sea and eaten by fish; and as a Consul, he'd obey the proper days of mourning, and then be free to marry into a family of higher status.

Before him, waiting on his every word, were men and women arrayed in rows of seats within the hall, those who considered themselves the most important in the front ranks, and those of lesser importance placed in serried rows towards the rear or standing on the outskirts of the room. In the very front of the hall sat the senior priests from the local Temple, sweating in their heavy vestments and looking ridiculous on such a hot and airless day. But in their middle, sat the High Priest, Joseph bar Kayafa, who wore a colored turban of blue, and over his body wore a striking blue, scarlet and purple ephod and golden breastplate containing rows of precious stones set in gold. His fingers were covered in gold rings set with precious gems. Joseph bar Kayafa's face was expressionless, unbowed by the majesty which overawed those who sat beside him.

Behind them sat the important men of the citizen's council of Jerusalem, some accompanied by their wives; these were the people who administered the decisions of the Roman authority at a local level. Scattered throughout the hall were his commanders of the local garrison, dressed in their armor and carrying their weaponry. These men weren't bowed by his authority, but sat in boredom, waiting for events to come to an end so that they could return to their rooms and refresh themselves.

And behind these worthies, listening acutely to the meaning of what was said, and left unsaid, were the advisors, clerks and tables of amanuenses, there to record every word uttered in the room, a copy for the Prefect and a copy for the Annals in Rome.

Before he began to speak, he picked up a goblet of wine, and drank a draft. A slave gave him a cloth with which he wiped his lips. Pilate took a deep breath, and came close to smiling when he saw many in the audience lean forward in their seats so that they didn't miss a word. He had never before felt more important, more in command of a situation or of himself.

He began quietly, so that the listeners had to continue to lean forward to hear properly. "Of all the provinces throughout the Empire which Rome governs, of all the peoples whom our Emperors have rescued from their barbarism and brought into the blessed light of civilization, none is as recalcitrant, intractable, headstrong and stubborn as you Jews. Not even the tribes of Gaul or Germania are as unmanageable as you."

Those fluent in Latin whispered a translation into the ears of their superiors; only Joseph bar Kayafa needed no translator, for he was fluent in Hebrew, Koine, Greek and Latin.

"The Zealots who attack my armies from the hills and mountains in the north, the madmen wandering around the deserts claiming to be sent by your god, who you call messiahs, to deliver you from Rome's rule, the surliness of your people who show their hatred towards my soldiers, even when they are building aqueducts and roads and bridges to make your inhospitable land habitable...you people are ungrateful and churlish. I'm inclined to write to my fellow governor in Syria and ask him to lend me his legions so that I can quell you and your rebellious nature and send your fighters, your women and children into the furthest corners of our Empire so that you can become slaves."

The audience looked at him in shock. They'd known that he usually began his audiences by telling everybody what was wrong with Israel, but to seriously threaten to bring down the Syrian legions was something they weren't expecting. This was a catastrophe in the making.

Pilate continued, "The madmen wandering naked in the desert and screaming about the end of times, are your problem, Priests of the Temple of the god you call Yahweh or however you pronounce that name. They're not my problem, although now they've become a problem for us all. There are few of them, but they preach subversion and can affect the simple minds of the populace. Do something about them, priests, or I'll send platoons into the lands beyond the Jordan River, and into the Negev Desert in the south, and they'll deal with them permanently. I won't crucify them. I wouldn't waste good trees on their scrawny bodies. Instead, I'll have their throats slit and then the vultures and the desert lions can feast on their miserable carcasses and in a few days, all that will be left of them and their prophesies will be bones.

"But the Zealots are a problem which is much greater and which will take the might of the Roman Army to quell, unless you control them yourselves. If I have to bring down a Legion of Rome's most experienced military men to comb through every hill, every valley and every cave to seek them out and execute them, then so be it. Do I need to remind you of the mercilessness of Rome when it comes to people revolting against us? Who here does not remember the terrible vengeance we wreaked against Spartacus a century ago, when we crucified six thousand of his misguided follower slaves along the Appian Way? How will your people feel, Judeans, if we crucify thousands of your Zealots along the road from Jerusalem to the sea?

"So now is the time for you, High Priest, and you who lead the citizens of this province, to go into the hills of Galilee and seek out the leaders of the Zealot revolt, and tell them to give in their weapons and we will treat them with justice. For if they don't, then listen to my words, you people of Judea." He took a deep breath so that the Jews in the audience concentrated in exactly what he was going to say, "Without mercy, with the justice for which Rome is renown throughout the world against those who oppose us, these Zealots will be destroyed; their families will be exiles; their homes burnt to the ground; their fields salted; their livestock slaughtered; and whoever is left alive when we have brought peace to this benighted land, will be sent into slavery."

There was absolute silence among the Jews in the audience chamber. The only words of approbation came from the military men in the room, who shouted their approval. Some even shouted out *"Hail Pilate. We who are in the army of Rome, salute you."*

He was surprised and delighted. It had not been since he'd first arrived in this nation that his men had called out in such admiration. In a way, he wished that his egregious wife Claudia Procola was here to see him and listen to the way in which his men acknowledged his standing. But the thought was momentary because there was the beautiful daughter of a Jewish merchant who was waiting for him in his private bedchamber.

Having ended his warnings, still in shock, the local Jews slowly bowed and left the audience chamber of Herod's Palace, leaving only a small contingent of his most senior military men and counsellors in the room. All except for the High Priest, the most important man in Judea not of Roman blood, Joseph bar Kayafa, who stood there, knowing that much of what Pilate had said was to shock Jerusalemites, and now that he was alone in audience, the real matters would be discussed.

"So, High Priest," said Pilate, "things have not been going well for you. Problems circle around your head like the vultures I spoke of before, who will soon be gorging on the bodies of these ridiculous men you call 'the anointed ones.' I'm here because I smell trouble in the air."

"Yes, times are difficult, Prefect, but the difficulties I have aren't caused by all these self-anointed messiahs, but by the Zealots, as well you know. And I don't call these madmen 'anointed ones,' Pilate. This is a title they've put into their own heads. The true messiah will make himself known to his people, Israel, and won't need a title. These false messiahs cover their bodies with ashes, they dab their foreheads with holy oil, and they hear voices in their heads which they claim to be the Almighty One, Blessed Be He. The only true messiah, which in our language means anointed in holy oil, is a man sent by Yahweh. He will be of the line of King David, descended through his father. He will gather the Jews back into Israel from far and wide and will bring about an era of peace. But more than this, Pilate; the true messiah will build the Third Temple, and..."

"Another temple? But you already have a perfectly good Temple on that mountain you call Zion," Pilate said.

"Though we worship at the Temple built by Herod, there are those who say that the Ark of the Covenant, containing the Ten Commandments given by God to Moses on Mount Sinai, will not return from its occultation until a third Temple is constructed where King David built his city, to the east of where the Temple now stands."

Pilate shook his head. "Occultation? Is that a Hebrew word?"

Surprised, the High Priest said, "No, Pilate. It is a word in your language, Latin. It means something which is hidden from view behind another object. The Ark was taken from the Temple of Solomon before the Babylonian exile when Nebuchadnezzar destroyed Jerusalem seven hundred years ago. Since then, it has been hidden from the view of mankind until God's Temple is rebuilt, and only Yahweh knows its whereabouts. So when the true Messiah comes to earth, he will build a Temple in the right place, and return the Ark to the Holy of Holies."

Pilate sighed, "I don't understand you Jews. Why do you only have one home for your god? You're like the Greeks with their Mount Olympus, which is where they say all of their gods reside. Why does your god have to have only one residence? We Romans are conquerors of the world, and so we have to take our gods with us, especially to the lands of the barbarians. That's why, where we build a temple to the worship of Jupiter or Zeus or Venus, that's where the God is. And the God can be in many places at the same time."

Joseph bar Kayafa smiled, and said softly, so that he didn't embarrass the Prefect, "But you Romans do have a home for your deities. You believe that when a citizen of Rome dies, he or she is met by the messenger Mercury, the son of Jupiter, and is taken to the River Styx that flows nine times around the underworld. Provided a fee is paid to Charon the ferryman, the dead can cross the river, where they are judged by Aenaeus, Minos and Rhadymanthas. Then the heroes are sent to the Fields of Elysium to commune throughout eternity with the gods, and ordinary people are sent to the Plain of Asphodel, where a god may, or may not be present. So you see, Pilate, you do have a place which your gods call home."

Pilate always enjoyed talking with the High Priest. His Latin was flawless and elegant, and his mind encompassed much of Roman tradition, often things which Pilate didn't know. Well, he was a soldier, not a scholar, and wasn't expected to know these things.

"True, but Elysium isn't the god's permanent home, like this Holy of Holies is your god Yahweh's home. Our gods wander through the world to protect their Roman subjects wherever they are in the Empire. But enough talk of gods. I've come to Jerusalem to discuss matters of importance with my commanders in the garrison here, and also with you, Joseph bar Kayafa. You're the *Pontifex Maximus* of your people. Your word is law. I want you to issue an edict forbidding these

Zealots from their incessant insurrectionary against my soldiers. They know the countryside better than anybody. They hide behind rocks on hillsides while we march through ravines, and then they suddenly emerge with blood curdling screams to shower us with arrows and spears and even rocks. By the time my men have scaled the cliffs to attack them and bring them to justice, they've disappeared and all we find are footprints. It has to stop. You have to bring these men under control," Pilate told him.

"Prefect," said the High Priest, "I do not...I cannot control them. They would no more listen to my entreaties or commands than they would listen to you. These are Jews, these Zealots, but they believe more in the nation of Israel than they do in the land of Israel as the home of Yahweh. They believe that I, and my fellow priests, are no more than attendants on our Roman masters. I try to ensure that we Jews remain safe, under your protection, by obeying the reasonable laws of Rome, provided these laws do not contradict the laws of God and Moses which we must follow, but these Zealots think I've sold my soul to you.

"Your predecessors, the Greeks didn't understand the importance of our one and true God and forced us to put a statue of their god king into our Temple, thereby defiling it. It led to a revolt and many of our people were killed. But so were many in the Seleucid army. That was a rebellion caused because our God Yahweh had been abused and our Temple corrupted.

"When Herod invited the Romans into Israel, you were sensible enough to allow us to pray as we have always prayed. Yet these Zealots aren't trying to purify the Temple. They're trying to free the land from Roman rule. Which is why they pay no heed to my words and ignore my edicts," said the High Priest.

"Then without an all-out war, in which much of your population will perish, what can I do?" asked Pilate quietly, so that his men didn't hear his question. "For understand me clearly, Joseph, if there is a war caused by these Zealots, it will not merely result in the deaths of many of your citizens. The Senate will instruct me to empty this land of all your Jews and exile you as slaves to the most distant parts of our empire...to Lusitania and Mauritania, and even to the ungodly

Britannia. This land will be laid fallow, your fields salted, your cities burned to the ground, your burial places dug up and the bones of your ancestors scattered for dogs and lions to eat. This is what Rome does to rebellious people. Control these Zealots, *Pontifex Maximus*, or this will be your fate."

"May our God forbid that it will come to this," said the High Priest, blanching white. Pilate shrugged, and said, "Perhaps you should offer a different prayer to your god." "You pray to your gods, Prefect, and I will pray to mine," answered Joseph bar Kayafa. Pilate sighed. "And these madmen wandering around the desert? These messiahs?" "Unlike the Zealots, these messiahs are not a problem. Crucify a few, and the rest will be terrified and come to their senses. Then they'll disappear back into their villages, clean themselves up and return to the lives they led. They're harmless. Touched by the sun, but harmless."

CHAPTER THIRTEEN

Jerusalem, Capital of Israel, the Roman Province of Iudea 28 CE, the second year of the Prefecture of Pontius Pilate

Miriam of Sephoris, mother of Jeshua ben Yosef of Nazareth, of the Tribe of Judah, did as her son had requested. In her community of Qumran, where women were considered the equal of men, and where she held a place of honor in the society, she would have been placed beside her son within the leadership of the group which had assembled to hear his words. But in their present society, of camel traders from the Negev, fishermen from Galilee, farmers from the north and traders Edom, cowherds and goatherds from the coast, iron workers and bakers, it was better that Miriam remained at the back of the assembly with the women.

Before he began to speak, and to the surprise of the men who sat at the front of the room, Jeshua apologized to his mother, and to the women who accompanied their husbands to the assembly for forcing them to sit at the back. "Until the kingdom of heaven is established on earth," he told them, "we will follow the customs of our faith, which decrees that women shall be separated from men in times of our rituals of prayer. But be aware, brothers and sisters, that in the place from which I come and where I have lived for these past twenty years, the Community of Essenes in Qumran on the shores of the Salt Sea, we do not separate men from women. Some Essenes, those who live in communities in other cities, are celibate and these do separate men and women, but you are all the creatures of the Father Yahweh and so when God's Kingdom comes, we will all pray together.

"And so I welcome you to this, the first assembly of those who wish to know and understand the rules of my community. Though community rule forbids us to tell you, who follow the Sadducees and the Pharisees and whom we call 'the breakers of the covenant', I have been visited by Almighty God Himself, and He has commanded me to spread the light of my community so that you can return to the covenant which Yahweh commanded our fathers Abraham, Isaac,

Jacob and Moses to keep. But before I begin, let me ask you to be silent for some moments, and to contemplate the infinity of Yahweh's love and compassion for us all."

The 50 or so men and women in the room shifted uncomfortably on their cushions. Some closed their eyes and bowed their heads towards the floor; others looked at Jeshua as he breathed deeply, his eyes closed, and a sense of peace and quiet seemed to descend on him.

Miriam sensed disquiet among some who were sitting in the audience. Neither she nor Jeshua knew these men or women. They had gathered in Jerusalem for the festival of the Passover, and were acquainted with the man whose tent they were sharing, Bartholomew Nathanael of the tribe of Judah. It was he, over the past four days, who had persuaded them to assemble in this room adjacent to the main building of the caravanserai, and listen to this remarkable preacher who had come out of the desert to preach the word of the Lord. Nathanael promised them that they would hear words spoken as they had never heard before.

And although she had heard her son preach many times, it was always in the community at Qumran. He had never preached outside of the Dead Sea area, and she wondered whether this audience would be as receptive as were the brothers and sisters who were in the community, men and women who had elected him for his wisdom, knowledge of the Books of Moses and his ethereal ability to commune with God, as the successor to their Teacher of Righteousness.

Her mind went back to an old priest on the banks of the Nile at Elephantine, when Jeshua was no more than a year old. He had spoken about an old Pharaoh whose name she'd forgotten after all these years, something like Aton or Akon or something, and his wife Neferti...Miriam couldn't remember whether or not that was her name; and how they'd had overturned the religious order of Egypt and it had caused terrible trouble. She desperately tried to remember what the old priest had told her; she knew it had something to do with Father Moses taking the Children of Israel out of Egypt and a hundred years later, the Pharaoh had gotten rid of all the false gods and left only one God, the sun god Ra.

Was her son Jeshua trying to do the same thing? He wasn't trying to introduce a new God into Israel; there was only one Hebrew God... Yahweh...but was her son attempting to overthrow the faith of the people, and introduce a new faith? Should she, his mother, stop it from happening? She knew that he didn't want to stop the worship of Yahweh, but was incensed by the corruption of the purity of the faith by the venality of the men in whose hands rested their religion. These men didn't hold Judaism in their hearts, said Jeshua, but their hands.

He especially detested the Sadducees and their rich lifestyles, their opulent garments and their expensive houses, full of ornaments and servants, while the rest of Israel was living in poor houses and strove hard each working day to put food on their family's tables. He abhorred the numbing doggedness of the Pharisees and their reliance of the letter of the law, insisting that Jews obey every word laid down by Abraham, Isaac Jacob and Father Moses, whereas Jeshua believed that in these times of Roman occupation, where so many were endangered, Jews should follow the spirit of the faith. If a Jew had to obey a Roman dictate which might contravene a Jewish law in order to save his life, then regardless of the absolutism of the Pharisees, that's what must be done.

And he loathed the Zealots, bands of criminals and ruffians who gathered together to attack the Romans with the sole purpose of killing enough foreign soldiers so that they would pack their saddlebags and tents and leave the country. But such a stance was contrary to the experience of oppressed peoples in Syria, beyond the Jordan, in Egypt and Gaul and Germania and other places where the Romans were in control. The Caesars had shown that the more you fought against the Roman armies and administrations, the more they built up their armies in order to crush the rebellion. It was said that Rome could never allow one of its armies to be defeated, because that would lead to uprisings throughout the world. Though he disliked the Roman presence in the land of the Hebrews, land given to Moses by Yahweh, only the Almighty could open the Roman heart and mind, and convince their army to leave and return to the homeland.

Miriam had asked her son what the Israelites should do about the Roman occupation, and he'd said to her that whatever was owed to

Caesar should be given to Caesar, and what was owed to God should be given up to God, and that Yahweh would see that it was good, and would lead His people to freedom and prosperity.

But now, her son Jeshua stood before the assembly in this room within the caravanserai, and as the congregation sat and waited for him to begin his sermon, Miriam was frightened that such statements could lead him into trouble. Just two nights earlier, they'd nearly been evicted from the inn because the innkeeper hadn't liked what Jeshua had said. Would they soon be evicted because of the talk he was about to give?

Then Miriam saw that her son was no longer looking down at the floor, deep in contemplation, but was looking up into the eyes of each and every one of the men and women in the audience. Though she had known him every day of his life, even she, his mother, felt that there was something deeply mystic about the way he looked at people. The intensity of his stare, the way in which his face seemed almost serene and beatific, gave people both a feeling of deep inner calm, and expectation that something momentous was about to happen. They were competing emotions, but somehow they were present in her heart, and in the hearts of his audience, at the same moment.

"Dear friends, brothers and sisters," he began. "You have come here to listen to my words, as you gather every Sabbath to hear the words of your priests and Rabbis. And you have come to Jerusalem both to celebrate the coming of the festival of the Passover, and to trade your goods.

"Most of you will visit the Temple in Jerusalem, not half a day's walk from where we are gathered. And you will do so in the hope and expectation that your presence in that once-Holy place will bring you closer to my Father, Yahweh.

"But do not be fooled, for as you walk upon the ground which lies encompassed within the walls of the Holy Temple, your feet will not be treading on holy ground. Just as King Solomon was not permitted by God to tread on the grounds of the Jebusite's pagan temple before it was destroyed by workmen from Lebanon a thousand years ago who came to build his temple, and then the bare earth was sanctified and made holy by Zadok the Priest, so you, brothers and sisters, will be treading on unholy ground when you walk through the Eastern Gate of the Temple."

There was unease in the congregation, and Miriam looked around in concern. These were not words which should be spoken aloud, in the company of strangers, and so close to Jerusalem. The Sadducee priests had spies everywhere. Some of the men were shaking their heads, and one was about to speak, when Jeshua continued, "It was Zadok, the High Priest and the descendant of Aaron, brother of Moses, who was told by God to sanctify the ground on which the Temple now stands, and who made it holy for the tabernacles of the Lord our God.

"And for generation upon generation, the sons of Zadok have been priests in the Temple and they kept it holy. And Yahweh was pleased. Even when we were exiled in Babylon, even when our land was conquered by the Assyrians and the Babylonians, we always returned to the Temple because it was holy and the home of our God.

"But all this changed when the Seleucids and the Greeks conquered us. Six generations ago, when the wicked Greek King, Antiochus Epiphanes conquered our lands, he slew many of our people, and in his arrogance, he installed an idol of the pagan god Zeus in our temple. But he did more than this. He installed a generation of false and wicked priests which broke the sacred thread that connected our Temple to the family of Zadok, and through Zadok to Aaron and to Moses the Lawgiver."

Many in the audience looked at each other, and nodded. Some could suddenly understand the essence of what this man, Jeshua, was saying. But why he was saying it, they didn't yet know.

"This is our history; this is known to you, as it is known to all Jewish men and women. But what is not known to you, and what I am come to tell you, is that the Priestly line has run unbroken from the time of Zadok, the first Cohen of King Solomon's Temple, even unto today," he said.

There was a gasp as the men and women in the room looked at him in astonishment.

"Yes, brethren, the linkage between the glory of King David and his son, King Solomon, and we who sit here today, was, is and will for all time remain unbroken. It is a line which remains to this day. The priestly descendant of Zadok left the Temple in Jerusalem at the time of the revolt of the Maccabees and fled to the purity of the desert and formed a community at Qumran on the shores of the Dead Salt Sea. A secret community of the pure and righteous, whose existence remains unknown to this day. This small community continued through the ages, until the High Priest of the Temple could no longer bear what was happening in God's name. So he went into exile and left the defiled Temple for the purity of the desert to rejoin the descendants of his family of the line of King David. He was Judah the Cohen, the Teacher of Righteousness. A hundred years later, I am his spiritual descendant."

There were audible gasps in the room. People were shocked. For one hundred and fifty years, the Sadducee priests in King Herod's Temple which stood on the mountain of Zion in Jerusalem, had assured the people that they were the rightful descendants of the priests of the King Solomon's Temple. And as the rightful heirs, they demanded tithes, taxes, fees and payments for allowing the people of Israel to worship there.

But now this man, this unknown desert-dweller, was saying that for six generations, the Jewish people had been lied to; that the priesthood of Jerusalem had perpetrated a heresy, a treachery against the Hebrew nation...against God Almighty. And that even today, in the desert not a few day's journey from where they were sitting, was a community in which the descendants of Zadok the Priest lived and prayed.

Miriam looked urgently at the gathering. Where there had been confusion, discontent, doubt and even anger when they had first listened to Jeshua's words, now there was wonderment. Men looked at their neighbors. Women looked at the men. All were wondering whether there could be any truth to what this man was saying. But his news was so astonishing, so bewildering, that nobody was willing to stand and challenge him.

Jeshua continued, "For generations, my community has hidden from the wicked priests in the Temple, knowing that to emerge and spread the true word of God would bring chaos and division and even death. But unlike Judah and all those who Sons of Zadok who followed him, I have no such doubts. Having joined the community and been anointed as its leader, it was my mission to continue the work of the true priests. But now God has told me that I have a new mission, which is to leave the community, and spread the word of my father, Yahweh, to the Jews of Israel. God told me to break the rules of the Essenes, to come out into the land of Israel, and to preach the light and the truth and the way.

"My father came to me in a vision. While I stood on the shores of the Salt Sea, He appeared to me as a mist of white, and told me to leave the comfort of my home, and to ascend the hills unto the very gates of Jerusalem. And so I have stepped out of the community. I have come unto the lands of Israel to cast out the false priests, the Sadducees, who pervert the sacred ground of the Holy Temple in Jerusalem. My father Yahweh told me that I am to cleanse the Temple of the wicked priests, and of the money changers and the sellers of animal sacrifices in preparation for the coming of the Messiah to redeem our lands. I am the way and the light to prepare a path for the Messiah who will enter Jerusalem and bring the Kingdom of Heaven onto the very ground where we stand.

"This was foretold by the Prophet Zachariah, who said, *'Rejoice daughter Zion; rejoice daughter Jerusalem. See your king comes to you, righteous and victorious, lowly and riding on a donkey, on a colt, the foal of a donkey.'"*

He looked at the gathering in the room, and asked quietly, "Will any of you join with me, in cleansing the courtyard of the Temple? In overturning the tables of the merchants and the money changers? Will any of you join me in purifying my father's house so that it can truly be a Temple for the Ark of the Covenant, the word of the Lord?"

The room fell into silence. Many were inspired by what this preacher had said, but they also knew the consequences. The Passover was a time when thousands of Jews came to Jerusalem to pray and celebrate the exodus from slavery in Egypt. But because so many crowded into the city, it was also a time when the Romans brought all available men to Jerusalem to put an immediate stop to any troublemaking.

Nobody spoke, until a young man, who had been sitting in the corner of the room stood, and said loudly, "I will join you. My name is Jude, son of Cleophas and Mary from Capernaum in the Galilee. I have listened to what you said, and if we are ever to land free for every Jewish soul, then we must bring Yahweh back to the Temple. So yes, Jeshua of Nazareth, I will stand beside you and overturn the tables of the money changers."

"Then," said Jeshua, "the Lord will bless you."

In another part of the room a second man stood up, and said, "I am James the Younger. Jude, that impulsive man, is my older brother. If he joins you, then I'll join you as well. He and I were sent by our parents from our village on the shores of the Sea of Galilee to Jerusalem in order to sacrifice white doves in the Temple and pray for good harvests for the coming year. But from what you've said, Jeshua of Nazareth, we will be praying to an empty House; that Yahweh isn't there and won't return until the true sons of Zadok the Priest are seated again on the chairs of the priests and the Ark of the Covenant is returned."

The room fell into silence as Jude and James the Younger resumed their seats. Jeshua waited for others to stand, but when none did so, he stood and said, "Blessed are you, my father Lord God, who gives me the strength and these good men the courage to overcome the wickedness of those who would profit from Your house."

Jerusalem, Capital of Israel, the following day

The three men arrived at the East gate of Jerusalem in the middle of the day just ahead of the older woman who rested on the rocks below to catch her breath. It had not been a hard walk from where they were lodging some miles out of Jerusalem, but the last part, ascending the road which led to the East Gate of the city, had been somewhat of a climb, especially as the sun was now becoming fierce.

They'd set out from the caravanserai after they'd said their *Schacharit* morning prayers; before leaving they broke the fast of the night with barley bread, olives, hen's eggs, fermented goat's and sheep's milk, dates and pomegranate, and a delicious beer which the innkeeper made from emmer wheat flavored with fruits. Jeshua had asked Matthew, the owner of the caravanserai, if they could take some of the ale, bread, olives and eggs to eat on their way to Jerusalem, and he'd agreed, provided that they paid him for them.

And as Jeshua, Jude and James rested a while, waiting for Miriam to regain sufficient strength to climb the short hill to the gate which led into the city, Jeshua told them, "Through this gate the Messiah, the prince of peace, will enter Jerusalem, riding on a donkey, and He will return Israel to the road of righteousness."

The two men looked at him questioningly. "This gate? Why this gate?" asked James.

Jeshua smiled. "You men of Galilee spend too much time with food and wine after your day's work, and not enough time reading the Holy books. The prophet Ezekiel said that one day, and that day is soon, the Lord will command that this gate be closed and that it will remain shut for all time because the Lord God of Israel has entered through it. And the prophet said in his vision that only one man, the Redeemer, the Prince of Israel, the man who will be the Messiah, may sit inside the gate to eat in the presence of the Lord, and only he may enter and leave through this gate. And my brothers, that day will soon be upon us."

Jude asked, "But who is this man? Is the Messiah already here?"

Jeshua didn't answer, but smiled, and turned as he saw his mother Miriam rise from the rocks below on which she was sitting, and walk up the hill towards them.

"She comes," Jeshua said.

The two other men turned and saw that Miriam was approaching. When she'd reached them, they joined the crowds of visitors trying to cram through the gate to enter Jerusalem's Temple. Because it was one of the greatest and most popular festivals in the Jewish year, many of the population of Israel wanted to pray in the holy Temple and offer their thanks to God for their freedom.

Slowly, one by one, the crowd shuffled forward as they approached closer and closer to the Eastern Gate. The sun was burning down on the pilgrims and the air was heavy with dust and flies. Men and women carrying trays of figs and dates walked up and down the lines. Other men with a couple of goblets and large vats of ale and water on their backs walked up and down the line selling their goods to thirsty men and women. Miriam was amused at their ability to pour the liquids. Just tipping their shoulders slightly was enough to send a thin stream of ale or water through a thin pipe and the vendor caught the stream in a goblet in front of him, without spilling a single drop.

As they ascended closer and closer to the huge gateway, they saw that the large gathering of men and women were being held up by ten Roman soldiers, who were scrutinizing everybody trying to enter the city, pulling some aside, and demanding details of identification.

Eventually, the three men and Miriam stood in the umbra of the gate, where two of the soldiers looked at them in suspicion.

"And where have you come from?" one of them asked.

Jeshua said, "We are visitors from an inn beyond the city, a half day's walk to the East. We have come to visit the Temple in this holy time of Passover."

"I don't care where you slept last night," said the soldier. "Where were you born and why have you come to Jerusalem?"

Jeshua said, "Friend, I was born in Nazareth; my mother is a daughter of Sephoris, and my two friends are from Capernaum on the shores of the Sea of Galilee. We are pilgrims, come to pray to our God in the Temple."

Jude and James remained silent, trying not to look concerned, and Miriam smiled at the soldier.

"Enter the city, Jews," the Roman said, "and don't cause any trouble."

They ascended further up the steep hill which led into the city through the archway of the gate. Slowing because of the huge numbers trying to reach the city, the four walked through the large gateway in the high stone walls, recently completed and begun sixty years earlier in the days of the reign of the infamous King Herod.

As they entered the streets leading to the Temple compound, they found moving ahead difficult. There were so many people gathered in the roadways, the alleys and the lanes which snaked in and around the temple, so many carts and donkeys and asses, so many soldiers pushing their way through the crowds, so much heat and dust and stench in the air, that even stepping forward was only possible with the movement of the crowd. Apart from being almost carried ahead by the throng, the only way to advance in such a press of people was to gently push a man or a woman, a goat or even a camel to one side. Some people, also trying to reach the Temple in order to buy a sacrifice and pray, looked around in annoyance at the tall, lean man who was trying to force his way through the crowd. Some snarled at him to wait his turn and be patient; others said nothing, but deliberately obstructed his way.

Jeshua was concerned that Miriam would be lost in the crush of people, but when he turned around and looked for her, he saw to his delight that both James and Jude were guarding her, flanking her on either side, and that they were just a couple of people behind him.

Turning left into a road identified by a sign high on the side of a building as 'Jericho Way,' they saw the vast white walls of Herod's Temple ahead of them, and to the left. Jeshua turned, and looked to see that his mother and her two companions had managed to traverse the pilgrims, residents and soldiers, and entered the road which led to one of the gates of the Temple compound. He caught James' eye, and indicated the way to the entry gate for 'Israelites,' Jews who were not members of the Cohen or Levite tribes.

James, who learned the previous night of Jeshua's ancestry, couldn't understand why his friend was forcing his way through the crowd to enter into that gate. As a descendant of King David, through his father Yosef, Jeshua was privileged, and could have walked through a far more spacious entry to the Temple, where the fortunate who were honored to be of that tribe could enter. Yet he chose to forge ahead of the crowd, and enter where the vast majority of Israelites walked.

And eventually, the four entered the Temple courtyard, a vast space, many times larger than the centers of most of the villages in Israel. At the opposite end of the courtyard, far in the distance, lay the entry steps to the Temple itself, guarded by golden lions and two vast nine-branched candelabrum on either side of the steps which led to the Holy of Holies. These were the Jewish Menorah, which Moses used as a symbol of God's light when the Jews left Egypt and wandered through the desert. Now, they were lit in the month of Kislev to celebrate the festival of Chanukah when, a century ago, the Maccabees defeated the Greeks because these pagan conquerors had defiled God's house by placing an idol to one of their gods inside the Holy of Holies of the Temple.

Jeshua looked around the massive square and at the colonnades and remembered the Temple all too well. Though it was twenty years ago, he had inscribed both the building, and the priests within it, in his memory. Though he was only a 13 year old boy at the time, he could still visualize the silly priest who had tried to have him removed from the Initiation ceremony because he asked too many questions; and he remembered Annas, son of Seth, the kindly High Priest who had sat in this very courtyard, and talked to him after he had been expelled, encouraging him to continue getting to know the Lord God.

Jeshua looked again at the Temple at the opposite end of the courtyard. Though the compound in which it was situated was huge, the Temple itself wasn't a vast building, especially compared to the gigantic gold and red temples which the Romans had built to some of their gods in the city of Sephoris. But nonetheless, it stood tall and impregnable, blinding white in the glare of the midday sun. On all four sides of the expansive courtyard were colonnades of walkways supported by columns of white Jerusalem stone. These corridors, high above Court of the Gentiles, and the height of two men above the place where the Israelites were permitted to congregate, housed the cloisters of the Temple, containing many offices and rooms of the Cohanim and the Levites who administered the Temple. Some were for scribes, some for adjudication of disputes, some offices were where the Sanhedrin, the court of justice of the Temple sat in judgment; and some of the offices were where the priests and Levites changed from street clothes into their religious vestments.

In the courtyard itself, crowded with a host of men, women and children, were dozens of carts and small shops, some with a canvas covering to protect the shopkeeper from the sun, others placed in the shadow of the walls. The carts and shops were selling pottery models of the Temple, clay toys in the shapes of lions and horses but painted to represent the uniforms in which the Levites and the Sadducees were dressed, or living animals in cages, like birds, or tethered goats and lambs to be purchased for sacrifice. And there were a dozen tables where men whose dress indicated that they came from distant nations, as well as local Jews, were exchanging Greek and Roman money for money without the graven image of a face which could be used to pay the Temple tax, such as those minted by the Romans in the city of Tyre in Lebanon.

Miriam looked at her son, and saw with concern that he was beginning to study what was happening in the Court of the Gentiles in a state of growing discomfort. She knew, from their conversation this morning, that he would try to change the way that the Sadducees and the Levites organized the worship of Yahweh, but that was just after the sun had risen, and in the quiet of the early morning of their tent in the Caravanserai. Now, though, in the midst of thousands of Israelites, here to pray to the Father, to sacrifice animals to ensure a prosperous and peaceful year, the circumstances were different.

And it wasn't only the Israelites who were here. There were the Temple guards in their prayer shawls, carrying large wooden staffs which they were using to push and separate groups. There were dozens of Sadducees and Levites trying to move the throng forwards towards the tables where goods were to be purchased and Temple taxes were to be paid...and of course, in the courtyard were dozens of Roman soldiers, with their iron helmets, their armor, their red cloaks and their fearsome swords and spears, walking through the crowds, and imperiously pushing people aside, just to show that they were the masters of the land.

Miriam, concerned at what Jeshua would do if one of the Temple guards, or worse, one of the Roman soldiers, approached him and treated him roughly, gently moved people out of the way and sidled over to where he was standing.

"Jeshua, my son, shouldn't we be making our way to the Temple in order to pray?"

She hadn't said that they should buy a sacrifice and hand it over to a Sadducee priest to sacrifice it, because she knew that it would upset her son. But he said nothing, and it was as though he hadn't realized that she was standing beside him. Instead, he was looking over the heads of the throng, and staring at the tables of merchants and money changers.

"They desecrate my Father's house. These money changers, these sellers of toys and trinkets, should be beyond the walls, outside, in the market places; not standing on the holiest of ground to where

King David brought the Hebrew people and King Solomon built his temple, and placed in it the Ark of the Covenant and the laws which Moses heard from the mouth of Yahweh."

She saw that her son's body was stiffening, the muscles in his face were becoming taut and his lips were pursed in determination.

"Jeshua, my beloved. I would like to go into the Temple now. It's so hot in this courtyard. I need shade."

He looked at her in sudden understanding and nodded. Turning to the two men by her side, Jeshua said to Jude and James, "Friends, will you take my mother to the Temple. There are things here that I need to do."

Jude nodded in agreement, but James, like Miriam, had noticed the way in which Jeshua seemed to have become tense since seeing the traders, merchants and money changers, and knowing about Rome's refusal to countenance any public disturbance, was concerned that Jeshua might bring the might of the occupiers down on his head. He didn't know what Jeshua was planning, but was acute enough to know trouble when he saw it. And he'd seen that look often enough in the eyes and attitude of his brother Jude to remain behind and prevent an incident, if he could.

Jude took Miriam by her arm, but she held back. "Jeshua, please join us. Don't stay out here. I should like to pray to Yahweh in the presence of my son."

"Mother," he said gently, "there are things here which must be done to set things right. If God permits, I will join you in body. If not, then I will walk beside you in spirit."

"You're frightening me," she said.

But James intervened. "Miriam, go inside into the Temple with my brother. I will stay behind here with Jeshua, and ensure that he is safe."

Jeshua was surprised, and said to James, "Brother, I need nobody to protect me. I have the Lord, my God, my Father, who sees all and who will keep me safe."

"Perhaps," said James, "but the Romans don't believe in our God, and they have a nasty habit of crucifying people who cause them trouble, so I'll stay with you while your mother and Jude precede us to the Temple."

"Go in peace, Mother. We will meet soon, in the house of my Father."

Jude again took her elbow and tried to encourage her to follow him, but she was still reluctant, and remained.

"Go, Mother. I ask you."

Miriam sighed, not knowing what to do. He had James, a good man, to stop him doing something which could get him into trouble with the Temple authorities, or God Forbid, the Romans. But she didn't want to go into the Temple without him, for though he was a man of peace, and never raised him voice, he had recently become increasingly unsettled, to the point of anger, when it came to what the priests were doing in the House of the Lord.

But Jude was insistent, and so she followed him. James and Jeshua stood together as crowds of people, like a sluggish stream, flowed around them; some were heading west towards the Temple complex; others were heading north towards where the tradesmen and merchants and money changers had set up their stalls.

"Come, brother, we will go and speak to the money changers," said Jeshua.

"Why?" asked James. "They have permission from the Temple authorities to be here. Why do you want to speak to them."

"Last night, we spoke about the defiling of the Lord's house by these merchants. They must be told that they have no place on this sacred ground. Trade is for the marketplace, not the Temple," he said.

"But that's not what you're going to cause them to leave, is it?" asked James. "You're intent on making trouble. That's the truth isn't it, Jeshua. You want to start a disturbance."

Jeshua shook his head. "I want these people to leave this place. And if I explain to them why they have no right here, they will surely leave and take their carts and wagons down to the marketplace."

James laughed. "This is the time of the feast of the Passover, Jeshua. This is one of the busiest times of the year for these people. Do you think they will willingly bid farewell to their trade and income just because of what you tell them? What even makes you think that they will listen to what a preacher from the desert will tell them; especially when the High Priest has given them permission to be here? Would you?"

"I would obey the dictates of my father Yahweh, and His commandment which Moses gave to us at the foot of Mount Sinai. Honor your father and your mother. Yahweh is Father to all the Jews of Israel. We dishonor him by buying and selling trinkets and toys and sacrifices in His home, like merchants in the market."

But at that moment, James was no longer listening. Instead, his attention had been diverted to a commotion close to where they were standing. Although the throng of people prevented him from seeing what it was, he noticed from within the crowd a man in rich priestly clothes wearing a tall turban and pushing his way through the multitude towards him.

As the gathering cleared a path for him, Jeshua also turned, and saw an obviously important man, preceded by a short, bald man, sweating in the heat of the day, marching like an imperious Roman commander directly towards them.

The short man, Malachi of Jaffa, pointed in their direction, saying loudly enough for all nearby to hear, "There he is, the man from Nazareth, and his companion. But not the Nazarene's mother or the other man I told you about."

The spy's fingers indicated Jeshua, who knew that the man marching towards him must be Joseph bar Kayafa, High Priest of Jerusalem. Joseph walked up to him, standing close before him, as if examining Jeshua's face.

"You are a man who calls himself Jeshua of Nazareth? Correct?"

Normally, ordinary Israelites cowered when Joseph addressed them. But Jeshua seemed to have the beginnings of a smile on his face, and looked anything but nervous.

"And you are a man who calls himself Joseph bar Kayafa. And your title as High Priest is what gives you the right to wear such sumptuous clothes."

Irritated both by his lack of fear and his impertinence, Joseph said again, "You are on Temple grounds. I do not answer your questions, but you answer mine. Are you Jeshua of Nazareth?"

By now the crowd was no longer sluggishly streaming around them but had come to a stop and was listening to every word of the extraordinary occurrence.

"I am the man you have named. But why do you seek me?"

"Follow me to my office. I want to talk with you," the High Priest said. He turned, and the crowd immediately parted to form an aisle, allowing him to walk back in the direction from which he'd come.

But before he could walk more than a few steps, Jeshua said, "I will not follow you, Joseph bar Kayafa. This is my Father's house. It is His commands I obey, not yours. You are a servant of the Lord, yet you act as though you have become master of His House. Beware of pride, High Priest. The Proverb says, 'When pride comes, then comes disgrace, but with humility comes wisdom.' You are surrounded by the men and women of Israel who seek guidance and wisdom in these times of anxiety and trouble. Yet all they see in your rich vestments, and your and your priests' bearing, is the sin of pride and the arrogance of fools."

The crowd gasped at this young man's audacity. Suddenly furious, Joseph bar Kayafa turned and said, "Be very careful, man of Nazareth. For such an offence against the High Priest, I could have you arrested and roped and hauled on your hands and knees before the court of the Sanhedrin."

But then another voice, this one from within the crowd, intervened. "The Sanhedrin is where some of your fellow priests might actually agree with what this young man has said."

The voice came from a man hidden by the crowd, somebody standing close to the High Priest but not yet visible. It was the weak and strangled voice of an old man. The crowd close to Joseph parted, and an elderly white-haired man, bent with age and supported on a wooden staff, but with a face which spoke of wisdom and experience, stepped into the space which had opened up. Jeshua recognized him immediately, although the old man's eyes were milky and unfocussed, and he looked carefully to see where Jeshua was standing. And then he saw him, looked at him closely, and recognized him.

Jeshua smiled, and said "Greetings, in the name of my Father. It is good to see you again Annas, son of Seth. It is twenty years since we met, here at this very spot. We last sat together and talked of many things, and despite the years, I have never forgotten what it was that you told me. I'm delighted to see you still alive, if frail."

"And I remember you, as well, Jeshua of Nazareth. I knew that you would return to this place. There was something of the mystic in you, though you were only a boy at the time. But something...something... there was something in you which I hadn't seen before in anybody, boy or man."

Annas nodded to himself, his mind defying the years as he remembered sitting near to a fountain in this courtyard, and being amazed by the boy's insights and knowledge. He breathed deeply, and said, "But you don't seem to have changed, Jeshua of Nazareth. You were disobedient and incorrigible all those years ago, and from the way you've just spoken to my son-in-law, the High Priest of Israel, I see that you are still being mischievous."

The old man was grinning, while the High Priest stood there in surprise and growing anger. Yet Annas understood his son-in-law's displeasure, especially in front of this crowd of Israelites, and so Annas gripped the High Priest's arm, and said, "Forgive the impetuosity of an old man, my revered son, but when I overheard this spy of yours, Malachi of Jaffa, tell you about Jeshua's presence on Temple grounds, I followed you. I wanted to see again if a boy who had caused so many problems in his Initiation had become a man who would cause difficulties for us. Well, Jeshua, will you cause problems for the Temple while you're in Jerusalem?"

"I am not the cause of the problems, Annas," he said, "I am here to ensure that the Lord's Temple is a place where Yahweh is given the reverence which is His due."

Angry at his impertinence, the High Priest said, "That is my responsibility, Nazarene, not yours. Nobody else, not the Romans nor the people of Israel, and especially not you, determines what does and does not happen in the Lord's Temple. Only me and my fellow priests. I remind you that any trouble in the Temple will be dealt with mercilessly. And if our laws mean that we are not capable of dealing with you, then we will ensure that you're taken before the Prefect of Israel, and tried under the law of the Romans. And may God Almighty help you then, Nazarene, for we will not be able," Joseph said.

But before Jeshua could respond, Annas said to the High Priest, "Twenty years ago, son-in-law, this man, Jeshua of Nazareth, made a fool of a foolish priest. It was right here, in this very Temple. Be wary of him, Joseph, for doesn't it say in the book of the gatherer, Ecclesiastes, that we should not be quick in our spirit to be angry, because anger rests in the bosom of fools. When he was a boy, he made a fool of one of our number; be careful that he doesn't do it a second time now that he's a man."

And Annas coughed, turned and walked back through the aisle created by the crowd. Joseph, the High Priest, continued to look contemptuously at Jeshua, but then turned and followed in his father-in-law's footsteps.

Suddenly the silence which had enveloped the assembly during the extraordinary interchange erupted into whispers and then loud conversation as the High Priest disappeared. Still in amazement, the people of Israel looked at Jeshua, wondering who he was, and why he had stood up so impertinently to the High Priest. But pressed forward by those at the rear who had not witnessed the exchange, the multitude started to flow again towards the traders, merchants and money changers, and others who had already brought sacrificial animals moved in procession towards the Temple.

Towards him, pushing against the stream of people, came his mother Miriam and Jude.

"I heard what happened just now. Between you and the High Priest. We should go, my son. I fear for your safety. This is not the place to be."

Jeshua looked at his mother, and remembered how she had looked all those years ago, when his father was still alive, before he became a leader of the Essenes, even far back to when he was a boy initiate in the Temple and she had come looking for him. Her hair then was a lustrous black. Today, it was streaked with white and grey. Then, her brown skin was smooth and even shone in the sun; today it was sallow and as brown as leather. He wondered what he looked like these days. When he was a boy, he would look into the still water of a lake and see his face. But for the past many years, the only body of water he'd seen was the Sea of Salt, and it was lifeless, milky white and there were no reflections from its surface.

Had he changed that much? Where was the boy, so full of wonder and God's grace, knowing so much yet prevented from speaking because the adults wouldn't listen to him? Where had that innocent boy gone? And now he was a man, a leader of the desert community of Essenes, he had confronted the High Priest, the most powerful man in Israel, and he had stood shoulder to shoulder, eye to eye and he knew that the Lord God, his Father, was beside him, giving him courage.

He nodded to his mother when he saw the look of concern in her eyes. He would not upset or worry her any further, and he would leave now, but Jeshua knew that he would return, perhaps tomorrow, perhaps after the Shabbat, or perhaps next year when he had more followers than Jude and his brother. Then he would begin his work of cleansing this den of thieves and return it to a house of prayer. But now wasn't the time.

CHAPTER FOURTEEN

The Palace of the Late King Herod 28 CE, the fourteenth year of the reign of the Emperor Tiberius

Sweating in the airless room, the sun beating down on the cushions close to where he sat on the extravagant and garish throne which was King Herod's pride and joy, Pontius Pilate, Prefect of Judea held the scroll tightly. He wanted to rip off the seal, read the words which Sejanus had written, and know his fate.

But out of courtesy, he had to wait until the ridiculous sycophants from Jerusalem's Council of Elders to finish their panegyric. They were currently heaping praise after praise on him for his wisdom, brilliance, justice and so many other aspects of his shining character that he was now ignoring everything they said, and wished their unctuous adulation would come to an end. Before they left, they would give him rich presents like gold and jewel encrusted spice boxes, or goblets made from Hebron glass, and hopefully, when he'd thanked them, they'd go away and not bother him again until the next time he came to this stinking and hideously overcrowded city. He'd sell the gifts to a dealer who'd give him a small amount, and sell them for a fortune in the market places of Rome.

Pilate noticed that the soldier messenger who'd carried the scroll from Rome was waiting at the opposite end of the Audience Hall, presumably in case Pilate had an urgent response which, after he'd eaten and slept, he could return to the coast to take the ship back to civilization and Sejanus.

An Emperor could dismiss whomsoever was before him, but for a Prefect to dismiss the worthies of the Province summarily might get back to the Senate, and then questions would be asked about his competence and ability to handle the many aspects of the diplomacy required. So for him to break the seal and read what Sejanus had to say before the sycophants had finished their interminable servile obsequiousness would have been an unforgiveable breach of protocol, and it would have reverberated around the city's walls for all time.

But eventually, the seven men bowed, wished him a long and trouble-free life in their appalling attempt at the Latin language, and departed. His major domo then came forward and in his stentorian voice, shouted, "The High Priest of Judea, Joseph bar Kayafa, seeks an audience with your Excellency."

The major domo turned to walk to the door and escort Joseph bar Kayafa into the Audience Hall, but to the surprise of his jaded captains and soldiers, Pilate said, "One moment. I have an important message from Rome which demands my immediate attention. Ask the High Priest to wait outside for a few moments."

Now people were suddenly attentive and looked at the Prefect as he broke open wax seal of the letter, indented with the Office of the Emperor, and unscrolled the document. Although he'd been a popular commander of a Legion in the Army, and was well-liked by his men, it had become clear and apparent from the early days of his Prefecture that Pilate was no administrator.

So although many of the men under his command enjoyed his company when he came to the barracks, few thought that he would last long. And perhaps this letter from Rome would spell his undoing. They looked at him in keen interest.

Pilate read the letter quickly. Then re-read it, trying to keep his face from showing signs of horror and distress.

Senatus Populusque Romanus

To Pontius Pilate, Prefect of the Empire's Province of Judea from the Noble Lucius Aelius Sejanus, Commander in Rome per pro Imperator Tiberius Julius Caesar.

In the name of the most glorious Imperator, Tiberius Julius Caesar, Ruler of the World and Pontifex Maximus, may the Gods grant the Emperor health, wealth and victory over his enemies

Greetings Pilate, Equestrian of the Pontii Family and Prefect of Judea.

We are again uneasy when We read of the disturbances caused by rebels in the Province which has been entrusted to you by the will and generosity of the Emperor and the consent of the Senate. These barbarians act against Our authority, dignity and rule.

You have been commanded by Us to quell these rebels in letters sent to you during your Prefecture. Yet you have failed, and still these malcontent renegades cause the deaths and mutilations of Our soldiers.

These rebellions shall cease within six months of your acknowledgement of your receipt of these orders, or We will order the Governor, the Noble Lucius Vitellius Veteris, son of the Quaestor Publius Vitellius, to instruct his Legate in Our Province of Syria to march south into your Province of Judea with his Legio XII Fulminata and cause these rebels to cease to exist. As will your Prefecture.

In the name and by command of the Emperor, Tiberius Julius Caesar, sealed under Our hand and with Our consent Lucius Aelius Sejanus Commander in Rome.

His mind quickly analyzed the import of the letter. If he failed to quell the rebels, he would be dismissed from this post and forced to return to Rome in disgrace, to the amusement of those in the Senate who knew him, and the fury of Claudia Procola's family, who saw him through the eyes of his wife, and who hated him as a result. Before he'd bought the Prefecture of Judea, they'd called him a failure and a man who couldn't support their daughter and give her and her family a lifestyle commensurate with her beauty and standing as a Roman matron. When he'd secured the post in Judea, they'd become much more friendly, anticipating rewards; but if his Prefecture became a disaster and he returned to Rome in debt, they'd pay an assassin a couple of golden *Aureus* to slit his throat and he'd end up floating down the Tiber, along with all the other failures. In that way, Claudia Procola would become an honorable widow, and able to find another husband, this one richer and more able to support her and her family.

If he were dismissed from his post by Sejanus, then there was no chance of his being able to pay back the money he'd borrowed to purchase the Prefecture. And if that was the case, and if somehow, he managed to survive the fury of Claudia Procola's family, then not only would he never be given another administrative position, but he would spend the rest of his life in servitude to the people who'd given him the money.

So his only possible avenue of moving forward, let alone being a success, was to quell the rebellion. If that meant by extreme violence, of crucifying hundreds of men, women and children, and leaving their bodies on crosses to rot on the road from Jerusalem to the sea, then so be it. He had no compunction in ordering the deaths of multitudes. It was the way in which Rome had conquered the world; yet somehow, he was still hopeful that the policy with which he had begun his Prefecture would still work. It had worked for him in the Army. Though authoritative, his command had been marked by his willingness to consult with his commanders, as opposed to many other military leaders who had made decisions based on their own instincts.

And consultation was what he'd done when he became Prefect; he'd discussed options to problems with his senior army and administrative staff, and when he'd gathered all the pertinent facts, he would make a decision. He considered this the best way of governing such a querulous nation, with so many factions, and with so many different divisions in the religion.

But if keeping his role was dependent on his acting like other Prefects and Procurators and Governors, being brutal and repressive, then so be it. He would open the doors of Hades and let the demons rampage throughout the country.

He was distracted by a cough. It was his major domo, seeking permission for him to being into the Audience Hall the august and imposing, and impatient, High Priest.

Pilate shook his head. "Not yet. Wait. Tell the High Priest that an urgent matter has arrived from Rome, and I will attend to him shortly."

The major domo nodded and left the room. Now all the eyes of the amanuenses and administrators were on him. He looked for the most senior military man in the room, but the Audience Hall was mainly full of administrators, as he'd met the previous night with his commanders, and they had returned to their barracks. This morning's audience was about petitions, dispensing justice and dealing with disputes. But there was one military person, whose insignia showed that he was a Cohort Tribune of middle rank, standing towards the back of the Hall.

"Tribunus Cohortis, step forward." The young man pushed his way through those before the thronal dais, and saluted. "Prefect?" "Your name?" asked Pontius Pilate. "Gnaeus Marcius Secundus, Prefect." "Well, Gnaeus Marcius, I will give you written orders which you will deliver. I want you to ride to the encampments of all the Auxilia and the Cohorts beyond the city walls, and give my instructions to my Commanders."

Pilate called over his amanuensis, and dictated a short note, which was then copied, rolled up, secured with Pilate's seal, and given to the young Tribune to take to his commanders. They were ordered to return to Jerusalem that night to discuss the beginning of a merciless assault against these damnable Zealots.

That done, Pilate began to feel a sense of relief. It was as though this was the first day when he was taking proper control of his cantankerous subjects. No more would he try to reason and accommodate. Instead, he would become the scourge of the nation of Judea, and these Jews would suffer. Rather them, he thought, then himself.

He nodded to the major domo, who immediately brought forward the tall, imperious and richly dressed figure who'd been standing in the archway, waiting to be given permission to enter.

Normally, he'd have apologized to the High Priest for keeping him waiting. But that was the Pontius Pilate of yesterday. Today, the Prefect Pontius Pilate was in command of a rebellious nation, and soon everybody who didn't obey the very word of Roman law would suffer the sword of authority he would be wielding.

"In the name of the one God of the Hebrew nation, I greet you, Prefect of Israel," said the High Priest. "I hope that your Excellency is well."

Pilate waved his hand in a gesture for the High Priest to state his requirement. Somewhat surprised that the normal accord of friendship was missing, Joseph bar Kayafa continued, "Some days ago, great Prefect, we were talking about these false messiahs who were wandering the deserts of Israel, preaching that the end times were here, and that the Kingdom of God was about to begin. These men, all of them insane, are causing great distress and anguish among my people. One of them even had the audacity to come to my Temple yesterday, and remonstrate against me.

"It is time, Prefect, that the might of the Roman Army came down and crushed the necks of these madmen, and showed the people of Israel that the only way to our Lord God is through worship at the Temple. I wish to prevail upon you to bring the majesty of the Roman law to bear against these men, and make an example of one or two of them to show the rest that their continued rabble rousing will end in their crucifixion," said Joseph.

Pilate cleared his throat. Normally, he would have tried to persuade the High Priest against such action, but after receiving the letter from Sejanus, he was in no mood for leniency.

"We'll begin with this trouble-maker who confronted you in your Temple. What is his name? He will be brought before me and tried. And you, Joseph bar Kayafa, will act as witness against him."

"Might I ask you not to arrest this particular messiah, great Prefect. This one isn't a madman screaming at the clouds in the desert. He is intelligent and knowledgeable, and I truly believe that he can be brought back onto the paths of righteousness. The man who confronted me is known to my father-in-law, the former High Priest Annas, who was appointed by your predecessor, Quirinius. My father-in-law believes that there is much goodness in this young man, but he has lost his way. To arrest and then to crucify this man will cause me much difficulty. So I beseech you to allow another to be tried and convicted. I will bring two madmen out of the desert and throw them before you for trial and conviction," said Joseph.

Indifferently, Pilate shrugged. "What you do is of little concern to me, Priest, but do it quickly for now is the moment to set the people of Judea on the proper path." Joseph looked at him in surprise, and Pilate continued, "Not the path you may wish for, Joseph bar Kayafa, but my path. And my path is full of stones and rocks and stumbling blocks."

Beit Netofa Valley, lower Galilee
(between Tiberias and Haifa), six months later

Every day, he surprised her more. Every day, she saw him grow as a person, a man revered by any he touched, followed increasingly by men and women whose lives he made better, just by his words, his love.

As they walked from village to village, town to town, he seemed to develop in confidence as the numbers of his followers increased. Six months ago, when they left Jerusalem after the Festival of the Passover in the month of Nissan, the sun was already hot in the middle of the day. These days, in the furnace which was the middle of the year, there were days when Miriam found it too unpleasant and hot to walk, and they would stay indoors, where crowds would gather around Jeshua and listen to his words of wisdom.

On days when the sun wasn't too hot, they walked north along the King's Highway and so far had rested for some weeks in the towns of Bethel, Shiloh and finally Nazareth, where they were reunited with many friends and there was even a reconciliation with some of Yosef's children and grandchildren. But it was Yosef's son, James who showed them the greatest warmth, giving them shelter among his family and food and even a donkey for Miriam to ride around the village.

It was now late in the month of Elul, and in the following month, Tishri, would fall the most joyous of all the Jewish commemorations, the remembrance of the moment that God had created the world, which was the Jewish new year, Yom Hazikkaron. And that was followed soon after by the awesome , sacred and solemn service of Yom HaKippurim, when the entire community would fast for a whole day both in penance and regret for the many sins which they had committed during the year. Only after proper penance could the Almighty One finish writing the Book of Life and predict who would live, who would die, who would prosper and who would suffer during the coming year.

Now that they had arrived in the village of Kfar Cana, where they would rest for a month and observe the ten days of awe between the new year and the Day of Atonement, Miriam listened intently to her son's first address to the gathering in the village's synagogue. To the fascinated villagers, gathered to hear the increasingly renown preacher, Jeshua explained that Yom HaKippurim was first performed on Mount Sinai after the Israelite's exodus from slavery in Egypt. The formidable and dreadful commemoration had been created because of the loss of faith of the Children of Israel in their God.

This preacher explained that after Yahweh had given Moses the Ten Commandments and the prophet and leader descended the Mountain to share the bounty with his people, he was incensed to see that in his absence they were worshipping an idol in the form of a golden calf. In his fury, Moses broke the tablets given to him by the Almighty and in begging forgiveness and a desire to make atonement, the people sprinkled ashes over their bodies and clothes and on their foreheads and fasted for a day and a night.

This and other forgotten aspects of their faith were the subjects which her son had chosen to discuss with the people of the village of Cana. After he'd spoken to the people and they were alone in the house where they were lodging, Jeshua suggested to his mother that now was a proper time to return to Jerusalem. Surprised, Miriam asked Jeshua why, especially as they had walked so far north. He explained that it was because the coming ceremony of Yom HaKippurim was the only time of the year that the High Priest, Joseph bar Kayafa, was allowed by God to enter the inner sanctum of the Holy of Holies. It was in this time, and in this place where the High Priest said special and unknowable prayers, sprinkled the blood of pure white heifers on the place where the Ark of the Covenant had once rested before its occultation, and the High Priest made atonement for the sins of his people as had Moses fifteen hundred years before. Jeshua told Miriam that he wanted to talk to Joseph bar Kayafa about these prayers, and God's reaction to them.

But when he'd seen the look of dismay on his mother's face, Jeshua realized how exhausted she was, relented and said that he would return another year to Jerusalem, and on that occasion, discuss this most sacred of rituals with the High Priest.

"When you are rested, mother, we will leave this village and walk eastwards, back to the Sea of Galilee, and visit the town of Capernaum.

I wish to see Jude and James again, for I have a mission to undertake, and I wish them, and others such as Nathaniel, Thomas, Judas and Peter to gather so that we can determine how best to achieve the task," said Jeshua.

"Task? You're always talking about your task, and your mission, my son, but you never tell me what it is."

Jeshua nodded, but remained silent.

Normally, Miriam wouldn't press her son any further, but for the past six months, he'd been slowly gathering a small number of men and women around him, decent and honorable people of whom Miriam had grown fond in the short time they'd been traveling with them. Men such as Judas who was given control of the group's funds which he carried and was skilled with the dagger called a sicarius; some were concerned about his association with the group, as they thought he was a member of the assassins who called themselves the Sicarii, but Judas insisted that he wasn't a man of violence, and his name Iscariot was derived from the Hebrew Ish Kariot, a man of Karioth, the town in the Galilee where he and his father were born.

Then there was Peter, whose name had been changed from Simon. He was a fisherman from the Sea of Galilee, born in the village of Beit Saida, and they had met in Jerusalem when Simon had come to sacrifice a young goat to Yahweh; but when he heard Jeshua preach, from that moment onwards, Simon had said that he no longer which to return to his old ways, but instead, as Jeshua told him, he would become a fisher of the people of Israel. From their first meeting, they had been firm friends, so much so that Jeshua had given him the nickname Peter, from the Latin for rock.

Then there was Mary Salome, who had changed her name from Miriam Shulamit in order to sound more Roman. She was the wife of Zebedee and her job was as midwife; but like others, she had been in Jerusalem to sacrifice to Yahweh and had been entranced by Jeshua's sermons in the streets approaching the Temple and had asked whether she could follow him. Jeshua had laid his hand upon her forehead and called her 'sister.' And from that moment, she was devoted to his every word.

Another woman had joined their expanding group after she had heard Jeshua speak, this time in an inn in the northern part of

Jerusalem. Her name, like Jeshua's mother, was also Miriam, but she had changed it into a Roman name and was now Mary. She came from a city on the western shores of the Sea of Galilee called Magdala, named after the Hebrew word *migdal* which meant 'tower.' Her town of Magdala was situated between Tiberias and Capernaum, and her husband, now dead, had become wealthy from exporting salted fish from the sea, to places far away in the Roman Empire. But as a widow, she had sold the business and all of his trade to others, and with her status and fortune, she could have lived a comfortable life; but instead she'd heard Jeshua's sermons in Jerusalem, and determined to spend her life, and part of her fortune, in ensuring that the Jews of Israel returned to the path of righteousness.

These four, with Jeshua and Miriam, now walked together along the length and breadth of Israel, talking, laughing, and learning. They followed Jeshua from town to town and had built a special affinity with her son. And soon, when they returned to the Sea of Galilee, they would join Jude and James to form a community of men and women, determined to save Israel from the Romans, and the Jewish people from the priests of the Temple.

Miriam felt no jealousy at all for Jeshua's closeness to the group, as he was always inviting her into the circle of friends, so that she would be involved in their conversation; but she refused more often than not, as the journey had made her tired and she wanted to sleep. But when she did participate in their discussions around the fire and beneath the canopy of stars, sipping wine and eating bread and cheeses and olives, it was always a time of relaxation and pleasantness for her. Jeshua would talk about the Teacher of Righteousness and the philosophy of the Essenes, of the different Manuals which the people of the community obeyed, of the rituals they followed and ideas to which they aspired.

And followers such as Peter and Judas, and especially Mary from Magdala, would question her son closely and pose difficult examples which they asked him to explain. It was during these discussions that Jeshua was so critical of the priests of the Temple, and how they had led the Children of Israel away from the paths which were ordained by Yahweh and told to Moses after the exodus from Egypt. Only the sons and daughters of Righteousness, followers of the Teacher, who had once been a priest of the Temple, but who had escaped from the wickedness to the shores of the Sea of Salt, only they were true followers of Yahweh.

When they had been in Cana for six days, lodged in rooms in a traveler's inn which Mary of Magdala willingly paid for, as she had paid for their lodging, food and drink since leaving Jerusalem, Jeshua called the group together that night in a field nearby. Judas had already lit a blazing fire, and Mary Salome had taken bread, cheeses, some fruits, two flagons of wine and olives from the inn's kitchen and prepared a small meal for the group.

After their evening Ma'ariv prayers, the group left the inn and walked into the field, where they saw the silhouetted outlines of Judas and Mary sitting by the fire. Jeshua and the others walked over, sat and refreshed themselves. When they had finished eating and drinking, Jeshua led them in a quick prayer of thanks to Yahweh for given them the food and wine, and said yet another special prayer of praise and thanks to Mary of Magdala for her generosity in supporting the group's needs and comforts, he cleared his throat, and then said,

"This morning, one of you asked me how I and my mother Miriam were initiated into the community of Essenes. When I told this follower of the rules of the Community, among which was that all things made known to the Sons of Righteousness must remain secret and hidden from the rest of the world, he seemed shocked that I would have abused the Rule, and he asked me why it was that I was disobeying my vows.

"In the time soon after the King, John Hycarnus had died, his son, Alexander Jannaeus, became ruler of Israel. This is the time before Herod, before the Romans, a hundred years ago. It was Alexander Jannaeus who was unfaithful to the word of Yahweh, and caused great anguish among the faithful. The High Priest in Jerusalem, long before Herod built his Temple, left the priesthood in disgust and horror at what was being done to our faith. The name of this faithful priest was Judah and with a small but devout following, he went to Qumran on the shores of the Dead Sea and re-founded a community of faithful and righteous. There were already people there from the days of our father Aaron, but their numbers had dwindled. He became the Teacher of Righteousness of this small but pious community. It was Judah the Wise who decreed that no word of the Essenes shall be preached beyond the boundaries of the Community, for he was certain that if word of the rules of the group of righteous became known to the priests in Jerusalem, they would have them imprisoned for heresy. So they continued to worship in secret. But that was before the reign of King Herod and the house of whores he built on top of the land where King Solomon built his Temple in the days following King David.

"After my father Yosef died, and returned to Yahweh, my mother was bereft, and so she and I traveled to the Dead Sea and we were admitted to the Community of the Essenes, promising to obey the Rules. In this way, both the Teacher of Righteousness' love and hatred were ours. He said that no man will argue or quarrel with the men of perdition, the Priests of the Temple; that we must keep the Teacher's council in secrecy in the midst of the men of deceit.

"That we must admonish with knowledge, truth and righteous commandments those who enter our Community. These initiates had forgotten, or were never taught to conduct themselves spiritually and in the laws of our God. In this way, our Teacher, though long dead, was able to guide those who had strayed from the path, and to instill them with knowledge and instruct them in the mysteries of wonder and truth when they became members of the community, so that they would behave decently with one another in all that had been revealed to them."

The followers of Jeshua were gathered around and listened to every word which he was telling them. There was something so melodic, so spiritual and comforting in the way he talked, that they willingly allowed themselves to be under his thrall.

Jeshua continued, "But even though I never left the community, those who came to us, or travelers seeking hospitality and nourishment in the harshness of the desert, told me of the way things were in Jerusalem and throughout Israel.

"It grieved me that in these times of oppression from our Roman conquerors, the Priests in Jerusalem and other cities were doing nothing to ease the plight of the Jewish people. And they were going further and further away from the path of righteousness ordained by Yahweh. So I grew to question this aspect of the Teacher's rule. It was wrong to allow hundreds of thousands of Jewish souls, living outside of our community, to be in peril for straying from the true path because they were misled by the evils of the priests. I doubted this rule of the Teacher of Righteousness, and for years I beat my breast until one day, I was standing alone by the shores of the Sea of Salt and a vision came to me..."

"Not alone," his mother interrupted, "You were not alone, for I was standing twenty cubits behind you, and I saw you encased in the Holy Light of Yahweh."

Jeshua smiled, "Yes, Yahweh came to me, and told me to go out into the community of Israel, to cleanse the Temple and to return the people to the paths of righteousness."

The group fell into silence, not knowing how to respond, until Mary of Magdala said, "Jeshua, how will you, alone, cleanse the Temple and return the people to the proper path? The Priests will never allow you to preach inside their Temple, and if you preach against the authority of the Temple on the streets of Israel, then the Romans will undoubtedly arrest you. How will you bring the people to you without being arrested?"

Jeshua smiled. "Alone? But I'm not alone, beloved sister. I am accompanied by Yahweh, our Father, and you, my friends. Between us, not the force of the Sadducees, nor the laws of the Pharisees, nor the rocks and stones of the Zealots, nor even the spears and arrows of the Roman Army can stop us."

And so Jeshua continued to talk to the group until he noticed that his mother Miriam was almost asleep. He said that they should put dust and earth on the fire until it was extinguished and return to the inn to pray and sleep.

The following evening, Jeshua was preparing to give a sermon in the small synagogue which was in the center of the village of Cana, when the local Rabbi came to the inn to speak with him. The Rabbi told him that there would be no congregation that night for him to speak to, because most of the villagers were attending the wedding of two young people, Matthew, son of a local farmer, to Berenice, daughter of the tool-maker.

So the friends relaxed in the inn, talking between themselves, until the Rabbi returned many hours later, looking anxious and distressed.

Surprised, Jeshua calmed him down, and asked him what had suddenly happened. As the group listened, the Rabbi said, "Sadly, the wedding party will soon be over. And there will be many unhappy people on what should be a joyous night."

Mary of Magdala asked, "Why Rabbi? What problem has arisen?"

The Rabbi explained that the problem was one of the differences in wealth between the bride's and the groom's families. That all of the money the bride's family could afford had already been spent on the wedding dowry and the cost of the wedding, and the wine had run out earlier in the evening. The groom's family was furious because they believed that they had been dishonored before the entire village. There was no money to pay for additional wine, and the bridegroom's father, already dissatisfied with the amount of dowry which the bride's family had paid, was growing increasingly incensed and was about to cause a serious argument.

Sad at what was happening and unwilling to allow a bride to be unhappy on her wedding day, Mary of Magdala ordered friends to stand, gather together and solve the problem. She immediately purchased six large flagons of wine from the innkeeper, swearing him to secrecy.

Carrying them, they all walked to where the food and drink had been prepared outside of the room where the wedding guests were assembled.

"Judas, Peter, quickly, empty those flagons of water onto the ground, and fill them with the wine from these flagons," she instructed them.

They did as they were told, and quickly, Mary of Magdala and Jeshua, along with Peter and Judas, carried the six water flagons into the hall.

In surprise, the room came to silence as the strangers suddenly walked in. To the surprise of the wedding guests, and most of all to the father and mother of the bride, Berenice, Mary said, "Forgive us interrupting you, but we are visitors to Cana, and we heard the Rabbi saying that there was no more wine left. But as we were passing outside, we noticed that somebody had wrongly filled these water jars with wine. So now there's plenty for everybody."

There was a roar of appreciation, and guests applauded, and rose to take the wine flagons from the newcomers and pour them liberally. The bride, Berenice, beamed a smile and shouted her appreciation at the strangers who had suddenly appeared.

Mary, Judas, Peter and the others returned to the inn, happy that they'd been able to reverse a dispute and an unhappy beginning to a marriage. As they were sitting and talking about the joy of doing good deeds, a young man, whom Jeshua had seen a number of times in the village, and who had attended some of his talks, entered the inn. He stood in the doorway, looking around diffidently.

Jeshua recognized his reluctance, smiled at the young man, and said, "You are welcome to join us."

The young man nodded his thanks, and walked over to where the group of friends were sitting. He introduced himself. "I am Nathanael, a man of this village."

Each introduced himself and herself to Nathanael, and invited him to sit and participate in the conversation. He listened to what was being said for several moments, but from the way he leaned forward, especially when Jeshua was speaking, it was apparent that there was something which he wanted to say.

Jeshua said, "Can we now hear from you, Nathanael, that we might know your thoughts."

But Nathanael shook his head, and said, "I'm poor with words. I don't know what to say. And I doubt that you would want to hear what I'm thinking."

Jeshua smiled, and reached out and touched him on the cheek. "Oh you of little faith in yourself. In doubting me and my friends, you doubt yourself. Yet you sit among us, drink with us, and are become one of us. My Father, Yahweh will come to your aid and assist you. Speak now, brother Nathanael, and your faith in yourself will be rewarded a hundred times over."

Mary Salome, Miriam, and Mary Magdalene all reached over and touched the young man's cloak. Peter and Judas also reached over and put their hands on Nathanael's arm to give him strength.

The young man from the village took a deep breath, and said, "I was born in this village seventeen years ago. I've never left it, except to go to Capernaum. I was going to marry Berenice, but her father said no because I haven't any money. Now there's nothing left for me in this village. I've listened to you, Jeshua of Nazareth, while you've been talking in the Synagogue and in the streets, and though I don't understand much of what you've said, I know that I want to find out more. I've mentioned you to my father, who once visited the town of your birth, but he questioned why I want to follow you. He said that he hadn't known of anything good to come from Nazareth. But listening to you, I think he is wrong, because now I know that you want us to turn from the path we're on to a new and better path, a path which leads to the Lord God. I told this to my father, and he laughed and said that if you were right, then I should follow you. But he also said that I should beware of being led along a false path. But I think your path is true, for though I don't understand much of what you so, I have often felt the same. So if you'll have me as your companion, I'll walk with you, and go where you go."

Mary Magdalene smiled, and squeezed his hand. "Like Ruth in the Scroll of her name."

Nathanael shook his head, not understanding.

Mary said, "Ruth was a pagan woman from the land of Moab who married a Jewish man. It's said that she was the great grandmother of our King David." Nathanael frowned. "Then our King David wasn't Jewish."

Jeshua smiled, and said quickly, "No, Nathanael, for though she was born as an idol worshipper, by marrying into a Jewish family, and accepting the power of our Lord, she herself wanted to become a Jew. She opened her heart to Yahweh and accepted Him as her God, and the Israelite people as her people. When her mother-in-law Naomi told her she was returning to Israel, Ruth begged to go with her, saying, *'Where you are going, I too will go, and where you will stay, I will stay. Your people will be my people and your God, my God. Where you die, there too will I die and where you're buried, I will be buried.'* This showed us, friend Nathanael, that regardless of the Greeks and the Romans whose feet are on our soil, this is our land, as given to us by God."

Nathanael listened, and nodded slowly, turning to Mary Magdalene and telling her, "Now I understand. There is so much I have to learn.

I'm truly sorry that I don't have your knowledge. When our Rabbi was trying to teach us, I was always thinking of other things. I don't have the learning that you have."

Jeshua again reached over and touched Nathanael's hand, saying to him, "My brother, you may walk with us, talk with us, and be with us. And we will learn from you and you will learn from us. As these others have learned from me, I am the way and the truth and the life. The only way in which you'll come to my Father, Yahweh, is through me. Not through the priests in the Temple, or even your Rabbi, good man that he is. I am the new way, and I will lead you and all Israel back onto the path of righteousness."

Nathanael smiled, and said softly, "Then I will sleep here tonight, with you all. And in the morning, I will tell my father that his son has a different path to follow than the path laid down by him."

CHAPTER SIXTEEN

The Road between Cana and Capernaum, two days later

A young, or strong man, a shepherd or a traveler, could have completed the journey in a single day; but because Miriam was tired and there was no reason for them to hurry, Jeshua and Mary of Magdala determined that the pace would be leisurely and if it took them two days to reach Capernaum, then so be it.

Mary had purchased two donkeys from a trader in Cana before they had left, and the group was using one of the donkeys as a pack animal to carry enough supplies that they didn't have to find an inn in which to sleep overnight, but could sleep in a field, making themselves food and taking with them sufficient to drink, if there were no brooks and clean water along the way.

Despite her resistance and determination to walk as one of the group, all insisted that Miriam ride on the second donkey, and as they left the town of Cana and climbed over the hill and through olive groves and in the rutted passage which took them out of the Beit Netofa Valley, Miriam listened with delight to the many voices which discussed aspects of what Jeshua had told them the previous night. Most had points they wanted clarified, or concerns which they wanted to raise. All except Nathanael, who remained quiet for the entire journey.

So when the voices were suddenly still for a period of time, as the group climbed to the top of the valley before its long descent towards the Sea of Galilee and Capernaum, Miriam asked, "So, Nathanael, what do you think about the discussion? Do you agree with Jeshua that in the Kingdom of Heaven, the first shall be last, and the last shall be first?"

The young man shrugged, and continued walking. Concerned that she had embarrassed him in front of the others, Miriam said, "I'm sorry, friend, if my asking you a question has upset you. In our group, there is no need to participate, unless you want to."

He looked up at her and smiled. "Miriam, I'm new to this company of friends. I have nothing to say which could be of interest. I'm happy just listening and learning."

Mary of Magdala intervened, "And that's wonderful if it's what you want to do, Nathanael. But Socrates, a great man in Greece who lived some four hundred years ago, said that the best way to learn is for a teacher to have a dialogue with his students, so that in the conversation he will learn as much from them as his students learn from him. He said that the best way to learn is to teach."

She looked at Nathanael, and saw that he was trying to understand what she'd just said.

"But how can a teacher have a conversation with his students?" he asked. "A teacher knows everything and a student is there to learn. When I was a boy in the schoolroom, we didn't talk. In fact, we were punished if we spoke. We just listened to what the rabbi was saying and we learned. Well, others did. I just waited for the lesson to be over because I was thinking about other things," Nathanael told her.

Peter and others laughed, enjoying the conversation. "Probably thinking about girls," Peter said.

Jeshua said, "My brother Nathanael, there is only one who knows all. He is omnipotent, all-knowing. He is our father. He is Yahweh. Though we are all his sons and daughters, no matter how much we know, we are all learning. So if you have thoughts from which we others can learn, then I invite you to speak to us of your thoughts. Perhaps you can begin in answer to my mother Miriam's question. In the Kingdom of Heaven, will the first be last, and the last be first?"

Nathanael looked at the others. It was the middle of the day, and the journey from the town of Cana to the ridge above the valley had been a long and uphill walk. Soon they would rest and eat their midday meal. But not until they'd breasted the hill and descended sufficiently so that they could find a stream or river beside which to lay and eat underneath the shade of an olive tree.

He thought about the question, and said, "I don't understand how the first can be last and the last, first. Surely if I enter the Kingdom of Heaven and I'm first, I can't be last. Can I?"

"But," said Jeshua, "when we say 'first', are we talking about a person's position in a line of men and women trying to enter the Kingdom? Or are we talking about something else? What if by first, we don't mean where somebody is standing. Rather, friend Nathanael, we mean somebody who has amassed great riches during his life, who has lived a life of luxury in Israel. One who has had a dozen servants and men to work his fields; who has never done a day's labor in his life? Or what if we're talking about a man who is commander of an Army, and whose life is devoted to giving orders which others have to carry out.

"In this world, the rich man and the commander are the first, but are they going to be the first in the Kingdom of Heaven?" asked Jeshua.

And a smile lit up Nathanael's face as the light of understanding dawned.

"No," he shouted. "No, they won't be first...well, they may be first in getting to the Kingdom because they'll have horses to carry them whereas I'll be walking. But when they get there, the Almighty One, Blessed be He, will ask them what they've done in their lives. And if they haven't led good lives, they won't be first into the Kingdom, will they, Jeshua. They'll probably be last behind those of us who have worked hard in the service of our community, or spent their lives being faithful to God."

The young man looked at the others to see if they agreed, and by the looks of joy on their faces, he knew that he was right.

"Blessed by my Father, Yahweh, who has lit the path of darkness, and let this good man Nathanael see clearly the way ahead," Jeshua said.

The journey continued, and by the time night came, the company was already walking downhill towards the shores of the Sea of Galilee. Though it was getting too dark to see the road ahead clearly, in the far distance, they could see some candles burning in the scattered houses. It presaged a settlement beyond the houses, which were probably where lived the owners of farms or groves. And that meant that Capernaum was half a day's walk.

As Mary Salome and Peter prepared the meal, Mary Magdalene looked around to find Miriam. She wanted to enquire how she had fared during the journey. She saw her in the distance, though in the falling light she was difficult to make out. Miriam was sitting on a rock ledge looking down into the valley, her back to the group and the fire which Judas and Nathanael had built from wood one of the donkeys had carried from Cana.

Mary walked over, and sat beside Jeshua's mother. She asked how she was feeling, and Miriam said that all was well. But there was something in her voice which troubled Mary.

"I feel that you are uneased. That you're troubled, Miriam." "No," said Miriam. "I'm alright."

The two women stared into the darkening distance, until Miriam said, "Talk to me about my son, Mary. You're older than the rest and a woman of wealth and maturity. You have seen more of life than the others. How do you think he is faring?"

Surprised, Mary answered, "He's an exceptional man. Extraordinary. I see the divine in him. That's why I'm following him. I think there's so much wisdom, so much love and warmth in him, that I feel a better person just being near to him. I've never met a man like him. I was always surrounded by men of trade and business all my life, who spoke of nothing but markets and profits and prices, and I thought that this is how men are. And then in Jerusalem last Passover, I listened to him talking to a crowd near to the Temple, and I was captured. I sought him out so that I could listen to him time and again. And each time I was in his audience and heard him speak, it was as if he was talking to me, and me alone."

"Yes," said Miriam. "That's the effect he has on people. I knew it when he was a boy. From the very beginning, he was different from other children. It was as if he was living in a different world. He would be here, yet somehow not here. It's so hard to explain."

Mary put her arm around Miriam's shoulders and drew her body towards hers. Miriam enjoyed the closeness to another. Not since her husband Yosef had died, had she been intimate with another person. She missed being touched, held, loved. She'd kissed and hugged women in the Community of Essenes, but such closeness and affection was a ritual, somehow more formal than this. Mary was sharing an intimate moment, a meeting of minds and bodies, and Miriam felt emotions flowing through her that she hadn't felt in a long while. It was the closeness to another human being, the fact that she was touching her, but not in the way in which she was kissed and hugged by Jeshua or Peter, Mary Salome or the others. These were hugs and kisses which were formal, the greeting of one member to another, contained within the intimacy of the group.

But Mary's hug was that of sisterhood, of one women who had experienced life's joys and disappointments, one who sat beside her and would share her troubles.

Softly, Mary whispered, "Are you scared of losing your son to us?"

She didn't reply immediately, although Mary's question made her think deeply. Instead she looked towards the town of Capernaum, even though its lights weren't visible beyond the ridge. But in the distance, she could see the pitch-black waters of the Sea of Galilee illuminated by the stars, deep, mysterious and unknowable.

"You, Mary, and the others are where he belongs," Miriam said. "Since he was a boy, he was always a leader; when other boys and girls in Nazareth were playing, he would be the one who they would follow. In his schoolroom in his town, it was always Jeshua who posed the most interesting and difficult questions to the rabbi...the rabbi even came to us one day and said that he had taught Jeshua all he could, and that we should consider taking him to Jerusalem so that he could learn more from those who were better able to teach the boy what he wanted to know.

"I should have known, from the moment he was conceived, that God had a special plan in mind for him. How else could I have born a child like him without..." She suddenly stopped herself, and remained silent, looking at Mary of Magdala to see if her inadvertent remark had been heard.

And though she too was looking into the distance, her thoughts appearing to be elsewhere, Mary asked, "His conception? Was there something unusual about his conception?"

"No! Nothing! I just meant that it felt as though his birth was... that God had...I was a young mother with an older husband. All those years ago, I was searching for a reason for why my life had turned in the way it had. That's all I meant."

Not willing to let the issue pass, Mary asked, gently, "Miriam, did your husband...when you first were married and alone, did he... force you?"

"NO! He was as gentle as a lamb. Though I fear I failed him. We were never...I mean, try as he might, he couldn't...I mean...look, I don't want to talk about it. Please."

Mary nodded and remained silent; but she was mystified. One day, when Miriam was more secure in their friendship, she would raise the subject again. But Miriam continued talking, as though a dam had burst its banks, and much that was left unsaid in her life was suddenly gushing out, "When my husband Yosef died, I was bereft and from that moment, I was alone with my son. Yosef's children were much older than Jeshua, some as old as me, some even older, and they caused so many arguments with me, that peace seemed to absent from the house. I sought peace by taking Jeshua with me when I went to the market, or sometimes we'd just go into the fields around Nazareth and sit, sometimes for the whole day, talking about God's good grace.

"Whenever I was in the house, Yosef's children, all but his youngest son James, would find a reason to quarrel me. I never seemed to find a way to befriend my husband's children from his first wife. I was young and unhappy, and Jeshua was only just an Initiate. So for years, I stayed in Nazareth, being treated by Yosef's family as a stranger, as a servant, even though I'd been their step-mother. They were rude, aggressive and took my things as though they were their own.

"When he was old enough, Jeshua took me away from my home in Nazareth and the ill-treatment I was suffering at the hands of Yosef's children, except his half-brother James, and we walked to the shores of the Dead Sea, to the Community where we lived all those years."

She looked at Mary Magdalene and smiled. "Oh, Mary, you can't imagine the peace and serenity I felt in that community. Yes, it had strict rules and my life was restricted, but for year after year, I remained in that community, reveling in the comfort of my friends, in the closeness to the Almighty and the love and security of the Community of Essenes. Until..."

Mary reached over and held her hand, and continued the conversation, "Until Jeshua was visited by Yahweh, and now he is traveling around all of Israel, defying the priests and the Romans, the Pharisees and the Zealots, and speaking to the people of the good times to come, provided we leave the path we're now treading and walk with him into the golden sunset of Yahweh's goodness," she said.

Miriam nodded, and asked softly, "And now can you understand why I am nervous? He is risking everything to bring about a better world. And if things go badly for him, what will become of us? What will become of me?"

"Of course, I understand your fear dearest sister. I am nervous for the same reason, as is Judas and Mary Salome. All but Peter who is like a rock and sees only hope in the world to come. For while we are now talking to small groups of Jews in synagogues, inns and on street corners and are unnoticed by the authorities, eventually, when we return to Jerusalem, we will talk to larger and larger crowds. And when that happens the ears of the Priests will be opened, as will the ears of the Romans. Our leader will be branded a troublemaker, a mischief-maker, a messiah, and he will be arrested, tried and crucified, like Prefect crucified those five messiahs just after Passover.

"Do you not think, sister, that I'm not worried about what will happen to us? Do you think that I want to end my days in prison or worse, looking up at the dozens of crosses the Romans erect outside the city walls, and seeing which agonized face is that of Jeshua of Nazareth?

"Sister Miriam, I fear every day of my life for Jeshua's safety and survival; but there is nothing that I would do to stop him. For what is the life of one man, or of a group of his followers, when we're bringing about the return of God's world and the ending, the cleansing, the elimination of this debased and false world in which we live?"

Miriam remained silent for some time, absorbing the import of what this mature and intelligent follower of her son had just said. But the reality couldn't be contained, and so Miriam asked, "So does this mean that my son will die so that the Jewish people can be brought back to the path of righteousness? Is that the sacrifice he must make for the sake of Yahweh?"

Mary's silence gave assent to the question. "So, if that is his sacrifice, then it is mine too," said Miriam.

CHAPTER SEVENTEEN

The Temple of Jerusalem, built by the Late King Herod 29 CE, the fifteenth year of the reign of the Emperor Tiberius

Joseph bar Kayafa, High Priest of Jerusalem, feared this moment. He put down the scroll he'd just been handed and looked up at the Roman soldier who had intruded into the Temple's offices without waiting for permission, pushing aside two priests and his scribe. Softly, so as not to show either fear at his summons or anger at the arrogance of the Roman, Joseph said, "Tell the Prefect that I shall be there."

"And you're ordered to come alone. No other priests. If you come with any other priests, they will be sent back. Understand?"

Joseph nodded, and the Roman soldier turned without a farewell greeting or salute and left.

He continued to look at the scroll, though the message had been as terse as was possible. There were no platitudes, such as...*To the most Holy and Eminent High Priest...there were no requests...The Prefect of Judea would be pleased if the High Priest would come to the Herodian Palace at...*

No. The message from Pilate was designed to be both derogatory and belittling, when he'd written just a terse...*Joseph bar Kayafa, you are hereby summoned by the Prefect of Judea to...*

But Joseph knew why he was being summoned. The past six months had been a disaster for the Roman army under the command of Pilate's Legionaries. Not only had they failed to quell the Zealots in the north and in the hills to the west of the Galilee, but it appeared that more and more Israelites were leaving their homes, farms and properties to join the renegades. The Zealots smelled victory. Defeat after defeat of troops of Centuries marching through the steep gorges and valleys in the Galilee, scores of Roman soldiers dead or badly wounded, and only a handful of Zealots captured and crucified.

And Joseph knew from his spies when the Prefect came to Jerusalem and resided in Herod's Palace and from those who worked in Pilates home in Caesarea, that the Emperor Tiberias, or possibly Sejanus, the man who seemed to have replaced the Emperor, was increasingly furious that the rebels were still active. For when there was rebellion, tax revenue dropped, and the people became restive for freedom.

It seemed, from what his spies told him, that swathes of the populations from Britannia, Germania, Gaul and other places were taking note of the Israelites' successes against the Roman army, and this was a very bad and serious thing, because it put the prospect of successful rebellion into the minds of indigenous people in other parts of the Empire who saw themselves as being trampled under the Roman heel.

And from what he was told, Pilate had suffered from the sharp tongue of Sejanus, and now was increasingly desperate that the Zealots continued to disobey Rome's authority. The Prefect of Judea was increasingly shouting, screaming, and threatening his commanders, his servants and even his wife, who still, it seemed, laughed in his face. But while once she'd done it in the privacy of their apartment, now she was doing openly in front of the servants, and his officers.

And suddenly, it appeared, in desperation, Pilate had made a surprise trip to Jerusalem to consult with his commanders and had ordered Joseph to appear before him tomorrow morning. And he'd been ordered to come at an hour just after dawn, when he would normally be in prayer. To defy Pilate would be to invite the High Priest's removal from office and probable arrest. To obey the order would be an offence to the Lord God and his absence from prayer would not only be noticed but would spread around the priesthood and used against him.

Would he put his personal safety before his duty to God and the Jewish people? There were others in the Temple who would love to replace him as High Priest; but if they did, they would fight Pilate, and then he would have all the excuse he needed to storm into the Temple and place an idol of Zeus or Venus in the Holy of Holies, as the Greeks had placed their idols a century earlier. Yet if he did go, then the talk behind his back would be that he was a servant of Rome and not of Yahweh, a man who couldn't be trusted, nor should be obeyed.

Joseph shook his head in dismay. There were many scrolls on his desk which demanded his attention, so he had to put the potential disaster of tomorrow out of his mind and concentrate on the immediacy of his duties. He picked up one at random and read it. It was from his spy in Galilee. And his heart dropped when he read that it referred to a troublemaker whom he thought had disappeared from his life forever, somebody he hadn't heard of in the better part of the year.

He closed his eyes and sat back in his chair, remembering the youth and his audacity earlier in the year. So much had happened, so many problems, that Joseph found it hard to place this Jeshua person in time and place. He remembered it had been in the Temple. It had been hot. And then he remembered. It was in the days of the celebration of the feast of the Passover, and the young man had appeared in the courtyard of the Gentiles. Joseph had gone down to order him to attend his office, but in front of hundreds of Jews, the arrogant man had refused. Joseph could have ordered him flogged, right then and there in front of the crowd of worshippers, in front of his own mother, but Annas, Joseph's father-in-law had intervened, and diffused the situation.

Joseph picked up the scroll and read it carefully. It appeared, according to his spy, that this Jeshua now had a small band of followers, men and women, and they were wandering from village to village, town to town in the north of Israel, giving sermons in synagogues, the homes of wealthy men, and even on street corners. The spy hadn't written down what Jeshua was saying, but it appeared that the crowds who came to hear him left his presence in a state of shock, as though they could barely breathe. They were quiet as they walked away from his sermons, as though in a dream. The spy couldn't really understand what this Jeshua person was saying, but it must have been very frightening, because of the awe-struck attitude of the people listening.

Well, thought Joseph, something would have to be done. He'd already ensured that a handful of these ridiculous people going around telling everybody that they were messiahs had been disposed of some months previously. Some had come out of the desert screaming that God would destroy them and send down the same fire and brimstone He'd used to destroy Sodom and Gomorrah; other madmen purporting to be messiahs had railed in town squares about the coming of the end times.

Five had been arrested for disturbing the peace of the land, and because of their blasphemy, they could have been sentenced by the Sanhedrin to death by stoning; but as he knew they would, other priests had resisted such a trial, and so he had bowed to their will when they argued that they be sent to Pilate as Prefect of Israel so that they could be tried under Roman law for breaching the peace of the land.

To the surprise and dismay of his priests, all five had been sentenced to death by crucifixion. And as Joseph had predicted when he'd discussed the tactic earlier that month with the Prefect, many men purporting to be messiahs had quietly slipped out of sight, returning to their families and homes, washing off the oil and ashes from their skin, and hoping that they would avoid a similar fate. Though there were still a few false messiahs wandering the desert, these were men touched by the sun, and almost nobody was paying attention to them.

Yet now this Jeshua, with his message that the Priests of the Temple were leading people away from the path to the Almighty, was again causing trouble, speaking to congregations and communities in the very worst place for such talk to take place, in the Galilee. Joseph shook his head in sadness. He'd hoped that five crucifixions might be enough to silence such nonsense. But it seemed that nothing would silence this young man, this Jeshua of Nazareth.

He would have to keep his eye on him, and ensure that he remained in the Galilee, where there were already so many problems for the Romans with the rebellious Zealots that some madman talking about pathways to righteousness might be overlooked. If not, then another crucifixion might be needed. And if that was the only way to ensure that Jewish people of Israel could be saved from Rome's wrath and the legions in Syria who could descend as a marauding army at a moment's notice, then what was the value of one life? Should this Jeshua need to be crucified, so be it, for he and the message he was so intent on spreading, would be forgotten the moment he took his last gasp, nailed to the cross.

Near to Capernaum, on the shore of the Sea of Galilee 29 CE, the fifteenth year of the reign of the Emperor Tiberius

The Greeks, when they were conquerors of the land before the arrival of the Romans, called the hill Mount Eremos, which meant solitary or without a population. But today, as he sat on a rock at the top of the hill and looked down at the hundreds of men, women and children who had come out of Capernaum and walked the two hours in the heat of the Sabbath day, after the morning services, in order to hear him, the place was crowded. Normally it was serene, a verdant swathe of grass which ran down to the quiet waters of the Sea of Galilee. Since arriving in the city, he had been here three times, and each time was inspired by its solitude, its quietness, and its closeness to the Creator. And when he was already known in the city and many asked him to talk to them about his path to Righteousness, he had decided that this was the place where the people could best understand the difference between God's path, communing with the beauty and purity of nature, and the path which the Priests were treading in the commerce of the city of Jerusalem and its debased Temple.

So unlike when he'd been here before, when he was alone with his thoughts, today it was crowded with people, and Jeshua, used to talking to people, realized that this day, and what he was about to say, could be the turning point of his mission. For when he was in a town or a village and stood on a small platform and spoke above the heads to a passing multitude in a street and many stopped to listen, or when he was offered a place before the Ark in a Synagogue, his audience was largely unknown to him.

But today, he knew many of these people. He and his friends had lived in Capernaum for five weeks, and as they walked around, and purchased goods, or talked to craftsmen, or assisted the elderly or the sick, he and his disciples had become recognized.

In the past two months, his group had acquired two more followers, Matthew, a resident of Capernaum, and a tax gatherer, and Philip, who had been born in Bethsaida, but now lived in Capernaum and worked as a fisherman. And so the large group became known to the residents of the city. Many times, as they were walking back to their lodgings, people who lived in Capernaum would smile and greet them. They would call them by name. They would hope they had a good night's rest, or that they would see them in the morning.

So as Jeshua looked out over the faces of the many who sat on the grasses, or ate food which they'd brought with them, he realized that, like a Rabbi talking to his familiar congregation, he too was about to give a sermon to people who called him 'friend.'

And it was different, for when he preached to strangers, few remained behind; yet after today, he would continue to see these same people in the streets and in their houses.

Which made his sermon all the more important; for if Jeshua wanted people to follow him onto the Path of Righteousness, then these were the people he had to convince.

He cleared his throat, and looked into the distance, beyond the shore of the Sea, beyond the blue water, and to the distant hills on the opposite side. Knowing he wanted to begin, Matthew stood and shouted, "Friends, fellow citizens of Capernaum, thank you all for coming. You have asked to listen to the words of Jeshua of Nazareth. The sermon is about to start. I ask you to pay attention to the man I and others have decided to follow, who will lead us onto the path of righteousness, Jeshua of Nazareth, beloved of God."

Jeshua stood, so that he could be seen by everybody, and said in a voice which was loud and commanding, "Friends, many people think that my mission, since leaving my community of Essenes on the shores of the Sea of Salt, is that I am come to abolish the Law and the Prophets. But they couldn't be more wrong. Because I've come to fulfil them. Let me make this plain. Until the Heavens and the Earth come to an end, not a single word or letter of the commandments of my Father, Yahweh, our Lord God, shall be altered by me, or by anybody. We are all the sons and daughters of Yahweh, and who would dare to alter the commands of their father? Because he who tries to alter the word of the Lord will be the last into Heaven; and he who teaches them shall be the greatest in Heaven. He or she who follows the path of Righteousness, true righteousness, and not that which is practiced by the Sadducees in the Temple, or the Pharisees who stray from the Law, that person will be first in Heaven.

"The day of the Temple in Jerusalem is coming to an end. I will destroy it, and in three days, I will build a new Temple. And that Temple will not be made of stones and mortar, but will be in your hearts. And you who follow me along the path of righteousness will carry that Temple in your hearts, wherever you go. So when you pray, don't be like the hypocrites of the Temple, the priests who love to stand and pray so that everybody can see what they're doing, and be in awe of them. Instead, when you pray, do so in private, because my Father, Almighty God, will see you pray and hear your prayers, and He will look into your hearts, and He will love you for it. So when you are alone in your home, pray with words like these...Our Father, who is in Heaven; hallowed is Your name; Your kingdom will come and Your will shall be done on Earth, as it is in Heaven. Give us today our daily bread so that we can eat, and forgive us what we owe, just as we forgive those who owe us money; don't lead us into temptation, but deliver us from evil, for Yours is the kingdom, the power and the glory forever and ever."

He stopped talking, and Jeshua could see that there were many in the congregation who didn't understand what he'd said, or were confused by his words. So he decided to bless them. All their lives, they'd been told that the Temple was where God lived, but as an Essene, he knew that God lived in the hearts of the righteous, and not in some building, however grandiose. For Yahweh was everywhere, and not in one place.

He held up his hands, closed his eyes, and said, "Blessed are the poor in spirit, for theirs is the kingdom of heaven. Blessed are mourners, for they shall be comforted; blessed are the meek, for the meek will inherit the earth; blessed are those who hunger for righteousness, for they will be satisfied if they follow my way; blessed are those who are merciful, because they will receive mercy; blessed are those who are pure in heart, for they shall see God; blessed are the peacemakers, for if you make peace, then you are the Sons of God, and blessed are those who are persecuted for following my path of Righteousness, for yours will be the kingdom of heaven. And finally, my friends, blessed are you if you are reviled and persecuted because you are following my way, the way of true righteousness. Rejoice, friends, for your reward will be in heaven. Remember that those who persecuted the prophets who came before me have not gained a place in heaven."

Jeshua opened his eyes, and saw that many were smiling. So he continued to bless the people and explain to them the beauty and simplicity of following the way of righteousness, and not the path which the men of perdition, the priests of the Temple and their Levite acolytes, were forging.

An hour later, when he had finished, Jeshua bade goodbye to many who were now wandering away, and slowly, contemplating his mission and in silence, walked back with his disciples on the road which led to Capernaum. As they walked, Miriam came to his side. Her silence indicated that she wanted to speak.

"So, beloved mother, what did you think of my sermon?" he asked.

"It was beautiful, Jeshua. Your father would have been so proud of you. I am so proud of you. Your words were like honey. But..."

Jeshua looked down at her. She was more stooped than she had been last month. Age was causing her body to bend. Miriam was growing frailer by the day, and so he would have to leave her soon in the care of a good person, so that he and his disciples could follow their path of destiny.

"You said 'but.' Was there something wrong with what I said, mother?"

Miriam sighed. "You told people that you will destroy the Temple, but rebuild it in three days. I know what you mean, but words, taking wrongly by people wishing us harm, can damage us and cause problems. Threatening to destroy the Temple will cause us to have enemies, even if you're talking about building it again in peoples' minds. And then you said to Yahweh that His kingdom will come and His will shall be done on earth as it is in Heaven. Won't this offend the Romans? They could take this to mean you're telling people to stop paying their taxes. I'm frightened for you, Jeshua my son. I'm frightened for us all."

Jeshua smiled and put his arm around his mother's shoulders. "I swear before God Almighty that you will be protected, mother. But it's right that you should be concerned. These are dangerous times, and although I'm telling people about the path to Righteousness, my words can be used against me. But don't be afraid. God is listening and looking after us, and He will protect us. Perhaps not all of us, but you and those I love. This, I swear to you."

She sighed, and saw that Mary of Magdala was walking just behind, listening. Miriam dropped back, and allowed her son to walk forward. When he was out of earshot, Mary said, "He's remarkable, Miriam. I've never heard such words from the lips of anybody. He paints a vision in the air, a vision of peace and perfection, which I can see so clearly when I listen to him."

Miriam nodded. And then Mary asked quietly, so that none of the disciples walking nearby could hear, "You said to Jeshua that his father would have been very proud of him, as are you. But there is the mark of the divine in him. Tell me truthfully, dearest friend; is he close to Yahweh? Has he been touched by God? Is the Almighty his father? Is that why he's..."

Her words tailed off, and Miriam continued to walk on. But her face was placid, as though she was lost in another time, another place. Only Miriam knew that the time was when she was a young girl in Sephoris, before she'd been sent to Nazareth to make Yosef the Widower's life more comfortable; when she was asleep in a meadow laying with a beautiful young man she loved, a young man named Malachai. And as she thought about that warm summer's day and how close he was to her, Miriam smiled.

Mary of Magdala wanted to repeat the question she'd asked about Jeshua's birth, but when she looked again at Miriam, she decided to hold her peace. One day, she would find out.

CHAPTER EIGHTEEN

The Temple of Jerusalem

A day after Jeshua and his disciples returned from his giving the sermon on the hill just outside of Capernaum, an exhausted man, dusty from the road and stinking from the sweat of the donkey he'd almost ridden to death traveling south and then the long climb east to reach Jerusalem, stood before the High Priest. He drank the goblet of wine so greedily that he immediately poured himself another. And then another to wash away the taste of the road and the stench of the beast.

But Joseph bar Kayafa didn't notice what the messenger who'd been sent by his spy, Abihu of Joppa, was doing. He was intent on reading what Abihu had written; and if it was transcribed accurately, and with no exaggeration, then the scroll contained either the most ridiculous words he'd read, or the most dangerous.

Were this to have been said after a drinking session at a feast, then the company of priests and Levites would have roared with laughter. But if this was said before an audience of ordinary Israelites, impoverished, downtrodden by the Roman soldiers, or having unwillingly been forced to pay their Temple tax, then the words could lead to an uprising. And nobody knew the power of words better than the High Priest.

When he'd finished reading what the spy had reported, he looked up at the messenger, and asked, "Is this an accurate reporting of what this person said?"

The messenger shrugged, and replied, "I don't know, sir. I just took the scroll from Abihu and rode here as fast as the donkey would carry me. I wasn't there when this person said these things."

Joseph looked at the scroll again. He couldn't argue against much of what the man is reported to have said. He had read many of the manuals which his spies had wrested from the Essene community, and a lot of what Jeshua of Nazareth had told the people of Capernaum was a repetition of similar sentiments said by the Teacher of Righteousness a century and a half ago.

But when he read a particular comment which Jeshua was reported to have made, that the meek shall inherit the world, this was something which could never be allowed. This was treasonous, a direct threat to the might of the Roman army, and if it became the byword of his followers, then once Pilate heard about it, the dogs of Hades would be unleashed against the Jews.

He continued to read what Jeshua had said to the hundreds of people gathered outside of the fishing town of Capernaum. He'd told them only that they should follow his path to righteousness, and that his way was more holy than the righteousness of the scribes, the Pharisees and the Sadducees. Only by following his way would the people enter into the kingdom of heaven! So if this man's advice was followed, Joseph wondered what then would be the value of purchasing sacrifices? And without the purchase of sacrifices, much of the revenue of the Temple would be lost. Surely by offering to God a sacrifice, that was ensuring His divine pleasure and entry into the kingdom of heaven. Wasn't that the lesson to be learned when God, on the very spot where Solomon had built his Temple, had stayed the hand of the patriarch Abram from killing his own son, Isaac, and substituting the sacrifice of a human being with the sacrifice of a ram.

But when he read further down the scroll, he was concerned that this Jeshua person was telling the people not to come to the Temple. He had told them to enter through the narrow gate. But there were no narrow gates which led into the Temple. He'd said that the wide gates led to broad roads which lead to destruction, but the small gate and narrow road can only be found by a few, and they led to life.

Was this telling the people to remain at home, and not visit the Temple? If so, it was something which must be stopped. Because when it was read with an earlier injunction, to beware of false prophets who come in sheep's clothing, but are actually wolves inside, then it was a reference to the vestments of the priests. And this was too much to tolerate. It was grounds for having the Temple guards arrest him, and drag him in chains before the Sanhedrin for trial and punishment.

But all this was as nothing, compared to the treasons he'd been uttering against the Romans in this sermon. If a Centurion had been listening to what this preacher had been saying, he'd have marched in, waving his sword, and stabbed Jeshua through the heart. The words had been uttered in public, to a multitude; Jeshua had told his congregation that no man could serve two masters because he'll hate one and love the other. No person could serve God and the desire for money. And that was far more than a criticism of the Temple, and its relationship with the Roman authorities. It was a threat to the Romans and their demand for taxes. It was an invitation for people to stop paying taxes because God will take care of them. But in this world, where the Roman soldiers could kill almost at will, this was an invitation to disaster.

No! No, he had to be stopped. His criticisms of the Temple could be dismissed as the ravings of a fool, and he could be shown the error of his thoughts. Joseph would tell him that the only way to prevent the sorts of massacres, decimations and genocides which the Roman army carried out, as with the Gauls and the Germanians, was cooperation. Pay taxes, ensure peace and all would live a normal and happy life... well, as happy as one could be as conquered people. But when the Romans faced insurrection, as they were facing from the Zealots, then the slightest insult or suspicion of treason would lead to a terrible retribution; the deaths of countless Jewish men, women and children; the excruciating crucifixion of dozens, possibly hundreds. He was all too aware of the retribution conducted against the Roman slave Spartacus a century ago, when 6000 men were crucified on the road between Rome and Capua. And that was what the High Priest was desperate to avoid.

All of these criticisms of Jeshua could be addressed; but that was before he'd seen this scroll sent by the spy Abihu of Joppa. For now he'd said these things in public, before a large community, there was every chance it could get back to Pilate through the Prefect's own spies.

If it meant the sacrifice of one misguided young man to put an end to his dangerous preaching, then a sacrifice would be made. And it would have to be Joseph who initiated it, because if it came to Pilate's ears before Joseph had a chance to inform him, then suspicion could fall onto the shoulders of the priests.

He looked up at the messenger, and thanked him, gave him a purse of money, and dismissed him. When he was alone, he re-read the scroll to ensure that he wasn't misinterpreting what it was that Jeshua was telling his congregation. When a priest gave the wrong reading of the scrolls of Moses, he would be counselled and forced to re-educate himself. So before he acted upon what Jeshua was teaching, he had to be certain that he was preaching heresy.

If Joseph, as High Priest, acted upon it, as every instinct in his body told him he should, then it would lead to the near-certainty of Jeshua's stoning to death by order of the Sanhedrin. If he was handed to the Romans, then crucifixion or exile into slavery were certain. The current hostility in the air in Israel, and Pilate's reaction to the Zealots would ensure that he crushed whatever opposition came into his reach; and with a simple preacher who had no weapons, and whose followers seemed to be middle-aged women, fishermen and simple artisans, the preacher made an irresistible and inconsequential victim. Pilate would make an example of him, as he'd made of the other messiahs earlier in the year.

Yet though their crucifixions were the right thing to do, Joseph still woke in the middle of the night in a sweat, thinking about the messianic Jews whose lives he'd been instrumental in ending. Yes, he'd done it in order to protect the Temple, and to stop Pilate from bringing down the Roman legions in Syria, but their deaths were still on his conscience. So, could he do it again? Could he cause the trial, torture and hideous death of another Jew, no matter how arrogant and annoying that Jew was?

And the answer was a simple 'yes.' If it meant sacrificing one man's life to save the lives of many, then yes, he could. He would. He would suffer criticism for his actions, but so be it. Some initially may be annoyed with him, but he knew with absolute certainty that the moment Jeshua was crucified and then his body tossed onto the rubbish pits in the Gehinnom Valley where, in ancient times, children had been sacrificed to the pagan gods, the self-proclaimed son of God and messiah would be forgotten in three or so days. Not even his followers would tarry in Jerusalem for more than a day but, like the followers of the other false messiahs, they would dissolve into the landscape in the hope of avoiding a similar fate.

After midday prayers, he wrote a note to Pilate, begging the Prefect to allow him an audience. The messenger returned soon afterwards, with a note which said curtly that Joseph was to come to Herodian Palace the following evening.

When he arrived at the appointed time, he was immediately shown into Pilate's private apartments. Joseph had been there a number of times before, and never felt comfortable. The walls were still painted with the murals which Herod had commissioned when he was trying to convince the children of Israel that he was their King. For he had contravened the second commandment which God had given to Moses on Mt. Sinai...*you will make no gravel image or any likeness of anything that is in the heaven above or that is in the earth beneath or that is in the water under the earth*...yet on these walls, as on the walls of Roman villas, were depictions of God's creatures. And not just lion or deer, cattle or olive groves, but murals which showed scenes God had strictly forbidden. Dozens of naked men and women, some of them cavorting in sexual positions. And Joseph had no doubt that Pilate instructed that the meeting should be held here, and not in the more formal Audience Hall, because he wanted to embarrass the High Priest and put him at a disadvantage.

After waiting in an antechamber for what seemed like an eternity, Pilate suddenly entered the room. Unlike in previous interviews, the dress the Prefect wore surprised the High Priest. He normally wore a military uniform when he was in Jerusalem, but today he was dressed in an off-white toga, its broad purple border indicating that he was presenting himself to Joseph as a magistrate.

"Well," Pilate said, without any greeting or formality. Joseph was shocked at the Prefect's coldness, which possibly was because the two men were alone in the room, or because the relationship they had developed from the time when Pilate was first appointed to Israel had devolved because of the Prefect's inability to control the assaults of the Zealots.

"Great Prefect, I bring you greetings from the Priesthood of Yahweh and the citizens of this nation and pray to our God that you are well and that your life is..."

"Yes. I know. Quickly, I'm very busy. You sought an urgent appointment with me. What's the issue?"

He cleared his throat. "Half a year ago, Great Prefect, I approached you because of problems which the Temple was suffering, or potentially suffering, because of some false messiahs who were leading the people astray and away from the paths of true worship of our God..."

Again, Pilate interrupted. "I dealt with that. I crucified five or so. Why? What's happened now?"

"Another man, one Jeshua of Nazareth, has appeared and is in the Galilee, and he's going around and causing the people to listen to his heretical words. And these words, Great Pilate, these things he's saying, are causing great anxiety in the populace. They could turn people away from their faith and reverence of the priesthood. They're..."

"They're your problem, Priest. Not mine. I've already dealt with this thing on your behalf. If you can't control your own people, perhaps I should replace you with one who can, as my predecessor Valerius Gratus disposed of your father-in-law Annas. I have enough problems with these Zealots, these madmen who oppose Rome's ownership of Judea. I don't care about these madmen spouting things which annoy you. Sort them out yourself. Take him before this court of yours, this Sanhedrin, and have him stoned to death or whatever you barbarians do. You have laws which can deal with men who oppose your god or your faith. Don't bother me with trivial issues."

At which he turned and walked out of the antechamber, leaving the High Priest alone, and wondering what to do next.

The Town of Nazareth

As Jeshua, who was born in Nazareth, walked through the main square, the numbers of people he had never seen before surprised him. The population of the town seemed to have grown since he'd left many years earlier as a young man, in order to protect his mother from her stepchildren following his father's death. Though he'd been back once since he and his mother had walked away from the Dead Sea community to spread the words of the Essenes throughout Israel, he had remained on the outskirts of the town where the family home was situated. Now that he and Miriam were back and preaching to the populace, he had decided to visit again to see if there could be any reconciliation with his step-brothers and sisters, and for the first time to meet his nieces and nephews born since Yosef had died and he and Miriam had left Nazareth. There had been no reconciliation. Though formally pleasant and polite, it was obvious to Jeshua and Miriam that they were not welcome in Nazareth, and so they quickly left.

Earlier in the week, before Jeshua and his disciples had left to journey to Nazareth, Miriam had objected to leaving Capernaum in order to walk the three days to the city of Jeshua's birth. Though she was on a donkey, her objection had little to do with the fact that the walk was mainly uphill; rather, she didn't want to return to Nazareth at all. It took Mary from Magdala to draw the reason from her, which she encouraged Miriam to tell the group on their last night in the inn in Capernaum.

"It's the town where I went as a young woman to be wed to Yosef the widower. The first time I went to the city was the first time I entered his house, and that was the day on which I was married and met his children by his first wife. I don't think they could have been more cold and unfriendly, and even cruel to me if they'd tried. All except one, Jeshua's half-brother James, who was young and didn't resent me. But the rest of the children..." She lapsed into silence.

"But we went there soon after we left Qumran," said Jeshua. "You seemed at ease. And though they didn't welcome us warmly, they were polite and hospitable."

"You say I was at ease? That was the woman you saw, my son. But inside that woman was a young girl, removed from the family she loved, forced to marry an older man she'd never met, and treated with contempt by his children. You saw your mother being polite to her step-children, but inside was a young girl burning with anger and resentment. When you were a baby, your step-brothers and sisters made my life a daily misery, all the time behind Yosef's back. He had no idea that anything was wrong, and I wasn't going to cause trouble by telling him. So I suffered for year after year. And now you want me to go back..."

"I have to go to Nazareth, Mother. But you should stay here. Perhaps Mary Magdalene or Mary Salome will remain with you while I'm gone."

"Why do you have to go there, Jeshua? Your ministry hasn't yet touched other towns and cities in the North. What of Simonias or Narbata? Why do you have to go again to Nazareth?" she asked.

Her son nodded, and said softly, but so that the others could hear, "The Romans have decreed that Nazareth shall be a center for the administration of Northern Galilee. When we lived there, the town numbered some 500 souls. Today, because of its increased importance, the town is becoming a city, and there are some 2000 Jews. Yet these Jews look more towards the synagogue for their guidance and instruction than they do towards the Temple of Jerusalem. If I can preach in the synagogue in Nazareth and make them realize the injustice which emanates out of the mouths of the Sadducee priests, then I can make the whole of Galilee follow me along the path of Righteousness. I must preach there, mother, for the sake of my mission."

But Miriam wouldn't stay behind in Capernaum, and so the large party followed Jeshua from the northern shore of the Sea of Galilee around the edge of the water towards Tiberias on the western coast where they refreshed themselves. It was a three hour climb to Cana, where they would spend the night. Then, the following day of climbing, ever climbing, they came to Nazareth, and instead of remaining on the outskirts where Yosef's home was situated, they walked into the center of the town.

With the funds which the wonderful Mary of Magdala was giving them and the treasury kept by Peter from donations they'd been given along the way, they were well able to afford rooms in the inn. Jeshua, his mother Miriam, Mary Salome, Peter, Jude, Judas and the others were all able to sleep in comfortable rooms in the inn in the middle of Nazareth.

That night, the three women slept together in a shared room at the rear of the inn, and the men, greater in number, slept in the largest room which overlooked the square in the middle of the town.

Their arrival was a cause of conversation among the townsfolk, and soon came to the ears of the Rabbi, who visited the inn to greet them. When he realized that one of the large party was Jeshua, who had preached so movingly in Cana some time ago, and who had miraculously managed to produce wine for a wedding feast, he invited him to preach in his Synagogue the following morning, which was the Sabbath.

That night, in his room, after his mother had lit the candles for the Friday night prayers and the beginning of the Sabbath, Jeshua asked Peter, Jude, Judas and James to go with him for a walk to the clifftops which overlooked the valleys below as the landscape rolled down to the harp-shaped Sea of Galilee. They sat on a high rock and looked over the moonlit landscape. On the far horizon, there was a glint of water. Perhaps it was the distant sea which Capernaum and Tiberias bordered, or perhaps one of the small tributaries which led into the body of water. The air was still and quiet as they sat. The men waited for Jeshua to speak. Eventually, after staring towards the East for some time, he said quietly, "Tomorrow, I will speak at the Synagogue here. Things will not go well. We should prepare to leave Nazareth quickly."

Surprised, Peter said, "But Master, you've spoken in synagogues many times, and the community is almost always enthusiastic and supportive. Why shouldn't things go well in Nazareth?"

"I was born here. I'm known here as a boy and a youth, not as a prophet. You will see what the reaction will be," he said.

"Are you saying this because you believe that your step-brothers will cause problems when you're talking?"

"They might. But trouble will come from the inhabitants. They will not like what I'm going to say."

Still amazed, Peter said, "What will you say? What you said in Cana and Capernaum caused no problems?"

He didn't answer for some time. When he did, it was so softly, that his words almost disappeared with the breeze. "I will quote from the scroll of the Prophet Isaiah."

Jude, who was listening carefully, said, "Good! They'll enjoy Isaiah. Reading his book always gives people hope for the future of Israel, provided we follow the path of the Lord." Jeshua looked across the top of the rock, and smiled at Jude. "Somehow, my friend, I think the people of Nazareth will like what I have to say to them, but not like the man who is saying it."

The following morning, the Synagogue was already full when the disciples and Jeshua walked inside. People shifted their positions on the wood and stone benches so that the newcomers could sit. The Rabbi was reading from one of the scrolls, and when he'd finished his portion, he looked around and acknowledged the presence of the strangers.

When it was time and he'd finished reading what Moses and the children of Israel had been doing in the desert after leaving Egypt, the Rabbi said to his congregation, "We are joined today by a man who has preached in the synagogues of the Galilee. He is known to us all, for he was born of this town, and now after many years, he and his mother and their friends have returned. I ask Jeshua of Nazareth to come forward and speak to us."

Jeshua stood, and everybody in the community, men in the front and women in the back and sides of the synagogue, all looked at him.

"Rabbi, thank you for inviting me. May I read from the words of the Prophet Isaiah as the introduction to my remarks to your congregation?"

The Rabbi nodded, and took out the relevant scroll from the ark, which he handed to Jeshua. Placing it on the table, Jeshua unrolled it to the section he wanted to read aloud. "My friends, today I want to talk with you about the Prophet Isaiah. You all know that he walked this very land seven hundred years ago. In those terrible days, Isaiah saw the rise of the evil new empire of Assyria, and the consequence of the fall of the Northern Kingdom of Israel. Only Judea, the southern land of King David and King Solomon, remained in the hands of the Jews and was the last place on earth which was faithful to the Lord Yahweh. Yet in their fear, many people strayed from the path of righteousness. They listened to false prophets and followed strange ways. In his hope for making the people of Israel return to the ways of the Lord, this is what the Prophet Isaiah said to the Children of Israel..."

Jeshua looked down, and began to read from the Scroll.

'...the Spirit of the Lord God is upon me because He has anointed me to preach good things to those who are fearful. He has sent me to give strength to the broken-hearted and to tell the oppressed that freedom is at hand, and the gates of the prison will be open. You will be called the Trees of Righteousness and the Lord will plant you firmly in your land in order to glorify Him. Where there is desolation, where there is waste and ruin, you will repair and make new cities. Strangers will stand and feed your flocks and the sons of your captors will be your ploughmen and will dress your vines.'

Now he looked up, and said, "Today, we are an oppressed people. We suffer under the iron heel of the Roman overlords. Though the Romans make us bend down to them with their spears and swords, their chariots and their fearsome war machines, all they can do is to break our bones and spill our blood. Every Jew who dies at their hands is a martyr sacrificed to their greed and desire for power and will sit beside Yahweh as He judges mankind.

"But the Romans are not the worst of our oppressors. No, my brothers and sisters. The worst of our oppressors are the Priests of the Temple, who break our spirits and conquer our minds. The Prophet Isaiah railed against the Kings of Assyria and cautioned the people of Israel for straying from Yahweh's path of Righteousness. And I, being heir to Isaiah's mantle, condemn the Priests of the Temple in Jerusalem, for leading astray the Jewish people from their faith in my Father, Yahweh."

Suddenly, where there had been silence and attention, suddenly there was conversation and questions in the congregation. People, who had been listening quietly and attentively, realized what he'd said; that he, Jeshua of Nazareth, was heir to Isaiah, one of Israel's greatest prophets. Some smiled at the young man's arrogance, but others were annoyed.

One man, the butcher of the town, a man known for his knowledge of the Jewish law, as well as his self-righteousness, stood and asked, "Did you just say that you were Isaiah's heir?"

Jeshua looked up and nodded. "I am heir to the Prophet. And to Elijah and Elisha."

"But you're Yosef the carpenter's son, may God rest his blessed soul. Like him, you're only a carpenter. You're not a priest. What gives you the right to say that you're the heir to the Prophets?" the butcher demanded.

Peter, sitting at the back of the Synagogue, looked at the congregation and felt a growing alarm. He was about to stand and defend Jeshua, but more and more people began to ask questions of the young preacher, and some were even shouting at him to sit down, and not be so arrogant.

The elderly Rabbi stood, held up his hands for silence, and said, "Friends, I beg of you, let Jeshua, who I have invited here to be our preacher, explain what he really meant to say. He doesn't mean that he's the heir to the Prophets; rather that he's here to interpret what the Prophets meant when they wrote their words. Isn't that right, Jeshua?"

But Jeshua smiled at the old man, and shook his head. "No, Rabbi. I mean that I am sent by my Father Yahweh to lead the Children of Israel out of their wilderness. I mean that God appeared to me on the shores of the Dead Sea and he commanded me to go forth from the Essene community and preach the word of that community. That is my mission. He told me that I am to go out to the people of Israel and lead them back onto the paths of Righteousness. Because of the false priests in the Temple, His children have strayed. You all have strayed by closing your ears to the Father, and instead you have been listening to the Pharisees and the Sadducees, the Levites of the Temple. The House of Yahweh is debased by those who purport to be His servants. But they don't serve Him. They serve themselves, and we, in turn, serve them. They dress in expensive clothes paid for by the money you give them; they force you to pay large amounts of taxes to support their lavish households and their sumptuous feasts; like the sycophants of Greece, they grow closer and closer to their Roman overlords, while the children of Israel wear iron chains around their necks; they demean the holiness of the Temple by allowing merchants and money-changers to do their commerce; and they force you to buy animals for sacrifice, yet Father Noah was charged by God to save His creatures before the great flood and the Almighty sees every living creature as sacred.

"And all this because the priests in the Temple have forged a narrow path to our Father Yahweh and are forcing you to walk in their footsteps. But it is wrong. Worship in the Temple is wrong. God is everywhere, not just in the Temple. Yet like the idol worshippers of Rome and Greece and Egypt who built huge temples to their false gods, so too do these Sadducees worship in an empty room and tell you that Yahweh is there. But Yahweh my father is omnipotent and ever-present.

"God has told me to bring down the Temple, and I will destroy it in three days; then I will rebuild it in the eyes of the Almighty. My Temple will be in your hearts, my friends. No matter where you are in this world, you will have my Father with you. You may journey north or south, to Lebanon or Syria, Egypt or Rome, but my Temple will be in your hearts, and you will..."

But he could say no more, because now men and women were on their feet, shouting at him, shaking their fists at him, and commanding him to be silent. The butcher shouted at the Rabbi that this man should be kicked out of the Synagogue because he was talking heresy for which he could be stoned to death, and so could they for listening. Other people joined with the butcher and started to demand his expulsion from the Synagogue. The Rabbi looked frightened. He'd never seen such anger in the eyes of his community.

Furious, the Rabbi looked at Jeshua, and said, "You must leave. Now. Go! Be gone from this holy place. And don't think of returning."

Jeshua nodded sadly, and said in an undertone to the Rabbi, "A prophet is never recognized in his home town."

And he slipped out of the side door to the Synagogue, meeting Peter, Jude, Miriam, Mary and the others in the laneway who quickly escorted him back to the inn.

The Temple of Jerusalem

Joseph bar Kayafa, High Priest of Jerusalem, sweated in the heat of the room. But he'd been sweating since early in the morning, even in the cool of the dark before the sun rose and made his room like the inside of a baker's oven. Annas, his father in law, had warned him of the heat inside the office of the High Priest because it was built on the Eastern side of the Temple. That meant it received the full force of the sun when it was high over the Mountains of Moab, and in the Summer months, it was like being inside King Solomon's furnace as his metal-workers smelted the copper out of the rocks which miners had dug from his mines near to Eilat.

And the reason he'd been in such a state in the darkness of a pre-dawn morning was because of a report he'd received the previous day concerning this maniac, this heretic, this wayward preacher who was traveling all over the Galilee stirring up the peasants with his simplistic nonsense about building a Temple in people's hearts.

While he was addressing small gatherings of inconsequential people, he wasn't really a threat; but if this latest report was to be believed, and there was no reason why it would be wrong, then his gatherings were not only getting larger, but causing increasing unrest in the populace. The group he'd addressed in Capernaum was large and much of what he'd said seemed to have been well received. The things he was saying were, of course, utterly wrong, contradicted the laws of Moses, and opposed the dictates of the priesthood, but in those early days of his preaching, he didn't seem to have caused too much dissent. But what did he expect would happen? That people would stop gathering and congregating to join in communal worship? That ordinary people had the capacity to pray to their God without the way being led by a priest or a rabbi?

And since this Jeshua had left the shores of the Sea of Galilee and was heading south, talking to larger and larger gatherings, his audiences had grown and now he was becoming increasingly reckless. It seemed to have started with those heretical things he'd said to a gathering in Nazareth, and then subsequent, as he came closer and closer to Jerusalem, his language had become more extreme, his words more sacrilegious. As his repute grew as a rabble-rouser, he gained an increasingly large following of the simple-minded, and that was a very serious problem, especially as Joseph's spy had noted that there were men in the audience who he recognized were Jews, but also acting for payment as Roman spies.

When his words came to the attention of Pontius Pilate, the Prefect wouldn't view the man's sermons as an assault against the Jewish faith, but as treason against Roman rule. And if that happened, especially in the Prefect's present mood, he would fly into a fury and dispatch three thousand soldiers with orders to slaughter everybody in sight.

Yet nearly a year ago, Joseph had approached the Prefect and his request for gentle intervention had been rejected. Had Pilate done what the High Priest had requested all those months ago when he'd sought the appointment, then only this reckless man Jeshua and perhaps one of two of his disciples, would have been executed. But now, now that there were hundreds, and possibly even thousands of Israelites who'd heard and been influenced by this man's false hope of redemption, the chances were that whole towns would be slaughtered and entire populations would die. Which meant that Joseph would have to try again to persuade Pilate to arrest Jeshua and some of his followers and stop the spread of this nonsense he was teaching.

Joseph again read some of what Jeshua had told the crowds in Joppa, then in Lydda, and most recently, a few days ago, in Emmaus. It was all so naïve as though a father was talking to his children. Rarely did he quote any of the books of Moses or the warnings of the Prophets, and if he did, he would twist their ageless warnings and advice to his own needs; never once did he talk about the Temple as being central to the Jewish religion; instead, he made up his own homilies and blessings, without the consent or authority of the Priesthood.

Joseph searched in the scroll to re-read what Jeshua was reported to have told his audiences...'*Blessed are the poor in spirit, for they shall inherit the Kingdom of Heaven!'* What did he mean by that? Why should those who had no strength of spirit inherit anything, and especially the Kingdom of Heaven? To be gathered up into God's heaven, one had to be strong and resolute and follow the letter of the faith. Those who led their religion, like him and his fellow priests, knew with absolute certainty that men and women who didn't believe fervently, or whose belief was weak and poor would never sit on the right hand of God! Instead, such heavenly seats would be reserved for a man of belief like himself or his father-in-law Annas, men who ensured that the faith was pure and unsullied?

Joseph shook his head in anger and read further into the scroll. Again, Jeshua had said something ridiculous, something which defied logic...*'blessed are the meek, for they shall inherit the earth.'* The earth, no less! Not inherit their father's house, or his animals or plot of land, but the whole earth! Yes, this might be his way of expressing an ideal, as Isaiah, Elijah, Elisha and others had talked of the totality of human experiences by their simply homilies. But how could the meek inherit anything? The only way to inherit the earth was like the Romans, with iron swords, spears and chariots.

What was this man Jeshua trying to do? Make the meek and the poor in spirit go out into the streets and confront the Romans by convincing them that they would inherit the earth and the Kingdom of Heaven? And how would they take the earth from the Romans? With grape vines and olive branches? It was a guarantee of a massacre. And it was contrary to everything which he and his fellow priests were teaching.

No! He had to be stopped. When this Jeshua was a solitary figure, traveling around and talking to a handful of people, he was a nuisance but he wasn't a serious threat; but now that he was gathering larger and larger followings, and especially now that he had so many disciples who could spread his message like a plague of locust, Joseph had to put a stop to his nonsense in order to avoid a catastrophe.

And this could not have come at a worse time, because everybody in Israel was preparing to celebrate the Festival of the Passover, the festival of freedom from slavery and oppression. Pilate knew all about this festival, because it was a time when the Jews of Israel looked at their Roman overlords and wondered whether they, like Father

Moses and Aaron, should seek a leader who would free them from the bondage of servitude.

He looked out of the window at the Courtyard of the Gentiles down below. Even though it was just an hour after dawn, and morning prayers hadn't yet begun, the square was already crowded. These days, possibly because of the Roman oppression, possibly because of the revolution of the Zealots and the false hope they gave to the people, the Temple had become increasingly central to the lives of the men and women of Jerusalem, and many of the surrounding towns and cities. Faith, since the time of the infamous King Herod, had been fading in the land of Israel. People seemed to have gone away from the worship of the Lord, despite the injunctions and condemnations which emanated from himself and the other Priests. There seemed to be a greater reliance of the people within themselves, rather than a reliance on Yahweh and His priests. Perhaps it went back as far as the Seleucids and their Greek philosophies of Epicureanism and Stoicism...he didn't know. But recently, he and the other priests had noticed that the people seemed to be coming back to the Temple and the worship of God Almighty. The harsher were the Romans, the more the faithful gathered to pray in the Temple. The faith seemed to be strengthening in them. And certainly, the purchase of sacrificial animals was very rewarding for the Temple's treasury.

And provided that things continued as they were, then there was every likelihood that Joseph and his generation, and possibly the next generation, could outlast the Romans. He'd seen conquerors come and go, and although Rome controlled the entire world, from Northern Gaul to the desert lands of Africa, from Lusitania in the West to Persia in the East, there was a chance that the empire would soon over-reach itself and shrink back, leaving its conquered people free to follow their own destiny.

But not today. And not tomorrow. And with this Jeshua the Nazarene wandering the land causing people to question both the Temple and their Roman masters, trouble was about to rise up. So, he as the leader of the Jewish people, would have to ensure that it was nipped in the bud...that the upstart Jeshua was forced to cease his heretical sermons, his treasonous statements. And the only way he could do that was to drag this man before the Sanhedrin and force him to recant his ways, promise to cease all proselytizing, and disappear from the public's mind forever, or suffer the consequences. And the consequences were deadly. Being stoned to death was a terrible way to die.

Joseph had tried to do it the Roman way so that no guilt for Jeshua's certain death could be ascribed to him and his fellow priests; but Pilate had declined to arrest, try and convict this heretic, and the Prefect had done it in the most imperious manner. So now it was up to the Sanhedrin to deal with this Jeshua of Nazareth. And that in itself was a problem, because the Sanhedrin almost never issued a death sentence, only for the gravest crimes such as idolatry and witchcraft. And two eye-witnesses would be required who had seen these abominations being conducted.

While Joseph had no doubt that he would find men willing to speak out against Jeshua, the likelihood of the Court finding against Jeshua for witchcraft was most unlikely. Which is why he so desperately needed Pontius Pilate to take over the arrest, prosecution and judgment of this heretic.

But if he wouldn't, then the Sanhedrin would have to do it. Well, so be it. But first, he had to try to persuade Pilate to get Rome to put an end to this man's heresy.

It took Joseph's messenger three days for the High Priest's letter of request to reach the Prefect of Judea, and a further three before he received a reply telling him that the appointment was made so that they would be together in seven days. In order to arrive in time, and rested, he would have to travel for three of those days to Caesarea, on the northern coast of Israel, because Pontius Pilate would not be coming to Jerusalem for over a month in order to be present at the Festival of the Passover. That meant that he wouldn't be traveling with his usual retinue of twenty or more men...priests, guards, treasurers, secretaries...but only two personal employees of the Temple who would act at his sentinels; and worse, it meant that he couldn't travel with a treasury because of robbers and bandits on the road. But it also meant that he would have to travel by horse instead of his usual beast, a donkey or a mule.

It was necessary for him to see Pilate, and so despite the cautions of his fellow priests, he and two men set off on horseback to descend from the heights of Jerusalem to the seaport of Joppa, and then on the coast road north to Caesarea. Initially, the journey was pleasant. It was good to leave the stench of Jerusalem for the open countryside of Israel; and it was pleasurable for him to enter the small towns like Emmaus and Lydda and see how the ordinary people lived. Greeted cordially by the townsfolk, he was invited into the homes of the local Rabbis to share in food and drink, and in Lydda, he conducted a morning service before setting off again with his tiny entourage to the sea, where he would rest for a while before the long journey north to the palace of the Prefect.

Exhausted after the hot and enervating journey, Joseph arrived in Caesarea a day later than he'd anticipated, having inadvertently been redirected from the coastal route north, and accidentally turned to a road leading to Antipatris, inland from the sea. When they entered the town and asked directions, the locals were amazed they had come from Jerusalem, and told them that there was a far more direct road which ran through Antipatris from the high country and the Kings Highway down to the coast and into Caesarea. Rarely having left Jerusalem, Joseph had thought that the correct route was to take the coastal road, and now realized that he could have saved himself a day's riding.

When he finally arrived in the late afternoon, Joseph was taken into the Palace by a guard and shown into his quarters. He was dusty, smelling of the horse, needing to immerse his body in water, a change of clothing, and a long night's rest. So, when one of his servants had laid out his vestments and he was in the middle of washing his face, hands and body with water from the basin in his chamber, he was perturbed when he thought he heard people entering his room unannounced.

He glanced behind him and was shocked to see Pontius Pilate and two others standing there. The Prefect was dressed in a *toga picta*, colored dark blue and embroidered with gold laurel leaves, as though he was a victorious Roman general returned from a campaign.

Standing almost naked except for a loin cloth, Joseph turned and tried to compose himself, immediately realizing from the expression on his face that Pilate had burst in, unannounced, in order to put the High Priest at a disadvantage.

Controlling his surprise, Joseph stood up straight, and bowed, saying, "Prefect, I bid you greetings. And I thank you for your hospitality in allowing me to sleep beneath your roof. Is not your glorious wife, the distinguished Claudia Procola with you? I would enjoy meeting her again."

"You will see my wife at dinner, High Priest. And I welcome you to my home. I apologize for entering your chamber without giving you forewarning, but I have urgent business to attend to this afternoon, and I wanted to ensure that you have everything you need. I hope you will join us for tonight's banquet. In your honor, my cooks have been hard at work. Our banquet tonight will be delicious. We have specially slaughtered birds such as a hoopoe, a heron and we've even paid tribute to you by butchering a whole pig. My family will be so hurt if you decline our invitation," said the Prefect.

The invitation to the banquet, whose food would have put Joseph in contravention of Judaism's dietary laws, was such a blatant insult that Pilate could barely restrain his smile.

"Excellency, it would be my greatest pleasure and privilege to come to your table. But while I will be there, I will be eating my own, much more simple, food. I have a problem with my stomach and rich food, and my physicians have forbidden me to eat anything other than simple bread and cheese with a small glass of wine. But I shall be delighted to sit at your table, and I will take great pleasure in watching you, the wondrous Claudia Procola and your friends and staff, eat what I'm certain will be a delicious banquet," he said. "I'm devastated that I will not be able to partake in your carefully-considered menu, but I know you would not wish me to become ill."

Looking closely at the Prefect, Joseph wondered what had happened in the past year to make their relationship devolve to such a low ebb. His position as High Priest was a gift of Rome, through its Prefect, and when Pilate had appointed him, they'd been both courteous to each other and friendly. But things had become terse recently, and now they were bordering on hostile.

Perhaps it was the constant attacks of the Zealots and the letters of criticism and condemnation which Pilate was receiving almost every month from Sejanus. Perhaps it was due to the never-ending arguments he was reported to be having with his wife Claudia Procola? But whatever the reason for Pilate's disposition, it was the reality of Joseph's life, and it made his visit to Caesarea even more dangerous. Pilate nodded curtly, turned and left.

The morning following the banquet, at which Claudia Procola had been both dismissive and hostile to the High Priest, Joseph attended the Audience Chamber at the appointed hour.

Pilate walked in, surrounded by a military guard, two amanuenses, and two advisors who Joseph assumed from their dress, were Greeks, while he had decided to come alone. The High Priest stood in the center of the room, facing the plinth, while Pilate sat, looking like an Emperor, surrounded by his entourage.

"I hope you enjoyed our banquet, High Priest, even though you ate none of our food."

"I enjoyed your hospitality, Excellency, even though your food smelled sumptuous. But my stomach is glad that I ate a simple meal, for had I indulged I would not be standing here today."

"Well, to business. You requested this meeting. What problem do you have?"

Joseph took a deep breath. "Prefect, a year ago, almost to the day, I came to you and asked you to put a stop to the many Jewish men, most touched by the sun, calling themselves messiahs. In my tongue, that means that they are anointed by holy oil. For us Jews, Excellency, their claims are a sacrilege, for to be a Messiah, one has to be of the line of King David, of blessed memory. Now, to become a..."

"But I've dealt with this. Jewish criminals are to be tried in Jewish courts and by Jewish law, unless they have uttered treason, or rebelled against the authority of Rome. We've already had this conversation, Priest. I crucified a number of these desert-dwelling madmen to assist you, even though they were yours, and not mine to try. We invented the crime of treason, but those deluded madmen had been struck by the sun, and should have been in a Jewish prison, not crucified on a Roman cross. But I acceded to your demands, and as I remember, a year ago, I told you that I had more important matters to deal with. Why are you bothering me with this again?"

"Because, Prefect, there is a man, one Jeshua of Nazareth, who not only offends against the faith of our God and our prophets, but also offends against Rome and Caesar.

This man speaks treason against the rule of Rome in Judea and must be stopped. I am here to petition you to have him, and perhaps one or two of his supporters, arrested and prevented from spreading their poison any further."

Joseph stopped speaking and looked closely to judge Pilate's reaction. But the man's face could have been carved in stone. It was completely emotionless. After a few moments, he motioned to his two Greek advisors to come forward, where he whispered into their ears. They nodded gravely, looked at Joseph, said something which he couldn't hear, and then stepped away.

"Firstly, Priest, as I have already said, Rome has done enough of your bidding. You were appointed by Rome, and you are the Empire's servant. So this man will be dealt with by your Jewish laws and tried by your Jewish courts. I know your game; you're trying to look innocent while you get me to do your dirty work and make the people hate us Romans more than they do already.

"Normally, I would dismiss you and this petition of yours without a second thought. But something that you said causes me concern, and that is this man's treason against my Emperor. I will not permit treason against the authority of Rome, but I am also aware that every Jew in Judea whispers into his neighbor's ears about our rule in this land. It's only natural for a conquered people to be resentful. And yes, if you aren't able to deal properly with this man, then I will put a stop to it. But in the first instance, Joseph bar Kayafa, do your job as the High Priest of this recalcitrant and troublesome part of our empire, and put an end yourself to this man's heresies and treasons. And if you aren't capable, then I'll have to do it for you. Now go, because I'm very busy and have much to do."

Joseph turned and left.

Jerusalem, one month later

The city was already full of worshippers who had come to celebrate the Festival of Passover. The Temple guards and officials had been warned by Joseph bar Kayafa to be on the lookout for a mob of men and women, some thirty in number and led by a Nazarene called Jeshua. Reports received from his spies told him that this man had been spreading his message and calling himself a messiah in every community, village and town between the north of Galilee and Jerusalem. Because of the interest and excitement he was causing among the disaffected communities in Israel, Joseph had been forced to employ ten more spies to ensure that whatever this mob did was recorded so that he had information he could use to prevent them from causing further trouble.

This Jeshua had gained more and more followers as he traveled from the Galilee in the north of Israel towards Jerusalem. His increasing numbers of followers were Jews who were growingly increasingly antagonistic to the constant demands for additional taxation which came out of Rome, not that the true population of Judea was known from the Census figures taken many years ago. The additional taxes were more of a burden than most people could shoulder.

And the Tetrach of Judea and Peraea, Herod Antipas had come from his seat in Beth Haran, east of Jordan, to his other land of Israel in order to be present in the Temple for the important festival. It was a time which, throughout his life, Joseph had always enjoyed as one of the most jubilant of all Jewish festivals; but now he felt nervous and guarded about the beginning of the Festival of Passover, and what could happen.

It wasn't just the Nazarene and his advance towards Jerusalem. It was the mood of the people. In past years, in the days of his forefathers, the Passover had been a time of unutterable pleasure, celebrating God's intervention on behalf of his people by releasing them from the bondage of the evil Pharaonic slave-masters. For the Jewish people, it was more than a time of manumission; it was the pivotal moment in the Jewish religion when Yahweh had granted His people not just their freedom, but also on Mt. Sinai the laws by which they would forever be Jews.

But in the past few years, as the Romans had tightened their grip on Israel and the Jewish people, as they'd squeezed blood from a stone, the people had become more and more resentful, angry, and rebellious. It wasn't just the Zealots in the Galilee; it was every farmer, every shopkeeper and every tradesman. Women and girls were raped by uncontrolled and insatiable soldiers, their commanders either turning a blind eye or participating. Children were impressed into slavery, and food stored to enable a family to survive drought was stolen by the Army's Quaestors and Masters of the Quarters, without concern to the reality of starvation by the citizenry.

So, although people flocked in increasing numbers to the Temple to celebrate the Festival, it was no longer a celebration of freedom, but increasingly it was seen as a reason to resist the rule of Rome a template for their people's freedom. For Rome was now being seen as a second Egypt, strangling the life out of Israelites and threatening them with starvation and extermination. And that was something which Joseph was determined to prevent.

He looked out of his office and saw that in the Court of the Gentiles, there were already hundreds and hundreds of worshippers, gathered to purchase birds and other small animals for sacrifice. The dust caused by the throng and the waves of heat in the air made it difficult to see properly, so he couldn't identify particular people, which is why he'd placed his spies among the crowds. Some of the worshippers were wearing their prayer shawls even before going inside the Temple buildings, their heads covered against the beating sun; some were changing money in the open courtyard, for Syrian, Lebanese and coins from Greek or Roman sources were stamped with human faces, defying the laws of Moses, and so couldn't be used in the Temple. That's why the money changers exchanged them for Israelite coins which had no graven images, and so didn't contravene the second commandment which was written in the twentieth chapter of the Scroll of the Exodus, in which God had commanded His Prophet to tell His people that *'Thou shall not make for yourself any idol, or any likeness of what is in the heaven above or on the earth beneath, or in the water under the earth.'*

And then Joseph, his senses honed from decades of caution and suspicion, noticed a movement. It was in the northern corner of the courtyard. It began as ripple, the crowd seeming to have a disturbance in their midst. But then it became a wave and seemed to spread from its center further towards the middle of the vast courtyard.

Joseph watched it in surprise; then in wonderment; and then, as the crowds seemed to turn and move away from whatever was the disturbance, Joseph grew alarmed. And when he saw Temple guards push their way through the multitude as the disturbance seemed to grow not only greater, but louder, the High Priest became annoyed. And something warned him that this wasn't just a minor squabble between pilgrims vying for the same sacrificial animal but was something more worrying.

He stood from his desk and walked over to the window in the north side of his office. There he could see more clearly. By now, the guard had pushed past half of the throng, and an aisle had opened as people sensed danger and moved out of the way. Despite the heat of the day and the dust in the air, Joseph could clearly make out a gang of men and women in front of the tables where money was exchanged and birds sold for sacrifice. Three of the tables were overturned and the contents strewn on the ground. Two of the tables belonged to Temple priests who made additional income by changing money for Israelite shekels. And the third table belonged to a Syrian merchant who paid for space to sell his spices and to act as a money-changer.

Mystified, Joseph looked more carefully at the interchange which was taking place between the priests, the money changer, and the leader of the rabble who had caused the mayhem. The priests had grabbed him by his cloak, and were shaking their fists at him, while the Syrian was on the floor, trying to retrieve his goods before people in the crowd helped themselves.

Yet the man, and it was too great a distance to see precisely who it was, wasn't fighting back. He was just standing them, speaking in what appeared to be a calm manner.

But Joseph had seen that man before; and the elderly woman who was standing beside him. Though she was bent from a lifetime of carrying and fetching, there was something proud about the way she was standing and facing the priests. She had no fear; she looked as confident as a celebrant before a congregation; she wasn't bowed into submission by the priests' authority.

His scalp tingled as a sudden fear spread through his body. The feelings which suffused him now were akin to those he'd felt when he'd met this boy, now a man, and his mother for the first time two decades earlier. He'd felt a prescience, a premonition, that these people would come back into his life to haunt him, and now they were here.

It was this heretic Jeshua; his mother Miriam. And an unholy group of followers who weren't in Jerusalem to celebrate the Passover, nor to worship in God's holy temple, but to upset the fine balance of his life and endanger the stability of priesthood which he loved with all his heart.

+

Miriam hadn't seen him as angry as this before. Always calm and placid, never showing his temper, she was stunned by the irritation in his voice. Although they were sitting in the cool shade of an inn on the outskirts of Jerusalem and slaking their thirsts with wine and pomegranate juice, Jeshua was still red-faced and incensed.

"I had every right to do what I did, Jeshua," said Peter. "You'd have been arrested and then where would we have been? And from what the priests were shouting at you, we'd have been arrested too. Do you want to see your beloved mother Miriam in prison?"

"Of course not," said Jeshua. "But to force me out of the Temple when I had only just begun my mission was wrong, Peter. That's why I was there."

"You didn't tell us you were going to cause mayhem, Jeshua. You didn't warn us that you were going to overturn the merchants' tables. If I'd known, my brother, I'd never have allowed you to go there. Not on a day when everybody is so tense and the guards are on notice from the authorities to arrest troublemakers."

"My brother, friends," said Jeshua, turning to the assembly of his apostles, "only I would have been taken by the guards. A stand had to be taken. My Father's house is no place for commerce and trade. How dare the priests allow money changers into its holy presence? Even if I had been arrested, they wouldn't have imprisoned me for long; not when I'd explained the reason that I was ridding the Temple of those people. Yes, they can continue their trade in the streets, but not inside the Temple. This is holy ground. Since the time of my ancestor, King David, and his son King Solomon the Wise, the land of the Temple has been holy. It was so holy and sacred that no Jew was permitted to cleanse the land of the pagan temple of the Canaanites who were there before. Men had to be called in from Lebanon before a Jew was allowed to tread upon its sacred soil.

"And that's why the priests in the Temple of today need to cleanse the holy site and made it fit for the worship of my people. And when that's done, the priests themselves, the Sadducees and the Pharisees, must go, leaving the Temple pure and untainted for those of us who have God in our hearts."

The group fell into silence, until Miriam said, "What you say, my beloved son, is true; but what Peter says is also true. These are perilous times, and tempers are short. If you'd been arrested and imprisoned, you might have been tried and, may God forgive these words, sentenced to death for disturbing the peace. You know what the Priests are like and they're in league with the Romans. And if that happened, what would become of us? Who would lead us? You can't be arrested. You are treading a path which is dangerous, and stumbling blocks are around every corner. Listen to Peter's counsel and protect yourself. I beg of you."

Jeshua rose from his seat and went to the front of the room. All turned towards him, waiting for him to speak.

"Mother, Peter, beloved followers...my apostles...I see looks of concern on your faces. And I, more than any other, understand your apprehensions. You would not be human, beloved of God our Father, were you not worried by what the future holds for us.

"But ask yourselves why I have called you my apostles. It is a word from the language of the Greeks, which means more than a messenger.

For all a messenger does is to carry a letter from one person to another. No, my beloveds, the true meaning of apostle, is one who is sent forth. And that is why you have been chosen.

"Yes, you are all apprehensive. But if you had stayed where I found you, some of you were toiling in the fields, some were fishermen, some were servants working in kitchens of rich people...had you still been there, you would be just as apprehensive of your futures. But think about your futures today, with me and your brothers and sisters. Where you came from, all you could do was to live to look forward to the next day. But with me, with your fellow apostles, you will be sent forth. You will carry my message to all of Israel. And if I am not here to help you, if I am arrested, as Peter fears so greatly, then you will be my messengers. You will carry my words to all corners of Israel. You will cause the people of Israel to rise up, and to cleanse the Temple of its rotten core.

"I may be arrested. I may be imprisoned. And yes, I may even be stoned to death or sold into slavery. But unlike all others, my friends, my death will have as much meaning as my life. For not only will I live eternally in the arms of my father Yahweh, but my words, sent forth through your mouths, mean that from this moment and forever, God and our Temple will be returned to His people and holiness will return to the land he swore unto our fathers he would give us. When my message becomes known, and the Jewish people rise up against the tyranny of the Sadducees and the Pharisees, the true enemies of the Children of God, then my Father Yahweh will return to this city and to this land, and sit eternally as our judge, our guide and our conscience. And it has already begun. Today, I overturned the tables of the money changers and the sellers of trinkets. Tomorrow I will preach at the gates which lead worshippers into the Temple courtyard and warn them of the horrors within which will offend their eyes. And soon, maybe after next Sabbath, I will enter the Temple and preach at the footsteps which lead up to the Holy of Holies and demand that the Priests come out and answer my accusations about their harlotry of our faith."

The apostles sat and looked at him in silence. Never before had he spoken of his death or the life his words would have when he was gone. All of them had assumed, when they'd willingly joined this most charismatic and seductive of men, that they were beginning a journey which would last for their lifetimes. They'd given up their work, their families, their possessions, to join a man who was unlike any other preacher they'd ever met; a man who had he answers to the questions they dared not ask themselves; a man who talked of a future free of servitude, free of pain and heartache, perhaps in this life or perhaps in the next, but something which would, without question, happen. And now he was talking about his death, leaving them...alone.

Stunned, they looked at each other, then round at his mother Miriam, whose face had turned white in shock. They looked back at Jeshua, but it was as though he wasn't present, as if he was in another place, another world. He was smiling, but he was looking up at the ceiling of the inn, as though he could see a vision which none of them could see.

It took Judas to ask the question which was on everybody's mind. "Brother Jeshua, you say that the Sadducees and the Pharisees are our enemy. Yes, they have perverted our faith and they must be replaced. But everybody knows it's the Romans who are the enemy of the Jews. It's the Romans who have their feet on our throat."

Jeshua turned and looked at the young man who came from Karioth, and smiled at him. "Oh Judas. You of little faith. Do you not know your holy book? Have you not understood the history of your people? In the past, since the time of our Father Moses, has not Yahweh always come to the aid of His people in times of trouble? Today is no different from when Moses led the Children of Israel into the wilderness of the Sinai and freedom from the enslavement of the Pharaohs. And so it will happen today. Do you not understand that God will smite the Romans, as he smote all of Israel's enemies from the time of the Egyptians to the time of the Greeks? As He will smite the Romans when the Holy land of Israel is freed from the grasp of the Priests and their Levite acolytes. How can our Father rid us of the Romans, when His land is occupied already by Jews who pervert His word and turned His people away from Him?"

Close to tears, Miriam asked, "But why does that mean that you must risk your life, Jeshua? Surely, if we worship Yahweh with an open heart and with true faith, He will come back to Israel and smite our foes. Why do you have to...to..."

She buried her head in her hands and sobbed quietly. Jeshua looked at her, pain etching his expression. "Mother...dearest mother... you gave me the most precious gift one person can give another, the gift of life. But no gift is forever, and no life is eternal. I do not hurry to my death, for there is so much I have to do, but I am in the loving hands of my Father Yahweh. And if my death can hasten a better world, then Yahweh will decide. He will decree and I will follow. But Yahweh has spoken to me in my prayers, and He has told me not to hide or skulk in the shadows like a frightened mouse as so many of our people are forced to do. Nor is there great danger in what I am doing, because my fight isn't with the Roman authorities, but with the Temple and those who pretend to serve God, while serving only themselves. If I come before the Romans, I will tell them that while ever they are masters in this land, then what is due to Caesar shall be rendered to Caesar. But what is God's, shall surely be rendered to God, and not to His priests. The Romans can have no cause for anger at me, and if I am able, I will tell them of the abuse which the Priests of the Temple are causing to the Israelite people...who are part of their empire...by their hubris."

Mary of Magdala shook her head, and said quietly, "No, my brother Jeshua, you are so very wrong. You expect the Romans to listen to your arguments with sympathy and understanding. You expect them to be like us, like normal people. But look at who the Romans are! Look at what they've achieved in conquering the world. They've enslaved all the nations of their empire; they rape the land, the women, and even little boys and girls; they enslave us, send us to the furthest corners of their empire, and leave those of us who remain in our lands without food, without money and without hope.

"And you think that these are the men who will listen to your voice of reason and do as you wish? Brother Jeshua, if you go before the Romans, you will go in chains. You will be humiliated, lashed, tortured. You may be enslaved or, God forbid, crucified for treason. Do you think that the Priests in their Temple aren't in league with the Prefect Pontius Pilate and his men? And when you're dragged before them, charged by the Temple with the crimes of sacrilege and disturbance, do you really think that those Jews who are servants of the Romans will allow you to speak?

"I'm begging of you, Jeshua, for the sake of your beloved mother Miriam and your followers and friends, for the sake of the message you have to bring to the Children of Israel, do not return to the Temple; do not anger the authorities; instead, do as you told us you would do when we were all in the Galilee...preach in synagogues and in private houses against the wickedness of the priests. Make the people rise up against those who have taken our faith from us. Go out into the community and spread your beautiful message on street corners, so that you don't come to the attention of the authorities. But don't try to pull down the walls of the Temple, for no single man can do that."

Jeshua nodded, and smiled. "Not a single man, my sister Mary. But God can. And God guides my hand and gives strength to my arm. Was it not Moses, whose strong hand and outstretched arm, guided by the Almighty, conquered the Egyptian army? Did not Joshua stop the sun in its path over Gibeon and the moon over the city of Aijalon? And if we read the words of the prophet Daniel, were not Shadrach, Meshach and Abed-nego saved from Babylon's fiery furnace? So too, I, Jeshua of Nazareth, have had my hand strengthened by Yahweh, and he is supporting my outstretched arm, and with my Father Yahweh's help, I will bring down the walls of this Temple, and set my people free."

In the silence which followed, the only noise which could be heard was Miriam, gently sobbing into her hands. Feeling desperately sorry for her distress, Jeshua was forced to tell her the entire truth of what he was planning.

"And mother, dearest mother, today's visit to the Temple was just the beginning. For tomorrow, despite your concerns and Peter's and the other's misgivings, we will return and create even greater to the money changers and sellers of sacrifice. Today was just a test. Nobody saw us properly, for our faces were hidden by our prayer shawls. But tomorrow, we will return in the early hours of the morning, and this time, we will cause a disturbance which will be heard throughout the whole of Israel, and for the rest of time."

The others listened in silence. Peter shook his head in dismay.

As the sun was rising above the mountains of Moab, and illuminating the rooftops and watchtowers above the city of Jerusalem so that they glowed in the pre-dawn like candles, Jeshua, Peter, Judas, Simon and the others walked in the shadows of houses until they were in sight of the outer walls of the Temple of Herod. The vast blocks of white stone were already luminous in the early light of the day, and the blistering heat which the walls retained from the previous day radiated into the cold hilltop air.

Soon, when the sun was well above the tops of the distant mountains, the Temple guards would open the gates to allow worshippers into the courtyard. Those who were queuing up had come early because they wanted to purchase the freshest doves and the plumpest pigeons, so that the Almighty, Blessed be He, would smile in appreciation of their sacrifices.

As Jeshua and his followers stood in the shadows, watching the entry door, twelve merchants arrived, their bags carried by their guards. From their weight, it was obvious that the bags were bursting with coins recently purchased from the mint of Israel. These Jewish coins would be used in exchange for currency from other nations which carried a human image, and so unable to be used in the Temple.

The merchants imperiously knocked on the huge wooden doors, which were opened in order to admit them so they could set up their tables in preparation for the day's trade. The moment the twelve were admitted, the door was immediately closed again. Jeshua looked at his colleagues, and said softly, "Now you see the face of our enemy's collaborators. But these merchants are not our enemy, for they only do the work which the priests will not allow to soil their hands. Yet they are happy to take the profits from the desecration of my father's house. When the priests have been driven out of the Temple, the money they put into their pockets will go, instead, to the widows and orphans who are in desperate need. Remember that, my brothers when we enter the Temple and do our work. These men are merchants, but they are only conducting their business, so they are not to be harmed. You know why we're here."

The others nodded, and continued to look at the door, waiting for them to open and admit the worshippers so they could purchase their sacrifices.

More and more Jewish men and women, some from Jerusalem and some, from their clothes, from other towns and cities who had journeyed to the holy city for the festival of the Passover, joined the crowd. Although the sun was still low over the Mountains of Moab, the heat and growing noise in the city was oppressive. Jerusalem always became crowded in this time of the celebration of the Passover, the festival of the Father's liberation of the Jews from slavery, but this year, there seemed to be vastly more people than ever before. Perhaps because of the brutality of the Roman rule, the Jews were crying out for the Lord to again intervene on behalf of his chosen people and liberate them from their oppressors.

And then, with the sound of trumpets from the parapet on top of the walls, the huge gates were opened, and the crowd began streaming in. Jeshua immediately joined the throng walking across the street in order to gain entry into the Temple. The others followed quickly so that they didn't lose their master in the press.

It had been five days since the mass of pilgrims began the Passover celebrations, and by this time, the Temple guards on the gate were so bored with the never-ending throng, that they barely looked at the faces of the men, women and children who were streaming into the courtyards. Only the guards at the top of the steps which led into the Temple itself, were more careful as to who they allowed across the portal.

Jeshua and the other men walked through the vast cedar doors of the Temple and were quickly surrounded by a huge press of people. They forced a way through the crowd towards the south eastern corner, where most of the traders and merchants and money changers had set up their stalls. As the men pushed their way through, the concentration of the worshippers grew so that they had to push and shove their way past, earning themselves angry looks and comments.

But eventually Jeshua was close to the carts where the merchants were desperately trying to satisfy the demands of the throng. At one of the stalls, dozens of men holding coins in their outstretched hands were pointing at caged pigeons, doves, geese and newly-born lambs, shouting at the merchants to sell them something which they particularly wanted. The cart on the left to the trader was owned by a money-changer, sitting on a stool beneath an awning shade, and guarded by two huge Nubian men whose eyes never left the piles of coins on the table, ensuring that no pilgrim was able to reach across and help himself to money to which he wasn't entitled to.

Further away to the east were more tables, these selling trinkets such as dolls in the shape of lambs and cows, or replicas of the scrolls which were used by the priests to tell the people the words of the Prophet Moses.

The trade was more than brisk; it was bordering on frantic. People were pushing and shoving to get to the front edge of the tables and carts so that they could buy what they wanted in order to make a supplication to Yahweh. The money changers were busy looking carefully at which coins they were offered in exchange for shekels, in case the coins were counterfeit. Even when they were satisfied and exchanged the coins for money which could be used in the Temple, often the transaction didn't end there. The worshipper would take the Israeli money, count it, and then complain that it wasn't enough.

But the money-changer never engaged in an argument. Instead, one of his Nubian guards would lift his hand, reach across the table, and push the pilgrim away; and the men who worked for the money-changer were so enormous, like Goliath who'd fought against King David, that the pilgrim turned and left, often muttering in discontent under his breath.

Suddenly, in the heat and noise of the trading area, Jeshua felt a hand on his shoulder and a voice in his ear.

"The size of those guards," whispered Peter. "They'll break you in two if you chose to argue with a money-changer. Better to take our quarrel against those who sell sacrificial animals."

Jeshua nodded in agreement. When his only weapons were words, he looked at the swords and knives which the guards carried on their person and realized that these were not men against whom he could win an argument. So he pushed his way to the front of the throng, earning snarls and angry words from those he'd moved aside, and was suddenly facing the merchant. The man looked red-faced from the noise, the heat and the dust, and was already impatient, although he'd only recently begun his day's trade.

"Well? Yes? Which animal do you want?" the merchant asked. "I want no animal," said Jeshua. Irritated, the merchant said, "Then step aside and let others make their choices." "Do you take money from those whose only desire is to worship Yahweh?" "What? Look, move off and let others..." "Why do you offend Yahweh by trading in His house?" asked Jeshua. "Why do I...? What are you talking about. Go away." "It offends my Father that you tarnish the glory of His Temple by common trading.

Do you not realize that to buy and sell goods, children's toys, change money is an transgression on Yahweh's...?"

"If you don't leave, I'll call the guards and have you taken away," shouted the merchant. "You're stopping other people from buying. Now go away, or else..."

Others were now looking in his direction and wondering why he was suddenly shouting at a customer. Even the money-changers, concentrating on their counting and their coins, looked over to see what was happening.

And when Jeshua reached down, with Peter on one side of the table, he in the center and Judas on the other side, and overturned it, scattering the cages of the birds and lambs all over the ground, the merchant let out a shriek.

Quickly, before anybody reacted to what they'd just done, the three men moved to the east, and without talking to the merchant, overturned his table of trinkets; then others in their party pushed their way through the crowds and overturned three other tables, full of merchandise, animals and trinkets.

Now there were yells of anger, fury and wrath. The merchants were struggling to keep their animals from escaping as their cages tumbled to the floor and broke open; pilgrims tried to stop Jeshua's followers from the destruction they were wreaking, but they were quick in accomplishing their allotted tasks, and the people were too surprised to react as they should have.

By the time seven of the merchant's tables had been overturned, Peter looked around and saw that there was a movement in the crowd from another corner of the Temple courtyard. Knowing that it was the guards who were pushing their way through the crowds as they reacted to the sudden disturbance, he shouted out, "Leave!" and the party of followers all pushed their ways roughly through the crowds and towards the cedar wood gate which led from the Temple into Jericho Road. The guards who had once been stationed on the doors had left their posts to push their way through to where the noise and shouting was happening, and so it was easy for Jeshua and his followers to leave the precincts of the Temple and escape into the narrow streets of the city.

Far from the Temple precincts, Jeshua and his colleagues didn't see the reaction to their sabotage at the courtyard. Instead, they sat and quietly drank at an inn on the road which led to Bethlehem, not daring to speak openly in case they were overheard, but inwardly congratulating themselves on striking such a decisive blow for the Lord.

+

But Joseph bar Kayafa, High Priest of Jerusalem knew who had disturbed the otherwise orderly rituals of the Temple and caused a commotion which prevented many worshippers from attending the morning prayers, an important ceremony to usher in the Passover. Whoever had done it the previous day had had the audacity to return, and repeat his criminal act. It was Jeshua, the Nazarene. And he would suffer for disturbing the peace and sanctity of the Temple.

As Joseph looked out of the upper casement window of his office when he heard the sudden disturbance below, even before he'd stood up from his desk, his every instinct confirmed to him that the troublemaker, Jeshua, son of Yosef of the town of Nazareth, was the cause and the instigator.

Up until this moment, Jeshua had used words and logic to prosecute his case for reform of the Temple. Words were something against which Joseph the priest could argue. But this was a step too far. Just as the old emperor Julius Caesar had crossed the River Rubicon, casting his dice and plunged Rome into civil war, Jeshua's assault on the sanctity of the Holy Temple threatened to plunge Israel into a war against itself. And if one section of the Israelite people were fighting against another section, it would provide an ideal opportunity for the Prefect, Pilate, to bring troops from Syria and destroy the Jewish nation altogether, something which the High Priest knew that he was hoping to do, if only to satisfy the demands of Sejanus. Unable to quell the Zealots, an uprising would be the excuse he required. Then he could return to Rome from a land he'd emptied of people and be appointed to another post.

So Joseph had to act, and act swiftly before these radical Nazarenes did something else which would cause people to rise up in righteous fury. Without waiting for the Captain of the Temple guards to report to him, he put on his cloak, and prepared to leave the Temple by the Levite's Gate. He would walk swiftly to the Praetorium of the Antonine Fortress, near to the Pool of Bathesda, and demand...yes, demand...an audience with Pontius Pilate.

The gentle words and calm persuasion of past encounters with the Prefect had run their course, and failed. Now it was time for swift action, and if that resulted in these stupid, heretical radicals suffering beatings, or torture or even death by stoning, then so be it. But one thing which Joseph would not do, and that was to arrest Jeshua himself. Though he had the power to arrest and try this heretic for his assault on the trade of the Temple, to do so would cause terrible unrest and division, and drive a wedge even further between the Priesthood and the people. No, this had to be an arrest of Rome, caused by a disturbance of the peace against the authority of the Emperor of Rome. Which meant that he and his fellow priests would be absolved of blame and punishment would be Roman, and not Jewish.

The sound could be heard from three streets away. When Jews walked, if there was any noise, it was the sound of the softness of leather shoes on compacted earth, accompanied by the gentle swish of cloaks. When Romans walked, especially a Century of Roman soldiers, marching in formation behind a Centurion on a horse, it was the angry sound of iron, the clanking of swords against scabbards, and the staccato beating of spears against metal shields designed to put the fear of Minerva and Mars into their enemies.

But as the eight men sat in the inn, praying in silence after their midday meal, the sound they heard was of a horse whinnying and feet marching towards them. This was no military machine come to do battle. This was a troop of Roman soldiers, come to arrest them, but in numbers sufficient to prevent any neighbors from coming to their aid.

Peter, Judas, James and Simon looked up in alarm. All eyes were suddenly on Jeshua. But when he opened his eyes, he merely smiled, and said softly, "They have come for me. They will not take you, for they know that I am the leader and they think that if they take me, then our mission will fall apart and you will disappear like a morning mist.

"But how little they know. Even with my departure, they don't realize that you will carry my words to Jericho and Bethlehem, Ashdod and even as far as Acco. And who knows, my brothers and sisters, if you have the strength, perhaps even beyond to the communities of Jews who live in Lebanon and Syria and Egypt. For even with my arrest, we have begun something which now cannot be stopped. The people of Israel have been shown what their faith should be. Yahweh, my father, has ordained that this day, and forever, the rule of the priests of the Temple will come to an end, and the true faith will flourish, like flowers in a spring meadow. The people will have back their faith, as Yahweh intended when he gave the ten commandments to Father Moses on the mountain of Sinai, and he told the people that they must obey God's laws. God entrusted the people with faith in Him, and the priests like Aaron and those who followed were nothing more than guides and teachers. If Moses was a leader of our people, he was like the sun, whose brilliance blinded us to all else; yet after he died, Yahweh entrusted the Jewish people to the leadership of Aaron, who was like the moon...we knew of his presence as a light above us, but he allowed the stars to shine brightly, each star being a Jewish man or woman, with none being brighter than the other.

"Our priests have become the sun, blinding us to all else and not allowing any of us to act and do and be...they control, they command, and they have taken our faith from us. But no more. Today, we have begun the battle to rescue our faith from the tyranny of the priests. We are the cold light of the moon. We're visible to all, but we permit the individual stars, the children of Israel, to shine as individuals."

They listened carefully to what Jeshua was saying, but despite his words, the others were growing in fear and trepidation as the sound of a column of men marching towards them, grew louder and louder. And then it stopped. The Romans were at the door to the inn, and the other patrons looked around in concern.

The door suddenly burst open, and standing in the doorway, though obscured by the sudden blinding light, was a huge man. He stood there for enough moments for him to know that all the customers in the inn were suddenly alarmed and intimidated, before he said in a stentorian voice, "Nazarene! Jeshua the Nazarene. Stand and come with me."

The other customers immediately looked towards the table where Jeshua and his colleagues were sitting. Nobody moved. The silence in the room spoke of their fears and the terror they felt. And then slowly, a slightly built tall man stood up from the table. Softly, in contrast to the booming voice of the Centurion, he said, "I am the man you seek. What do you want with me?"

The Centurion looked at him, and said, "I have orders to take you to the Prefect of Judea. Come with me immediately."

"Why am I being brought before him?" Jeshua asked.

"You don't asked questions. You do what you're told, Jew. Now come with me immediately."

The Centurion turned and went back to his troop, who were waiting in two straight lines, backs to each other, with their spears angled outwards to intimidate any crowd which might gather to oppose them. But anybody who was on the street had disappeared immediately they heard the marching footsteps of the Century coming towards them. The road to and from the inn was deserted.

The Centurion waited by his horse until Jeshua emerged, shielding his eyes from the brilliant early afternoon sun which was beginning its descent into the distant waters of HaYam HaGadol, the sea which the Romans said was at the center of the earth and which they called in their tongue the Mare Interim, the Mediterranean.

He was suddenly surrounded by the 80 Roman soldiers who immediately went into formation so that he was forced to walk in the middle of the two ranks of men. Then the Centurion mounted his horse, and began the slow march up the hills and back into the city proper of Jerusalem, where he would hand over the prisoner to the keeper of the Antonine Fortress and be done with him. Then he could return to his game of Ludus Aleae, which he'd been forced to abandon when the commander of the fortress had ordered him to take a Century of troops and go to arrest this prisoner. The dice were falling in his favor and he fancied that he'd win tonight.

Miriam, mother of an imprisoned son, sat in silence as she was told the news by her friend, Mary of Magdala, of Jeshua's arrest. When Mary had finished telling her of Jeshua's bravery in front of the Centurion and how her son had protected his followers from arrest, the mother merely sat and stared out of the window.

"Beloved friend, did you hear what I said?" she asked of Miriam. "Our leader, Jeshua, your son, has been arrested."

Again, there was no movement in her body or face, not even a flicker of concern, the creasing of her forehead, the raising of an eyebrow. Just a blank stare, as if she was deaf to all outside influences.

"Miriam? Is there anything I can do?" Then Miriam's eyes flickered, and slowly, she turned to face Mary. "And so it begins," Jeshua's mother said softly. "And so it begins." Mary smiled, and placed a hand on Miriam's arm. "It's all a mistake. They couldn't know that it was Jeshua who led the assault on the Temple. Nobody was there to identify him, and his followers pulled him away before the guards arrived. His arrest is a co-incidence, I'm certain. Without proof, the Prefect won't be able to do anything, and I'm certain that our beloved Jeshua will soon be back with us."

Miriam looked at her friend, and smiled. "I will go to him. He is in the Roman garrison, and so I will go to him."

"No! You mustn't. It'll only endanger you. Wait here for his release. It'll only be a day, or a few days at the most."

Miriam stood, and began to walk towards the door. Mary stood, and shouted, "Don't! Don't go, Miriam. You'll be arrested. You know the Romans. Cause them any problems, and we'll never see you again."

But she left the inn and hurried in the late afternoon heat up the hills towards the gate in the walls of Jerusalem. By the time she was inside the city, she was out of breath and sweating in her haste. She stopped at a water station, and drank greedily from the chained cup. With, her breath returning, Miriam hurried further up the hills, through the narrow laneways crowded with men and women, towards the Pool of Bathesda, and the Praetorium of the Antonine Fortress. It was close to the Jaffa Gate on the opposite side of the city, which meant that she had to wind her way through the streets and brush past the throng of traders and shoppers and men with huge flasks on their backs, selling pomegranate and orange juice to thirsty wanderers. But eventually, she stood in awe as she looked up at the massive stones which were the walls of the fortress.

She was so anxious, she didn't even realize how nervous she had suddenly become. But when she came to the vast wooden gates of the Fortress, the height of three men, guarded by a dozen Roman soldiers, she suddenly realized how foolhardy she had been. Yet inside this place was her son. And in all their lives, from the day of his birth to the day of his arrest, they had never been separated. Not when she was still married to Yosef of Nazareth; not when they'd escaped the madness of Herod and lived all those years in Egypt; not when she was a widow and Jeshua had urged her to come with him into the deserts beside the Dead Sea and live among the Essenes; and certainly not now, when he was alone in a Roman prison cell.

She gathered up her courage, took several deep breaths, and in the deepening shadows as evening came upon the city, walked up to one of the guards. He looked at her in suspicion, even though he towered over her. His pilum was planted in the ground and stood vertically in his hand. She glanced above his head at its tip, the sharp, vicious spear rising high above her head into the darkening sky. He carried a shield to protect his body.

"Well?"

"I wish to see my son. He was arrested by your men earlier today, outside the walls of Jerusalem and brought here after the noonday meal. I am his mother. I want to see him."

The soldier continued to look at her, saying nothing. His fixed stare undermined what little confidence she tried to exude.

"May I go through the gate?" "No. Go away," he said curtly.

She stood her ground, took a deep breath and said, "I am his mother. You cannot separate a man from his mother. If you were in prison, wouldn't your mother want to see you?"

"Don't talk about my mother. But if you're that keen to see him, then go to the gate and speak to the Tesserarius who's just coming on duty for the night."

Having no idea to what the guard was referring, Miriam walked uncertainly from the guard to the small door in the large wooden gate, and there found a man in a senior Roman uniform. His back was turned to her, speaking to another soldier, but as she approached, he turned, and looked at her.

"Yes? What do you want here?" he asked. His voice, his language was more refined than the other soldier, and Miriam suddenly felt more confident.

"Sir, are you the headman of this fort?"

He smiled. "No, my rank is Tesserarius. I'm the night watch commander. What do you want here?"

And Miriam explained why she wanted to see her son.

The Tesserarius listened, and nodded. "Yes, I know of this Jeshua from Nazareth. He's in a cell in the Northern tower. The Day Watch Commander told me of his arrest. But you can't see him. I'm sorry. I know you're his mother, but the High Priest of the Temple, Joseph bar Kayafa, was here this afternoon, and after he'd left, the Prefect issued an order that no person is allowed to see the prisoner. He's to be tried by Pilate tomorrow morning for treason and sedition. I'm very sorry. I suggest you go home, and pray for his soul."

Miriam looked at the Commander, trying to comprehend what his words meant. She'd rushed here assuming that she'd talk to people, make them understand that Jeshua was a good and God-fearing man, and return with him. But this man was talking about a trial. For treason. And then the enormity of what he'd just said seeped into her conscious mind. It was so hot. The sun was merciless. And the stench of the city suddenly became overwhelming. She tried to breathe, but suddenly found that she couldn't. And as she looked at the Tesserarius, he seemed to enter and leave her focus. Until everything was suddenly very distant and black.

The men ran to her assistant and on the orders of the Night Watch Commander, carried her inside the Fortress, laying her down in the Watch Commander's cubicle inside the gate. It was a small room, with just a chair and a table, but the Tesserarius cleared the table of its scrolls, inks and wax tablets, and lay the aged woman on top. He raised her head slightly, and poured a drink of water into her pallid lips.

Slowly, her eyelids flickered, and she blinked to try to focus on where she was. Then she stared up into the face of the Commander, and frowned.

"I'm so sorry, your Excellency. I don't know...I must have..."

"You fainted, Lady. I'm sorry to have delivered the news to you, but it caused you to collapse. Sit in this office quietly for a few minutes, and continue to drink water. Then when you're feeling better, I'll have some men escort you to where you live."

He turned, and began to leave the room, when Miriam said, "Sir. Please. Don't go."

She struggled to sit up, and said to him, "You seem a kindly man. I am a mother. My son is in your prison. He will be frightened. You said he will be tried by your Prefect. But why? What has he done? I don't understand any of this."

"Lady, from what I've been told, your son committed wanton destruction in the Temple yonder," he said, pointing to the East. "He assaulted people, and in the company of others, behaved in a treasonous manner, against the rightful peace and tranquility of the Empire. For that offence against the rule of Rome, he will be sentenced to death. I'm sorry. The trial will be tomorrow, and the sentence will be carried out immediately thereafter. I'm truly sorry, but you have to accept Roman justice and that means obeying Roman rule."

She shook her head. "I'm not an educated woman, Excellency, but surely the Sanhedrin court of the Holy Temple must try him. If he did what you say, then he did it on Temple grounds, where the High Priest is in command. It's for the High Priest to try him. Isn't it?"

The Tesserarius shrugged. "Perhaps. But the High Priest came here today to speak with our Prefect, and he's handed the matter to Pontius Pilate. That is his right. So the trial will take place according to Roman justice and Roman rule. I don't know why your *Pontifex Maximus* made that decision, but there it is. And unfortunately for your son, Lady, there will be no difference in the outcome. Whether we Romans send him into the arena to fight a Gladiator or against wild beasts, or whether we have him crucified, or if your High Priest has him stoned to death under Jewish law, he will just as surely die. He committed crimes in your Temple, and for that he must pay the price. As a Jewish peasant, he'll probably be crucified, as we crucify thieves and robbers, in order to warn others not to raise their fists against the majesty of Rome.

"I'm truly sorry, Lady, but soon your son will be dead, and the sooner you accept that, the better it will be for you. For him, there's no hope. Now, I have to get on with my duties." He left the office, and she heard him give orders for his men to watch over her, and then to escort her back to where she came from.

The Hill of the Skull, outside the walls of the City of Jerusalem, the following afternoon

Her heart was almost breaking as she ascended the hill. Mary of Magdala, who accompanied her, turned and looked over Jerusalem, seeing its towers and roofs standing proudly against the white stones from which the city was constructed. On the horizon, to the North, were black clouds which presaged a thunderstorm. Gathering her breath from the climb, she turned back to look at the top of the hill, where the crucifixes had been planted.

It was a hideous place, used by the Romans for their many executions, tortures, strangulations and crucifixions. Since the beginning of their occupation a hundred years ago, so many Jews had been crucified or otherwise killed up here that the people had renamed it the Hill of the Skulls. Forbidden to gather their dead and allow them a ritual burial in greater abuse of the rights of their faith and those they had killed, the Roman authorities simply cut down the bodies of the crucified, threw them on the ground, and let them rot, food for dogs and birds.

Mary looked at Miriam's back as she paced up the hill to see if she could tend to the needs of her son Jeshua. She had to catch up with her, because she didn't want her to arrive at her son's dying body without the comfort of a friend to share in the misery. Looking upwards to the crown of the hill, Jeshua could be seen, along with some other Jews who had been found guilty of some crime and were being crucified alongside him. His body was limp on the cross, hanging down, held in place only by the cruel nails which had been driven through his wrists and ankles. His body twitched from time to time, but Mary was sure that the pain of the nails, and the feeling of drowning because he couldn't breathe properly, had caused him to faint.

Mary walked quickly, and caught up with her friend. "Dearest..." she said to Miriam, but then couldn't think of anything else to say. Miriam turned as she walked, and smiled. "We must be strong for him," she said, panting. "If we show distress, it'll distress him more in these final moments." Mary nodded.

Then Miriam asked, "Do you know how long a man can survive. How long before Yahweh shows mercy and takes his soul?"

"They say that some strong men can last a day, sometimes two. But most faint with the pain, and water fills their lungs and death soon takes them."

Miriam nodded, and slowed her pace. As the two women walked up the hill, they saw that a soldier had been positioned beside the dying men in order to prevent friends or relatives from taking down the prisoners before they died and absconding with them.

By the time they reached the top of the hill, they were both out of breath. They looked up at Jeshua, whose eyes were closed and whose body hung limp on the cross, straining against the nails which held him in place on the upright and the crossbeams. His arrest, his secret trial, his humiliation and now his crucifixion, suddenly impinged themselves upon Miriam's mind. She stood there, looking up at her son's comatose body. Mary stood beside her, knowing to say nothing, but to let the enormity of this moment settle on Miriam's head.

The silence of the afternoon was interrupted by the soldier saying, "What do you women want here? Leave immediately. Nobody is allowed on this hill."

Mary said, "We are friends of this man," pointing to the cross upon which Jeshua was affixed. "This lady is his mother. She has come to see if she can ease his agony."

"This isn't a place for a mother. He'll die soon enough. Go back down and grieve for him in private. There's nothing you can do for him."

Miriam looked at the soldier, and, as she'd asked the guard at the Antonia Fortress the previous day, said, "If you were nailed to the cross, surely you'd want some relief from your mother. Wouldn't you, soldier?"

He remained silent, looking at the two women, knowing that they were no danger to him. Then he said, "I never knew my mother. She died giving birth to me. But yes, I suppose that if I were a criminal and was condemned to death by the Prefect, I would want my mother to be here."

From the cross, Jeshua, his eyes still closed, and his body still wracked in pain, moaned. Perhaps, in his unconsciousness, he'd heard his mother's voice.

"Is there nothing you can do, Soldier, to help my son? Please! Help relieve the suffering and the pain."

The soldier looked at the grieving woman, their faces gaunt and drawn, and thought back to the kindly aunt who'd taken him in and been a mother to him in the early years of his life.

"I'm sorry, Lady. I'm not allowed to..." "Please!" begged Miriam, beginning to sob. "Please..." Taking pity, he said, "All I can do is to hasten his death." Mary said, "That will ease his burden, and ours." The soldier nodded, and walked the few paces to Jeshua's body. His head sagging in unconsciousness, his wrists no longer bleeding from the wounds of the nails, his entire body was suspended on the cross. Occasionally, they saw his chest suddenly rise as he tried to gasp for breath against the weight of his body and the fluid which had filled his lungs. Although neither woman had witnessed a crucifixion, they knew instinctively that Jeshua was drowning in his own body fluids, and that death would not be long.

The soldier sighed as he saw the grief and horror on the women's faces, looked down the hill to make sure that nobody could witness what he was about to do, and took a few paces to his right. Holding his long pilum in both hands, he positioned the spear so that it was touching the man's ribcage, and then sharply thrust it upwards, so that it entered his lungs. Blood and other liquids spurted out of the wound, and the soldier withdrew the spear. Turning to the two women, he said, "Death will be very soon, now. You should go down to the city. I will call men to help me take down his body."

Mary and Miriam nodded. Then Miriam said, "Thank you for easing my son's pain. I will pray for you tonight, soldier. What is your name?"

"Spurius Lucianus Balbus, Lady. They called me Balbus because as a child I lisped, and the name stuck."

She nodded in gratitude. It was the first time she'd felt even the semblance of relief since she'd been escorted back to her lodgings from the Fortress the previous day. "Then, Spurius Lucianus, I will ask my Jewish God Yahweh to hasten your return to your homeland and to your family."

Miriam closed her eyes, facing the dying body of her son, and silently entreated Yahweh to hasten his death and the end of his suffering, and take his soul up into the heavens.

Then, sobbing, she turned, and walked slowly down the hill. Mary followed in her footsteps.

CHAPTER TWENTY ONE

An inn on the outskirts of Jerusalem, the following afternoon

She knew he was dead, and on the previous evening, when she'd returned from the Hill of the Skull, drenched to the skin because of the torrential thunderstorm, she'd immediately begun the mourning ritual. Miriam had wanted so desperately to honor her son's memory by burying him, as she'd buried her husband Yosef so long ago. She'd wanted to have his family or friends carry his body on a pallet, clothed in pure white with his prayer shawl wrapped around him, intertwined in the folds with spices such as myrrh, Frankincense and aloes. He'd be carried to the family burial cave outside the city of Nazareth, and there he'd be entombed with his family's ancestors, so that his soul would be in the company of his family and his people. It was necessary for him to be buried with his people. She recalled the words of the old man, Barzillai of Gilead, friend of King David, who refused to journey with him because he was close to death and wanted to die in his own city beside the grave of his father and mother.

But then in shame and greater grief, Miriam remembered that a lifetime ago, she had given birth to Jeshua, and that Yosef wasn't his father, but even though she remained a virgin, it was the fluids from the young lad from Sephoris, the city of her birth, which had given her Jeshua. And now she was so much older, the lad's name escaped her.

Entering the inn, she had found a low stool to sit upon, and scooped ashes from the cold fire, and spread them on her forehead and cheeks to show the world that she was a mother, mourning for her dead son. But where was her son's body? It should have been washed by the women of the town, cleansed of impurities so that it met Yahweh in a state of purity; then wrapped in white linen, then his prayer shawl, and then the rich spices and perfumes spread over to ensure his loving acceptance by the Lord.

But Miriam knew, with a dreadful certainty, that her son's dead body was lying on the cold wet earth of the Hill of the Skull, filthy from yesterday's rains, his raiment sodden, covered in mud and slime.

And that his flesh was, even now, being torn to pieces by dogs and mountain lions and carrion eating vultures; like the vultures she'd always feared when she was a young girl and knew that these evil birds presaged the death of a hapless animal.

So she sat there on her low stool, as Jeshua's friends and followers, and even strangers in the inn where she was staying came up to her and said a prayer for the dead as they stood before her.

Those who had followed him since he and Miriam had emerged from their seclusion among the Essenes on the shores of the Dead Sea, people like Peter and Judas, Mark and Phillip, Matthew and Mary of Magdala all came and sat with her. Even the men, rugged fishermen or farmers, had tears in their eyes, and Mary could barely restrain herself from weeping.

As she sat on her stool, morose and tearful and contemplating her future, she noticed that the other men in Jeshua's circle of followers were sometimes huddling in a corner of the inn, deep in conversation. It happened several times during the day after her son had been crucified, as well as on the following day.

When Mary came to sit with her on the morning of the third day of her bereavement, Miriam whispered into her ear, "Why are they speaking in whispers? What are they talking about?"

"Beloved, don't concern yourself with these things at a time like this. King Solomon the Wise said we should not mourn too long and be fixed in our grief. And in our blessed book of Koheleth, did not the son of King David say that one generation passes away and another generation comes, but the earth abides forever?"

Miriam nodded, and said, "And in that same book, did not the sages say that there is a time to be born and a time to die? What son dies before his mother? What is the righteousness in Yahweh taking my son Jeshua from me before I'm too old to live?"

"Dearest friend," said Mary, "in that book, does it not say also that there is a time to weep and a time to laugh; a time to mourn and a time to dance? Now is your time to weep, to mourn. Soon enough will come time to ask what these men are talking about, and why they're whispering. Today, your only task is to sit on a low stool, covered in ashes, and remember our beloved Jeshua."

"Yes," said Miriam. "He was our beloved, for he belonged to us all. His goodness, kindness and brilliance were the sun which showed us the path through the darkness of this world."

Mary reached over and kissed her on the cheek. She uttered a small prayer for Miriam's continued health and strength, and then withdrew to leave the mother to her thoughts about her dead son.

When she'd gone, Peter, the follower closest to Jeshua, came and sat beside her. "Dear friend, how is it with you?"

Miriam shrugged. "As you would expect," she said softly.

Peter nodded. "Miriam, I need to tell you something, to bring a little brightness into the dark world you're living in. I know you've been observing me, Judas, Simon, Matthew and the others talking on the other side of the room. And I know that you've been curious about what we've been saying to each other. The question foremost in our minds, now that our beloved leader has been gathered into the bosom of Yahweh, is what will become of the things which he has taught us? With his death, does that mean we can no longer cleanse the Temple of the evil which pervades it? Now that he no longer walks among us, does that mean the Jewish people must again be the prey of avaricious priests, of charlatans, of the sellers of trinkets? And does it mean that we Jews can have no hope in a future of an Israel ruled by God, and not by those in the Temple who pretend to speak in His name?"

Miriam shook her head. "I...I don't..."

"We've been discussing our future since Jeshua was taken from us. I heard you talking to Mary just now, and quoting from the Book of Koheleth. I know that blessed book like I know the back of my hand, and there's another verse, soon after the one she quoted. It says, 'A time to rend and a time to sew; a time to keep silence and a time to speak.' This is our time to speak. That's what we've been discussing. Now that Jeshua can no longer speak for us, it is we who must speak for ourselves. And for our people. For if we don't, then his life, his mission, will all have been in vain."

She smiled. "How will you accomplish this? Who will be the new Jeshua?"

"There will be no new Jeshua. The Almighty touched him in a unique way. I'm never heard any man before who stirred my very soul like him. Nobody could replace him. But I have listened to everything he has said, and before he was crucified, he told me and that others that we should take his mantle, like Elisha took Elijah's mantle, and we should spread his word. None of us will ever be like him, but at least his words and thoughts will be spread throughout the Jewish land, and even to Jewish communities in other countries. His words, his thoughts, will live on forever more."

She reached over and held his hand in gratitude. Then she asked, "So who will lead you? Every group has to have a leader."

Peter shook his head. "Jeshua said that he was first, but among equals. We are all leaders...and followers. Each one of us has studied his ways, and all of us are able to stand before a congregation, and talk to them of what should be, and not what is. We've all been inspired by his vision. Now he is no longer with us, we will take that vision, and change our world for the better. And..."

Miriam frowned. "And...?"

Peter smiled. "Often on our walks, when we spoke, Jeshua told us of his affection for his half-brother James. I have sent for James to come here, for two reasons. The first is that a member of your family should look after your needs, and he is the only one with whom you hold any affection. And the second reason is that being from the same father, it occurred to me that James might be enough like Jeshua carry the mission on his back."

Miriam stared at him for long moments. Peter wondered what he'd said that had caused this reaction of surprise...and even distress.

But then Miriam smiled, and said, "If Yahweh wills it, then let it be so. Yahweh sees into the hearts and minds of men and women, and He knows what is right, and what is wrong. I shall look forward to James coming here."

+

It took five days for the messenger sent by Peter to reach Nazareth, and a further eight days for James, older step-brother of Jeshua, to bid his family farewell, and travel to Jerusalem. He walked the roads which took him along the ridges of the hills which were the backbone of Israel, stopping off to sleep in inns along the way.

When he arrived at the inn where the messenger had told him to meet his step-mother Miriam, he was exhausted, in desperate need of a wash, and refreshments. He didn't want to meet his step-mother, who he hadn't seen since the previous year, looking like a camel trader. So he walked further and took lodgings for the evening in a hostelry inside the city of Jerusalem, where he changed his clothes, refreshed himself and slept in comfort for the first time in a week. Not that there was a need to see Miriam quickly. She would have finished the seven days of intense mourning for her son Jeshua, and would now be entering the thirty-day period of reflection and thanksgiving for his life. So seeing her in the morning, when he was properly dressed and rested, would be of greater benefit to her, and to him.

Properly presentable, James walked from the Horse Gate in the walls to the east of the Temple of Jerusalem, down the hill towards the settlement where he had been told by the messenger that Miriam and the other followers of Jeshua were in residence. It was a short walk and when the sun was already high above the Mountains of Moab in the land of the Nabateans, he arrived at the inn. The door was already open, welcoming travelers to or from the City, and he could smell the freshly baked bread and even the aromatic spices which the innkeeper had used to flavor the figs, pomegranates and grapes which would be bathed in soured goat's milk.

He entered the inn, and his eyes tried to adjust to the darkness, compared with the brilliance of the sun outside. As the figures became more and more distinct, James searched the large dining room for Miriam. And he saw a diminutive figure sitting in a corner beside the cold and unlit fire. With her sat an elderly matron, holding her hand and comforting her. To the left was a group of three or four men, talking quietly among themselves. His eyes still blinded from the outside sunlight, he didn't recognize her at first, but realized that this must be his step-mother, Miriam. After his father Yosef had died, and his sisters and brothers had been cruelly indifferent and said heartless things to her about belonging and remaining in Nazareth, she had left the family with Jeshua, and he didn't think he'd ever see her again. So it was a surprise that she and Jeshua had visited Nazareth twice in the past two years.

He remained close to the door, looking at her as memories flooded back to him. She had been kind and loving when he'd first met her. As a young girl, only a year older than him, she'd come from Sephoris to marry his widowed father, and all of the family, except Yosef and himself, had treated her with callous indifference, bordering on hostility. James had done everything he could to make her feel welcome, and as he had grown older, following the birth of their son Jeshua, he had protected her from the spitefulness of his older sisters. Then the three of them, Yosef, Miriam and the baby Jeshua had disappeared suddenly to Egypt. It was said that they'd fled the madness of the old king Herod, but he still didn't understand why.

And then, when Yosef had died many years later, when Jeshua was a young man, the two of them had gone again. It was said that they'd descended into the pit of Gehenna, which was the Sea of Salt, and lived there as hermits for many many years. Now they were back. He'd heard Jeshua preach, and knew him as a captivating speaker, a charismatic and vital man, somebody he'd like to know better.

But suddenly, James had been told by the messenger that his half-brother had been crucified by the cruel Romans for treason and sedition and Yahweh knew whatever else, and Miriam was not only a widow, but alone in the world. And the messenger had told him that some man named Peter wanted to speak with him about a matter which was urgent, burning, and concerning the future of the Jewish faith.

Here he was. There was his step-mother Miriam. And one of the men in the group near to her, James assumed, was this man Peter. He didn't know whether to go up and accost them or wait until his mother saw him. But if she was debilitated by the death of her son, then...

He walked over, and the group of men turned around. His step mother looked up and frowned. Then she beamed a smile. "James? Thank God Almighty in heaven that you've arrived. Friends, this is my son, James. Jeshua's brother."

She stood, and walked over to hug him. They were immediately joined by the four men, who all introduced themselves. Last to grasp his hand was Peter, who stood beyond the group, smiling.

"You and our beloved Miriam must have a great deal to discuss. We will leave you both in peace, and when it's time for the midday meal, we will come together, you and me, and I will tell you why I've sent for you," said Peter.

The four men left the inn to walk to nearby Jerusalem, where they would listen to the crowds and see if there was any mention of the crucifixions recently carried out by the Romans. Such sentences of death were carried out every few days by the authorities, mainly against those Zealots who the army managed to capture, against anyone insane enough to threaten or harm a Roman soldier, and especially against a common thief. In the old days, before the reign of the Prefect Pilate and his predecessor, the fourth Prefect, Valerius Gratus, such men were sent to Syria to be torn to death in the arena by wild beasts or hacked to death by gladiators. But such transportation was deemed too expensive by the Emperor Tiberius because of falling taxation revenues due to poor administration, and so he had decreed that criminals were now executed where they were tried and found guilty.

As they left the inn, the woman sitting beside Miriam also stood so that James could sit where she had been seated. He and Miriam sat, and began talking about what she and Jeshua had been doing since they left Nazareth the previous year. And she told him more about their lives following the death of Yosef. She discussed their sojourn with the Essenes in their community at Qumran, by the shores of the Sea of Salt. She told James how her beloved son had quickly established himself as a natural leader of the community, and when the old leader had died, he had been given the mantle, which he wore with pride. Jeshua had established a loving, open and benign rule of the Community, which had not only thrived, but had attracted others from Jerusalem and further afield, who were increasingly distressed by life under the Romans, and the authoritarian rule of the Sadducees in the Temple of God.

But when she began to tell her step-son about Jeshua's vision of Yahweh by the shores of the Dead Sea, and their subsequent journey out of the valley and into the heights of Jerusalem to begin their mission of bringing an end to the rule of the Priests, she began to cry. He reached over and comforted her.

"Mother," he said, even though Miriam was a year older than him, "I was in the synagogue in Nazareth when I heard Jeshua preach. The crowd was hostile and hateful, but before he was thrown out, I listened to both what he said, and the way in which he said it. I kept asking myself whether this was the same lad I'd seen grow up as a baby into boyhood, and then into the youth who took you to the Qumran community. Mother, he was extraordinary. I could have listened to him for hours, had the crowd not turned on him. What he was saying about the priests in the Temple..."

Sobbing, she nodded and whispered in James' ear, "He was so deeply offended by the abuse of the priests; by their authority over the people of Israel, their control of the faith...and in the end, it brought him undone. All my blessed son ever wanted was for the people to have back their faith, to pray directly to our God and not to do it with the permission of the priests."

She couldn't continue, she was sobbing so hard. Nor could she recount to James of Jeshua's assault on the Temple, his arrest by the Roman Century or her inability to see and comfort him before his trial, sentencing and crucifixion. It had all been carried out in such haste. The Prefect, Pilate, who was only away from his capital of Caesarea and in the city of Jerusalem because of the potential for riots during the Passover, wanted troublemakers to be dealt with swiftly, and out of sight of the rest of the Jewish people.

And so her son's beautiful life had been brought to an end. She didn't know where his body was, nor could she take it to the family's cave near to Nazareth where it could be wrapped in pure linen, covered in spices and oils, and then, when the flesh had rotted and only his bones were left, they would be placed in an ossuary with his name inscribed on the outside forever more. Bereft by her son's death and tortured by not being able to reclaim his body for the many strewn and left as carrion by the Romans on the Hill of the Skull, Miriam was barely able to bear the burden of grief she felt.

"What can I do, mother, to ease your grief?" James asked. "I have a wife and family in Nazareth, and I work as a shepherd with my own flock of sheep and some goats. But I also have two men who I pay to help me, and so I can leave my work and my children are old enough to help their mother. So I can help you, should you need me. What can I do to assist you?"

She looked at him, tears in her eyes, and remembered his kindness towards her when she was a young girl and had come up from her home in Sephoris to marry Yosef. Of all Yosef's children, he was the only one who welcomed her and showed her any compassion.

Tears again welled up in her eyes, and she hugged him. "Just be with me, James, until the burden of this grief begins to lift from my old shoulders."

James remained sitting beside Miriam for much of the morning. When the men had returned from Jerusalem, Peter said, "Come with me, brother, and we will sit outside in the shade of the vines, and talk."

When they were seated, and the innkeeper had brought them a flagon of wine, Peter said to James, "How much has Miriam told you about what Jeshua has been doing in these past few years?"

So he told Peter what his step-mother had said. Peter nodded. "But that is only half of what has happened. Jeshua was the most compelling man I've ever known. I would sit and listen to the way he spoke to ordinary Jews, men and women and children, and he raised them up so that they could see Heaven. His eyes, his face, his gentleness, his calm but insistent voice; yes, they were all enthralling; but it was what he said which stays in the mind and changes the way we see ourselves. Unlike the prophets of old, who threatened us with eternal damnation if we failed to follow God's path, Jeshua words were those of love and peace and hope. For him, it was through goodness, charity and love of ones neighbor more than oneself, which were the keys to the kingdom of heaven."

James nodded, and said, "Yes, I was there in Nazareth when he spoke. I know what you mean."

Peter smiled and reflected on how Jeshua had taught him so much in the time they'd been together. He continued, "You know, James, that your brother Jeshua was fond of the books of Moses, and especially the third of his books, called Viyikra, which comes from its first words, *'He called...'* It angered him that the Romans call it Leviticus, after those things which belong to the Priests. He was deeply saddened by what the Priests had become, and kept reminding us of the greatest of our sages, Hillel who once said that what is hateful to you, do not do to your fellow: this is the whole Torah; the rest is the explanation.

"James, you have listened to him, and you must know how listening to him for just moments could enthrall you; his words washed over you like a warm bath. He convinced many of us...ten...to give up our lives and to follow him, but not once did he ask us to do it. He told us of the kingdom of heaven and what our lives could be like, and we gave up what we'd once been, and became servants of our people.

"It was his mission to cleanse the Temple of the priests, to bring back our Jewish faith into our homes, into our synagogues, and away from the Sadducees. And for us to follow the golden rule of Hillel to do to others as we wished them to do to us.

"He began a movement here, James, which was about to grow into something which couldn't be stopped, not by the priests or the Levites or even the Romans. He, your step-brother, was about to revitalize our faith. He was another Moses, another Elijah, another Isaiah, but a prophet of love, and not of damnation."

James sat and looked at Peter in astonishment. He tried to associate the young and clever step-brother he'd taken under his wing, a youth who was often just staring into the heavens, and made James wonder what he was thinking, with the Prophet that Peter was describing. It was such a transformation that it would require the intervention of Yahweh...and his thoughts stopped there, because it was the edge of blasphemy. Miriam had already said that he'd been visited by Yahweh on the shores of the Sea of Salt. And now this man Peter was saying that Jeshua, his own brother, was a Prophet like Moses and Isaiah. No, it couldn't be.

Peter continued, "Which is why I've asked you to come here." James looked at him in surprise. "None of his disciples can take up his mantle. Only a blood relative can continue his work. We can help you, aid you, spread the word of Jeshua, but as a leader, none of us has the quality which comes from birth...your birth, James. For you and Jeshua share Yosef as a father. So his seed was implanted into you, and into Jeshua. You, brother of Jeshua, must become our leader. That is why you have come. You will lead this congregation of ours into Jerusalem. And you will grow our numbers like the grass in the fields until we can properly challenge the Sadducees and the Levites in the Temple.

"We have learned not to antagonize the Romans because it led to Jeshua's crucifixion. So, you will be our preacher. You will be our learned leader. We will teach you everything that Jeshua said, and did, and thought. Because you are Jeshua's brother, people will listen to you, and they will follow. And you will continue his work."

East of Jericho, on the edge of the valley
leading to the Dead Sea, one month later

Miriam of Nazareth, widow of Yosef, mother of Jeshua and step-mother of James, stood before the vastness of the valley into which she was about to descend. She had left the ancient city of Jericho and was walking east towards the vast scar in Israel's face which was the valley where she had lived all those years. Directly in front of her were the ancient mountains of Moab and the land of the Nabateans.

She knew this valley so well. At the bottom of it, hot and pestilential, yet strangely familiar and comforting, was the Sea of Salt, the Dead Sea, which the Greeks, when they had been in control of Israel, called Lake Asphaltites.

But in the many years she'd lived beside it in the community of Qumran, Miriam preferred the name by which it was known to the Essenes, the Sea of Lot's Wife. As Yahweh was bringing destruction to the evil cities of Sodom and Gomorrah for their immoral ways, He had allowed the good man, Lot and his family to escape, with the injunction that they must not look back and witness the death of their townsfolk. But Lot's wife, Ado, had disobeyed God's word and had looked back to see the fire and pumice rain down from the heavens. And the punishment for her sin of disobedience was to be turned into a pillar of salt.

Miriam had always felt an empathy with the tragic woman. Did she look back because of her sorrow that so many people, despite their sinful ways, had been put to death? Or was it because, deep in her soul, she regretted leaving the city of Sodom because she secretly hungered for the life of freedom and immorality and lust? Was that why Yahweh turned her into a pillar of salt? Because she was lustful and unworthy of being saved? What did that say about Miriam, and the life she'd led?

She always felt that she was much like Ado. Her early life, though respectful and pleasant, had been full of lustful thoughts, which she'd done her best to bury, but which kept resurfacing when she looked at a young man from the city of Sephoris, or even when she saw Roman soldiers, whose tunics enabled her to see their fine muscular legs.

And when she became a young woman, she'd enjoyed herself with the body of the young man, Malachai, with whom she'd been so deeply in love. She'd run with him through the fields, laid with him in the meadows under the burning sun, and allowed him to kiss her on the lips and the neck.

As she and James walked towards the lip of the valley before descending, she thought back to those carefree days of her childhood. And then shame and embarrassment suddenly suffused her as she remembered how she'd fallen asleep in the field and woken to find her garments pulled to one side and Malachai's fluids at the top of her legs. He swore he hadn't entered her and begged her forgiveness, but the fury she felt at his violation of her while she slept was still raw in her mind, even after these many years.

She smiled when she thought of Yosef, her elderly husband, and his eventual acceptance of Malachai's son as his own. And to Yosef's great credit, he loved Jeshua with all his heart, and never once thought of him in any way differently from his other children.

"You're deep in thought, Miriam," said James.

His voice startled her. She'd been walking along the path without noticing her surroundings. She was leaving the world of the living, of her recent joyous and painful experiences, and descending into the world where she'd found peace and harmony, friendships and understanding in the nether world of the Essenes. Yet although this was a harsh and unforgiving world, it was the one she hungered for. It was as though the descent into the deep valley, bordered by steep walls, somehow shut her off from the evils of the upper world, from the dangers of men like the Romans, the priests of the Temple, the liars and cheats and thieves, the deceivers and manipulators and charlatans of the upper world. Down here, in the depths of the earth, where life was lived on the edge of a knife, one lived by the rules of the environment. Eat, drink, stay out of the sun, pray, obey, serve and love your neighbor. Simple, elegant rules by which to lead a life. A life free of the regulations of the Romans and the decrees of the Sanhedrin and the Temple.

Yes, she thought, this was the life she wanted to live now. She had lost her first true love, Malachai, she'd lost her family in Sephoris, she'd lost her treasured husband Yosef, and now she'd lost her beloved son Jeshua. What was left for her, other than to live and die in a community which asked nothing of her other than her observance of God's requirements?

"What are you thinking?" asked James.

"Nothing. And everything. I was thinking about the twists and turns of my life. Of my world before I met your father; of my life with him; and the world which your brother Jeshua and I tried to create. I'm an old woman, and all that's left to me are my memories and the warmth of my thoughts."

"You're not old, Miriam. Methuselah lived until he was 969. You're only...what?"

"I have suffered for nearly 50 years on this earth," she told him. "Fifty years of toil, hard work, and fear of the Lord, and of the Romans. But I have also enjoyed fifty years of devotion to my family and friends, and my love of Yahweh."

"Then why," asked James, "in what time is left to you, do you want to shut yourself away in some place by the shores of a place full of pestilence? Why not live your life in the open, in Jerusalem? Why not return with me to Nazareth where I live, and my wife and I and our children will love you as once my father loved you as the companion of his end days?"

As she walked, careful not to trip on the rocks which were strewn in the road, she smiled. To live in comfort with people she would grow to love, in the peace and tranquility of Nazareth. It was a quiet town, too far from important roads and cities to be of any importance to the Romans. But no matter how peaceful, how comforting, nowhere other than in the desert, beside the Salt Sea, would she be able to escape the whirlwind which had been started by her son, Jeshua. For Peter had told her that James would now lead the group in Jerusalem, and that he and others would take Jeshua's words and spread them throughout Israel. And that others would take up the words and continue the movement until the Temple was cleansed of the Priests and the Levites and the faith of Yahweh was returned to the Jewish people.

And when that was accomplished, then the sect of the Essenes, which Jeshua had taken against the rules into the wide world, would be made manifest. It was a faith in which there were only good men and women, and there were no priests, only teachers of righteousness to lead the community. In the desert, among the Essenes, the people spoke one to one with God. Which is as it should have been. Which is what Yahweh decreed.

For when Father Moses brought down the commandments from the top of Mount Sinai, wasn't the very first order of the Lord, "You shall have no other gods but me."

Everybody assumed that the Lord was referring to the idols of the Egyptians and the Caananites and the Jebusites; but only the Essenes realized that when Yahweh said 'no other gods', he was talking about the Priests. It was an injunction to the children of Israel that Moses and his brother Aaron, the first of the priests, and those who followed him such as Zadok and Ahimaaz and Azariah were only men. Yet today, the priests of the Temple looked upon themselves as gods.

Which was why Miriam had determined that she would live out the rest of her days in the desert, among the community of Essenes, her brothers and sisters. For when the storm broke over Jerusalem and Bethlehem and Emmaus, as it would when Peter and the others began to turn the people away from the Temple, Miriam didn't want to see the clouds. She just wanted the purity of the desert, it's endless cloudless days, and nights full of stars which showed her the great and good majesty of the Lord.

The End

CPSIA information can be obtained
at www.ICGtesting.com
Printed in the USA
LVHW020834281022
731799LV00009B/504